The phone finally rings. Micah glares at it like it's a rattlesnake shaking its ass and Trace chuckles.

"Yep," Trace says, answering with the phone in one hand and the cigar in the other.

An intoxicatingly familiar voice answers, "Report."

"Similar situation to last year," Trace says, letting the regret come through in his voice. "My boys are fucked. I'm lookin' for help. I get that it'll cost me. Whatever it is, I'll pay."

He feels the connection, stretched over miles of land and leagues of ocean, crackling through thin air. It makes him sad, and older than he is. Taking another puff on the cigar, he forces it all down where it belongs and listens to someone who knows him better than anyone else alive as they read between his lines.

"Been a long, damn time, kid," Trace says softly.

The longer it takes for a response to come, the more Trace understands why.

"Okay. You know what to do. I'll get back to you as soon as I can. Keep your phone handy."

"Will do, babe," Trace replies. "Thanks."

He knows how strange he must sound to Micah. He suspects he looks strange, too, and not like himself at all. Wouldn't be surprising, since he doesn't feel like Trace. More than ever, Trace feels like a persona that doesn't fit as well as it needs to. The seams are splitting

Also recommended...

You may also enjoy these other ForbiddenFiction works:

Antidote by Jack L. Pyke
Sequel to the in the amazing BDSM novel, *Don't...*, and crossover with Lynn Kelling's *Deliver Us* series. Part of the shared world of The Society of Masters.

Videos of Jack having sex with a man who mutilated teenagers for fun should have stayed dead and buried, just like the man who filmed them. Yet when footage of Jack's past starts appearing on Internet porn sites, Jack's whole world is again turned on its head. Jack's sex life is now on camera for a whole new audience. (M/M)
http://forbiddenfiction.com/library/story/JP2-1.000170

Consort: House of Silence 3 by J.A. Jaken
On the surface, the business of the infamous House of Silence is obvious enough, but its carefully cultivated veneer of political neutrality is threatened when a lover from Master Charon's youth arrives with an urgent message from the queen, prompting jealousy from Reiji and putting the whole house on edge. The House's unique resources are called upon to investigate one of the local cabals which is overstepping its bounds, snatching up disproportionate amounts of territory and capital beyond its domain. When Tam goes missing, Charon and the boys are caught up in a web of intrigue, peril, and sensuality that may end up costing them their lives. (M/M)
http://forbidden-fiction.com/library/story/JAJ-1.000198

Forgive Us
Book 3 of Deliver Us

Lynn Kelling

ForbiddenFiction
www.forbiddenfiction.com

an imprint of

Fantastic Fiction Publishing
www.fantasticfictionpublishing.com

FORGIVE US
A Forbidden Fiction book

Fantastic Fiction Publishing
Hayward, California

© Lynn Kelling, 2014

All rights reserved. No part of this work may be used or reproduced in any manner whatsoever without permission from the publisher, except as allowed by fair use. For more information, contact publisher@forbiddenfiction.com.

CREDITS
Editor: Rylan Hunter and D.M. Atkins
Cover Design: Siolnatine
Cover Art: KrisCole at Dreamstime
Production Editor: Erika L Firanc
Proofreading: Kaye O'Malley and Kailin Morgan

SKU: LK1-000197-02 FFP
ISBN: 978-1-62234-162-7

Published in the United States of America

DISCLAIMER

This book is a work of fiction which contains explicit erotic content; it is intended for mature readers. Do not read this if it's not legal for you.

All the characters, locations and events herein are fictional. While elements of existing locations or historical characters or events may be used fictitiously, any resemblance to actual people, places or events is coincidental.

This story depicts fictional BDSM; it is not intended to be used as an instruction manual. It contains descriptions of erotic acts that may be immoral, illegal, or unsafe. The characters are not models for the Safe, Sane and Consensual forms embraced by most current practitioners of BDSM. The author takes license with the use of BDSM for dramatic effect. Do not take the events in this story as proof of the plausibility or safety of any particular practice.

For Jack.

Contents

The Truth About Trace 1
Damage Control 10
Lying and Leaving 17
A Slave Afraid 24
In Love and Loss 36
Edge of Madness 47
The Danger of Secrets 54
Threesome 61
Confession and Consequences 69
Straight Answers 77
The Unspeakable 85
What Ben Gives Kyle 95
Call of Need 104
Love in the Dark 110
Bright Eyes 117
Introductions 123
Access Points 132
New Threats, Old Instincts 142
Gabriel's Submission 151
First Impressions 161
Patrick, Master's Sub 170
Observations 177
Life of the Party 184

Darrek, Collared	197
At the Mercy of the Masters	204
Helpless Surrender	216
Supervised Visitation	226
Knowing Trace	234
At Long Last	243
The Old and the New	250
Master Gabe, Master Gray	260
Darrek's Submission	268
Dominating Jack	277
Just a Kiss	286
Micah, Inside and Out	296
Without a Trace	307
Just a Letter	312
Contact	324
Answers	335
Talisman	345
See It to Believe It	355
Slow Surrender	364
Patrick's Family	374
Parting Gifts	382
Company	389
Acknowledgments	402
About the Author	403
About the Publisher	404

Chapter 1
The Truth About Trace

The ritual Trace has to go through before he can make the phone call is always the same. He drives to the nearest large shopping center and parks his motorcycle in a crowded area of the parking lot. With his backpack, he walks between the cars rather than down the aisle, goes into the shopping center and heads right for the bathroom. Once inside a locked stall, he changes into a different shirt and adds a scarf and a hat which he uses to hide his long hair, tucking it up inside. He puts the old shirt and the backpack into another duffel bag that had been inside the backpack. When he emerges from the bathroom, he walks a little straighter, a little slower and smiles less, watching everyone around him warily. The physical transformation itself always feels like coming home again. For a vagabond at heart like him, there's undeniable familiarity in the moving and metamorphosis. No matter how firmly anchored his heart may be, the need to venture outward or reexamine which truths to tell, or conceal, is a lingering plague.

Through the shopping center and out the opposite side of the building than that through which he entered, he calls for a taxi. The taxi is then instructed to get on the highway and drive for about thirty three minutes before pulling off at the closest exit.

He has the driver keep the meter running and walks off into the fields or trees wherever they've stopped, not going too far that he loses sight of the taxi. The open air, isolation, and ability to easily see in all directions without obstruction helps calm his increasingly paranoid nature. Then, using a new, disposable, pre-paid cellphone, he dials the number from memory. He can only truly relax once the conversation has begun. Getting lost in the role he plays, and the comfort of trust formed diligently over the span of years, for a moment, nothing else exists except for the masculine voice on the other end of the line.

"Have I told you how sexy your accent is?" the voice tells him.

"Only a million bloody times, mate," he chuckles. When he speaks, the pitch of his voice is slightly higher than it was pre-transformation. But, since it's his normal register, it feels as soothing as a deep breath. It can be exhausting to constantly, consciously alter one's way of speaking, but that's just one of the costs of a good disguise. "How's the missus?"

"*Big*."

"Oof," he groans.

"No, no. I mean she's pregnant. Still can't believe it, really. We heard the heartbeat again yesterday, though, so it's real."

Fear subtly tenses his friend and informant's voice, sharpening the words like they were being scraped over a stone. Yasha Lachinov has been a voice on the other end of the phone for a long time now. Since the two of them have quite a lot in common, the conversation is always easy and good.

"That's fucking fantastic," he says sincerely. "Congratulations, mate."

"Thanks Patrick," is the sighed reply. "But that means I'm out. I'm done. That's why I asked you to call. I couldn't do this to you over email. I'm so sorry. I just can't take the risk anymore."

"I understand." The news hurts, and makes speaking normally more of a challenge. How many years, total, has it been? Fifteen? Twenty? And now Yasha is going to fade away into obscurity like so many others, lost to time and circumstance. A true friendship is over, possibly forever. They will never speak again, most likely. It would be too dangerous. "Stay safe, my friend. Do what you need to do. *Nothing* is more important than family."

"I don't hear much these days anyway," Yasha says. "I'm out of the loop. Have been for months, but… It would have been nice, just once, to get the chance to shake your hand. You're a good man. It's been an honor to know you, sir."

He hates how upset he is after ending the call. It's like the clothes, the voice, and the name all scheme to undo over a decade's work at learning how to be strong.

After yelling, "*Fuck!*" loudly enough to startle some nearby sparrows, he tries to compose himself. He finds a fairly large rock and sets the cellphone down upon it. Driving the heel of his boot into the casing, he stomps until he hears the splintering crack, then leaves in the broken pieces were they lie. Slowly, he walks back to the taxi idling by the side of the road.

The ritual in reverse is hell. It's like coming down with a crash from a beautiful high, or waking up after amazing sex next to a stranger who's drooling in their sleep. It's too much like the *old* rituals — clean up in the bathroom, make sure the fee is taken care of, and the customer is satisfied, then that long, cold walk out of the hotel, or wherever he happened to be, back to his life left feeling just a little bit more used, a little more soiled and ruined.

The taxi drops him back at the shopping center. He gets changed back into his original clothes without making eye contact with his reflection. It feels too much like vertigo.

The bike is where he left it, and the first thing he checks is the saddle bag. With a relieved sigh, he discovers his cell is still taped to the inside and hasn't been stolen while he was gone. He never takes it with him when he has risky business to handle, due to possibly unfounded concerns of his location being traced on the off chance that his contact has been compromised. Mainly, though, it's the memories of needing to be reachable at all times when servicing clients that cause him to leave the cell behind. When he's slipping inside old identities, it's better to do so without carrying along unnecessary stressors. He doesn't work for anyone anymore. That's a fact he repeats to himself, often. The freedom found in that truth is empowering. It steadies his nerves to choose to be unreachable when he's already taking risks that leave him on edge.

But then, once business is handled, his current responsibilities mandate he have the means to check on those who are depending on him. As soon as he has the phone in his hand and touches a button to awaken the damned thing, he is reminded why he can't abandon it entirely, even when he most wants to. There are messages waiting for him, mostly from Gabriel Hunter, his boy.

From an hour ago: *'Someone broke into the house. I need your help.'*

From forty-five minutes ago: *'The cops are here. Where are you?'*

From twenty minutes ago: *'I don't know what to do about Darrek.'*

All of them cause his chest to feel too tight, every subsequent message making the dread of added responsibility a little worse. Beneath it all is the never-ending apprehension for the safety of his family, and the inescapable frustration born of rotten circumstances.

"Goddammit. Perfect fuckin' timing." He dials Ben Knox as he gets on the bike. He can't call Gabriel. The ringing alone would do more harm than good.

Ben answers after the first ring. Another bad sign.

"Benny," Trace says. "I'm headed over to see him. He texted you?"

"Yeah. Last ditch effort, I guess. The hell have you been, man?"

"Busy. I'm on my way. Gonna stop by your place after for a talk, so make your boy comfy before I get there. Understood?"

"Yep."

The storm he'd temporarily stepped out of to make the phone call is swirling faster than ever. It's always swirling lately, buffeting him, the debris of his life and his kids' lives clipping him as it wings by. The shrieking wind of shitty fate has been getting worse, more violent, and harder to escape. It's all out of control.

The need for constant, daily maintenance of the lives of those who rely on him really started to kick Trace's ass with the decision to keep Darrek Grealey and Kyle Roth away from each other, without any knowledge of what the other is up to while simultaneously not sacrificing Ben and Gabriel's friendship in the process. Only through much finagling and a lot of effort on Trace's part has he been able to keep everyone happy and functioning.

Then, Jerry had tried to call Darrek. When Darrek wouldn't answer, Jerry kept trying to call. It has sent Darrek right up to the edge of a mental cliff, not able to stand up to his father and abuser, or able to completely escape him either. The ideas Darrek imagines to be the unknown reasons for the call make things worse. Gabriel tries to manage Darrek's constantly shifting level of unease and find a way to fix the problem, but so far things have only gotten steadily worse.

Gabriel. Trace focuses on Gabriel.

Right away, his conscience starts to give him hell for things he's done with Gabriel in the recent past—like acting the part of Daddy during sex involving Gabriel's total submission after an urgent phonecall from Ben made on Gabriel's behalf.

Sex doesn't solve everything, you stupid shit. You showed that boy the respect he deserves for a goddamned decade and one desperate phonecall is all it takes to end it? Really? You should be better than that by now. That's the shit that got your heart broken. That's the shit that destroys hope and happiness. Your boy is on the line now, because of you and your fucking inability to keep it in your pants.

It's always amused and disturbed him that he can sometimes hear Trace's voice in his head, separate and distinct from his own inner mental dialogue. The part of him that is Trace, yelling at the rest of him which isn't, is a uniquely twisted exercise in self-recrimination. When it comes to his relationship with Gabriel, Ben, or Micah, the voice of Trace tends to speak up and kick him in the ass. Trace—just one of his distinct, multiple identities—didn't occur naturally, but is rather a conscious creation and a blend of a few different guys he used to run with as a teenage thug in New York. He scrambled their attitudes, their accents, and their manners of speaking and made them his own. It took a while for it to feel normal in practice. To be honest, it still doesn't, always.

Perhaps it is because he can't be who he really is, freed of labels or distinct personas, with anyone else anymore that he is forced to disassociate himself in private, quiet moments. When alone, he has no name, and no specific identity. He's many people at once and none of them at all. Secretly tired of performing to please, he hopes one day to be able to drop the act entirely. The likelihood of that ever happening, though, is quite slim.

The ride to Gabriel's home is short. He pulls up and parks in the driveway. The garage is open, the radio blasting inside. Darrek is in there, pencil in his hand, which is hanging at his side. He stares at a piece of wood on the worktable in front of him, but doesn't move, doesn't blink.

Going to the front door, instead, Trace raises his hand to knock, but it's opened before he can. Gabriel practically throws himself forward into the hug, his eyes teary.

"Hey, beautiful," Trace sighs, gathering Gabriel in his arms, taking a second to simply enjoy the proof that his boy is whole and safe.

"Thank you for coming."

"Sorry I'm late. I miss the party?"

Gabriel detangles himself, straightens and looks slightly embarrassed.

"I know this isn't your problem, but—"

"Hey, I get it. Let's talk inside," he suggests, wanting to at least put a closed door between them and Darrek.

Gabriel leads them into the hall, then the kitchen. The gun is there, above the bookcase where Gabriel leaves it. Trace can see the shine of its black metal, if he looks.

"He was upstairs in the bathroom, shaving," Gabriel says, pacing back and forth by the counter, glancing now and then at the yard and the dog sniffing around in the grass of the lawn. "It was two hours before he was expecting me home and he knows I'm never early. Not with the way my workload's been. He said the house was quiet. Sierra was asleep by his feet, near the heat outlet in the bathroom. She perked up. Barked once. Then the alarm started to blare."

Gabriel exhales, running a hand over his mouth. He's shaking, his eyes too big with fear. This is the stuff he can't show Darrek. This is the stuff he only shows Trace.

"I don't know if it's a good thing or a bad one," Gabriel laughs hysterically, sounding on the verge of tears. "But he shut and locked the bathroom door. He just barricaded himself in there with Sierra, and sat with his back to the door, curled up like that. When he heard sirens, he finally came out and opened the door before they could break it down to get inside. At least he didn't have the gun."

Better to hide than to run face-first into trouble, especially with where

Darrek's head's been.

"Did they find any evidence?"

"No," Gabriel says with exasperation. "No forced entry. Nothing. Darrek didn't even hear footsteps or any sounds of someone moving around. They were certain it's faulty wiring and the system just needs to be replaced. We only got it put in recently, so it makes sense, but...."

"But what?"

Gabriel hesitates, then finishes, saying, "But there's a photo of me and Dare in the hall downstairs, on the bookshelf by the door. It was turned face down."

"Babydoll, that doesn't mean—"

"There's another photo in our bedroom. Our *bedroom*, Trace. It was turned face down, too. What are the odds of those two things getting knocked over when the cops were wandering around, and nothing else? Nothing else was touched! It's not right. I mean, they didn't take anything. They didn't leave anything. They didn't try to break down the bathroom door. It's creepy. And I'm so scared for him."

Gabriel looks at Trace with a pleading expression, and the need is there. It's right there, visible, tangible. Gabriel wants Trace to touch, to comfort, and take charge. The trouble is, Gabriel is completely oblivious to the inner struggles going on inside the man he only knows as Trace. Trace would never take advantage of Gabriel in a sexual way. Trace sees himself as Gabriel's guardian and father. But Patrick would perform with pleasure if it was needed and demanded of him. When Ben called, Trace slipped, let Patrick take over. It was a mistake he's been trying to live with, and striving not to repeat. Ever since, Trace has been reprimanding Patrick for his weakness in repeatedly resorting to sex as a solution to almost every problem.

"How do I make him safe?" Gabriel asks, looking desperate. "What do I do, here? *This is breaking him.*"

"You still having the issue with the phone?"

"Yes. It rings constantly. The caller ID usually comes up as Unavailable. Sometimes it's the Grealeys. Dare won't answer their calls since that first time when it turned out it was his father, and he won't let me answer either. The idea of me talking to Jerry sends his anxiety level through the roof. When I do answer the phone, most times there's no one on the other end. Sometimes I think I hear breathing."

"Christ," Trace sighs, rolling it over in his head, trying to not let the new worries get swept up in the storm in there, to keep hold of things until he finds something useful to say, some way to help his boy.

For how long did you crave a real family of your own, and here you are, fucking it up, like usual. Then again, all you're good for is a fuck, right, Patrick?

"He's convinced this is Jerry. Jerry on the phone. Jerry showing up at the house. But Jerry has *no reason* to come after him like this," Gabriel hisses, his voice low, his gaze on the closed door to the garage. "But *Harry* has a reason to come after me. What if Harry found out it was my friends who cut him up? What if this is revenge? What if he's coming after me and trying to—"

It's not Harry.

"Hey. Enough," Trace says. "You're being paranoid. You need to keep it together for Dare. We'll figure this out. You keep the alarm on the house active. Schedule an appointment for the system to be replaced, as soon as possible. You keep Dare out of here as much as you can. Keep him away from the phones. Keep your routine as normal as you possibly can. Keep things *normal*. You're his Master. If he needs to submit to you for his own comfort, so he can draw comfort from his trust in you, then *use that*. Push him that way. Test his limits in a way he's familiar with. It'll help him see what a fighter he is when he needs to be, and keep his head here, instead of with the worry."

"Okay," Gabriel nods, latching on to the suggestions. "Yeah, okay."

By the time Trace is able to leave, reassured Gabriel has it together, he sees Darrek in the garage, in exactly the same position as he was before.

"Hey," Trace calls over the din from the radio, probably turned up to drown out the sound of ringing telephones. "Hang in there, okay? Don't let the bastards get ya down, kid. We'll figure this out."

Darrek turns to look at Trace, but doesn't reply at first. Then, he just nods once. The demons are right there, under the surface, scratching away at the kid's sanity, feeding him nightmare possibilities on an endless loop, no doubt.

"Yessir," Darrek murmurs.

He's surrounded by every kind of power tool, hatchet, or blunt instrument he could want, in order to defend himself, and it makes it a little easier for Trace to leave Darrek there. Astride the bike, Trace watches Darrek turn back to stare at his unfinished work, then takes off down the road in search of Ben.

Chapter 2
Damage Control

The separation that had been established between Darrek and Kyle is having strange effects on their little group. Ben and Gabriel aren't speaking as often as they would, usually only when absolutely necessary. Trace is their go-between. Trace is the glue connecting Ben to Gabriel, and Kyle and Darrek to Micah. Whereas the Doms view things one way, the subs have their own spin. Trace has been encouraging Kyle and Darrek each to speak to Micah about whatever is on their mind. Though most of them are switches, Micah's status as Trace's sub has him the most in the lead role within the circle of submissives. He's the only one who's been a safe confidant. Kyle and Darrek don't get news about each other. That's to help facilitate their healing processes in the wake of everything that happened involving Darrek's recovered memories about the abuse by Jerry upon him and Kyle.

Trouble is, Ben still needs to get news about Gabriel. It's a stupid fucking game of whisper down the lane, since Ben and Trace can't call Gabriel without the phone ringing and sending Darrek into a panic.

Upon arriving at Ben and Kyle's home, Trace pulls up the winding drive which loops around the house. The garage opens up on the fields behind their house. There's no one else back there, so it's private. That's why Trace is never surprised when he arrives to find the garage door wide open, exposing Kyle bound or shackled in various positions inside the makeshift dungeon.

Ben is waiting impatiently by the opened door, and Trace smiles at him in greeting. Shutting off the bike and walking up to

Ben, Trace spies Kyle. He's naked and shackled to a St. Andrew's cross, his arms and legs spread wide, his head fallen forward so his honey blond hair hangs in front of his blindfolded eyes. Holding up a finger to Ben, Trace approaches Kyle to take a closer look. Kyle doesn't show any sign of detecting his presence until Trace is right in front of him.

There are noise-cancelling headphones over Kyle's ears. A series of clips have been attached in a curving line from just beneath his arms to his nipples on both sides. Smaller clips ring his cock and balls. Reaching out with a hand, Trace brushes the smaller clips and grins at Kyle's grimace. Shifting around the cross a little, Trace gropes behind Kyle and feels the vibrating plug buried deeply in his ass.

"Comfy?" he asks at a normal volume. "Answer, slave."

There's no reply besides the grimace and a happy little twitch of Kyle's pinched dick.

With a shrug, Trace heads back to Ben and says, "Nice work, kid."

"What the fuck happened?" Ben demands, looking highly disturbed, his arms folded tightly over his chest. "This wasn't another false alarm, was it?"

"Not sure, to be honest. Gabey's convinced someone was actually inside and turned over two photos of him and Dare. One in the hall downstairs, one in the bedroom. The cops are convinced the whole thing is just shitty wiring and there's no one trying to get in. Dare locked himself in the bathroom with the dog until Gabey and the cavalry showed up, sirens a-blazin'. Dare thinks it's Jerry. Gabe thinks it's Harry."

"Harry'd make more sense, don't you think?"

"Maybe. Maybe not. You two noticed anything weird lately? If it's Jerry, you'd think he'd be after this one as much as the other," Trace murmurs, gesturing to Kyle.

"No, no phone calls with a mouth breather on the other end."

"You two need to get a security system installed. A good one."

"So you think it's Jerry?"

"I don't fuckin' know," Trace groans. "Come on, help me out here. Nothin' out of the norm? This one's acting fine?"

Ben glances over his shoulder at Kyle. "Well, he's been a little quiet. A little more serious than usual, but I've been chalking that up to missing Dare, since he denies it when I ask him what's up. But, he'd tell me if something creepy had happened."

"Would he?"

"Fuck you," Ben says angrily.

"Hey," Trace says, putting up his hands, palm out, "I ain't a damn mind reader. My gut tells me this ain't Harry, so that leaves one other possibility. And over my dead body does anything else happen to these kids."

"Why do you think it's not Harry?" Ben frowns. "He's the one we tortured for information. He's got motive."

"You're gonna have to trust me on this one, Benny. Up until today, I was writing the whole thing off as a nasty coincidence, not a threat. I mean, maybe they got themselves on some solicitor's hot list or it's a wrong number issue. A couple of days ago, they got that call from the cops saying the alarm had been triggered when they weren't home, but they didn't find anything concrete then either. But now… that kid, barricading himself in like that? The goddamned photographs? I don't like it."

"Yeah," Ben groans, turning to stare at Kyle as he's wont to do when he starts to get worried about him. It warms Trace's heart to see that sort of loyalty and love. If there's anything worth fighting for, it's that sort of ingrained, instinctive concern for another human being. Finding someone who's willing to tie their heart to yours for the duration is the biggest gift you could ever ask for.

"Keep him close for a while," Trace says. "I'll be in touch."

"Thanks, boss."

Mostly because it's on the way, but also because the part of him that isn't Trace is just as riled as the rest of him, Trace stops by his house on the way to Micah's. He needs to stop and take a breath. The house is his home base. It's where he recharges and remembers he has somewhere he belongs now. No more constant running, hiding more than living. Now, he has a place of his own to defend and protect at all cost. It's his beloved sanctuary from the ceaseless storm, a quiet rebellion against a life that keeps trying to make him feel like he can belong nowhere, to no one.

But, when he gets home, it's not deserted, like he expects. Instead, he discovers Micah's motorcycle in the driveway. Trace takes a moment to look at the bike, sitting on the pavement like it belongs there, as much as anything else. Never in his life has Trace had a lover who would run to him when things got tough. Gabriel did, and does, but Trace wouldn't expect any different from the boy he gave shelter to when the world turned him out. And Gabriel isn't a lover. Not really. But Micah is. He's a lover in the truest sense of the word, giving his heart too completely, therefore leaving himself vulnerable to hurt.

The way Micah's instinct is to come closer rather than take off is a blessing so wonderful, Trace stands in awe of it most days. Some might resent the intrusion or brazen assumption they'd be welcome, no matter the time or reason for the visit, but Trace has always been the one doing the running toward. And his lovers were always the ones turning him out. To need so desperately a welcoming presence, and be denied it, is a pain he's unwilling to ever inflict on another living soul.

Walking inside, he spots Micah in the living room, sitting tensely on the edge of the couch with his hands folded. Like a switch is flipped, Micah reacts instantly to Trace's arrival. First there's eye contact, and Trace feels how clearly Micah sees him. No matter what Micah may be going through, he does Trace the honor of putting it all aside for a moment in order to acknowledge him. It's yet another aspect of Micah's personality Trace treasures. With a past and present so full of shadows and secrets, it means the world to Trace that Micah makes the selfless effort to know and appreciate his lover. Sometimes, it's the little things that make all the difference.

The turmoil in Micah's expression tells Trace the problems are rushing back in. Micah stands, walks up to Trace, and kneels. He folds his hands behind his back, then bows. There's a bad look on his face, and it makes Trace's stomach churn in a way the rest of the day's bad news hasn't.

"Stand up. Relax," he tells Micah, speaking with authority in order to cut through anything causing Micah to doubt himself.

"Sir." Micah gets to his feet, standing straight as an arrow, his caramel-brown eyes unfocused, his attention caught on something internal. A frown line creases Micah's brow and dark circles are visible under his eyes. Trace knows the worry about Kyle, Darrek, and Gabriel has been eating at Micah, but that doesn't explain the look of him entirely. There has to be something else going on, but Trace can't handle anything else. There's already too much wrong.

With a heavy, exhausted sigh, Trace wraps a hand around Micah's jaw. It's warm and rough to the touch, covered in dark stubble. The tilt of his head, the downward cast of his gorgeous eyes, ringed with dark, thick eyelashes, the sensual shape of his lips—it's so intoxicating. There's something there, Trace knows, in the spark of *rightness* between them. The balance of give and take, the equality of what each of them brings and gives away freely to the other, makes sense in so many ways everything else does not. It's more effective shelter from the forces seeking to harm them than any house or physical structure could ever be. Simple, pure, safety and unconditional acceptance is what they each provide.

Together at last, they can each breathe a little easier. The weight of dread lessens, if only for a moment.

"Can I just check something real quick, before we talk? Didn't think you'd be here, love. It'll only take a minute."

"Of course," Micah murmurs, barely audible, looking like he's trying not to cry, making Trace want to scream with rage at the unfairness of it all.

This fuckin' day. This fuckin' life.

Trace walks into the adjoining room where his computer is plugged in. He boots it up and keeps Micah in view while he waits. Dressed in khaki pants and a pristine, button-down, light blue shirt which suits his olive complexion perfectly, Micah stands there in the middle of the room like someone's been beating on him. His outward appearance is so refined, but inside he's in pieces, held together with wisps of hope. It's a look Trace might not know, but Patrick does. That thousand yard stare, the wear and tear on the soul, it implies bad shit and hard times.

Turning his attention to the task at hand with effort, instinct telling him to go, and love Micah's pain away, no matter what it takes to make it happen, Trace forces himself to focus on his desk. Booting up his computer and opening his internet browser, Trace checks an email account—the one he shares with Yasha to pass messages back and forth safely.

The account has been deleted.

"Fuck," he hisses, pounding a fist on the desk, wanting to scream again, but managing not to. It's expected but shitty nonetheless. If Yasha is really out of the game, the biggest, best way to make a clean break is to delete all of the accounts tying him to people like Patrick.

He checks the next email account that comes to mind, and the next, and the next. He goes through the whole mental list, finishing with the one he shares with Nicholai, the man who had been Patrick's Master. The accounts are all the same. No change, no new messages. The latest messages are the ones Patrick left for the others. None have been read. No activity. No new information. It's as quiet as the grave.

It's not good.

The feeling of being stranded on an island in the middle of nowhere, with no one aware of where he is or how he's surviving, used to be comforting. It's not anymore. Now isolation only breeds desperation and dread, and mostly because his island now has multiple inhabitants, all of them counting on him to get them through. Little do they know they're relying on such a basketcase.

"Okay. It's okay. Priorities. Protect the family. Keep the kids safe," he murmurs under his breath, a mantra. There's a locked file on his desktop. He clicks on it, types in the password. Information spills out, flooding the screen. It's all there—beautiful, glorious fact. He skims it, just to ground himself, to remember what's true. The information on that screen narrows the possibilities about what could be happening with Gabriel and Darrek. But he can't tell them about it. He can't tell anybody.

At least his focus has been narrowed. The path he must take becomes clearer.

He closes the file. He closes his browser. He shuts down the machine.

At last, he doesn't have to fight the pull on his heartstrings any longer. He leaves the rest of his worries behind and goes to find out what's wrong with Micah.

Chapter 3
Lying and Leaving

The first time Patrick fell in love was when he was little more than a boy, a dumb teenage kid with a crush on a girl that landed both of them in water so hot, Patrick fled across the ocean to another continent just to get clear of the steam. Once he was in London, Patrick began to love another, a man named Nicholai Zhukov who was a Master Dom with an organization known as the Master's Circle. Nicholai helped train young Patrick as a Dom and introduced him to the fantastically kinky world of BDSM. But loving a man and being *in love* with a man were different conditions of the heart. The first man Patrick had ever been completely in love *with* met him immediately after the worst decade of Patrick's life. Patrick was in his early thirties. The man he fell so deeply for was much younger, in his early twenties.

His name was Gray Raoul.

Ten years of hell had changed Patrick. He'd fled the hot water of his adolescence only to tumble into the deepest, darkest pit. There, he'd roasted over flames for too many years, serving sick human beings and doing whatever was required of him for their pleasure. He was a slave, a whore, a pawn, and when he'd returned to London, he'd lost the ability to trust or respect anyone.

Beloved Nicholai had been there, waiting, and willing to help Patrick heal. Serving Nicholai as his Master's sub, Patrick began the slow, torturous process of remembering how to care about himself and why it was worth trying to entrust his heart, mind, and body to another human being. Patrick had been a broken man. Yet, there'd been hope. Nicholai had deemed him off-limits. Patrick was not to be touched by anyone, but especially by the other Doms of the Master's Circle.

Gray hadn't listened to Nicholai's decree. Enchanted by the challenge, Gray had been a young, headstrong, confident playboy learning to be a Master Dom, and he'd been unspeakably hot. In a time of his life when he hadn't known if there was anything left in the world worth wanting, or even getting out of bed for, Patrick had met Gray. Gray became his reason to want to try again. Nicholai was his teacher, but Gray was his muse. Gray's attempts at seduction, despite Nicholai's explicit orders, were Patrick's hope. So, he fell. He found himself in Gray's bed, again and again.

He was being taken advantage of in new ways, willingly. He hadn't known, then, how much it would cost him.

It was one of the most luxurious bedrooms Patrick had ever been in, and he'd been through a lot of them. The floor to ceiling windows overlooking the gardens, the rich fabrics of the curtains tied back to let the mid-morning light in, the handwoven carpets atop glistening hardwood floors, and the four-poster bed with its thick duvet, down pillows, and silk sheets—it was blessedly different than the impersonal, well-used hotel rooms he was used to.

The best thing about Gray was his quietness and intensity. Nothing about him was careless. Despite the ten year age difference, Patrick was always taken slightly aback by the fierceness of Gray's intelligence. It helped him forget the details and just *feel*.

Gray pushed Trace, naked, up against the bedpost so that his hands wrapped the wood, his stance wide. A strap was wound around the post, twisted, then wrapped around Patrick's wrists. Pulled tight, the strap bound him there. Skin prickling with awareness of where he was, who he was with, and how helpless he suddenly was, Patrick didn't have it in him to hide his reticence, his arousal, or his darkness. The dark was always with him then, tempting him to say fuck it all and do what was easy, and what felt good.

Gray gripped Patrick's jaw in a firm hold, forcing his chin up and around. Teeth scraped over the ridge of bone, down the column of his neck, then bit down at the junction of his shoulder.

Nicholai would see the bite. He would know. Gray bit harder, palming Patrick's erection, growling as Patrick gave in to instinct to thrust; undulating, pushing into the contact. The pain helped him focus, kept him present. Gray licked the bite, kissed the mark. Patrick shamelessly fucked the hand wrapping his shaft.

"Nicholai," Gray said in a low shiver of sound by Patrick's ear. "He give you a proper fuck this morning?"

"Yeah, proper," Patrick chuckled. "He gives it hard, just like everything else, bright eyes. And you? How do you give it?"

"Me? Harder."

Rubbing down the planes of Patrick's lean body, scratching hard enough to leave faint red lines, Gray gripped Patrick's hipbones. With a bruising hold, he pulled back and pressed forward at the same time, grinding against Patrick's ass. His cock was thick, hot and steely. Instinct took over.

Patrick tilted his hips on the next push. Gray's head caught and pressed right where Patrick needed it to, and it made Gray grin. Humming hungrily, he caught Patrick's mouth in a kiss over his shoulder. It was lips and breath and gasping, aching as Gray steadied himself with a hand at the root, holding the angles of their positions. Fuck, but it hurt, and Patrick chased the hurt, pushing back as Gray drove inward, making him take it, and making him moan. Like everything else with them, it was rough and urgent. Gray fit himself inside Patrick in defiance of everything, and everyone. He had no right to do what he was doing. But, once he was there, inside, Patrick wouldn't let him go.

Starting to move, riding the thick, gorgeous length of him, Patrick knew just how to rock backward into Gray's impatient thrusts to make it good, to drag against his gland and take his pleasure for himself. Their eyes locked, briefly, and what Gray saw then made him chuckle. It was like he needed the dark, was drawn to it. Maybe Gray sought to fuck Patrick because he was told he couldn't, but, once the act had commenced, it was Patrick that fucked Gray. Hands bound, ass stuffed with Gray's cock, Patrick moaned and kissed and did that which he'd been doing for so long, perfecting technique every day for too many years.

That could have been all, but whenever Patrick began to fade, to shut out specifics and only move, yielding, giving his body over, divorced from mind, Gray would grab hold, bite down, and wring pleasure in new ways. And it kept Patrick there. The mental game was just as important as the physical one.

Gray was sliding easily by the end, as Patrick throbbed, hugged tightly around his possessor's cock, claiming that which claimed him. Forehead pressed against the back of Patrick's head, Gray pushed, and pushed and came with a heavy exhale. They stayed like that, with Gray nuzzling Patrick's dark, thick, short hair and pressing a tender kiss to the nape of his neck. It was intimate enough to be frightening.

Patrick began to drift, to detach himself, to think of cleaning up and leaving, his route from the room, the best way to travel, undetected….

Gray pulled out, loosened the strap binding Patrick's wrists, and turned his captive around to face him. Those deep-blue eyes glistened with mischief and knowing. He was still so engaged, even though the act itself was complete. Gray was never off. He was always on, and Patrick loved that about him as much as it hurt to be truly, deeply, seen.

When Gray looked at Patrick, Gray saw him. He saw *all* of him.

Patrick stared into those lapis lazuli eyes and let Gray see enough to force him to back off. That endless slideshow of faces washed over Patrick's memory, all of those who'd bought the right to touch him, then threw him away once spent. And still Gray stared. He stared even harder, hand gripped beneath Patrick's jaw, holding him there to be kissed deeply and roughly. Their foreheads touched as Patrick teared up, the heartache like an open, gaping wound and still Gray wouldn't leave. A few gentle kisses trailed over Patrick's smoothly shaven jaw to the end of his chin, then Gray's hand caressed down the center of Patrick's body to find his cock.

The hand release was just as intense—a bombardment of sensation for the sole purpose of proving himself, of trying to outdo so many others, even though Patrick didn't care about any of that at all. The only thing that mattered was how clearly Gray looked at him, and how he didn't flinch away, or second guess.

That was what damned them. Gray saw too much, and Patrick made the mistake of hoping that this time, love would be enough to make it last. But it was the love itself that frightened Gray more than the damage. So, he let go, and Patrick once more was left used and discarded.

The quietness of Micah scares Trace. It feels like the beginning of an ending, and he hates those, so he's slow to ask. There's so much he's trying to hold together, and Micah is what's holding *him* together. To lose him in any sense would be too much. But, Trace knows enough to know when someone's needs change.

"This is about Lily, isn't it?" he says upon returning to where Micah still stands and leaning in to catch the scent of him. His nose brushes the softness of Micah's cheek and Micah reaches up to weave his fingers in Trace's long hair. The gentle touch sends a tingle rushing under Trace's skin. Feeling Micah tense, sensing his frown, Trace leans in more to catch Micah's kiss.

Is he leaving me for her? Has he finally decided?

Like Gray, Micah is smarter than he should be. He sees more than most and he's hardly ever intimidated. He dedicates the time needed to the things deemed most important to him. There are too many similarities between them to not be scared.

He gets a better look at Micah's face and how rattled he is. The threads holding him in one piece are frayed and unraveling. His eyes are too glassy, his lips too tight, his jaw clenched, and just beneath the surface... wildness.

"Talk to me, love," Trace begs. "Please."

Lowering his gaze, bowing his head, Micah shakes it.

"She won't sleep next to me. She sleeps somewhere else... her lover. She won't...." he gives a mean smile, full of teeth and bitterness. "She won't look at me. Her gaze slides right off like there's nothing in me to catch her notice anymore and...."

Micah blows out a breath.

"I deserve it! No wonder she feels better with Saoirse instead of lying next to me, pretending she can't tell I'm shutting her out, too. She should be with someone who makes her happy, makes her smile. She's been through hell and when I'm around her, I feel like I'm drawing her back down there instead of letting her move past it. She's been trying *so hard* to make progress but I am *lying* to her about *important* things," Micah says with barely concealed rage, but at whom or what, Trace can't tell.

"Then stop lying," Trace answers. As unlikely a turn-on as it is, Micah's humility pushes every one of Trace's buttons. To be a man so self-possessed, so successful and capable, but willing to readily admit to faults is one of the most attractive things about him. It also distinguishes Micah from Gray. Gray was always right, about everything, and it drove Patrick nuts. But Micah, with his brilliance, unassuming sexiness, and humanity, only pulls Patrick—and Trace—in closer and closer, until there's nothing but heat and breath between them.

"*It's not as easy as that.*" Micah's eyes flash. Then he pushes all of the torment about Lilianna back, behind walls and layers of civility and control. The effort of doing that makes him look even more tired. "I didn't come here to talk about it. I didn't want to talk about this, I just wanted *you*. I wanted…."

Trace grabs him, pulling him in, hard, kissing his breath away. It breaks through some of those barriers. Then, Micah is on him and taking over. He pushes Trace over to the couch, then down. He straddles Trace's lap, sinking down, grinding against him. Raking his fingers through Trace's hair, Micah moans into the kiss, releasing so much built-up tension that Trace feels the relief too.

There's so much beauty in the way Micah is able to completely surrender to Trace. The love in the submission makes it mean more than it has with anyone Trace has ever been paired with. To be trusted as much as Micah trusts him, with his body, heart, and mind, helps Trace feel how lucky he is rather than how burdened. With his past loves, Trace was always the one doing the surrendering, and it never quite gave him what he needed, deep down. Maybe there wasn't as much mutual trust then as he liked to think there was, but it's not the case with Micah. With him, there's a luxurious abundance of it, enough to get swept away in.

They kiss and touch, but it doesn't go anywhere, because it doesn't need to. It's enough to be close and shake off the loneliness. Micah pours some of his frustration into his passion and Trace invites every moment of it. Another difference between Gray and Micah, past and present, is with Micah, there's no end goal. Their feelings, their passion has always been and will always be driven by present moments. Too much of why Trace and Micah each suffer is because of the past. Everything that worries them has to do with the future, so they ignore where they came from and where they're going and just exist, together. They're messy and imperfect, but it's worked so far. Trace knows all of the chaos swirling around them has nothing to do with the current moment. It's all speculation and old pain.

"You feel so good," Micah sighs between kisses.

"You taste like oranges," Trace tells him.

Micah laughs and says, "I haven't been anywhere near oranges. Guess I'm naturally fruity."

"Hey, you said it. Not me," Trace smiles. Micah smiles back and kisses him harder.

Holding Micah, kissing him, trying to soothe away his frown lines with light brushes of his lips or rough caresses of his hands, Trace tries to keep him there, where they have everything that matters.

For a little while, Trace has him. Palming Micah's ass, encouraging every sexy little undulation as Micah rocks against Trace's groin, Trace watches him, wondering. He wants to grab hold of Micah the way Gray used to grab hold of Patrick. Sometimes, it would work. Gray could keep him from slipping into the dark for a few, precious minutes. Trace sees Micah slipping. Experience tells him sex isn't the answer. The only thing that will help is patience and love. It might not be enough. He still might slip away for good, but Trace knows he has to try.

Chapter 4
A Slave Afraid

The phone is ringing again. The landline. Though the answering machine is in a box in the closet with some of the wires ripped out, the phone itself is still plugged in, so it just rings and rings without ever being picked up.

It doesn't always ring. There were a few days of blessed, though tense, silence before it started up again.

Darrek has the gun in his hand, and he's not sure why. He likes the weight of it and the feel of the cool, slick, hard metal inside his grip. Wearing an old pair of jeans, his leather collar buckled around his neck, he sits on a chair in the living room, facing the phone and the door. His back is to the wall.

It occurs to him that the timer for dinner should be going off soon. Then he'll need to take the casserole out of the oven before it's overdone. His training and responsibility to his Master lets that much filter past the shrill rattle in his eardrums, echoing off of the walls of the empty house.

Five rings.

Six.

Seven.

He's breathing hard and his eyes burn. His back is tight like he's bracing himself, waiting for the slicing lash of a belt across his bare skin, or the slam of a door on his wrist. Sierra, their golden retriever, comes over to him, her nails clicking softly on the floorboards to nuzzle his leg with concern. After a sniff or two, she settles down at his feet, laying her head on her paws. Eyes upturned, she beseeches him but keeps her body between him and danger. That makes him

wish he didn't have the gun.
Eight rings.
Nine.
"No. No. Enough."
He stands and sets the gun—a Glock 30—on top of the tall bookcase in the hall, out of sight but in reach, and goes right to the phone. It rings again. Reaching for the jack, he pulls it out of the wall.
The phone goes silent.
He exhales heavily. After a moment in which he lets himself begin to calm, Darrek returns to Sierra and sits with her, stroking her back and murmuring, "Good girl. Such a good girl."

Thirty minutes later, the casserole is cooling on the kitchen counter; Darrek is naked and kneeling by the door, awaiting Gabriel and the phone's next ring. He hears Gabriel's Discovery pull into the driveway and audibly tracks his movements from the vehicle to the front door of their house. Part of his mind—the cruel part—whispers that it's not Gabriel at all, though he recognizes the engine sound and the squeaky brakes. The glimmer of doubt is what prevents him from keeping his head bowed as his Master enters their home after a ten-hour shift at work at his studio, Daring Angel Photography.

All he needs is the glimpse of Gabriel's polished shoes. Once he gets it, Darrek's heartbeat slows to a more normal pace. His right arm and shoulder muscles gradually relax and he stops wanting to get up and get the gun again.

Sierra gives a happy little bark and hurries up to Gabriel, her tongue lolling out as she greets him and gets a nice head scratch for her troubles.

"Hey baby, you taking care of the big lug for me, huh? Good girl."

Sierra barks again, then runs to the back door, looking expectantly over a shoulder as she waits to be let out.

"Okay, okay. I'm comin'," Gabriel sighs, sounding more tired than he should. There's always something about the way Gabriel speaks around Darrek lately that makes it seem like he's *trying* to sound normal instead of actually sounding normal. Darrek is fairly sure that's the paranoia talking, or maybe Gabriel is just managing to muster courage in a more successful way than Darrek.

Darrek knows he should get up, take Gabriel's coat and bag, ask him how his day was, but his legs won't heed commands from his brain. They stay folded beneath him, his arms heavy, knees weak, and spine prickling with certainty that the phone will start ringing again any moment and he'll lose it for good. His mind will snap cleanly under the strain.

Gabriel's hand lovingly caresses the side of Darrek's jaw as he passes with a murmured, "C'mere."

It's good to keep his gaze down, Darrek decides. It keeps him from seeing if Gabriel is glancing around the house, checking for anything that's off, feeding the madness that's always with Darrek now, like Jerry is right outside, listening, waiting, or maybe crouched in one of the closets, or standing behind a door, holding a knife, or a belt.

After a few long strides, Gabriel is at the back door. He unlocks it; unfastening the chain and opening it up. Sierra rushes out into the fenced yard. Gabriel closes the door behind her. Darrek wants him to lock the door again, but he doesn't.

As Gabriel's gaze drifts over to the unplugged phone line, seeing that it is, in fact, still unplugged, Darrek is able to move at last. The casserole is his primary concern. He stands, walking to the kitchen. Ignoring the look he glimpses on Gabriel's face, he gets out a plate and scoops onto it a serving of chicken and vegetables in cream sauce with toasted breadcrumbs on top. After setting this on the table, he moves to get the opened wine bottle from the fridge, but is stopped by Gabriel's hand on his arm.

Stilling himself, eyes averted, Darrek just stands there as Gabriel folds him up in a hug. Slightly wind-chilled fingers caress over Darrek's bare back and Gabriel's lips press a kiss to Darrek's shoulder.

"Please sit with me," Gabriel asks gently, a breath of sound.

"I need this," Darrek manages, his voice coming out rougher than he expected. He adds, "Sir," as an afterthought.

"Look at me, Dare."

There's a five inch difference in height between them. Gabriel is the shorter, as well as the slighter one. In almost every way, Gabriel looks sweeter, gentler, and more innocent than Darrek. Appearances can be deceiving, though. A slim, startlingly pretty body can sometimes disguise a powerfully determined, wise, strong and well-fortified spirit. Even simply standing in Gabriel's arms, Darrek can feel the steady strength of his partner. He needs that too, desperately.

He looks into Gabriel's grey-blue eyes, at the perfectly casual, sexy tousle of his dark hair and struggles not to grimace at the claws of stress and fear shredding Gabriel's paper-thin façade. They're both struggling, and coping in their own ways.

Gabriel asks, "The phone was ringing, wasn't it? Did you leave the gun alone, like I asked? That's for emergencies *only*."

Gabriel's voice is low and carries, pressing the will, triggering instincts that have become ingrained in Darrek's psyche in their two and a half years together. Knowing his Master can read the answers well enough in his expression, Darrek lets silence speak his guilt.

"You need this?" Gabriel asks.

"Yes, Master," Darrek answers tightly with a nod.

"Okay," Gabriel relents. "Restraints?"

"Please."

The phone upstairs begins to ring, the one not yet unplugged. Instantly, Darrek starts to cry.

"Hey," Gabriel says in a sharp, rasping command, demanding Darrek's attention. "Who's in charge here? Huh?"

"Y-you."

"Louder!"

"You."

"On your knees. Right there," Gabriel orders, pointing at a patch of tile beside the table. "Don't move an inch. Don't fucking even think about touching the gun. You hear me?"

Wiping his eyes on the back of his arm, Darrek gets in position, trying to tune it all out, to go inward, but he hears it all anyway — the heavy footsteps up the stairs as Gabriel goes, then crossing through the bedroom, the silencing of the other phone and the subsequent footsteps into the second bedroom where a creaking door tells Darrek that the cabinet has been unlocked.

He's already getting hard by the time Gabriel returns with the restraints. Chest rising and falling, eyes unfocused, body on display for his Master to do with what he likes, Darrek shivers pleasantly when Gabriel tells him, "Face down on the floor, slave. Hands behind your back. Knees bent."

Two of four cuffs go on his wrists, binding them together. The other two wrap his ankles, effectively hogtieing him.

"Try to move."

He does, but can't do much with his arms bound behind him and his legs bent back as they are. Briefly, a soft, cold panic washes through him at being so immobilized, but then Gabriel's hand moves over the skin of Darrek's left arm, soothing. Telling himself to accept the position, to adjust to it and take comfort in Gabriel's fierce care, slowly, Darrek calms again.

"Deep, even breaths," Gabriel says in a pacifying, butter-smooth voice that instinctively sends a prickle of nervousness crawling up Darrek's balls.

A chain is snapped onto the back of his collar, connecting it to the cuffs. There's enough slack that he's not going to choke himself, but he can feel it, the tension on the leather wrapping his neck.

"Good," Gabriel praises, still with that unnerving tone. "Breathe. Inhale. Now. And out."

Without any warning or prep, an object is inserted swiftly into his anus, making him gasp. Gabriel spreads his buttocks with a hand and presses it farther into him as Darrek grunts, his body struggling to adjust to the pressure and fullness.

"*Breathe*, slave," Gabriel snaps.

Shuddering, Darrek feels the object widen dramatically, but Gabriel doesn't ease up, he forces it inside Darrek's ass. It continues to slide through his sphincter and he's panting, crying out a little with each exhale. Then the object is fully seated in him. A moment later, Gabriel turns it on and it starts to vibrate.

"Oh fuck," Darrek moans. His dick is guided to point back between his legs and Gabriel strokes it until Darrek is completely erect. His cock pushes at the tile floor, trying to rise, making Darrek want to lift his ass up and make room, but it's not enough. It doesn't help at all. Gabriel stands, knees popping.

"And now, I eat," Gabriel sighs, going to the sink to wash up. "Smells delicious, by the way. Thank you."

Unable to see a clock, Darrek has no way to gauge time. All he knows is the silence of the phone and the soft sounds of Gabriel's fork moving against his plate as he eats his dinner and sips his wine.

Sierra begins to scratch at the back door, wanting to be let in. Body thrumming, covered in a light film of sweat, muscles straining in the bonds and his dick aching from being so hard for so long, Darrek can only groan as the dog is let in and immediately comes over to lick his face.

"She's worried about you," Gabriel says, watching.

"Sierra, go lay down!" Darrek says gruffly, grimacing against the wet drag of her tongue.

"C'mere, girl," Gabriel says, taking her by the collar and leading her away.

"Did you lock the door?" Darrek asks when Gabriel returns. "Is the alarm on?"

"Speak only when spoken to, slave. Starting now. But yes, I did and yes, it is. Calm down."

"Yes, Sir."

Another stretch of time passes as Gabriel finishes up. Unhurriedly, he clears the table, then washes his plate, silverware and wine glass in the sink, leaving Darrek to stew in his own juices for a while.

By the time Gabriel is unfastening the ankle cuffs, Darrek can't move anything. The vibrator is still up his ass. The collar is still chained to his wrists. His legs and arms ache and his dick hasn't lost any interest. It sticks up uncomfortably between his legs as Gabriel helps Darrek kneel, then stand.

"Walk. Take your time," he says with a hand holding Darrek's linked wrists.

They move through the kitchen to the hall beside the living room, then up the stairs to the second bedroom.

Gabriel leaves him standing in the middle of the room. It's their personal playroom and makeshift dungeon. As Gabriel turns on lights and gets things ready, Darrek's eyes scan the handcrafted sex furniture and cabinets stocked with every piece of toy, lubricant, whip, flogger, restraint, or miscellaneous gear imaginable.

"Get the whip. Hit me," Darrek hisses.

Gabriel breathes out a humorless laugh. "Yeah, bet you'd like that, huh? Guess what, slave? You're not in charge. We do this *my* way. You want punishment for disobeying my orders? Fine. I'll punish you. But I want you to know who it is making you hurt. You know who I am? Who am I?"

"Master," Darrek growls.

"Ask nicely," Gabriel teases with a cold smile. "Beg me, bitch."

"Please hurt me, Master. Please punish me for taking down the gun and holding it against your orders." "Sit in the chair," Gabriel sighs, pointing to it.

Dread tightens Darrek's chest and makes him want to void his bladder. That's good. It distracts him, brings him out of his head and into the moment. He walks to the indicated chair and sits. It's no more than a narrow piece of wood under his ass, pressing the vibrator into his rectum uncomfortably. It also has a headrest, though, fixed to the wall. The headrest cups under his skull, holding his head in place and leaving a space for his arms behind him. Gabriel pulls a leather strap across his forehead and buckles it tightly, keeping his head perfectly still against the headrest.

Breathing harder, chest heaving with growing fright, Darrek watches his Master bind his legs in place, too. Straps go over each thigh, beneath each knee, over each ankle, binding them perfectly to the chair and keeping his legs spread. His balls hang, heavy and full between his legs and his cock sticks up, waiting. The prospect of imminent pain doesn't wilt his erection at all.

When Gabriel fits a ball gag between Darrek's teeth and straps that on too, his worry notches up. Biting down on the firm rubber, he practices his breathing exercises and tracks Gabriel as he moves around the dungeon.

Of course, Gabriel doesn't even try to hide what he has selected. It's something he's threatened many times but never actually used on Darrek. Darrek has seen videos, though, of times Gabriel used it on other submissives when he worked as a Dominant, professionally, at Diadem.

Trembling uncontrollably, Darrek whimpers against the gag as Gabriel coats the sound with lube. A moment later, additional lube is swiped over the slit in Darrek's cock, then worked inside with the pad of Gabriel's finger.

"You... are *really* gonna hate this," Gabriel says with a steady, determined sort of promise in his eyes. Darrek holds his gaze a little longer, understanding that Gabriel wants him angry and physically uncomfortable so that there's no room left in his head for fear of what may be lurking outside the house or on the other end of the telephone line. And Darrek wants that too, enough to go willingly, eagerly along with whatever his Master has planned. They might not be in control of what's been happening with the calls and the house alarm, but they have control of the scene and themselves. It's a good thing to be reminded of.

The sound is seven inches long and 5/16 inch in diameter, trailing a black wire, which connects it to the power box. The thickness of it and the promise of not only being stuffed with the sound but also the imagined pain from the electric shock makes Darrek's thighs quiver. He fights the restraints, but he's in tightly. Grunting and whimpering against the gag, he stares helplessly as Gabriel brings the end of the sound to the tip of his dick, steadying the organ with a hand.

Blowing out hard through his nose, eyes rolling up as the dull, narrow end of the sound lowers into his opening, parting it, Darrek moans thickly. The trembling increases as the pain starts, the sound passing into his urethra a millimeter at a time. With a focused expression of concentration, Gabriel's gaze is fixed to Darrek's penis as he holds the metal rod and lets gravity pull it into the narrow opening. It burrows deeper and deeper into him.

Soon, Darrek is shouting. It's muffled by the rubber ball and he pulls on his arms, making the collar tighten on his windpipe. He hates the feel of the sound pushing so far into his penis, but his legs are trapped. That damned chair immobilizes him completely.

Gabriel doesn't rush. Slowly, steadily, diligently, he waits for Darrek's member to take the rod. When it's all the way in, Darrek is woozy with hurt, throbbing with his heartbeat, which radiates from his dick, through his groin and up into his gut, twisting it sickeningly with cramps that tense his body from thighs to midsection.

"How's that feel, slave? You like that? Should I get a thicker one? Or maybe bring Trace over here for a replay of the first time we met? That'd be sweet, wouldn't it? A trip down memory lane."

He can't answer. The breath tears from him. Sweat drips down his face, down his neck and chest. The leather bites into skin at all of the places where Darrek is pulling at the straps.

Gabriel squeezes up and down his slave's stuffed cock a few times, causing Darrek to whine pleading sounds, interspersed with hard grunts and growls. He wishes Gabriel had taken the damned vibrator out before doing this, because it's keeping him hard, forcing him to find the pleasure in the pain.

Then Gabriel lets go and turns on the sound.

A shrill, abrupt scream wrenches from Darrek's chest. His whole body tightens from the electric surge coursing up through the inside of his penis and directly into his lower abdomen. Every muscle tenses. His body locks up, making the cords of his neck stand out as he bites down hard on the gag. His face grows hot, turning red, his body straining, straining as hard as it can against the onslaught.

"Breathe, baby," Gabriel hushes. "Learn to like it or I put some pads on your balls too, and I have a few different plugs for your ass I can hook up to this little box. This is *nothing*. This is *easy*."

Darrek exhales sharply, then sucks another breath.

"No, better than that. Breathe or I make it worse."

The dial turns as the charge increases. Darrek chokes off a desperate sound and begins taking shallow, shaking, uneven breaths.

"Steady 'em out. Now."

Growling, biting hard on the gag, eyes rolled up in his head, he manages to take a few, even, deeper breaths and still the surge barrages his body.

Gabriel turns the electricity off.

Darrek goes limp in the bonds, sagging, gasping for air. As Gabriel goes back to stroking him, watching his hand move on the reddened column, filled obscenely with silver, Darrek can't deny how good it feels.

Gabriel loosens the gag and pulls it from Darrek's lips to hang around his throat instead.

"Tell me you love it, bitch."

"I love it," Darrek gasps.

"Say please."

"Please—ahhh!"

Gabriel has let go again and turned on the charge. Gritting his teeth, snarling against the pain, Darrek fights back against it, blowing breaths through his lips.

"Good, baby," Gabriel praises. "Look at you. Gorgeous. Just a little more, okay?"

The surge gets stronger.

"Can't," Darrek manages, face hot and red, his whole body burning as he bears down, his hands in fists.

"You want to say the safeword?"

Darrek nods.

Gabriel turns the dial down.

"Say it."

Darrek growls, blowing another breath out, shakily.

"Hurts," he whimpers.

"Nope. That's not it," Gabriel tsks, turning the dial backup. Darrek screams.

The pain consumes him, incinerating every thought, every care and worry. Nothing matters but the lightning bolts frying his aching cock from the inside out. By the time Gabriel shuts off the power and begins to pull the sound out, Darrek is fairly delirious, without much fight left in him at all.

With a throaty cry, he watches as all seven inches of the sound are pulled very slowly out of his urethra, leaving the opening stretched wider. Immediately, Gabriel lowers his mouth onto Darrek's cock, sucking it as Darrek bears down again with a gruff protest of, "Please don't. *Please*," because he knows Gabriel has no intention of giving him permission to orgasm. It's just more torture, but this time in the form of pleasure rather than pain.

Ignoring him, Gabriel takes a few long pulls. His mouth comes off with a wet pop and his hand works the shaft as he glances up at Darrek.

"You know what I want, right?" Gabriel asks quietly.

Jaw clenched, staring up at the ceiling, Darrek nods.

The restraints all come off. He's aching everywhere, head to toe, but shuffles into the other bedroom. Laying down on the edge of the bed, Darrek draws his legs up, holding the knees and presenting his ass.

"Please fuck me, Master," Darrek asks with a wavering voice.

Without ceremony, Gabriel steps up to him and tugs the vibrator out. With his cock in hand, Gabriel enters Darrek in one smooth thrust. The sex is rough and Gabriel stays deeply inside him. Gabriel has an angry expression on his face as they fuck and Darrek bears it, lying as quietly as he can while Gabriel takes him as hard and fast as he wants.

He hears Gabriel's soft cry as he comes. It makes Darrek's stomach swoop happily, painting the whole scene with bittersweet emotion and a profound, inexpressibly devoted love.

Vision blurring, eyes burning again, Darrek feels Gabriel pull out. Then Gabriel undresses completely and climbs onto the bed, lying on his stomach with his legs spread wide.

It's become part of their routine, an established give and take that helps them balance the new rules defining the boundaries of their relationship. Gabriel lets Darrek know when he needs physical comfort of his own. They know it's not safe for Gabriel to submit to Darrek, and Darrek isn't even sure if Gabriel would want that anymore. But it's a given that Gabriel can't always be in control. Sometimes it's not enough to be Master, and Gabriel just needs to feel loved and less alone in quieter ways, once he's confident that Darrek's needs have been met first. After every scene ends, and the Master and slave roles fall away, they become, simply, lovers again. And Darrek loves Gabriel so that he's less afraid, too.

"Thank you for that," Darrek murmurs. "I feel better now."

"Good. I'll reheat some food for you after we shower, okay? But first…"

"Yeah," Darrek smiles. "I know."

Darrek shifts, rolling onto his knees and crawls over to him, settling between Gabriel's legs. Slipping a hand under Gabriel's hips, Darrek draws them up at an angle and aligns himself to Gabriel's opening. Darrek's cock is wet with saliva and lube, but Gabriel isn't prepped, so he goes slowly, adding a little pressure and giving Ga-

briel's slim, smaller body a chance to adjust and accept him.
With a low, broken moan that puts steel in Darrek's cock, the head breaches Gabriel, nestling in his body. His hand flattened on Gabriel's pelvis, lips peppering kisses over his neck, shoulder and head, Darrek works his way into Gabriel with gentle pushes. Once they're fully joined, Darrek guides Gabriel's hands up over his head, holding the wrists together there as he caresses down the side of his lithe body. Gabriel quivers and gasps.

"Love you, Gabe," Darrek whispers.

Gabriel presses down onto him, back arching slightly, skin pebbling with goosebumps as Darrek's grip on his wrists tightens. With a blissful gasp, Gabriel begs, "*More.*"

Chapter 5
In Love and Loss

Ten Years Ago

Micah is seriously, diligently trying to lose himself in the moment. It's late. They'd had a quiet dinner at home and danced barefoot in the kitchen to music from the radio before retreating to the bedroom. Crouched by the foot of their bed with his head nestled between Lilianna's firm, smooth, caramel-colored thighs, he kisses and licks her. He's fairly certain he's doing a good job at giving her pleasure, and not only because his wife is quite vocal about what she likes and how she likes it. With his eyes closed, his mind free of worries or cares, Micah gets lost in the beautiful, sexy woman who is to him everything warm and good, and pushes his tongue in deeper.

"Oh!" Lilianna exclaims, not really like someone who's about to get off, but, rather, someone who just remembered that thing they forgot, which has been bugging them all day.

Sighing, Micah lifts his head to see her face. On her back, gazing happily at the ceiling, one hand tangled in her long, dark hair and the other gripping the top of her leg, Lilianna makes a curious humming sound.

"You always sound so surprised," Micah observes, squinting warily at her. He's not as exasperated as he could be, at least not until she begins to giggle. "The giggling doesn't help my confidence here, either."

"I'm sorry," she apologizes and it sounds sincere, but she's still laughing even though she's trying very hard to compose herself and make her expression a serious one. It's not really working.

Rolling his eyes and settling back down, he caresses her silky soft skin. As he nuzzles against her inner thigh, dragging kisses here and there, he hears her say conversationally, "You know, the first time I was with a guy, as in, you know, close encounters with a penis, the biggest surprise was—"

"Oh, here it comes."

"It moves!" she says brightly, giggling even more helplessly. He gives it up for the moment at least and climbs up to lie atop her, gazing with frustrated wonder at her sweet face. "It moves on its own. Like a... like a *snake*."

"Jesus, Lil," he sighs with dull amazement. It does make him smile, though, but he does his best not to laugh with her, as much as he wants to. His pride demands it. "*That's* what you think about while I'm tonguing your clit? Some guy's twitchy johnson?"

Lost in the giggle fit, she argues, "I mean, they don't tell you that!"

Squinting again, he asks, "Who is 'they'? Your parents? They never sat you down when you were a young girl, perhaps on the way back from church, to have the all-important twitchy johnson talk? And now you're snorting. Fantastic."

She covers her face with her hands, snorting and laughing hysterically.

He makes himself comfortable, because there's no telling how long it'll take her to settle down again. He consoles himself with the knowledge that he's got a naked, aroused, hot as hell and very leggy woman wrapping herself around him.

"I love you," she grins happily.

"Can we move on now? We done?"

"Yes," she says, calming down and raking her fingers through his hair, drawing her legs more snugly around his lower back. He reaches down between their bodies and lines himself up with her.

"Wait!" she says abruptly, her eyes lighting up.

"Wait?" he echoes, confused again.

"I want to do something for you too," she explains, making that sweetly imploring face she knows he can't resist. Her voice softens. Like the temptress she is, she tries to hypnotize him into agreeing before she properly explains herself and her motives.

Letting go of his dick and planting the hand instead on the bed by her side, he asks pointedly, "What do you think this is, lady?"

Her smile only grows, and she's like a cat brushing against him, purring softly and he knows where this is going, or he has a good idea at least.

"No, I mean it," Lilianna says. "C'mere."

She has him and she rolls them. He doesn't fight it. In fact, once they're on their sides, he shifts onto his stomach, holding his face in his hands. Speaking against his palms, he groans, "Lil…"

She kisses along the side of his jaw, down his neck and around the back of his shoulder. Her hand skims down the length of his back, her dainty fingers tickling over his skin. Down the side of his thigh, over to between his legs she rubs lightly. Drawing the hand up his inner thigh to the crease of his ass, she slides her index finger into him in one push.

"I want to," she says breathlessly, eagerly and with plenty of intent. The finger pumps inside the clenched ring of muscle. "Please? *Please?*"

A few minutes later, she has the damned harness strapped on and he's full to bursting with the lube-slicked phallus attached to it. Crying out roughly, panting, sweating, he can't bring himself to look at her, not when he's in such a state—humiliated and aroused, vulnerable and wild—and keeps his face turned down toward the bed as she rides him in smooth strokes. The thing that makes his skin pebble and stiffens his cock, sliding easily in her small fist, is how much Lilianna is obviously getting off on this, maybe even more than the cunnilingus. She moans like the dildo is part of her and she can feel Micah's ass gripping the shaft, and yes, it's unspeakably hot.

She takes him up the edge, pumping the toy into him, jacking his dick harder and faster until he shouts, "Fuck!" Shuddering with his release, feeling her small fingers play in the hot fluid of his spend, he gasps, "I love you too."

"Mm," she hums happily, "there it is. Say thank you, and mean it." It's not a request, it's an order. But she has him and there is no fighting her, not when she gets like this. She owns him completely.

"Thank you," he answers, meaning it entirely. He still can't glance back at her, though. Blushing, he tries to hold in small panting sounds and grunts as she keeps going, rocking against him in just the right way.

"God, I *really* love you," she chuckles when he shivers and arches on the bed, pushing back onto the toy.

"Fuck," he rasps, but it doesn't matter. He's lost and nothing else exists but her.

―◻―◻―◻―

Present Day

It's terrifying what time can do to you. Sometimes, no matter how many material possessions you accumulate, or accomplishments you achieve, it still adds up to not much worth anything. Micah sits in his large, fine house—nicer than any of his friends' houses—in an office where the walls are lined with his framed and immaculately displayed degrees, photos of professional triumphs such as the company he built from the ground up, then sold for millions of dollars in profit, his bank accounts filled with as much money as he will ever need. He wishes it all could help fix what's wrong inside of him and with his marriage. He wishes it all meant something to him anymore.

His hand, trembling, rests on the remote control for the video screen perched on the elegant desk in front of him. He has no thought of Lilianna other than, for once, hoping she stays away instead of just expecting her to. Typically, he's praying for her return, her attention, or her care. But she doesn't care. She doesn't *care*, and why should she? Her husband isn't just having an affair behind her back with another man who she thinks is just a friend they have threesomes with once in a while. Now he's gone and fallen in love. Micah feels more alive with Trace than he has with Lilianna in years. Every time he looks at her, he feels the lies he's telling constantly now, like silent, unseen barbs shot into her back, driving her away to someone else. Saoirse wasn't there through the torture and loss, so she still has the ability to have a conversation with Lilianna that isn't layered with subtle bitterness and accusation.

They used to be happy together. Micah and Lilianna would laugh and find the humor in any situation. It made it easier to get through the tough times. But humor doesn't get you through hellish nightmares chewing up their lives, gutting their hope. Lilianna turns her face from Micah now. Out of self-preservation, she lowers her gaze, closes him out, and he doesn't know if he can ever get her back. He can't take it. He's sick of living beside the woman who used to be his best friend in the world, constantly reminded how their closeness has withered because of the mistakes he's made. Now, with Lilianna looking elsewhere for sex, love, and trust, Micah has been left to fend for himself, trying to piece back together the tattered scraps of their world, losing a little more every day of the one person who was supposed to be his best friend forever.

The office door is securely locked against her, but she won't try to come in anyway. She probably left the house entirely in order to not be anywhere near him. He doesn't blame her. She's never been able to tolerate him when he gets like this, because now Micah is the poison, corrupting everything he touches. He deserves pain. He deserves everything he's suffered through and more.

Call Trace.

Guilt is a pang in his chest, because he knows he won't call. Not today.

It's Moira's birthday.

You should have reminded him, a voice barks angrily. The voice sounds a little like Ben, enough to make the corner of Micah's mouth twitch in an almost-smile. *He's human, you silly bitch. He forgets shit just like everyone else.*

They should be having a party. There should be family and friends gathered in celebration, laughter and presents, shining, colorful balloons and a big, decadent cake. They should be so happy.

But all they have is this. This large, fine house, silent as a tomb; this office littered with accolades that count for nothing, except money he doesn't spend, with honor that feels hollow; and a pathetic man who used to be a good husband, and a father.

Submitting helps. In fact, it's one of the only things that helps him cope and continue to get out of bed every day. Conversely, dominating helps him vent, purging some of the tightly bottled emotion inside him. Plus, he gets a rush off of it like nothing else. The ways he enjoys submitting and dominating are really quite different. The pleasure of each originates from opposite ends of the spectrum of his identity. But really, there is only one way to crack the hard shell formed around his emotional core, and get to what is trapped inside.

Oh, how he wants to be back there when life was so good, holding his baby in his arms, seeing her smile, hearing her laugh, and taking her hand. He's so mad it's gone, like it never was, like it was erased, like *she* was erased. He *knows* it was real. It was the best of him, the best of *both* of them—those years, that wonderful little girl.

With one press of his finger, and a click of one button, he presses play and the delicate sound of old, recorded, gentle laughter fills the air.

The effect is quick and devastating.

It comes erupting up from the depths in a hot spray that splatters the fine walls, the trophies and trappings of sanity. Everything bubbles, boils and melts, coursing to the floors, burning through those too, eating through earth and rock, dripping down even unto hell itself.

Micah doesn't know why he does it to himself, watching the videos, driving himself to madness with the proof of what could have been and will never be, but he does, and the screams come from way, way down, below the fury and the pain and the unfairness of it all.

Because there is nothing else of her left.

She would have been six.

Zippered pouch in hand, Trace slams the door of his truck closed, exhaling a heavy breath. His dark hair, interspersed with plenty of gray, is loose about his shoulders but the bandana tied around his head keeps it out of his eyes. The fall weather gives the air some bite, but even though he's wearing a sleeveless shirt and no jacket, he doesn't mind the cold.

He's left the truck's engine running. The sound of the radio through the window's glass is muffled. His boots crunch over loose gravel and dirt of the long, winding drive which reaches around to the back of the property. That's where he parked. The sun is bright, the wind blowing gently. Lilianna sits on the back step, elbows on her knees, quaking subtly, like she's recovering from shock, and sucks hard on the end of a burnt-down cigarette. Her long, dark hair is pulled tightly back, her almond-shaped, exotic-looking eyes focused on nothing.

The breeze quiets for a moment and Trace is sure he can hear Micah, deep within the house. He shouldn't be able to, but it is what it is.

Lilianna had sent him a simple, coded text—*MM911*—maybe twenty seconds after Trace remembered on his own, slamming a fist in frustration with himself against the beat-up old Ford in his garage, which he'd been tinkering with at the time.

Life is shitty like that sometimes. Blame it on the chaos, or his waning ability to manage so much at once, or his age. He knows he's not perfect, but he should be better than this. For Micah especially, he should.

"Hey, beautiful," he says in greeting to Lilianna. It's full of apology and a resigned, tired sort of sorrow. "He in the office again?"

She nods without looking anywhere near his face, one knee bouncing, making quite a picture there, huddled like she's just waiting for her own house to swoop in from behind like a giant monster to gobble her up.

Yeah, ain't I her proud, white knight come to save her?

He knows it's not his place to tell her about Micah's feelings and infidelities. That's something Micah needs to own up to himself, hopefully sooner than later. Still, he hates seeing her question herself on such fundamental levels, especially after everything she's already been through with Moira. She's endured the most awful kind of loss, one no one ever should have to face. Now she's losing Micah, too, and, little does she know, Trace is the one stealing him away.

Maybe he shouldn't, for her sake, but he does set his hand briefly on her shoulder as he passes. Without having to look, he knows her cheeks are free from tears. They hollow as she draws smoke into her lungs, eyes still diligently averted. He hates that quaking, though. It makes him angry at many things at once, wishing there was something there to fight and rip apart with his bare hands, for the sake of everyone he knows who's in pain from impossible, intangible things.

Feeling each and every one of his forty-nine years, he takes another deep breath and walks past Lilianna, toward the back door.

"Go on in the truck, now," he tells her. After a sideways glance at that cigarette, he adds, "Leave those windows up."

Lilianna is up and on the move before he's even able to turn the door's knob.

As soon as the door is ajar, he hears the screaming more clearly. It's primal and coming from the far corner of the first floor.

Trace quickens his pace, boots clicking on the slick wood floors, the wailing growing stronger and stronger as he approaches. As soon as he's at the door, he draws his lock picking kit out of the pouch. Crouching, he gets to work. Last year, Micah installed a reinforced lock on that door, despite Trace's assurances that it wouldn't make much difference. Trace would be able to get in anyway, and Lilianna would never bother to try.

With his hands busy, he tries to turn his thoughts inward rather than listen, but behind the screams, he hears it, soft and awful. A child's giggling.

Trace slams a palm against the door, twice, in warning, rattling it in the frame.

He gets the lock, turns the knob, and eases the door open. A scan of the wrecked room reveals Micah to Trace's left. Micah is on the floor, back to the wall. His dark, olive skin is slick with a light sheen of sweat, his brown eyes glistening, and the whites now red. Face covered in tears, hiccupping on his cries, because god knows how long this has been going on, he looks wild, crazed, and way, way beyond reason's reach.

Christ, if only she would listen to him, now and then. If only she would try. None of this is his fault. Not like he thinks it is. Maybe, if they were both kinder to each other, it wouldn't have to get this bad. It wouldn't even get close.

Stepping over some shattered glass from photo frames bashed in on walls or thrown around, Trace approaches Micah slowly.

"You know how this goes, slave," Trace warns, using every bit of volume and command he can muster. He's glad for his early morning workout, since it means his blood is already pumping, his body honed and ready to do battle with the demons in the room. They're some real sons of bitches, too. He knows from experience. "You fight me, and it'll only make it worse for you."

Micah doesn't respond, except to blast Trace's eardrums with a yell that comes from way down in his gut. He doesn't look over, either. His eyes are glued on the video screen. A quick scan of the room for the remote finds it in a corner, in fragments.

Well, shit.

Setting the pouch in his hand on the edge of the desk, Trace withdraws a few items, namely a syringe, a vial, disinfectant and a cotton swab. He plunges the needle into the vial, fills the syringe and then holds the fucking thing between his teeth so that his hands are free to wrestle his slave, should he fight back. He soaks the swab and decides on the best approach.

Trace really, really wants to turn the video off, and not just for Micah's sake, but it would waste time he doesn't have. Micah has never looked this bad before. It gets worse every year as Micah gets a little closer to the frayed end of his rope, and it makes Trace dread the year to come because it sounds like Micah's throat is bleeding from making so much noise. Each yell is shredded and painful. Trace almost expects a fine spray of red to accompany it on each exhale. Maybe he's screaming to cover up the sounds coming from the video, or the recriminations being voiced in his own head, or out of terror of what's still to come. There's no way to know. Sometimes, it all gets to be so much; all that's left is to lash out, blindly.

"Okay, fuck it," Trace sighs, muttering around the syringe, smooth between his teeth.

Luckily Micah doesn't fight back much. He must have expended most of his energy while causing all of the damage in the room, hitting everything but the screen, because Trace feels the exhaustion in Micah's slim body when he gets an arm, twists it behind Micah's back and pushes him face down to the floor. Trace sits, straddling

Micah's ass and swabs the side of his pinned right arm. A second later, the needle is jabbed into the muscle of his bicep, the plunger pushed to disperse the tranquilizer.

Growling, fighting back a little more just as the drug sweeps over his system, Micah finally, slowly, quiets. Dissolving into whimpered hiccups, he's malleable as Trace shifts off of him and sits against the wall, drawing Micah up into his arms.

He rocks Micah gently as the drugs make it harder to move, harder to cry out. Kissing Micah's temple, wiping his face dry, Trace, like Lilianna, looks everywhere but at the thing that fills his mind and heart.

The video plays on a loop, taken on Moira's last birthday, in her hospital room. Lilianna is the one behind the camera, making witty commentary, sounding so confident and hopeful. She's a beacon of positivity. Moira is center-screen, her body wasted away from the leukemia to almost nothing, her hair gone, but her smile wide and beautiful as she hugs her teddy and kisses her daddy.

Micah sobs softly, then seems to calm, especially once Trace covers Micah's eyes with a hand.

It takes Trace longer than he'd ever admit, to find the off button for the damn screen. When he does find it, he almost rips the screen from the wall and throws the fucking thing out the window just to be rid of it. If he didn't know Micah has hidden many backup copies of the videos, he would have.

Micah is limp as Trace heaves him up and takes him out of the office, carrying him to the guest room down the hall. Laying him down on the bed, making him comfortable and checking his vitals, Trace does everything possible for Micah before leaving him alone for a moment in search of Lilianna.

He doesn't get farther than the kitchen on his way to the back door and the truck, because there she is, unable to stay put for long. He can tell she's only inside so she can go and get even farther away. The cab of Trace's truck isn't nearly as isolated as Lilianna would like. He figures she'd sensed things had gone quiet inside the house and came in search of her means of real escape. Would she stay if Micah was able to ask it of her? Maybe it would be too little, too late. Trace knows they've been living at odds with each other for a long time, both of them carrying blame they shouldn't.

"You're shaking like a leaf," he says, finding her standing by the kitchen counter near the door, digging through a purse. Her cheeks are still dry but there's that god-awful look in her eyes that says the ability to cry anymore would be a blessing she can no longer expect.

He knows how this goes, too, well enough to know it's not worth saying what he'd rather say. What Micah is going through in regards to their daughter's untimely death is not Lilianna's fault, though she might feel it is. The reasons why Moira died and the state of his marriage to Lilianna isn't Micah's fault either, though Micah is convinced it is. This is all just something they need to endure and process, somehow, as long as they keep drawing breath. They're the ones left here, alive. That's the truth. Hating it doesn't change it.

Trace could go to her, hold her if he didn't know she'd fight him harder even than Micah, just because she can. Maybe he should, anyway. Maybe it would help her to fight a little, the way Micah does.

But she doesn't look at him, so he stays where he is, reading her signs.

"I need to get out of here, get some air," she says, even her voice quaking. She finds her keys and her phone, then heads for the door without looking back. "You'll stay with him?"

Halfway out the door already, she doesn't wait for Trace's reply. She just runs.

The door shuts behind her.

"Yeah, I ain't leavin' him, Lil," Trace says to no one, only the ghosts. "Guess one day you'll figure that out, too, huh?"

Chapter 6
Edge of Madness

Hours pass, during which Trace patiently sits on a chair beside the bed where Micah is curled up on his side. His body relaxed, weighed down with the effects of the tranquilizer, Micah dozes. When his eyes stay open for a longer period of time, looking like there's some life behind them, too, Trace catches his gaze and holds it. It's easy to feel, then, how much Micah needs Trace to be strong for him. The job of showing Micah the path to take to get him clear of his self-made torments is one Lilianna can't handle. Not with the way things have gotten. Only Trace can help Micah.

"You with me, now, slave?"

"Yes, Master," Micah replies readily. And God, it's thin—the tattered remnants of a voice.

Thinking if Micah had enough fight in him to destroy his office, maybe he can muster up enough spirit to fight for himself a little, too, Trace says, "If you are, then show me. Get on your knees."

Micah struggles upright, the strength in his arms nearly failing him as the tranquilizer makes them harder to command. His legs slump to the floorboards. Trace is ready to catch him if need be as Micah tumbles to the ground, but lands soundly on his kneecaps with a grimace. His arms hang at his sides for a moment, his head is bowed. Then he makes a valiant effort to clasp his hands behind his back.

"If you can't, then don't," Trace says, hating to see the struggle. "Tilt your chin up. Look at me."

Micah drags his gaze up. His warm, watchful brown eyes are the last part of him still crying out with dire, vicious need when they look up at Trace.

"Hit me," Micah hisses, his voice sounding raked over hot coals. "Hit me, you fucker. You should hate me too, just like she does. *Hit me!*"

"Bet that's what you want, huh, you little shit? Bet you'd *love* all of that pain. If you start begging me for the barn's rafters, too, I'll get the fucking gag out. You'll wear it for days on end until you're not even sure your jaw *works* anymore, and then you'll wear it some more. So shut the fuck up. I've heard enough. All I want is your neck."

He watches Micah's chest rise and fall with each quick, labored breath, eyes blazing, soul screaming.

One, thick, terrible tear falls and Trace acts swiftly upon seeing it. He steps up to Micah, drawing the collar from his back pocket. Micah looks at it briefly, like a starving man offered sustenance at long last, and another tear falls. His chin snaps up as he stretches his neck, waiting, hoping — hoping so very much.

When the leather fits around his throat, clasping snugly, a shuddering, nearly orgasmic exhale leaves Micah. It's a tangible symbol of their commitment to each other. It's *them* — their love, their peace. He draws a deep, steadying inhale through his nose, blows it out past his lips, then does it again while Trace's fingers work at the lock. Once it engages, Micah whimpers and sags slightly with relief so profound it seems to make him dizzy.

Trace hooks his index finger in one of the metal loops on the side of the collar, using it to keep Micah upright, caressing through his short, dark hair. The pure, absolute surrender in him leaves Trace breathless, and more resolved than ever to do whatever is in his power to help. Micah has given him body and soul. Trace knows he has to give Micah the same honor in return, devoting himself in every conceivable way to the exquisite man in his care. He just has to figure out how.

While his slave bravely fights an entirely internal battle, with such intense gratitude for Trace's aid, and his love, that Trace can see from the expression on Micah's face and in the shine of his eyes that there aren't words big enough to even get close, Trace holds him up. Micah sobs, gasps, snarls and tries hard to push past the memories of what he's done and how he's failed. On his knees at Trace's feet, Micah looks ready to dissolve into a puddle there, so he can leak through the floorboards into the earth and melt away to nothing. Trace knows how that is, to feel done with the trials of life, to be so used and mistreated, the act of simply staying in one piece is too much of an effort. So, he holds Micah up.

"Yours," Micah manages, after a while. The simplest, biggest vow he could possibly make. "Anything. Always."

For a few minutes, Trace can't reply. That need to hit, to hurt something that deserves the hurt, is back and strong. He's sick to death of adversaries he can't lay hands on.

"Knowing her, she won't be back for a while. Maybe days," Trace tells him, tenderly. He knows he needs to be truthful, but doesn't want to sway Micah toward abandoning Lilianna for Trace's sake if that's not what Micah truly wants.

Bypassing this, Micah swears, "Yours, Master. Anything."

"You *will* tell her about us. You'll find a way. Soon," Trace warns. It's not just their hearts on the line. "Waiting to tell her only makes it worse. She doesn't deserve to be hurt again. Not like this, and I know you know it. You've been selfish. Greedy. *Mean.*"

Trace yanks on the collar, hard enough to make breathing a challenge. Micah doesn't fight it, or protest, but just hangs there, his mouth working soundlessly. Easing up, Trace takes a chain from the nightstand at his side, hooking one end to the collar and winding the other around his hand.

"Yes, Sir," Micah says in agreement. He falls to hands and knees as he gulps air, though Trace keeps the tension on the leash tight enough for Micah to feel it. "I'm sorry."

"You're coming home with me. You'll service me. You will *obey*. You will not speak unless spoken to. You will wear my collar, and nothing else. You will not eat, piss, think, worry, or fucking breathe unless I want you to. You are *mine*, in every sense."

"*Please*, Master," Micah sobs, begging, desperate for it.

"Good boy. Crawl to my fucking truck, as slowly as you need to, because if you damage your body, *my* property, there will be hell to pay and you best damn believe it."

Forgive Us

A few hours later, after eating something and keeping busy with chores Trace gives him—sterilizing gear, reorganizing Diadem's video library to be more easily searched according to content and kink, breaking down some old equipment for parts, Micah grows restless again. His movements slow, his focus dulls, and his posture sags. Trace sees all of it. The loss of distraction and fading influence of the drugs is making Micah's pain rise closer to the surface.

Micah stands naked in the middle of the hallway, wearing a disoriented, heartbroken expression. Knowing exactly how it feels to be as adrift as Micah seems to be, Trace's resolve to be Micah's anchor drives him to act, and help. With a sigh, Trace tells him, "Get on the bed. Now. *Now*, slave. Go! Move your ass!"

The sharp command gets Micah going. He stands straighter and looks more alert, hearing the bite in Trace's voice. That's good. That's a lot better than dull, rotting pain. Trace's former Master, Nicholai, used to be the one he relied on to snap him out of it in moments when the past overwhelmed the present. It would be a wonderful way to complete the cycle to be able to show Micah how to heal his own wounds by leaning on someone who loves him unconditionally. Trace doesn't know what he would have done without Nicholai, even if he didn't always listen to what Nicholai was trying to teach him. All he can hope is that Micah is smarter and less of a rebel than Patrick used to be.

Micah gets to the bedroom, crawling up onto the bed. Trace notes that his slave's breathing is heavier and his eyes averted. Following behind, Trace grabs a leather strap from its hook on the wall. He can tell Micah is watching from the corner of his eye when he starts grunting softly with apprehension. On his knees near the foot of the bed, hands balled in tight fists, Micah arches with a swallowed cry as the leather lashes across his shoulder blades. The skin is instantly red.

"Down! Ass up!"

Swinging again, Trace hits in a perfect horizontal line across the thickest part of Micah's ass. With another swallowed yell, Micah tenses up, hands over his head as he gathers fistfuls of his hair in his hands and buries his face in the bedding.

"Legs apart!"

The next lash is harder. Micah flinches violently, huffing and moaning as shrill whines slip in now and then. He widens his stance, trembling.

Another strike and he clenches up tight, tucking his hips forward.

"Ass out! Unclench!"

Two strikes, back and forth, one for each side and Micah's breathing is out of control. Trace can tell he's in real agony, so he waits a few seconds. It doesn't really help as the anticipation of the next hit grows exponentially the longer Trace holds out. Staring at Micah's striped ass and the sweat breaking out over the length of his body, Trace feeds on the anger, letting it infuse the muscles of his arm, strengthening his grip on the strap.

When Micah breaks, crying out hoarsely, "More damn it," Trace acts. The strap snaps loudly against flesh four times until Micah is gasping with his sore, raw vocal chords, not sounding like himself at all. Micah writhes and tries to stay in the position as Trace unfastens his pants, taking his cock out, spreading lube to coat it thickly. He steps behind Micah, takes him by the hips and fits his tip against Micah's unprepped hole.

The pause as Trace waits, letting Micah feel him there, is a gentle warning of what's coming. It's going to hurt, but Trace knows Micah inside and out and plays him easily, knowing when to ease up or go in harder. Without being asked, Micah stretches out his arms in front of himself, fingers splayed, like he's praying, bowing to some unseen god and Trace begins to work his erection into Micah's tightened body.

Trace is careful not to do damage, with plenty of experience at consensually taking Micah by force. Trace scratches, slaps and kneads the tender, welt-covered flesh of Micah's buttocks, bombarding him with sensation, overloading his system to hold him there mentally. With shallow, hard, quick thrusts once he's buried balls deep, Trace pounds his slave's ass until he comes with a growled moan, coating Micah's passage with his seed.

Right away, Trace gathers him up, guiding Micah upright and enveloping him in a tender embrace. Kissing Micah's neck, caressing his sweat-slicked, heaving chest, holding him close, Trace laments, "This was my fault. I forgot. *I* did this to you."

Micah hisses, clawing at the flexed muscles of Trace's arms, bearing down even as Trace keeps him stuffed full. The first sob is strong and comes up from a deep, dark place. Trace just holds him tighter, nuzzling Micah's neck, containing the fight. The next sob edges into a scream and Trace's vision blurs. He blinks it clear, chest burning, aching to fix this, but unable to, ever.

"*It hurts,*" Micah seethes through gritted teeth. Wound up in Trace, Micah's slim body feels like it's trying to tear itself apart, so Trace squeezes around it to hold it together for him.

"I know, love," Trace sighs. "Let it go. Please. You're killing yourself like this."

For a long time, they stay like that, wrapped up in each other. There's nowhere else Trace would rather be and with the strength with which Micah keeps him locked in the embrace, Trace knows the feeling is mutual. Eventually, Trace eases Micah down so they can lie together, hoping sleep will come. For little stretches, Micah fades off, but surfaces silently, eyes opened but glazed over. Trace never lets him go.

If only he hadn't loved Lily so much. If only he didn't still.

The sun sinks lower in the sky.

Trace thinks about how hard Micah tries to keep it together all of the time, for his wife, for appearances' sake, and in order to live the lie that everything is fine, everything is under control. That's why the blow-ups happen. If Micah could admit to his failings and let off steam in healthy ways, in small amounts, it wouldn't get this bad.

But who is Trace to judge? He's dealing with the same problem of trying to do too much without letting on that, inside, the walls are crumbling. He's not doing much better than Micah. Maybe they both need to work on owning up to their failings. If only they could figure out how to do it without losing everything in the process. There's undeniable sanctuary in secrecy.

Breaking the stillness, the silence, Micah asks with his ravaged voice, "What if there's nothing good left with Lily? What if I tell her the truth about me and you and it's the last straw? What if it's too much to forgive this time?"

"You know the answer."

Trace folds their fingers more tightly together. They're on their sides, with Micah pulled snugly with his back tucked to Trace's chest. Another one of those awful sounds blooms from low in Micah's throat and Trace touches his lips to Micah's head.

"I can't lose her, too," Micah whispers.

"She might not be yours to keep anymore. If she goes, you have a place. Always. You know that."

"I still love her," Micah confesses. "As much as I ever have."

"Doesn't mean you're good for each other. Talk to her. You're just making yourself nuts."

Lying there, trying to keep his mind active and think of other things he can do for his lover, Trace plans a dinner consisting of Micah's favorite foods. Mentally, he checks whether he has all of the ingredients needed to make a curry and whether he has the right wine in the cellar. If not, he'll have to ask Ben or Kyle for a favor, since Trace doesn't intend to go anywhere for a while. Micah is his top priority for the duration. He'll close Diadem for a few days, if needed.

"You need any of your things? I think I got the important stuff on my way out."

"Everything I need is already here," Micah murmurs, giving Trace's arms a gentle squeeze. The words sound cracked and bleeding but at least Micah's body feels more relaxed.

"Some tea with lemon'll help that. We're out of lemons, so lemme call Benny—"

"Don't," he argues. "I don't need him knowing I've gotten this bad."

"You know how much he cares about you. He would never judge you harshly, love," Trace retorts softly, glancing around. His phone is on the dresser by the door. "Stay there," he says, getting up to retrieve it. "He owes us one anyway."

"I'll help with the tea. I don't want to be in bed anymore. I need to... to... I don't know. I "

"Hey," Trace interrupts, hearing Micah's frustration. One look from Micah and Trace gives in with a surrendering, "Okay, fine." He's pushed enough for one day after all.

Chapter 7
The Danger of Secrets

"You know," Micah says. "I can't help but notice an imbalance, here."

Trace hadn't called Ben after all, giving in to Micah's desire for privacy. The mug filled with tea, sans the lemon they don't have, warms Micah's hands. The tea itself heats his worn body, helping his throat feel slightly better. Trace has finished making dinner and Micah ate what he could. The tea helps more than the food, but it's Trace's fierce loving care and steadfast company that helps most. Contrasted with Lilianna, the way Trace will stay by Micah's side through anything speaks of a profound loyalty Micah almost can't comprehend. He's not sure what he's ever done to deserve such a man, or his love.

"Mmm," Trace grunts, tapping fingers on the tabletop, leaned back in his chair. He looks so relaxed and on guard at the same time, just cool, sexy, and confident. Watching him, wondering about him, Micah feels his many questions rise to the surface, needing to be voiced. If he can't talk to Lilianna, he at least wants to be able to be honest with Trace.

"You know *all* about my shit. The good, the evil, my most twisted, awful secrets... they're all out there. I confessed, let you in." He thinks of Lilianna, how in love they used to be when they first met in college. He was a small town kid figuring out the complexities of his sexual orientation. She was wiser, patient, charming, and best of all, funny. They were friends first, but life, bad luck, and grief wore the foundation of friendship away and scraped the love thin. Knowing that, having lived through it, he takes a new view on his relationship with Trace.

Truthfulness is vitally important to Micah. Without full disclosure and full acceptance, they aren't going anywhere, as Master and slave or as lovers. When Lilianna stopped confiding in her husband, Micah knew it was the beginning of the end. If Trace means to hold on to Micah, and Micah knows he does, there has to be something more to tip the scales.

"Look," Micah says, "I know you love me. I know you trust me. But you *don't* trust me."

There's a pause and Micah watches Trace become more uncomfortable than Micah has ever seen him before. It doesn't take much, because Micah has never seen Trace look the least bit ill at ease with anything. The direst threat usually only gets a cocky smirk from him. Obviously, Micah has found one of Trace's few vulnerabilities with his accusation.

Micah decides to start with what he does know, from what little Trace has mentioned. "What's The Company? What did you do when you worked for them? Why won't you talk about it? Why won't you mention their name to any of our friends? You won't even mention them to Ben and Gabe."

The look Trace gives him then makes Micah afraid, because it seems like Trace is actively increasing the emotional distance rather than lessening it. Remembering what he has put himself through that long day, the hell he'd sunk into, the raw state of his heart, Micah begins to lose hold of hope and slip back into a bad place. So, he reaches out to the only person left who can save him.

"I can't do this," Micah admits thickly, hating the tears, tired of them. "I've lost *so much* and I don't have anything left. I don't have Lily. I don't have *you*. I don't have Moir—"

Trace takes Micah's hand, holds it, and says in soft breath of command, infused with such devotion and understanding, "*Stop*, love. Please."

They're leaning over the small table in the kitchen, with the light hanging down from the ceiling illuminating their joined hands. Used plates, forks and glasses litter the table top. The house is a darkness wrapped around them, listening, waiting.

"There's a reason I don't talk about this shit. My job is to protect you. *All* of you."

When he doesn't continue, just keeps giving Micah a hard, unreadable stare, Micah asks, "From *what*?"

"All the past is good for is to fuck us over. Tell me that ain't true," Trace dares defensively.

"I need this," Micah begs. "Please."

Trace sighs heavily.

"Shit," Trace curses, standing. After a trip to the liquor cabinet, he returns with a bottle of scotch and a clean glass. Pouring himself some, he sips, and sets the glass back down with a clatter.

"The reason I don't tell you some shit is because knowing it would put you in harrm's way. I won't have you in harm's way. Not *you*. Not *now*, when things are so...."

"What are you talking about? Me and Lily?"

"No," Trace says with a sour expression, taking another drink, slicing his hand through the air to dismiss the suggestion. "'Course not."

"What does 'of course not' mean? What 'things' are you talking about?"

"Things! Everything. Shit. See, everything I say is just gettin' my ass in more trouble. I've had a lot on my mind. I'm tryin' to keep all of this separate and organized but it's all going to hell, fast, and I'm startin' to fuck up. I'm trying to keep *everyone* safe. Not just you."

"So this is about the others? Are you talking about the stuff going on at Gabe and Dare's house? Or the isolation of Kyle and Dare after everything that happened with them?"

"*Jesus*," Trace groans, exuding discomfort, looking like he knows he's trapped right up against a wall he built himself, a long time ago. "Yes, okay?"

"Yes," Micah echoes with surprise. "All of it? How can it be about all of it? Just tell me about The Company."

"I can't!" Trace says, sounding like he's arguing with himself rather than Micah. It doesn't make sense. Trace makes a frustrated growl. "Okay. Okay, smartass. If we're doing this, we need to start with the basics. Common knowledge in some parts of the world, especially the BDSM world we like to think of ourselves as part of. You ever heard of the Master's Circle?"

Recognition sparks in Micah's brain, but it's dull, hard to get hold of. "Rumors," Micah replies. "That's it. But it's not real, it's just something people in the lifestyle talk about to freak each other out."

"What do you think it is?" Trace asks leadingly.

"I don't know," he answers honestly. "Some organization that controls all of the Doms and subs, and regulates the whole scene from some covert place. It's not *real*. It's not...."

Trace just looks at him levelly and takes another sip.

"I was trained," Trace starts with another sigh, "by a Master Dom named Nicholai Zhukov, at the Master's Circle headquarters in London. This goes way back to when I was just a kid. Nicholai ain't around anymore. He's retired. Been replaced by new blood. Younger. Weirder. More of a pain in my ass."

"Holy fuck, you're serious about this, aren't you?" Micah says with awe.

"Do I look like I'm telling a goddamned bedtime story?" Trace asks. "You say you want to know more about me, so this is about me. This is how I got to be a Dom. And you're my collared sub, so you've got a right to know this shit. You're right about that. *Some* people are less than fucking forthcoming with details, and I ain't them. I mean there's a difference between keeping people safe and being a grade A asshole, right?"

"What are you talking about?"

"I'm talking about you, asking me direct questions, and me giving you answers, like a decent person does. You appreciate that, don't you?"

"These aren't answers. Who are you mad at? Are you mad at *me*?"

"No! Of course not. Fuck."

"Who are you mad at?"

"I'll get to that later," Trace says, waving the topic away, taking another drink. "Where the fuck were we?"

"The Master's Circle."

"Right. Those assholes. I saw an... opportunity, you could call it. So, I took it. Signed a contract as a Dom for hire with The Company. They run a nationwide prostitution ring catering only to the richest fat cats around. Clients are heavily screened before they're given access. We're talking politicians, white-collar criminals, billionaires, movie stars, mobsters, terrorists, you name it. Anyone who had the money to pay and didn't have any diseases or murderous tendencies got a pass. Contracts for the employees are ten-years a pop. I did my ten, got paid, and got out. It was a long goddamned ten years and it fucked with me in every way a man can be fucked with, so I took some time off after. Spent time recovering at headquarters in London, with the Master's Circle. It was the only place that felt safe anymore. Hell, the MC is filled with Masters from MI5, the Metropolitan Police, the army, you name it. Having guys like that watch your ass takes some of the unsavory sort of heat off, so that's where I went—back to the MC. Back to Nicholai."

A strange expression crosses Trace's face. Frowning, head lowered, he clears his throat, then says, "Nicholai convinced me it'd be best to make a fresh start. When I got back to the states, I met Benny and we founded Diadem. It sounded like it'd be a good time. I wanted to have my own place, my own rules, no fuckin' Master's Circle breathing down my neck. I was sick and tired of people telling me what to do, how to do it, why, where, and to whom. When it wasn't the Master Doms from the MC, it was those corrupt shits at The Company. I wanted to get away from *all of it*. You know the rest. We found Gabey. Became a family."

Frowning back at Trace, mouth tight, thoughts in turmoil, Micah lets the awkward silence stretch out for quite a while before reacting. At first, his reaction is too big to process. The shock is gigantic. Trace waits patiently, as he's always been easily able to do. For the first time, Micah begins to glimpse the reasons why Trace is so good at being tolerant and patient with what he wants.

Finally, Micah says with passionate concern, "Don't take this the wrong way, but why would you do that to yourself? You were a prostitute for *ten years?*"

"Had my reasons."

"My god, Trace. I can't even imagine what you went through. Would you undo it if you could?"

"Don't ask me those types of questions. You wouldn't like me asking you the same thing."

With disbelief, Micah says, "And you've told no one?"

"Yeah, and it's gonna stay that way. If I want people to know, I'll be the one to tell 'em. Understood?"

"They should know this," Micah says urgently. "Ben, Gabe—why would you *not* tell them?"

"Would you want to tell *your* kids you whored for a decade? Don't make me repeat myself. It's done. You wanted to know, so you know."

There it is, Micah thinks. *Papa Trace, putting himself last so he can fill the role he's appointed himself, and take care of everyone else first. And meanwhile, no one's taking care of him. I should have asked about this sooner. He's been suffering and I didn't even know. No one did. And here I was, thinking it was only Lily I was hurting with my selfishness.*

As it always has, it warms Micah's heart a little, knowing Trace guards with such fierce paternal love the people he's gathered around him, filling his life. Ben might only be a few years younger than Trace, but he's still one of Trace's beloved 'kids', someone who Trace would do absolutely anything to safeguard. Imagining what Trace must have gone through, being trained by some powerful Dominants in England, then being shipped off to sexually service the wealthy, with no input in what he does or is done to him, of course it makes sense that Trace seems so much older, so much more experienced. It's because he is.

But there's one person who does not so easily fall under the umbrella of Trace's familial care. It's someone Trace has been involved with for as long as he's been with Micah. When it began, it used to be about sex, exclusively. Now, though, who knows what it is? The lines have blurred beyond recognition.

Micah asks, "What about Lily?"

Trace rolls his eyes, holds his head in a hand. "*I'll* tell her. Need I say, also, that you are not to breathe a word of this to anyone? Keep it to yourself."

"No problem," Micah says, looking at Trace in new ways, letting his imagination run wild.

"And don't give me that fuckin' daydreamy look either. It's not a role play scenario, it's my damn life."

"Explains a lot, I've gotta say," Micah says over the rim of his mug.

With a faint smile, Trace says, "Yeah, well, you don't get this good without some serious goddamned practice at your fuckin' craft."

"I hear that."

Chapter 8

Threesome

A couple of days later, Micah is still staying with Trace when Lilianna reappears and stops by to check on him. It puts a smile on Micah's face when Lilianna runs up to hug him and say how much she's missed him, because he can tell it's sincere. Though she's careful not to ask what Micah's been up to in the meantime, she happily fills him in on the latest news from work and the errands she's managed to complete. Not a word is mentioned about the day she left, Moira's birthday. Micah's foggy memories of it fill every awkward lull in the conversation.

Not an hour into the visit, Trace and Lilianna are heavily in conversation in the living room after Trace pulls her aside to fill her in on some aspects of his past. Micah lingers in the doorway, already privy to everything being discussed. He steps back to give Trace the chance to catch Micah's wife up on some of the recent confessions he's made about his past. Strangely, that's always been the way between the three of them. Trace is the mediator of the group, the one to speak privately to each of the others, then work out a compromise or solution. Lilianna is the one who initially brought Trace into their bedroom. Trace is the one who has pulled the strings to keep himself there. The longer the three of them are together, with whatever definitions you want to use, the more Micah is aware of how his wife and Trace call the shots, in their own ways, leaving Micah to step back and follow their commands.

Even now, with Trace's secrets being revealed at long last, telling Lilianna is something that needs to happen between Trace and Lilianna. Sometimes Micah feels he belongs to his wife. Sometimes he feels he belongs, instead, to Trace. Sometimes he belongs to both of them, equally, together, submissively waiting for them to come to an agreement or understanding. They respect him and his needs, and he trusts them to have control. Or, at least that's the way it's supposed to work. Lately, he's not so sure he's getting the respect and trust he deserves from his wife. The trouble comes from figuring out a way to speak up for himself without ruining everything. But, the longer he waits to say something to her, the harder it is to do so.

A half-empty glass of Trace's scotch is in Micah's hand, the alcohol already consumed and burning away some of Micah's reservations. They have a lot to talk about, but maybe some truth doesn't have to be conveyed in words. The three of them have always been better at getting to know things through more physical expressions anyway.

Lilianna knows her husband is there, but hasn't glanced his way in a while. The startling nature of Trace's news, as well as his natural intensity, are certainly going to demand Lilianna's attention. Micah knows it. It's better for her to deal with Trace first, before opening up the radius of her focus large enough to include Micah, too. Let her be concerned and talk it out. Micah has already been through it. Trace and Lilianna are close enough to handle this privately.

Lilianna is wearing a crimson blouse and a black skirt and looks as beautiful as she always does, her voluptuous, hourglass figure filling out clothes better than any other woman Micah has ever laid eyes on. Trace looks just as good, though. His thickly muscled arms are on display, his suntanned skin and carefully trimmed, dark facial hair. One look at Trace, the strength in his body and the casual, lustful willingness in his eyes makes Micah, and many other people too—men and women alike—go weak in the knees. He'll kick your ass or fuck it into the ground, depending on what his mood may be. Surrendering to that kind of power is one of the greatest luxuries Micah has ever experienced.

He can hear the concern in his wife's voice and isn't surprised when she moves closer to Trace, straddling his lap. It's a position, ironically, that Micah recently occupied, not that Lilianna knows it. She thinks Micah only indulges in sex with Trace when she's there, too. That's one of the biggest untold truths tearing them apart, but the extent of Micah's love for Trace is doing even more damage.

They begin to kiss and Trace's hands are on her right away — slipping up inside her shirt, pulling the bra out of the way to free her breasts, rubbing up her thighs, tugging her closer so that her crotch is flush against him as he rocks up into her. Micah sips his drink and sees Trace's fingers twist sharply under the shirt where they appear to be closed around Lilianna's nipple. She makes a soft, angry exhale and he knows it's with small, welcome pain.

Seeing them together still excites Micah, but in different ways than it used to. It no longer feels as thrillingly taboo to see Trace and Lilianna screw around. It's become comfortable. What isn't comfortable is how freely Trace incorporates Micah in their sexual escapades without consulting him first about specifics. He likes to push Micah right up against his safeword. That's probably to force Micah's hand and make him come clean about where his heart truly lies. But whatever Trace may want from him, Micah is willing to go along with it, discomfort or no. He can take anything Trace throws his way, and enjoy the debauchery while it lasts. It won't hurry him up if he's not ready to commit to confessions that could ruin his marriage.

He's ripped from his thoughts as Lilianna's fingernails scratch over Micah's chest. He hadn't even noticed her cross to him. She takes a handful of his shirt and pulls on it, passing by him with a smile and taking him along with her.

"Bedroom. Move it," Trace says, following behind.

"So, I guess she took the news well, then," Micah says, downing the rest of his scotch and grimacing at the taste.

No sooner is he through the bedroom doorway than Trace is pulling off Micah's shirt. Lilianna's mouth moves hungrily over the new, pink scratches on Micah's skin and she makes a few more as she sinks to her knees at his feet, yanking open his fly. She tongues his tip and Trace pins Micah's hands behind his head, watching the show and caressing through Lilianna's long dark hair.

"Okay, okay," Trace says, hurrying things long. "Get on the bed already."

"Cuffs?" Lilianna asks, taking off her shirt and bra, then shimmying out of her skirt and panties.

"Already attached to the headboard. What can I say? I like to be prepared."

"Of course you do," she grins. "Cock ring?"

"Yeah. I've got a good one here somewhere."

Naked, her breasts full and heavy with dark, small nipples, her pussy waxed nearly bare like she was expecting this and spent time getting ready for it, Lilianna manhandles Micah onto the bed. She pushes him up to sit with his back to the headboard. His wrists are put in the cuffs so that they're bound behind his head. His head buzzes from the booze. The lingering weight of sadness keeps him from protesting or making smartass comments as Trace tosses a few condoms on the bed. Next he tosses the cock ring. Lilianna wastes no time working it onto Micah, getting his balls through, then carefully squeezing his dick through as well.

It's incredibly uncomfortable and he fights not to writhe as they both smirk down at him.

"Comfy?" she asks Micah while crawling up his body, giving him a slow kiss that's mostly lips and the tips of their tongues before slinking back down. She teases a trail down his chest and abdomen with her tongue as Trace moves up behind her. He nudges her thighs apart and his fingers go right for her sex. Micah can't see what he's doing but can read Lilianna's reactions quite clearly.

He sighs with annoyance, and maybe a little jealousy, as she chases a quick climax—the first of many, probably—with the help of Trace's middle finger. Meanwhile, she swallows the head of Micah's cock and twists her middle finger up his ass.

"Fuck!" Micah complains. "Lube! Come on!"

She chuckles, then hums, then whimpers, her hips twitching as she gets closer to orgasm. Trace steadies her with a hand on her back and seems to really go for it. Lilianna's noises get wilder and she takes out her torturous ecstasy by fingering the hell out of Micah's asshole. He grunts and bites his lip, wincing a little and trying to thrust farther into her mouth.

With a telltale choked sigh, he knows she's come.

"Well, that's one for me," she giggles after pulling off of his cock, then takes a long lick up the underside.

Trace, still not wasting any time, pushes a dollop of lube through Lilianna's sphincter with two fingers and says, "Yeah, that's to loosen you up a little, darlin'. You don't mind, right? I'm kind of after one thing."

The fingers pump into her efficiently, and Micah sympathizes, knowing the feeling. She moans, frowning slightly as she starts sucking him, her hand twisting on his shaft.

"Gentle, please," Micah says to Trace, tiredly.

"Oh, are you in charge?"

"I said please."

Removing his fingers, Trace wipes them clean and rolls on one of the condoms, looking right into Micah's eyes as he does it. Then he moves up closer, behind Lilianna, and starts to enter her. She makes an anguished little cry and Micah closes his eyes, tuning some of it out, but unable to ignore Lilianna's attention to his bound cock, nor the finger rotating in and prying at his ass. Once Trace is seated and moving more easily, taking her slowly, Lilianna works her mouth more intensely on Micah's dick, deep-throating him.

"Easy! Fuck!" he grimaces, needing to come, unable to because of the ring constricting him.

She ignores him, of course. After a minute or two, she pulls off and starts to pump the hell out of him with her hand. He gasps, pushing up off the bed. She just slips another finger into his ass and hums happily.

Trace puts an end to it by pulling out, holding himself by the root and taking off the condom.

"Mic, your turn, sweetheart. Babe, get him out of the cuffs."

Once they're off, he's pushed and pulled by two sets of hands, bending him over in front of Trace who coats his own dick in some lube, but no condom. Lilianna kisses Micah, coaxing his jaws open wide, teasing his tongue with hers. He gasps roughly into her mouth when Trace breaches him. The sounds get her going again, kissing him harder. She's always gotten off on watching men fuck him, and especially Trace. It's nothing new. Trace forces him to take his whole cock at once and Micah cries out, with Lilianna guiding him down, down, down, until his gasping mouth is between her legs. He tongues her clit, using two digits to finger her while she gets to watch Trace fuck him, no holds barred. She leaves scratches over his back and Trace kneads his ass, giving it everything he's got.

Lilianna cries out her second orgasm and Micah abruptly stops getting lost in the easy sweep of it all.

Not like this. Not this time. He can't pretend it's all the same as it was before, when they first came together, that he hasn't changed and isn't the man he now knows he is.

Like he can feel time slowing down, the great wheel of life turning less quickly for once, he discovers, ready or not, it's time. He wipes his mouth and takes a steadying breath. Feeling Trace's movements within him, Micah says, "Stop. Red!"

He's distantly aware of Trace pulling out, of them both asking if he's okay and what's wrong. For a long moment it all gets lost in a buzz of white noise until he pushes through to clarity. When Micah comes back to himself, he realizes Trace has him upright on his knees and Lilianna is looking into his eyes with concern, touching his chest and measuring his pulse.

Taking her hand, kissing the knuckles, he fights not to fall back through memory and relive all of the wonderful ways she's been his devoted partner through so very much. He tells them both, without confidence or certainty, "I want the collar."

Micah feels Trace understand right away what's going on from the way his breath moves over Micah's neck and the energy radiating from his body. He's become even more attuned to Trace's rhythms than his wife's. It says a lot about why the ache of regret in his heart is so strong.

"Collar?" Lilianna asks, confused.

Trace asks, "You sure, love?"

Love how he calls me love, Micah thinks fondly, fleetingly.

"Yes. I am," he answers, meeting Lilianna's hurt glare, dead on.

Trace leaves them there to get the collar from a dresser drawer. Returning with it, he fastens it around Micah's neck, a perfect fit.

Micah may have submitted to Lilianna for most of their marriage, but he never wore a collar for her. Not once.

"How long?" she asks softly, looking only at Micah and looking so hard it feels as rough and sharp as her nails had, raking his chest.

"Long enough," he admits. "I love him, Lil, but I loved you first. I'll love you always."

She breathes out a wounded ghost of a laugh. "God, I'm stupid."

When she tries to pull free of his grasp, he holds her there. "No. You're anything but that. I didn't do this to hurt you. I'm not trying to exclude you, either. Or leave you. I'm just admitting I need this from Trace. Please."

He lets her go. Her head is bowed and embarrassment colors her cheeks.

"Lily," he calls.

Gathering her clothes, she yanks them on a piece at a time. Micah starts to go to her, but sways, so Trace goes in his place, telling Micah, "Stay."

They whisper to each other in the doorway. All Micah can hear is the accusation in her voice, not the words themselves. But then she seems to soften when Trace doesn't stop explaining and gives every sign of hearing where she's coming from. The steadfastness in Trace must be something that appeals to Lilianna, too, Micah realizes. It makes sense when you're someone who never stays still; it helps to surround yourself with those who are constant and reliable. She lets Trace kiss her and pull her in for a hug. Mostly dressed, she finally meets Micah's gaze and says, "I'm not mad, okay? I get it. I just need some air, and to sleep in my own bed. Are you coming home? I'd like you to."

"Tomorrow. Promise."

She nods once, then goes.

Trace doesn't say a thing after she has gone. The house is quiet again.

Micah tries to feel more ashamed of himself for hurting Lilianna in such a way. But he finds he can't. There's too much built-up resentment from the ways she hurt him, too. The whole situation simply feels as miserable as it always has. Everything, suddenly, has changed, but at the same time nothing has changed.

Trace returns to bed, eases Micah down, enters him and takes off the cock ring. In minutes, Micah is exclaiming his powerful climax, quivering around Trace, held in his tight, skilled grasp, giving his body over completely for his lover's pleasure. Trace bites down on his shoulder while Micah's body convulses subtly with aftershocks. All of the ways Trace holds him, takes him, and keeps him seduce Micah, helplessly, and he nearly drowns in the force of the white, cleansing fire consuming him, body and soul.

Chapter 9
Confession and Consequences

Ever since the decision was made to keep Kyle and Darrek apart while they heal and recover from revelations about their shared childhood sexual abuse, both of them have been, independently, spending more time with Micah. Trace understands how much the three men have in common, since all of them have been collared by their respective Doms and are working to build a life around that in their own ways. It's an added benefit when Kyle or Darrek stops by—though it's always one or the other—because it allows Trace to discreetly supervise how things are going, if they're getting better or worse. Neither Kyle nor Darrek would ever come to Trace directly, unless there was no other choice. That's mainly due to being intimidated. If they knew how much Trace truly, actively cares for their wellbeing, they might be less reticent. But, if they knew the *whole* truth, they'd likely be more scared of him than ever.

The toll has obviously been taken in ending Kyle and Darrek's close friendship, whether it's official, or final, or not. Both of them have gotten quieter, more withdrawn, more guarded. They seem healthier, though, to Trace. The fear of each other is gone. All that's left is the heartache. The two of them really did love each other; he has no doubt of that. It's what keeps them close, even though they can't be together. The permanence of Gabriel and Ben's friendship—if you can label it friendship when they call each other "brother" and often meet for sex with the consent of their partners—helps Kyle and Darrek find their peace with the way things have turned out. At least they're near to each other, and get word with ease about how the other is doing.

Trace knows the comfort some solid information can bring.

When Darrek comes by Trace's house after a frantic call to Micah, asking to talk, Trace makes sure to stay busy nearby, within earshot. He lays out a bunch of gear from Diadem on the table that needs to be fixed or maintained after all of the wear and tear, and takes a seat. Quietly, he gets to work, listening intently all the while. Once in a while, he glances up, but every time he does, he doesn't like what he sees at all.

Micah and Darrek are just a few feet away in the living room, sharing a pair of beers. The house is quiet, without a television or music to fill it with excess noise. Outside, it's raining. When Darrek arrived it was a drizzle. Now it's coming down hard. The drumming of the raindrops on the roof and windows is the only thing challenging Trace's ability to eavesdrop.

"So," Darrek begins, hesitating, "you know how I told you I got a call? Or, calls, I guess. So many damn calls." His left leg bounces restlessly. He chews on his fingernails. There are bags under his eyes, and a weary paleness to his face. Trace notices how Darrek keeps glancing nervously at the house phone, a landline.

Speaking slowly, his perfect calm a counterpoint to Darrek's unmistakable anxiousness, Micah replies, "The message from Jerry, your dad?"

"Yeah," Darrek answers. He smiles but looks like he's about to cry, and angry he's about to cry. Staring at the phone again, he pushes both of his hands through his hair like he wants to rip it from his scalp. It's damn hard to watch. Trace can hear the strain in Darrek's voice and the way he's being driven to get some of this off his chest to someone who doesn't have to live with it every day.

Thinking about how certain Gabriel has become the person stalking them is Harry, and how that could affect Darrek, who is certain it's Jerry, Trace sees in the proof of Darrek's body language, how awful the situation has become. Because whoever is doing this is not Harry. It has to be Jerry. And if it's Jerry… what does that mean for poor Darrek and Kyle, through hell and back down in it again before they'd even truly broken free?

He tries to imagine how he'd feel, right after finishing his ten years with The Company, if they'd dragged him back into another contract for another decade. He'd be looking a lot like Darrek is, sitting there on that old couch, dying inside.

He'd have been beyond desperate for help—any kind of it.

"You said you didn't listen to the message past the first word or two," Micah says.

"I ripped the damn thing out of the wall to turn it off, even after I hit stop and erase. It was like I could still hear him anyway. Then I opened it up with a screwdriver and tore some of the guts out—wires and stuff, just to be sure." There's a pause during which Darrek scratches roughly at his head and almost gets up, staring at the phone, and Trace is sure if Darrek had a screwdriver in his pocket, he'd take that phone apart too, just in case. "I had it all worked out in my head, you know? I'd been working up the courage to call and tell him I remembered. I remember all of it, if I try, but I try not to—remember it, I mean. But, it's there. I don't want it to be, but it's in my head now. The more I thought about telling him the truth, though, the angrier I got. I wanted to tell him to go kill himself and do the world a favor. Real nice, huh? But... that's not even the worst part. Maybe I shouldn't tell you this. I, um... I also thought about going down there, with the gun, hiding somewhere I could see him, but not too close, you know, and...."

"But you didn't," Micah observes, filling in the blank Darrek leaves there. Darrek makes a bad sort of hysterical laugh and bites at his lip.

"Course not. I wouldn't. I wouldn't do that."

As someone who has lived through Micah's troubles with his own family history, Trace knows he must sympathize with Darrek's torment, even if Darrek's issues are brought of abuse and Micah's of a child's terminal illness. When it comes right down to it, pain is pain, no matter the breed or flavor.

There's a pause, then Darrek adds, quietly, as if to himself, "Kyle might have. Kyle...."

Trace stops pretending to work and holds his head in his hands, wrestling with the frustration of not being able to do anything constructive to resolve the problem. It tears him up inside. From the other room, he hears soft noises as Micah comforts Darrek when he loses control for a moment, sniffling, weeping, then trying to take a few deep breaths.

"We don't even know this is Jerry, okay? We *don't*. You're so close to this you can't see the bigger picture, but those things the fear tells you are true are all in your head. You're psyching yourself out. Don't worry about Kyle. He's doing great," Micah says. "You did the right thing. Space is good for both of you. It doesn't mean you can't care about him. He knows you do. Trust me."

After another deep, shaky breath, Darrek says, "I'm sorry. It just sucks. A lot. It's too much to deal with. There're too many questions. Too much waiting. I feel like I'm just waiting for something awful to happen."

"I know."

"And I haven't even said what I wanted to yet. Man. Okay. Whew."

"Take your time. I'm not going to kick you out or anything."

"Thanks for letting me come by and all. I know I'm probably interrupting. I mean, you've got your own things going on and—"

"No, it's fine. I've been wearing this for almost a week straight now." They're talking about the collar, Trace realizes. The one he locks in place around Micah's throat every morning, whether he'd slept over or not. Either way, they see each other bright and early at Diadem. "It messes with your head, as you know."

"Yeah. I do," Darrek agrees. "But it's good. It helps, more than anything else does a lot of the time."

"Keep going," Micah encourages. "You sound better now."

"Okay. Well, after that message, the phone rang and rang all day. The answering machine couldn't pick it up, so it just kept on ringing. It was all day. It made me crazy, so I unplugged the phones, but then I started to worry they'd somehow get my cell number or decide to drive or fly up here, that he'd show up at my home. Or track down Kyle. I mean, my god. It's been a nightmare and there's no good way out. Gabriel wanted to answer the calls, take the chance to tell Jerry a few things or just make the call himself, but I couldn't let him do that. It can't happen that way. Jerry has always made me feel so powerless, the last thing I need is to send someone else in there to be a man for me while I cower in silence. I mean, I love that Gabe wants to, but this is *my* fight. Bringing him into it would only make it worse in *so many* ways. If anyone should be standing the fuck up to Jerry, to make him feel every bit of the pain he's brought down on me, give it right back to him with interest, it's me." Darrek exhales heavily, gets choked up and starts crying as he speaks, and says, "But then the alarm went off when we weren't there. And then it happened while I... And I *couldn't... I couldn't even—*"

"Dare," Micah interrupts.

But Darrek barrels on. "For a week or two there, the phone was silent. Gabriel agreed to keep a gun by the door, in case Jerry showed up. At f-first I left it there. But t-then the phone started to ring again. No one else calls the landline. We only have it because it's part of the package we have for internet and cable. And the caller ID... It said the number was unavailable, but it was *him* again. Mic, I *know* it was. It's been *days* and the phone won't stop ringing. Every time I plug it back in, it starts. I... I'm *so scared*. I'm really scared he's going to come after me, and I don't know what he'd do. I don't know why he'd want to hurt me like this, why he hurt me like he did before. It just doesn't *make sense*. And as much as I fantasize about being the one to put a bullet between his eyes, *I can't do this! I can't.*"

It's the last straw. Trace listens as Darrek, without Gabriel there to prop him up, breaks down into pieces and Micah is left to deal with the aftermath. Trace sees Darrek curled up around himself, like he's waiting for the lash of a belt, or the sound of his father's voice, telling him to hurt Kyle, or else. He's sobbing, trying not to, then, feeling worse for seeming weak, gets even more upset.

Calm settles over Trace. The decision is made swiftly, easily. Trace knows it'll cause his kids more pain to do what he's planning to do, but it's the only solution left. Gabriel can't fix this for Darrek. He can't even start to try. The relentless calls from a specifically unlisted number, the break-ins at the house—it's not just aimed at Darrek. It's both him and Gabriel who have been targeted. Maybe Jerry is going after the man who's fucking his son, dominating him in ways Jerry wants to be able to dominate Darrek. Maybe the point isn't to hurt Darrek at all, but to scare him into helplessness before striking out at Gabriel.

It's getting way too dangerous, going way too far. It calls for help Gabriel and Darrek don't have the means to ask for. Trace

Forgive Us

won't let his kids live in fear from the unknown, not when all signs point to impending violence, and not when he has ways of swiftly resolving all of the terror and uncertainty.

Trace is also absolutely willing to deal with his own aftermath. If Micah, who was in an extremely desperate emotional state only days ago, can try to help Darrek cope with the stress and turmoil of needing to confront the man who tortured, beat and scarred him, Trace can do his part, too. He'll have them all to face afterward. He knows that. But maybe it's time to stop the lying, and let some truth free in a bigger way.

Standing, pushing his chair back, he goes to wash his hands at the sink. He picks up a hand towel and dries them carefully, then walks into the other room.

Darrek's eyes lock onto him immediately. Trace knows Darrek always slips back into that nervous, submissive state when they're faced with each other, more so than with anyone else, even his own Master. Using that, Trace steps right up to him. With only a crook of his finger, he gets Darrek, whose breath is hitching with tears, to stand. Darrek is taller than Trace, but weaker in every way that counts. He lets Trace look hard into his eyes, though, and Trace is proud of him for it, because there's no hiding anything. Trace sees it all—every word of what he's confessed to Micah and much more as well. All of the things he would say to Jerry if he could, the things he would use to hurt his father, to bring him down to the place of hellish existence he's put both Darrek and Kyle in, so Jerry could feel the burn of the pit's flames for a while. It's only fair. It's justice.

Trace doesn't say a word, but he does let Darrek see the resolution in his face, and the steady, eerie calm. For a while Darrek simply stares, trembling from exhaustion and hopelessness. There's a dead sort of acceptance in him Trace doesn't like at all. There's always been sweetness to Darrek, and Trace sees it being ground out of him by his growing certainty of the horrors to come. It's the same sort of look he imagines Darrek had when he was getting ready to cut his own throat, so Trace stares back, letting Darrek see some of what he intends to do. It's a glimpse, no more.

Trace pats the side of Darrek's face, then hooks the hand around Darrek's ear, drawing him in a fraction of an inch. Darrek tenses, breathing through his nose, lips sealed tight. There is no protest, though; only tension, bracing for whatever is on its way.

Pulling his phone from his pocket, Trace dials a number.

"Hey sweetheart. Got your boy here. He needs you. Nah, he's dandy, just going through shit you already know about. Yep. Okay."

Trace says to Micah, looking right at Darrek as he hangs up, "Got another call to make, but it'll wait until after Gabey picks him up."

A few minutes later, Gabriel's Discovery swings into the driveway. He runs up to the house, getting soaked in the downpour.

"Everything all right?!" Gabriel shouts through the thunder.

"Abso-fuckin-lutely, beautiful," Trace grins, liking the way the rain drips from the ends of Gabriel's hair. He reaches out and takes a handful of it, drawing his boy in close, out of the storm. Gabriel bows his head slightly, glancing back into the house while Trace's fingers brush down his jaw. "You okay?"

"Yeah," Gabriel nods, breathing harder from the hurry but staying right where Trace has put him, reacting to each caress without thinking, inviting more instinctively by leaning in to every touch. That kind of trust is a miraculous thing in Trace's eyes. He hates himself for taking advantage of it.

"Your boy's in bad fuckin' shape. Take him out for me. Have a nice dinner. See a movie. Try to keep him out of the damn house for a few days and definitely keep the gun and the fucking knives locked away. Maybe you even stay at a hotel for a few nights."

He pushes a few folded bills into Gabriel's front pants pocket.

"When's your next therapy appointment?" he asks when Gabriel doesn't say anything, just seems like he's waiting for Trace to drag him into the garage and fuck him raw over the hood of a car to ease some of the frustrated ache and help him feel cared for.

"Tomorrow," Gabriel answers. "Both of us."

"Good. Make sure you both get there."

Fleetingly, he sees Gabriel sigh and let down his walls. The strong Dominant, owner of his own business, capable of easily taking men apart in wickedly effective ways, fades away. This leaves behind only Trace's vulnerable boy, the one who showed up homeless and forsaken a little over ten years ago. That mad scramble of unquenchable need to belong, be loved, be safe, is right there, in his eyes. He lets Trace see it, and it's tantalizing.

Then it's gone. Trace lets go. Gabriel goes into the house and returns with Darrek in hand. The sight of their fingers woven so tightly together makes it easier for Trace to let them leave. They both look steadier for being connected like that.

They get into the SUV and slowly drive off.

"Ah, shit," Trace sighs.

Chapter 10
Straight Answers

"Who are you calling?" Micah asks, sounding suspicious as hell, proving he's starting to learn how to read Trace like an expert.

Trace tells him, "I need you to be quiet as a fuckin' mouse right now, got it? If you want to be here for this, you *listen*."

He hooks his index finger in the collar's front ring, giving it a tug to remind Micah of his current position.

"Yes, sir," Micah murmurs, his eyes a little too wide, a tiny frown line creasing his brow as he tracks Trace's every move.

With a deep sigh, Trace dials a number from memory rather than selecting a saved contact in his phone. All of his most important phone numbers are ones he memorizes. It would be too dangerous to leave them lying around for anyone to find.

After two rings, Rachel picks up.

"How may I help you?"

"Hey darlin'. Tell him October thirteenth for me. Thanks a heap."

"Of course."

Then he hangs up, looking down his nose at Micah, setting the phone on the table.

"What... the fuck... was that?"

Shaking his head in answer, Trace selects a cigar, trims the end and lights it up. Taking a few puffs on it, he lets the buzz calm his nerves.

Minutes pass. The phone finally rings. Micah glares at it like it's a rattlesnake shaking its ass and Trace chuckles.

"Yep," Trace says, answering with the phone in one hand and

the cigar in the other.

An intoxicatingly familiar voice answers, "Report."

"Similar situation to last year," Trace says, letting the regret come through in his voice. "My boys are fucked. I'm lookin' for help. I get that it'll cost me. Whatever it is, I'll pay."

He feels the connection, stretched over miles of land and leagues of ocean, crackling through thin air. It makes him sad, and older than he is. Taking another puff on the cigar, he forces it all down where it belongs and listens to someone who knows him better than anyone else alive as they read between his lines.

"Been a long, damn time, kid," Trace says softly.

The longer it takes for a response to come, the more Trace understands why.

"Okay. You know what to do. I'll get back to you as soon as I can. Keep your phone handy."

"Will do, babe," Trace replies. "Thanks."

He knows how strange he must sound to Micah. He suspects he looks strange, too, and not like himself at all. Wouldn't be surprising, since he doesn't feel like Trace. More than ever, Trace feels like a persona that doesn't fit as well as it needs to. The seams are splitting.

Suddenly more sentimental than he even gets with Gabriel, the man who simultaneously is and is not Trace can't try to hide it, and he can't yet explain it either. The phone is set on the table again. He clears his throat and averts his eyes.

"Get the laptop for me?" he says quietly.

Micah goes without a word, fetching the computer from the desk, bringing it over, opening it up in front of Trace. He's patiently, apprehensively waiting for the explanation Trace owes him. The focus in his dark, gorgeous eyes just makes Trace want to pull him near and kiss him for hours.

As he waits for the PC to boot up, then as he opens email, Trace readies himself to endure a few questions from his confused submissive.

The first, hesitant query is, "What's October thirteenth?"

"Our anniversary. It's code so he knows I'm calling about a personal matter."

"Who?"

"Hard to fuckin' say, love," Trace answers with an expression of pure apology.

He gets the email program opened and logs in with the shared username and password. The account, like so many of his others used for communicating with friends within and without The Company, is one only the two of them know about, and can access. It's how they pass information back and forth without it being detected by anyone. Starting a new email draft, Trace types out Jerry Grealey's information. Trace has memorized the address and looked up the social security number just in case of the precise situation he currently finds himself in. After that, he adds a few awful sentences explaining why, knowing he probably adds them for his own benefit, only.

Saving the draft, he sits back and waits for another hard question.

"What happened last year?"

Trace sucks on the cigar, blows smoke. It's hard to figure out how much to say. In his mind's eye, he sees the contents of that locked file on his PC, which contains the collected findings of the private detective he secretly hired to track Harry, as well as a transcription of what Trace knows thanks to a certain ex-lover whose voice warmed the phone line mere moments ago. It all started as a way to make sure Harry didn't connect the abduction and torture Trace, Ben, and Micah committed to Gabriel, and to make sure Harry stayed far away. It didn't end where he thought it would.

"Harry, Gabe's stepfather, that kiddie fucker, showed up in an E.R. with the scars we gave him all burned off and drunk off his ass. Proximity-wise, he was too fucking close for my liking, and the way he'd burned the scars away made me suspect he was trying to get up to his old tricks. I made a similar call, then, and had him taken care of. Harry ain't a problem anymore."

"You had him murdered," Micah says hollowly, shocked.

"Should have done it sooner. Would have if I could."

"You're having Darrek's father murdered," Micah realizes.

Trace squints at him through the smoke, glancing now and then at the drafts folder.

"This is my family, Micah," Trace says steadily. "I take care of mine."

"Does anyone *know*? About Harry? About.... Who is this guy? Who did you call? How do you know him? Is he from The Company? Is he—?"

"He's with the Master's Circle. A Master Dom and an old friend. He's got resources at his disposal most people don't."

"Because of the Master's Circle?"

"No, this is separate from that. The MC is just how we met. I do him favors, he does me favors. Haven't seen him in years."

"He's a criminal?"

Trace laughs, smokes his cigar. "No," he answers without explanation.

"What's his name?"

Memories, so many memories, wash over him like warm rain. Lingering in those rooms at headquarters, Trace remembers being always on edge, not knowing who to trust, other than Nicholai, and then finding *him*. The seduction was intense. Those lapis lazuli eyes, the deceptively gentle voice, the passion in him, the way he could touch, and the ways he let Trace in, even when he was trying not to....

"Gray Raoul."

"You were lovers." Micah's expression changes with the revelation, the frown shifting into something less accusatory.

"Enough," Trace says gruffly. "*Enough.*"

The remembered feel of Gray under Trace's hands, the way everything had been exposed between them. Nothing was sacred. It was supposed to just be about sex, and breaking the rules which Nicholai had chained him with. Too fast, they realized there was real depth to the way they connected, and it got dangerous in a lot of different ways. That was before Gray had so much to hide, before he closed himself off, and he had surrendered, for a moment, to what they shared. It was so long ago, though. Too many years stretched out between them, for far too long.

Funny how he can still feel it, the betrayal, the way Gray shut him out, left him out in the cold like a whore who'd overstayed his welcome. Fuck, but that was hard.

Has he really not gotten over it yet? Is it possible?

The reason why is clear. Gray might be good at letting people go, but Patrick never was, and Trace can't dream of trying.

Trace comes back to himself slowly, recognizing that Micah has come to him and is now kneeling at his feet, gazing up at him with concern and affection. Micah places a warm, steady hand on Trace's chest and Trace overlays it with his own, gratefully.

"Guess we've all lost people along the way," Micah says with tenderness.

Leaning forward, holding Micah's hand, Trace kisses the silken hair on top of Micah's head and fights his way back to the present, where he has someone who really cares about him, in all of the right ways. There's nothing left for him in the past.

The call comes not even twenty-four hours later. Gray sounds different this time. Something is wrong. That's clear right away.

"No action needed," Gray says. "Client had a stroke. He'd been hospitalized two weeks ago. Transient ischemic, a mild one. The second one was worse. He fell and broke his neck a few days ago."

The news hits hard, like a brutal punch from a blind spot.

"Oh fuck," Trace groans. "*Fuck!* God, now I have to tell Darrek, don't I?"

"Clearly it's not ideal timing, but I'm afraid I have my own situation to deal with. I'm calling in a favor. You'll have the details, but expect a personal visit with Diadem's scheduled psychological analysis of you and your staff."

"Wait, what fucking psych analysis are you talking about? What sort of personal visit? From *you*? When?"

"Soon. *Very* soon."

"Jesus. Thanks for the advanced warning," Trace said sarcastically. "You coming alone?"

"No. Your company has a website. Who maintains it? Your boy?"

"Yeah. He used to. Been training us rookies to do what he does easy."

"Good. I'll need to meet with him."

"No shit? Huh. That'll be a kick in the ass, won't it? Okay. I'll have to catch you up on a few things later. See ya soon, kiddo. Lookin' forward to it."

"Likewise," Gray says with what sounds like gladness before ending the call.

Trace stares at the phone for a while, dumbstruck, before going to check email.

Kyle asks, "Why do you look like that?"

"Good fortune with the genetics roulette wheel," Ben mutters, turning the car off of the main road. Just a few more blocks left to go before they reach their destination.

"What aren't you telling me?"

"Quite a lot, actually. For instance, I had a dream last night where you had pointy, furry cat ears and a tail. Really fucking unsettling and vivid."

"Are you ever going to give me a straight answer?"

"Those are straight answers."

"Your eyebrows have been scrunched together since Micah called. You're driving us to Darrek's house. That's breaking rule number *one*. Nothing breaks rule number one. Not even a zombie apocalypse or alien invasion."

"You read all of that fine print, huh?"

"I'm thorough. Especially when it comes to weirdly detailed instructions on what I can and can't do."

Kyle continues to stare at Ben and the worrisome frown line etched between his eyebrows. It's obvious how freaked out Ben is, and it should probably disturb Kyle quite a lot, since there are few things that can truly freak Ben out. That, combined with their destination, is like detecting a nuclear bomb headed straight for their remarkably peaceful life.

Things are about to be blown to smithereens. Ben's new rules, the new order they've been living with for months, it's all going away and Ben is doing everything he can to keep Kyle in the dark, for the moment at least. Kyle suspects once they get to Darrek's house, things will get a lot clearer, fast.

Interestingly, Kyle isn't worried about it at all. There's not a whole lot that can worry him anymore. Pretty much everything he could worry about has already happened to him. Survival has instilled the blond haired, blue-eyed, angel-faced foreman and full-time submissive with a disproportionate amount of bravery. Even the prospect of seeing Gabriel and Darrek excites him. There's no tickle of dread. He keeps looking inward for one, but it hasn't manifested so far. Maybe that's because Ben will be there, and there's no way anything remotely bad will happen to Kyle while Ben is there. If there's anything that can be said for Benjamin Knox, it's that he handles his shit. Thoroughly. And Kyle is and has been priority number one for a long time.

The more it becomes apparent to Kyle how safe he is in Ben's care, how blessedly free from judgment or scorn, without even the smallest glimmer of possibility anything Kyle does would ever cause Ben to stop loving him as fiercely as he does, the more Kyle has learned he can push back. He tests the rules, teases a toe over the lines just to see how Ben is going to draw him back.

If Ben is the one instigating this, Kyle has his unspoken blessing to do whatever the hell he wants in the meantime, because Ben trusts him. Kyle knows his own limits now. Certainty of what he will tolerate, and what he won't, is as clear as day, all the time.

"You realize you're one notch away from that bizarre near-comatose state of shock you were in at the hospital that time? When you just kept staring at me? You hardly blinked. You were running on core systems only. You even dismantled your ability to speak for a while just so that you could stare at me harder. It was fucking eerie, you know that, right? What could Micah have possibly said to you to get this reaction? Why are we going here, Ben? Ben?"

He won't glance in Kyle's direction. They turn onto Darrek and Gabriel's road. Ben stays mum.

"If you're trying to keep me calm, you're doing a pretty bad job," Kyle says with a sigh. Trace's truck is in the driveway already as they pull up to the house. That's interesting.

"You are calm," Ben murmurs, shutting the engine off.

"Yeah, that's neat, isn't it?"

Ben turns sideways, looking at Kyle with that frown line firmly in place.

"Do you need a hug or something?" Kyle wonders aloud. An expression passes over Ben's face, there and gone, which makes Kyle's stomach do a nervous little swoop. "I should be worried, shouldn't I?" he realizes.

"I'm staying right with you," Ben promises.

"Stop it," Kyle says with less confidence, pulling his hand out of reach when Ben goes to take it. "Why are we here, Ben? Tell me."

"Because you need to be here for this. It was Trace's call."

"Be here for what?"

Ben's gaze drifts sideways, to the house. Trace has come out onto the front stoop, Kyle sees, looking the same way he always does—like he just got done either fixing a car, fucking a slave into unconsciousness or kicking someone's ass until they've forgotten their own name. He also looks impatient.

"Ben," Kyle warns, his heart beating faster, as Ben takes his hand.

"I love you, okay?"

"Stop it! Did Darrek get hurt? Is that what this is? Was there an accident?"

His voice wavers and Ben takes his face in both hands.

"No. Darrek is fine. Gabriel is fine. This is something else, but it affects all of us. So let's do this. Just like ripping off a band aid."

"I don't like it," Kyle says, losing his grip on the calm.

"Me either."

Chapter 11
The Unspeakable

The last time Darrek felt this out of his depth, he was in the lower level of Diadem, having waited on what he thought was a female Dominatrix named Gabey, but suddenly with a man sending him to his knees, fondling him, promising release and turning his life upside down. Something tells Darrek, though, that the release at the end of this visit will be nothing like it was the last time.

Trace is guarding the entryway, hurrying Ben and Kyle inside with hard stares and simmering impatience. Micah and Lilianna are in quiet conversation in the corner. Sitting on the floor in front of the couch, between Gabriel's feet, waiting with Gabriel's arms wound around his neck from behind, Darrek is wracked with a sense of foreboding so intense it threatens to overwhelm him.

What is this? What's happening?

Trace, Micah and Lilianna had showed up at the door with troubled expressions and whispers of news to be shared, but not until everyone was together.

The worst part is how disturbed Trace appears. Trace is never upset. He's the one always in control, never coming close to losing his composure, ever, not even with every nightmare that's been thrown their way. Yet, there he is, arms folded, hand over his mouth, brow furrowed, eyes haunted.

It's made Gabriel become suddenly quiet and obedient. He has no answers for Darrek, so he just holds Darrek, and waits, as they all wait.

"Why are you here? Why are they coming?" Gabriel had asked Trace when he mentioned Ben and Kyle.

"*You trust me, beautiful?*" Trace had responded, with more remorse than seemed possible for a man who had always been out of the reach of such human emotions as regret and grief.

"*Always,*" Gabriel had sworn.

"*Then trust me now. Please.*"

It feels like a dream when Ben and Kyle walk into the house, peeling off jackets, hanging them on the banister before venturing into the living room. Gabriel's hands on Darrek's chest are heavy, keeping him down as Ben and Kyle cross to them. Ben leans down, kissing Gabriel's cheek. Kyle offers Darrek a hand to shake.

"This freaking you out too?" Kyle asks.

"Yeah," Darrek admits, shaking with him. It's surreal to be sharing such a civil, normal handshake with someone who has been such a complicated part of Darrek's life as far back as he can remember. It's good though. The goodness surprises him more than anything else, as does the easy smile that Kyle gives him. Just seeing him there, looking healthy, strong, and happy does wonders for Darrek. The highly anticipated drama which Trace is about to lay on them feels much easier to handle, just for having gotten that assurance of Kyle's wellbeing.

Kyle lets go of Darrek's hand and Ben takes it instead, pumping it twice. Ben doesn't say anything but wears a complex, heavy look as he gazes down at Darrek. Kyle, in turn, is looking with mistrust at Ben's solemn expression. Darrek glances between Ben and Kyle, feeling more unsettled by the moment.

"I don't like this," Kyle says.

"Me either," Gabriel echoes as they all turn to Trace.

With the front door locked, Trace walks into the room and sighs heavily. He chews on his bottom lip and plants his hands on his hips, clearly struggling to say what he has gathered them all to hear.

"So, I've been trying to figure out how to say this," Trace begins. "Some of it has to do with things I've never shared with you. *Any* of you. They're things I kept to myself for your own good, but the time has passed for secrets. Especially moments like this. We all know where secrets get you, anyway. But, we're family. We take care of each other, the best way we can, even though we've all made mistakes. God knows, none of us are saints."

Perfect silence has descended upon them. Darrek glances at each of their faces. Lilianna and Micah know something, and whatever they know is making them drift closer to each other, clutching paper cups filled with coffee. Ben is watching Trace, but all of his attention is focused on Kyle. It's evident from the way he keeps Kyle a step behind him, as if trying to physically guard Kyle from the news. Their hands are linked, Kyle's eyes unfocused. Darrek absentmindedly caresses Gabriel's hands where they lay on his upper chest. He knows what it is to be afraid, with plentiful experience with being still and silent and keeping his head down while stronger, more willful men than him prepare to teach him a thing or two which they've decided he needs to know. Without a thought for himself, he worries about Gabriel and about Kyle, knowing how this must be testing each of them, wanting to save them from further pain.

"Ah, god," Trace groans, making Darrek's heart pound, his fingers gripping Gabriel's hand more tightly.

Trace looks up, looks right at Darrek and says, "Jerry's dead."

I heard him wrong, Darrek thinks. *He said someone else. It just sounded like —*

"He died in a hospital a few days ago. That's probably why your phone's been ringing. He was sick, being treated for a stroke, but they knew it was only a matter of time. He had a second, massive stroke, and he fell and broke his neck. He's gone, Dare. *He's gone.*"

The logical part of his brain is still working, somehow. He remembers how in the past month or so, he's gotten a few letters with the Grealey address on the envelope in the upper left corner. He hadn't even thought about it. He tore up every single one before opening the envelopes. They were probably from his mom. He recognized her handwriting on the envelope, after all, but he'd always thought what if they weren't *really* from her? And why would he have wanted to know anything she had to tell him anyway, when she'd never been there to protect him from Jerry? And he'd never given his family his email address. They didn't know how to contact his friends, either. But they could call. They could keep trying to call, over and over again.

Darrek grunts, stands without thinking, easily breaking free of

Gabriel's hold.

"You did something," Darrek hisses, blinking his eyes clear as things blur and shift. His voice is unsteady, weak. "*You did this.*"

"No. I swear," Trace insists.

"H-he... He's dead? He's r-really...."

Kyle is there, suddenly, hugging Darrek. Darrek gets a glimpse of Kyle's face, the face of the boy who was with him through it all, fighting at his side, sticking up for him when no one else could or would, against all logic and reason. Then Darrek simply hugs Kyle back, holding him tightly, exhaling heavily against that blond hair, which smells just like it always did, like home and safety.

"Oh," Darrek says lamely, piecing it together. The message from Jerry. The repeated, relentless calls, the absence of a visitor when Darrek waited, certain one would be coming. "He's gone."

Part of Darrek realizes Gabriel and Ben are both there, watching him hug Kyle, neither he nor Kyle letting go. Both Gabriel and Ben are ready, probably, to pry them apart if need be.

Darrek relaxes his grip on Kyle, but Kyle just holds on tighter. He hears it then—Kyle is crying, so Darrek holds the back of his oldest, dearest friend's head and presses a kiss to the top of it. Taking a deep breath, Darrek lets it out, ignoring the tears slipping down his cheeks. He does it again, and again, until Ben steps forward and puts a hand on Kyle's shoulder.

"C'mere. Come on," Ben coaxes.

It takes another few, long moments, but then Kyle steps back and stares up into Darrek's face. There's fury, but it's righteous and brilliant as he says thickly, "*God* killed him. God *killed* Jerry."

"Enough," Ben scolds, but Darrek feels the words hit him anyway. They steal his breath.

Standing there, shaking, he's glad when Gabriel steps into his arms and enfolds him in a hug.

"I'm sorry," Gabriel whispers. "I'm so sorry, baby."

"What's with the goddamned look on your face? There's fucking more, isn't there," Ben says angrily to Trace. "You've gotta be *kidding*. What else, Trace? Huh? What fucking else could you *possibly*—?"

"Jerry ain't the only one," Trace murmurs.

Everything stops.

For an impossible second, there's nothing, then Ben spitting, "You motherfucking—"

"Harry's dead, too."

"Holy...." Kyle gasps.

"What?" Darrek flounders, feeling Gabriel bolt from his arms, flying at Trace.

Gabriel runs at Trace, knocking him backward, his arm cocked. Trace gets a good grip on the arm, though, and they struggle as Trace restrains him while Gabriel's furor nearly enables him to overpower Trace again and again. Wrestling, struggling, Trace growls, "What the fuck did I always promise you, huh? I *promised you* he'd be gone. It wasn't talk! It wasn't boasting! It was a fucking *promise*. I had him followed, okay? I hired a pro to keep tabs on that scum to make *damn* sure he didn't *think* of coming near you again. You know what I found out? Huh? That piece of shit burned off the scars we gave him and showed back up to keep poisoning the world. He thought he could get back in the game, so, yes. I had him taken out. It wasn't me that did it. I just made a call. It was *a year ago*, Gabey! It's old news! I knew it was time to tell you, though. You deserve to know. Both of those scumbags are a non-factor now. They can't hurt you anymore! They can't hurt *anyone* anymore! I ain't sorry. Hate me if you need to, but protecting my family is more important than anything."

"A *year*?! A fucking...." Gabriel exclaims breathlessly. He gets an arm free and punches Trace in the eye.

"Ah, shit," Trace hisses, holding his face as Gabriel gives it up. Hands on his knees, breathless and hunched over, he squints up at Trace.

"How'd you know about Jerry? You were gonna do him too, weren't you? But you found out *God* did your dirty work for you."

"God's an efficient son of a bitch sometimes. Hell of a thing," Trace says.

Darrek sees Kyle crouched on the floor, hands folded in front of his mouth. Ben is standing agape next to him.

"Jesus," Gabriel pants.

"You actually did it. You took a hit out on my father." Darrek says, needing to say it aloud to help make it feel true, to make the surreal-ness go away.

"Tried to. After everything you and Kyle went through, and with everything that's been happening lately, it was time. Guess I'm not the only one who felt that way. But I'm not done. There's more."

"There's *more*?!" Ben exclaims, laughing a little hysterically. "There's no one else to kill! Who... What...?"

"Maybe you should let it breathe," Micah suggests, speaking directly to Trace.

"This is a lot for them," Lilianna agrees. "The rest of it...."

"He's going to be here *tomorrow*," Trace argues, shaken and shouting with frustration. "I don't have *time* to let them piss around and cry and hug and be sad for fuckers who don't deserve their grief. He needs Gabe's help and he's not coming alone. He represents the MC. Do you know what that means? Diadem only exists because they allow it to. When a Dom or a sub becomes a problem, or *causes* a problem, they are *handled*. The problems get *solved*. This is fucking serious shit and it involves *all of us*. We've not exactly been following the rulebook here, kids. All of us have done shit or are still doing shit that the MC would not like. That is *fact*. It has *nothing* to do with Jerry or Harry. It has to do with *us*. That's what fucking concerns me. That's what we've *really* got to worry about right now."

"What the good, sparkly, bleeding fuck are you talking about you goddamned crazy son of a bitch," Ben asks softly. "*Who's* coming tomorrow?"

"Oh, Jesus," Trace sighs, testing the eye Gabriel punched, alternately blinking it and opening it wide.

Darrek goes to Gabriel, taking him by the hand and leading him over to the couch again where they both sit. Darrek winds an arm behind Gabriel, pulling him close and murmuring, "Is this really happening?"

"Honestly, I don't know," Gabriel says. They look at one another briefly, seeing a lot, saying even more without needing a single word. Darrek pulls Gabriel in for a brief kiss and exhales beside his ear, just needing to feel him there, close, tangible and rational.

"Good. Sit," Trace says encouragingly. To Ben and Kyle he says, "You two sit, too."

"Can I get anyone a drink?" Lilianna offers.

"A couple waters would be great," Gabriel tells her.

"No problem, hon."

Ben claims the oversized stuffed chair. He pulls Kyle down to sit on his lap, winding Kyle up in his arms, resting his chin on Kyle's shoulder.

After bottles of water are passed around, Trace grabs a chair and goes through his story piece by piece. He explains about The Company and his time with the Master's Circle, only saying enough to paint the picture, not quite enough to answer all of the many questions popping up in Darrek's head. When he gets to Gray, all Trace says is, "He's a good man. He's broken his own share of the damned MC rules when it was convenient for him, so he's got no right to fuck me over with them. He's also an expert Dom with a *lot* of power and influence, and he's been a friend for a long, long time. Well, okay, he used to be a lot more than that, but we've both moved on since."

No one says anything. Darrek keeps catching Kyle's eye and he mainly feels numb. Gabriel is as still as a statue at his side and Ben seems dumbstruck. The awkward silence stretches on and on. When Gabriel takes Darrek's hand and clasps a hand to Darrek's cheek, pulling him in for a moment like he's giving Darrek a safe place in him to escape to, it helps Darrek breathe a little easier.

"What does this have to do with Harry and Jerry?" Gabriel asks, almost too quietly to hear.

"Is this guy a thug or something? Is he the one that bumped 'em off?" Ben demands.

With a hard, unyielding glare, Trace says, "He ain't a thug. He's the farthest thing from it. You heard of MI5?"

"No way," Kyle says, a smile playing at his lips as Darrek struggles to catch up. He doesn't have the faintest clue what MI5 is. "You used to fuck James Bond?"

"Christ," Trace sighs, rubbing his sore eye.

"James Bond killed Harry?" Gabriel squints.

"*He's not—*" Trace starts, talking too loudly. He softens his volume with effort and continues. "He's not James Bond, for fuck's sake, besides the fact that Bond was MI6 and Gray's MI5, homeland security. He won't take kindly to being called MI6."

Kyle asks, "Are we talking Pierce Brosnan or Daniel Craig?"

"More like Sean Connery," Trace grumbles. Pointing a finger, he says, "But you tell him I said that, and I will deny it to my fucking death bed."

"But young Sean Connery, right?"

"He's ten goddamned years younger than me. What do you think?"

"Sweet. Who's he bringing?"

"He's involved in a triad with a Master's sub named Jack Harrison and a regular Joe finance guy named Jan Richards. They'll be here too."

"Are they hot? Can I touch them?"

"Hey!" Ben exclaims, arms wide. "I'm right here you know. You're perched on my damn lap."

Kyle turns sideways and asks Ben directly, "So can I? I promise to only fuck them a little bit."

He holds up two fingers pinched close together and puts on his best smile. It makes Darrek smile too.

"You really think James Bond is going to let you fuck his Master's sub and boy toy?"

"Gray does like to watch," Trace murmurs, giving Ben a look.

"Are we really discussing this right now?" Gabriel barks. "Seriously? This guy *murdered* Harry. He was *going* to murder Jerry."

"He knew what Harry did," Trace explains. "And Jerry. He knows about all of you and what you mean to me. Gray did this for me, so if you want to be mad at anyone about it, lay it at my feet. You think Gray's life is all sunshine and roses? You think he hasn't seen shit? He knows how to handle a situation. He handled the situation. He's the one who told me about Jerry. He also needs your help, which he will explain in greater detail once he's here. It's not for me to say. But I would like you all to meet them. There'll be formal introductions tomorrow.

"Micah and Lily have offered to host a party at their place, two nights from now, which I'd like you all to attend. Blow off some steam; forget some of this shit for a few days. It'll be good for us. Now, I'm asking you, as a personal favor, to welcome Jack and Jan. I had a message from Gray telling me a little about them and what to expect. This visit is hard for them. Jan isn't a part of the MC scene. He's not a Dom or a sub. And Jack will need certain things to be comfortable here. He's got severe OCD and ODD — that's Obsessive Compulsive Disorder and Oppositional Defiance Disorder — and I am making it my personal mission to make sure whatever he needs, he gets. Like all of us, Jack has lived through some major shit and he has no idea what he's walking into here."

Trace stands, stretching some stiffness from his body.

"I'm sorry this is all hitting at once," he says with apology. "But no one will ever hurt my family and get away with it. That is my motherfucking guarantee. I know I haven't shared my history with you as much as I should have, but Gray *is* my history. We've been living out in the wild here, apart from the rest of the MC community. I think it's time we civilize ourselves and try to learn a thing or two before we get our asses in any more trouble. Couldn't hurt to have a few more friends in our corners either. Now, I'll understand if you wanna tell me to go fuck myself, but I love each and every one of ya. That's it. That's what I needed to say."

Gabriel is holding Darrek's hand tightly. As Darrek sags more into the couch, Gabriel sits forward, sitting straighter, getting stronger as the initial shock wears off a little more and he falls easily back into the role of Master, and taking control so Darrek doesn't have to.

"You wanna hit me again, baby boy, before I get out of your hair?"

Gabriel shakes his head. Turning to Darrek, Gabriel asks, "You wanna free punch while he's giving 'em out so easy?"

Darrek shakes his head, but asks Trace, "Would you have told us, if your plan went the way you wanted it to? If things hadn't gotten screwed up, would you have ever told us about our fathers?"

"Hard to say, kid," Trace answers. "Hard to fuckin' say. I am sorry for what you're going through. I'm sorry as hell for every bit of it and that's the damn truth. You didn't deserve this." He points at Kyle. "Neither did you." Then at Gabriel, his voice wavering,

"And neither did *you*."

"Please get out," Gabriel says softly, calmly. His fingers weaved with Darrek's, Gabriel presses a gentle kiss to the knuckles.

Ben walks past, and rests a hand, briefly, on Gabriel's shoulder in goodbye. Kyle gives Darrek a sideways glance and a subtle nod. A moment later, they're gone. Micah and Lilianna leave quietly, without fuss. Trace is the last one out.

"Gabriel," Trace beckons, his voice sounding full, rich and demanding.

Wearily, Gabriel rolls his eyes, then stands. Darrek stands as well.

With great reluctance, Gabriel walks to Trace and lets himself be gathered up in Trace's arms. "I love you, boy. Let this leave you lighter. Please." He kisses Gabriel's cheek, then lets go.

"Darrek," Trace calls next.

"Sir?"

"C'mere already," he says, gesturing, softening.

Hesitating even more than Gabriel, Darrek goes, very slowly. Trace sighs, hugging Darrek, then giving his cheek a kiss, too. With Darrek's face in his hands, Trace says, "You survived him, kid. His part in your life is done. Grieve if you have to, but put it behind you. Put it there and keep moving forward. There's a lot of good in life yet to find. I'll leave ya's be, but I will be calling tomorrow."

When he's gone and the house is emptied of all but the two of them, Darrek goes back to the couch, sitting heavily. Gabriel follows, sitting on Darrek's lap, facing him, wrapping his smaller body around him and whispering, "It's okay. We're okay. Love you. Love you so much."

Gabriel's fingers trail through Darrek's hair, making him shiver.

"Let's just stay like this for a while, okay?" Gabriel asks.

"Okay."

Chapter 12
What Ben Gives Kyle

The news delivered by Trace in the Grealey-Hunter living room does strange things to the dynamic between Ben and Kyle. When they get home, it seems all Ben wants to do is have a drink, sit somewhere comfortable with their cat, Kyle Junior, and have an easy, stress-free evening while they each adjust to new realities. However, all Kyle wants to do is submit to Ben and test his limits.

"I'm not in the mood," Ben argues.

"Oh please," Kyle scoffs. "You're *always* in the mood. You're in the mood at the DMV, and when you're helping old ladies through the door at the shopping center, and when you're in rush hour traffic…"

"Well, there's a first for everything. Shouldn't you be sad? Or upset? Or in shock?"

"Don't tell me how I should feel, Ben."

Ben has taken exactly one sip of Malbec, which he swirls inside a large, round wine glass. That's when Kyle realizes he's not in the mood either. He's not in the mood to be denied something he knows will make him feel better, and safer, and more able to deal with the next day, hour or minute.

"Fine." Kyle says. "I'm gonna go get ready. Then I'll go play by myself in the garage. Junior can keep me company."

"I'm not letting you masturbate in front of the cat!" Ben hollers after him as he goes upstairs. "You'll scar him for life! He's still a kitten, you know!"

As he closes the bathroom door, Kyle hears a bang and a shouted, "God damn it, Kyle!" Smiling with triumph, he begins his clean-up routine.

When he emerges from the bathroom, Ben is in the bedroom with a tray laden with supplies.

"Slave! Bed! Now!"

"Really?" Kyle sighs, folding his arms. "Are we Neanderthals? Try a multiword sentence."

"Get your ass on the fucking bed, now, before I change my mind and permanently dispose of the padlocked chest in the closet and all of its contents. How's that sentence? You like that?"

The chest is full of the things Ben has decided Kyle cannot be exposed to anymore—things like knives, scalpels, speculums, and catheter kits. They're all things Kyle has enjoyed in the past, but have now been deemed too dangerous to use. They've only been locked up and not thrown out because Ben has allowed Kyle to hope eventually, with time, he might be healthy enough to be exposed to them again in a controlled way. If Kyle keeps pressing his luck, though, he knows Ben will do as threatened and squelch that hope.

"Yes, Master," Kyle says with an obedient, submissive purr.

"On your back, head on the pillows," Ben instructs. "And if I see even a glimmer of fucked-up-edness in your eyes while we do this, I'm ending it. Got it?"

"Got it," Kyle says softly, with the ghost of a smile. He steps out of his cotton pants and fastens his collar around his neck.

The overprotective side of Ben constantly fascinates Kyle. It's been getting more intense by the day. For a while, Kyle assumed it was a passing phase, that once Ben saw Kyle was recovering, and space from Gabriel and Darrek was helping just as much as his regular therapy appointments, he would relax a little. But that's not so at all. It's like every day, every moment, they're walking down a path together. Each step draws Ben closer to a mindset where Kyle is not a submissive at all, only a cherished true love with a past so dark it makes Ben not want to hurt Kyle in any way, ever again. It doesn't matter if Ben, at his core, is a BDSM enthusiast and a skilled Dominant, or that Kyle craves submitting as much as Ben craves dominating. His love for Kyle outweighs everything. It didn't used to.

Recently, Kyle has been wondering if they'll get to a bend in their path where Ben will begin to refuse to engage in scenes like this, and will refuse to let Kyle submit to anyone. Maybe he would let Kyle screw around with other men to blow off steam, as long as it was safe and controlled, but the restraints, the pain, and the surrendering of all control would go away forever.

Kyle knows, in some ways, he learned to submit out of self-preservation, not choice. He has wondered what life would be like if he stopped submitting entirely, and if he could be okay with that. Fear that he *could* be okay with it is why he pushes back. He tempts Ben to engage in scenes with him. Luckily for Kyle, if Ben has one weakness, it's Kyle, naked, ready and willing.

"You're funny," Kyle tells him, getting in position as Ben moves around the bed, fastening straps and restraints to the frame.

"Yeah, well you're not funny," Ben counters, sounding sullen and defeated. "At all."

"Why not the garage? Why the bedroom?"

"It's cold in there."

"I can do cold. You once fed many ice cubes into my ass. That was pretty damn cold."

"You'll be more comfortable in here."

"Maybe I don't want to be comfortable."

Ben stops fiddling with a strap, his jaw clenched, and Kyle watches as he mentally counts to ten, letting go of the anger.

"You're not going to scare me, you know," he tells Ben. "I trust you. I know you're not Jerry. Jerry's worm food."

It was too much, too far, Kyle discovers suddenly as Ben leaves the bedroom entirely, and fast.

"Ben! Come on! Please?! This helps me! You want to help me, right? I'm not giving up everything I enjoy for that shit. I trust *you*. Let me show you that! I'm not going to break! I'm a grown up!"

Ben comes back just as quickly. Grabbing Kyle by the arm, he turns it over to expose the scars on the inside of the forearm, from wrist to elbow.

"You were a grown up when this happened, too. You didn't tell me something was wrong first. You didn't use a safeword. You just decided it was enough without giving me the *chance* to help and I know things are different now. *You're different*. Well, guess what, peaches? *I'm* different, too. I will not do *anything* that would in *any way* make you feel bad, because you've already had to feel *so fucking bad*, Kyle. And it's *enough*! It's ENOUGH."

"I love you, you know," Kyle smiles. Ben lets out an aggravated yell; Kyle pulls him down and hugs him. "Now fucking restrain me already."

Yielding, Ben does as Kyle asks. His wrists are bound loosely above his head, cuffed and chained to the headboard. His legs are another story. Ben pulls them apart in a wide V, fastening each ankle in a leather cuff and attaching straps which he pulls tight with no slack whatsoever. It forces Kyle's legs apart and back, folding his body in half. The position exposes his genitals, his ass—everything. It also gives Ben an unobstructed view of Kyle's face in order to better judge his mood and anxiety level.

"Wow, this position *sucks*. Good job!" Kyle says happily.

Ben settles on the bed, kneeling by Kyle's ass. The tray is right there for easy access. There's a cloth covering it so Kyle can't see what Ben has brought to play with.

"Why are you happy?" Ben asks. "Seriously, why? You were in the room with the rest of us. I saw you—and allowed you to—hug Darrek. You cried. Where did that go, huh?"

"Am I supposed to be sad for him? Am I?" Kyle challenges. "Am I supposed to mourn Harry, too?"

"You threatened to leave me if I ever went after that fucking human trash. The idea of me going after him scared you *so much,* and now you're just fine with it?"

"I never wanted your judgment," Kyle says softly, losing the smile. "I can't change what I did, or what happened to me. I don't want anyone looking at all of that and deciding on their own who gets to pay and how. It's not our place to judge. *God* judged Jerry. He died because it was his time. Now, he's gone. He won't be haunting Darrek. He won't be haunting me, either. He's just gone. That makes me happy. *Very* happy."

"What about Harry?"

Kyle shrugs. "You didn't do it. It's done with. This isn't about me trusting Trace or this new guy. It's about you and me. We're cool. I have no problem with us. We're done talking about it."

"Oh are we?" Ben asks with a supremely smartass tone. "Well, since you're in charge and everything, I guess you're right. Why don't I create some atmosphere to get us in the mood, then?"

From under the cover on the tray, Ben produces a few candles. They're white and thick. Two are plain but one is beeswax. He lights them and sets them on a small glass tray on the nightstand.

"Oh shit," Kyle chuckles.

"Why don't we start with a massage?" Ben suggests, still being a smartass. He produces a bottle of mineral oil and starts to rub it into Kyle's legs, working his way up them, slowly. His hands coat Kyle's calves, the undersides of his knees, and his thighs. When he gets to Kyle's groin, he uses a liberal amount of the oil on his ass, getting some in the crease, working it over his balls and shaft, then moving up over Kyle's pelvis before going on to his chest and arms. Before long, Kyle's whole body glistens with the slick fluid and his skin tingles from Ben's rough touches, covering him, lingering long after the fingers have moved to new places.

"Funny how you mentioned the ice," Ben observes with a frown of concentration, drawing an ice bucket from the tray, too. He plucks a single cube from it before replacing the lid to keep the rest cold. Trailing the cube through Kyle's crack, Ben smiles deviously. "I was going to save these for after, for cooling the wax, but I think that cocky fucking tone in your voice needs a little work."

The cube stops on Kyle's hole, water dripping down to his back in trickles. Ben pushes and the cube begins to pass through the ring of muscle.

"Fuck, I hate that shit," Kyle hisses, pulling uselessly on the restraints. "Do you know how fucking uncomfortable—AHH!"

The cube is pushed into him. Ben's index finger moves it deeper.

"Oh, woops! That one got away from me! Maybe I should get the forceps out to pull it back? What do you think, slave? You want the cube or the clamps?"

"Fuck," Kyle hisses, squirming. "Ahh, *fuck*... You're b-bluffing. You don't really...."

"Oh, don't I?"

Ben pushes back a corner of the cloth, revealing an assortment of medical clamps. Humming through the fear and the cold, bearing down on the cube to push it out, gasping at the spreading, searing, biting, vicious chill, he shakes his head as Ben takes two of the smaller clamps and attaches them to Kyle's nipples, pulling on each with his fingers to stretch the skin before closing the metal on them, letting the clamps rest against his chest. Kyle's dick twitches, swelling, and Ben picks up a much larger set of forceps.

"You're not really going to...."

Without a word, Ben presses a hand against Kyle's ass, pulling it open with his fingers. The end of the metal clamps are inserted and opened up once they're inside him to grab the cube rather than push it deeper.

"*Oh fuck,*" Kyle gasps, more shrilly, his voice climbing and his breath growing shallower as the forceps reach up into his rectum. Grunting, throwing his head back, he's helpless but to bear it as he's pried open and filled obscenely with the medical equipment. Then Ben slowly withdraws them, taking his sweet old time getting the forceps back through his sphincter.

Panting, sweating a little, Kyle shudders and says, less bravely, "Next time, leave the cube in."

Grinning wickedly, Ben says, "And what makes you think you get to decide what I do next time? You know, it's been a while since I played with *these*." He grabs Kyle by the balls, giving them a tug and a twist. Kyle's breath leaves him. He's got nowhere to go, no way to keep Ben from tormenting him whatever way he wants to, having instigated this and all. The only thing he can do is peek up through his bound legs as Ben takes a complicated ball stretcher from the mystery tray.

"God, I fucking *hate* that one," he laments as Ben fastens the first of two thick stainless steel locking rings around the base of Kyle's scrotum, feeding his balls through one. Two metal rods attach the rings to each other. By turning the nut with the hex key on the outside of the other ring, you can draw the rings apart to stretch the scrotum. Of course, that's not all the toy can do.

"What do you say, slave?" Ben asks. "Stretch 'em or crush 'em? Or, you know, *both*. I've got time. Hell, I've got all night."

"Fuck you," Kyle growls as Ben feeds his balls through the second ring, locking that in place as well. He doesn't watch as Ben spreads the rings apart with the hex key. The skin stretches, forcing his balls away from his body with the first ring flush against his groin and the second behind his testicles. The more Ben turns the key, the more space is created between the rings.

Soon, Kyle is whining back in his throat. Ben rubs Kyle's balls, the skin pulled smooth, while he screws the spikes into his flesh through the second ring.

"Had enough yet?" Ben asks. "Gonna pussy out on me before we've really started?"

He keeps turning the key, and just as Kyle thinks the rings must be at their limit, they shift a little farther. Throbbing, unable to think past the pressure in his balls, Kyle can only grunt and gasp. Ben leaves him like that, spread and stretched to his limit, clamps bruising his nipples, as he draws the biggest butt plug Kyle has ever seen from under the cloth.

"You motherfucker," Kyle groans, barely with time to brace himself for it as Ben slicks the toy with lube and begins to feed it to him. It's ridged all the way up its eleven inches in length, from the fairly narrow tip to the three and three quarters inch diameter end.

At first only the plastic head enters. Ben holds it there and grabs a candle. Tensing up, Kyle tracks the flame as Ben moves it over Kyle's chest and drips a long, snaking line down his sternum to his navel. Wax falls hot against the oiled skin and Kyle bears down, gritting his teeth against the burning while Ben screws the massive plug a little deeper into his ass. It leaves him gasping, head spinning, and feeling absolutely, completely at Ben's mercy.

The pressure in his ass builds. Kyle's balls ache and the wax drips in another long, weaving line up the underside of his left leg, from ass to ankle. Kyle wants to draw away, but can't. Humming against the feel of each burning drip, focused on it more than anything else, he knows Ben's working his way up his ass, but can't do anything about that either. All he can do is cry out or growl or pull at the straps spreading him wide.

Once his other leg is decorated with its own long, drizzled line of cooling wax, Kyle is panting, dizzy with it all.

"Look, slave," Ben beckons. Kyle doesn't want to, really, but he does.

The huge plug is protruding from his ass, with a ridiculously amount still left to go, and so wide it makes Kyle moan instantly. The stainless steel trap on his balls shines in the candlelight, the flesh reddened and skin tight. The wax along his belly is white and hardening fast. Ben brings the candle to hover over Kyle's cock, his other hand steadying and pushing at the plug, trying to work a little more into him.

"God, you *suck*," Kyle moans, waiting for it. The wax drips slowly from the candle's flame, landing on the shaft of his penis. With a shrill, bitten-back cry, Kyle exclaims his useless protest. Hot wax keeps falling, drawing a line up to the head of his cock, where it hurts so much tears come to Kyle's eyes, then back down the underside of his shaft to his tortured balls. "Mmm… no, don't… please…"

The wax dribbles over the steel, over the stretched skin, over his trapped, reddened, sore testicles and Kyle can only shout and strain and cry as the heat dulls and the phallus stretches his ass, filling him to bursting, making him certain that he's never been so full, stuffed so wide.

Writhing, becoming delirious, he doesn't see Ben remove the forceps on his nipples. Blood rushes to the area, making the hurt grow, blooming in brilliant colors. Wax drips, coating his left nipple, then his right. The phallus pushes deeper and Kyle chokes on his cries. Stroking Kyle's dick, Ben pumps it as wax flakes off. The phallus is worked into his ass, bit by bit, making Kyle shout, making him desperate to come.

Ben lets go of Kyle's dick and the beeswax candle is in his hand.

"No, no Ben, no, please," Kyle moans and it's dripping over his hip and his mouth works around a shriek that won't come out. The wax from that candle is so much hotter. Ben drips it over Kyle's ass, covering each cheek in liquid fire and his eyes roll up.

The phallus tugs back out and Kyle gasps, shouts, and is filled a moment later by Ben's cock, which fucks him in long, slow strokes.

Kyle wants the ball stretcher off and begs Ben for it, but Ben just fondles him while riding his ass and scratching off pieces of cooled wax. A hand falls in a loud, painful smack against the side of his butt. Kyle tenses around Ben's cock, making him hiss and curse, causing him to thrust harder. Ben keeps spanking him. Nipples throbbing, balls throbbing, ass throbbing, skin tingling everywhere, Kyle feels Ben come, unloading with a hard snap of his hips and a grimace.

The ball stretcher comes off, and Kyle sobs with relief. Ben peels the wax off of Kyle's dick, cooling it with an ice cube that brings welcome but bitter coolness, making him writhe again, straining the bonds holding him down. Ice cubes drag everywhere, over his arms, his legs, his torso and nipples. Next, Ben runs a comb over his skin, prying the wax free. Kyle pants and sweats, his erection stiff and begging to be touched or sucked—something, anything.

Worn out and blissful, Kyle can only lie there, needing to come so badly he can only make soft pleading, purring sounds as Ben frees his aching legs from the straps, guiding them down to the bed.

Eyes closed, body exhausted, simply needing, Kyle doesn't anticipate it when Ben straddles him and sinks down onto his cock.

Humming, purring, eyes rolled up, arms in shackles, he feels Ben riding him and chases up into each downward push, taking as much of Ben as he can, planting his feet and fucking with all of his need. Kyle comes with a whimper, nuzzling Ben's touch as it skitters down his face, over his lips, down his neck and chest.

They kiss and Kyle comes down slowly, wanting to maintain the high, ever so reluctant to let it go.

"So, not in the mood, huh?" Kyle teases Ben.

"What can I say?" Ben replies with a grin. "You motivate me."

Chapter 13
Call of Need

Sitting in his home office, Ben stares at his cellphone for a while before actually placing the call. He can hear the water running through the house's pipes as Kyle showers on the second floor. Unable to stop thinking about everything Trace had told them about Harry, Jerry, Trace's past and their soon-to-arrive visitors, Ben can't even decide which piece of news is most worrisome.

The line rings in his ear.

It's picked up with a low, murmured, "Yeah?"

"Hunter," Ben says in greeting, his voice just as hushed. He has no idea what to say, but simply hearing Gabriel makes him feel a little better about the whole thing. Trace just blew Gabriel and Darrek's lives apart and left them to pick up the pieces. It's Ben's unspoken responsibility to check in and see how they're doing. Kyle isn't the only one he worries about these days.

"Knox," Gabriel replies. It's slightly muffled. Ben tries to envision where Gabriel is and what he could be doing.

Neither of them says anything.

"'Sup?" Ben asks, eventually.

"Oh, you know. Stuff."

"What'cha doin'?"

"Laying here."

"Where's here?"

"The bed."

"You alone?"

"No," Darrek replies from nearby, close enough to have heard Ben's question at least.

"Good. What can I do?"

"Nothing." That's Gabriel again.

"Talk to me. Give me something."

"I'm not even mad at him, you know?"

"Trace?"

"Yeah. I'm just... frustrated. And I resent the hell out of it that he made this decision without even asking me. I'm fucking sick of people doing things without my permission."

"You're glad he's gone though, right? I mean, *I* am. One less thing to worry about."

"I can't even wrap my head around it," Gabriel sighs.

"How's Dare? Can he still hear me? How you doin', ya big lug?"

"Shitty," Darrek answers. "Shocked. It doesn't feel real. I mean, they're just words. Can't really decide if I want to kiss Trace or punch his other eye."

Ben smiles. "Yeah, that was fun. Look, you guys call if you need anything, okay? I mean it."

"Yep. Thanks Benny," Gabriel says.

They hang up. Ben drops the phone onto the desktop and runs his hands back through his hair, exhaling heavily and leaning back in his chair. The water has stopped. Kyle must be done with the shower. Ben decides to give him a few minutes to himself to work some of this shit out, because fuck if Ben knows what to do about it.

―◻―◻―◻―

The first thing Kyle does is find the obituary online, using his phone. He sees the funeral is planned for the day after tomorrow. The Grealeys have a lot of out of state relatives, so that, combined with the irksome difficulty of being unable to get a hold of Darrek, has probably left them padding time a bit.

He sits there, naked, on the edge of the bathtub, staring at the screen, reading the words over and over again. Jerry Grealey. Born. Died. Husband, father, and grandfather. Preacher. Survived by Steven, Darrek, and many others.

Facts are printed there like they tell the whole story of Jerry's life, like *that's* the summary of his accomplishments. But the more Kyle stares at those words, those simple, straightforward labels, the more the memories come back.

He's twelve, lying naked and spread on Darrek's bed, with Darrek's face pressed gently against Kyle's groin, his tears dampening the skin as he cries and obeys the commands being shouted from the foot of the bed, by the man standing over them both, wielding the belt, scripture, and arousal, using all three to torture and scar. And Kyle can only lie there, naked, taking it, allowing it, for Darrek's sake, from Darrek's father—Jerry Grealey, who to most was just a father, just a grandfather, just a preacher and upstanding member of the community. Kyle's twelve, and he's on his hands and knees, being fucked, being raped, and lashes of the belt quicken the thrusts, sharpen Kyle's cries as Darrek screams and the pain blooms.

The words blur as his hand shakes. He presses a button to clear the screen. Instead, he goes through his contact list.

Finding the person he needs, he hesitates, grunting against the bitter taste of bile rising in his throat. Shaking his head with force, like it could help clear it of the nightmares of his adolescence, Kyle knows the decision is his, and his alone. Does he let the lies stand? Does he let Jerry Grealey have the honorable funeral his wife and family have planned for him? Or does he try to interject some truth, tell people who that man really was on the inside? He could try to hack the website, add some words of his own to the obituary, like pedophile, child abuser, and monster. They'd just take it down, though. The people who need to know, wouldn't know.

So he thinks of Ben, and what Ben helped Trace and Micah do when they followed Gabriel home. They abducted Gabriel's stepfather, gave him marks to carry with him so that the people who needed to know what he really was, would know. And maybe more than he ever has before, Kyle understands why they did it.

This time, though, Kyle doesn't have collaborators. He won't get Ben involved, or Trace, or Micah. Or even Darrek. This deed is Kyle's alone to tackle.

Well, he thinks, *maybe I do have one collaborator.*

He remembers Nicky with a fond smile—his rich, caramel-colored skin, the taste of his kiss, the sweetness of the way he made love. More, he remembers the way Nicky once lied for him, covering over the truth with ease and an innocent grin, going along with the fabrications Kyle wove around them to hide what was really happening.

Nicky.

In high school, they snuck around together, slipping away to kiss or touch or fuck. Nicky was younger, off Darrek's radar until he almost walked in on Kyle and Nicky going at it in the pool in Kyle's parents' backyard on prom night. Maybe Darrek suspected even then, because he never liked Nicky, and always reacted with jealousy whenever Nicky was near or even mentioned. So, Kyle has never talked about Nicky to his best friend since, even though they've kept in touch since Kyle moved away. Nicky has been someone Kyle knew he could trust and count on with parts of himself almost no one else knew about. Their secrets bonded them. They've been a safe place for each other for a long time.

Kyle places the call, holds the phone to his ear, and sighs. His knee bounces with nervousness and he bites at his lip.

"Kyle?" a familiar voice, still full of that innate sweetness, asks upon answering.

"Hey, Nicky. How are you?"

"Good. Doin' good. You?"

"Well," he chuckles uneasily, blowing out a breath and trying to calm down. "I've got a really big favor to ask you, actually. You haven't moved, have you?"

"Nope, still a townie," Nicky confesses.

"Good. You uh, hear about Darrek Grealey's dad dying?"

"Yeah, I heard rumors about that, I think. Sucks."

"No, it doesn't actually," Kyle murmurs. "Look, Nicky, if I could get down there and do this myself, I would."

"You got some loose ends or something? With the funeral? I ever tell you my cousin, James, works there? That's who I heard the rumor from. Small town and all. He was there when the body arrived."

Kyle does, in fact, remember tales of Nicky's cousin, working in the morgue. James would tell stories to his younger cousins, like

Nicky, of seeing dead bodies every day, and the types of things done to those bodies in preparation for burial or cremation. Stories like that were high entertainment to teenagers or young men, looking for a good scare or some freaky shit to whisper about.

"Yeah," Kyle agrees. "I ever tell you about why Darrek got a cast on his hand when he was twelve? His dad slammed a door on it, intentionally, to teach him a lesson."

"Jesus Christ," Nicky hisses. "His dad did that?"

"That's not all he did. Jerry had a thing for watching little boys get raped. Guess how I know?"

"Kyle…" Nicky gasps, sounding breathless. "Fuck, you're not kidding, are you?"

Wiping angrily at his eyes, sniffling as his nose starts to run, too, Kyle takes a steadying breath.

"You okay, man?"

"No," Kyle rasps. "I'm not. Jerry wasn't a good man, Nicky. The shit I've endured because of him… The shit Darrek has, too… God, how many years has it been? And it's *still* a day to day process, trying to get past it. For *years*, we were terrorized. He *got off* on it. He was sick and evil. He doesn't deserve a nice funeral service, or honor, or respect. No one knows he abused us — no one that counts. What I'm about to ask you to do, man, I know it's a lot. I know you could get in a lot of trouble. I'm willing to pay whatever you think it's worth. I've got money. I've got things besides money, too, if your tastes skew in other directions. But that man — he made me feel like I was nothing for so long, just something corrupt and fun to hurt. I want to take some of that back. That's all. He's dead anyway. It's just his legacy I'm looking to shake up a little. But it's your call, okay? Tell me to fuck off. Hang up and forget you ever knew me."

There's a pause. Kyle waits for the click of the line going dead, squeezing his eyes shut.

Then, softly, tenderly, Nicky asks, "What do you need?"

Something knotted tight inside Kyle's chest comes loose, and he laughs, crying. "You have *no idea* what this means to me."

"My ex was abused as a kid. Believe me, I've got an idea," Nicky tells him. "What do you need?"

With a quiet moan, a release of some more tension, Kyle begins to feel steadier and gathers together the details of his plan in his head. "Thank you, Nic. Okay, um, it's up to you how much you're comfortable with. I'll leave it in your hands."

"Baby, anything goes," Nicky says with a chuckle. "You know me."

"How trustworthy is James?"

"James handles *corpses* for a living. If there was ever someone who knew how to keep a secret...."

"Awesome," Kyle grins, feeling the pieces come together, and feeling more empowered than he could have dreamed.

Chapter 14
Love in the Dark

Micah, Lilianna and Trace are all quiet when they return to the house—Micah and Lilianna's. Micah can tell Trace is in a keyed up, heightened emotional state. After all, he has just given Gabriel every reason in the world to hate and shun him, forever. In the name of being truthful, he's sacrificed his own happiness in order to help his boy find peace. Maybe more than anyone, Micah appreciates the grand selflessness of the gesture. It makes Micah wonder what else Trace has done without saying a word to anyone, to help or protect their little group. It also makes Micah want to step up and do his part to show Trace he's valued, and his contributions don't go unnoticed. But Trace's nerves are frayed. He doesn't want to talk. His eye has swollen up and his pride is even more wounded.

In need of company and comfort, rather than solitude and dread, he's asked to stay with them. It's Lilianna's decision to invite Trace to spend the night, as it always is when Trace is allowed to share their bed. After grabbing a quick bite to eat and a beer or two, they retire to the bedroom.

Lilianna uses the en suite first, locking herself in. Hearing the click of the lock, Micah catches Trace's gaze from over a shoulder. He doesn't blame her for shutting them out, or wanting her space, not after the way he'd shared the news he's been collared by Trace. But that little, insignificant lock feels like just another thing keeping them apart.

Trace comes up to Micah, who's sitting on the edge of the bed, too shellshocked to even want to get undressed. He grabs hold of the hem of Micah's shirt and pulls it over his head for him. Pressing Micah back to the bed after the shirt has been tossed toward the hamper, Trace follows him down, lying on top of him for a brief, indulgent moment, just to kiss and hold him, skin against skin. Every point of contact sparks, making Micah crave *more*, willing to do anything to get it.

When the water in the bathroom sink shuts off and the light switch is flicked, Trace rolls and sits up, working his boots off. Lilianna opens the door and finds them quite innocently engaged. Lying there, Micah watches the sensual way she moves, going from bathroom to dresser to nightstand. She's wearing a miniscule pair of cotton shorts and a tank top, her hair tied back in a loose bun at the back of her head. He's always thought she's absolutely beautiful in the quiet moments when she's not trying to impress, only needing to be herself and be comfortable, but it's like watching someone through a window. There's something there, between you, and you can't cross over without breaking something.

They all get in bed. Trace lies in the middle, between them — figuratively and literally. He kisses each of them goodnight. Lilianna rolls over, facing away from both of them where she clings to her side of the bed. Micah also rolls to face away from his other two bedmates, but Trace is facing him, and spoons up behind him quite closely. He lies so closely, in fact, the feel of Trace's hardness against him soon gets Micah's blood pumping, his heartbeat quickening. Sleep won't take him. The strength of his want is dizzying.

A restless hour or so passes by. Micah can hear the gentle rise and fall of Lilianna's breath, and knows she's asleep. Still, he doesn't do anything. He won't presume to think Trace is in the mood to do anything, or assume he'd want to under the circumstances. There's been so much betrayal already.

In the end, he can't help it. The more he tunes in to the feel of Trace behind him, the solidity of his body, the weight of his muscular arm slung around Micah's chest, the heaviness of his cock pressed against Micah's ass, the more aroused he becomes. It's a slight movement, just a gentle press backward, a fluid rolling of his hips.

Right away, Trace's hand slides down Micah's body, moving from his chest to his pelvis, palming Micah. Trace rocks forward.

Micah savors the insistent drag of Trace's cock through the crease of his ass, wanting his boxer briefs out of the way so he can feel even more. Trace thrusts again and Micah presses back to meet him, turning his face so his heavy exhale is muffled by the pillow rather than released, dangerously, to the air of the room. His cock stiffens with Trace's hand hooked around the root, straining the ability of his underwear to contain his erection. When Trace begins fondling him through the cotton, Micah bites down on his lip in his attempts to stay silent. Quivering, he pushes fractionally into that firm, rough hand kneading him, knowing he's soaking the briefs with pre-come. Trace's cock grinds even harder against his ass.

Trace is the one who decides.

He lets go, moves slightly away, then pushes Micah over, onto his stomach. Trace moves to lie on top of him, hooking his fingers in the briefs, tugging them down low to expose Micah's ass. Micah's legs are nudged apart as Trace settles there, between them. Two fingers, licked wet, are worked into Micah's ass, coaxing it open. Throughout the whole process, Micah swallows every plaintive cry, staying silent, letting his mouth work soundlessly through the ache. He keeps his ass pushed up, inviting the probing movements of the fingers sheathed within it.

He doesn't glance over at Lilianna often, just now and then to make sure she's still asleep. Thankfully, Micah knows she's not easily roused. That doesn't make it any more excusable, but he can't bring himself to stop.

Trace begins to force his cock through Micah's hastily prepped opening, entering him with a slow, steady push, and it's glorious. One of Trace's hands clamps tightly over Micah's mouth to hold in any cry, not wanting to wake Lilianna. It helps, especially when Trace goes deeper and Micah can't help but let out a soft moan.

They make love silently, moving as slowly and as little as possible, and climax together. Trace drags open-mouthed kisses over Micah's shoulder and neck. Stuffed full, Micah clenches around Trace's cock, loving the feeling of being so completely possessed. For a little while, Trace just caresses Micah, covering him with the gentle, explorative touches of his fingertips and fingernails. Soon he's hard enough to go again and Micah reaches back to grab a fistful of Trace's hair, denying the cries of pleasure he wants to make as Trace begins to move again, rocking into Micah again and again. Silently, secretly, he worships Micah's body, and Micah savors every second.

The next morning, Micah exists in a pleasant daze, feeling quite starkly the effects of Trace's attention the night before.

Sitting in the expansive, pristine, white kitchen, filled with sunlight, in a house both enormous and mostly devoid of the usual signs of life — for now at least — Micah admires the colorful bruising of Trace's black eye. Lilianna has gone out on a supply run, leaving them, again, without her. At least it allows them to speak freely as they figure out how to proceed. The day's planned momentous events seem daunting.

"It's your call whether you want to be collared or not for the party," Trace tells him. "Kyle and Dare will be collared. It was their choice. I don't know about Jack. You're acting as host, though, so if you're more comfortable focusing on that, then that's what we'll do."

"What about today?"

"Today you wear it. I intend Gray to see you're mine, no question about it. He'll respect it. It's important."

"Okay," Micah nods, his stomach swooping with nerves and excitement. After being so often abandoned in love, ever hesitant to let on exactly how much his attractions and fantasies involve people of his own gender, it's deliciously intoxicating to have Trace be so eager to stake his claim in Micah in such an important, public way. "I'll do whatever you need. After everything you've done to pull me out of my own head, I'm happy to help. It really means a lot that you've stuck around this past week or so. It's nice to feel like I'm important to you, because you're really important to me. I'd love to wear your collar in front of them, today."

Trace's fingers move over Micah's jaw, along his throat, admiringly. The skim of warm skin against skin is like a tantalizing taste, provoking even more fantasies. It's amazing how simply being around Trace makes Micah lust wantonly after possibilities which, before, seemed utterly impossible or ridiculous. He's always had a vivid imagination and only with Trace as his Master has he felt so eager to explore every glimmer of a dream.

"Hopefully they're fine to stay here, with us," Trace says. "We can put 'em in the spare rooms, or maybe they'll only need one of 'em. Who knows? I'll stay here, too, as long as they're around. If we want to be together, like last night, it might be better to be discreet. I won't pressure you into submitting, even if Lil isn't here. I promise you that—for your comfort and also because if we get into a scene, Gray will wanna be there."

Voyeurism. Exhibitionism. Humiliation. Willingly made helpless as the most powerful of men play with his naked, willing body….

Tingling, creeping anxiousness crawls over Micah's skin. He lowers his gaze. He almost can't imagine such a thing—submitting to Trace while Trace's ex, a Master Dom, supervises, possibly participates or takes over. It would be the ultimate fantasy, a heady ordeal to test all of his limits. In any other circumstance it would make no sense to expect Micah to perform sexually in front of a partner's ex, but Gray is a representative of the Master's Circle. His job is to evaluate the Doms of Diadem. There's no getting around it, as awkward or taboo as it might be.

"Yes, sir," Micah murmurs.

After a beat, Trace gets a funny, thoughtful sort of look. Then it's gone.

"What?"

"Nothin', really." Trace says, shaking his head briefly. "Lil hates that I fuck you raw. You know that? Maybe she had a feeling about what we were up to last night, or maybe it's just been bugging her since you told her about the collar, but she said a few things this morning while you showered, before she left. I told her it's not her call anymore. She didn't say much else after that. We need to talk this shit out, the three of us. It's just the sucky timing of it all that's gonna make it a challenge. Don't think any of us have the energy to face having it out when our guests are about to invade our peaceful oasis of tranquility." Trace gives a bitter laugh and sets his jaw. There's a hard, foreboding glint in his eyes. "But you? Me? Her? We need to sit down and talk once the time is right. I don't like hurting her any more than you do. But the way she doesn't even bother asking you how you're doing, how she takes off, over and over again—I don't like it. She spends more time with her lover than she does with you, and that's been going on *long* before I came into the picture. Now that she knows about us, I can tell it's hurting her in ways she didn't expect. But she's been hurting *you*. She doesn't get that. She can't expect you to wait here, in an empty bed, while she's out there sleeping with someone else, then condemn you for—"

"Hey," Micah says softly. "I know. Sore subject for you, huh?"

"Don't defend her," Trace scolds.

"I'm not."

"*She made her choice*," Trace says passionately. "Don't you see that?"

"You're assuming. And you're just trying to defend... whatever this is between us. I don't even know what to call it. It doesn't feel like it's enough to just call you Master. Not anymore. The title isn't big enough for all of the feelings I have. That's the problem with me and Lily, I guess, in a nutshell."

"You're more than a slave to me, too, love. Hell of a lot more." Trace's fingers skim over Micah's throat. "I never wanted to just be a slave, either," Trace says quietly, introspectively. "Just a slave. Just a Master. Fucking labels."

"I know why Lily's sore about us going bareback, though," Micah says, circling back around to Trace's earlier comment. "Lil and I haven't had sex without a condom since long before Moira died. Lily's on the pill and all, but still. It's like we both need that barrier to keep us in our comfort zones. Makes it feel colder, though," Micah confesses. "It's like all of the ways we hold back from each other are symbolized by that piece of latex. I like feeling you against me, with nothing in between."

"Me too, love," Trace says fondly, leaning in to kiss him on the lips.

Micah wonders, and not for the first time, if Trace has had sex with Lilianna because of her own unique allure, or if it's because she's a part of Micah, and in his search to conquer every aspect of Micah, body, and soul, Lilianna has merely gotten swept up in Trace's quest to have it all. But it doesn't really matter. All that counts is the love Trace always leaves behind to fill the empty spaces in Micah's heart.

Micah's not sure what to do about Lilianna, or if he's ready to face what's right in front of him. For the moment, it's enough to hold on to Trace in order to get through, and see where their path is trying to take them, whether they like it or not.

Chapter 15
Bright Eyes

Trace waits for Gray in the front room of Diadem. The blinds on all of the windows there are open, letting shafts of bright sunlight through, but not a light bulb in the building is on. All is dark, still, and rather uninviting beyond the reception area. The midday sun is left to try to reach inside and banish the shadows.

It's quiet—too quiet, like the indrawn breath between screams. Your ears are still ringing from the last, anticipating more. All the tense pause means is you better hold on to your ass if you know what's good for you.

No one else is around. Diadem is closed for the day. Trace made the calls, first thing. He didn't want anyone else on the property when the initial meeting takes place. Things are complicated enough as it is anyway. He can't imagine what Ben is dealing with at home, let alone Gabriel. All of it falls at Trace's feet. He's apprehensive about what the Master's Circle will have to say about Diadem. He's the one who built it, after all. Him and Benny. And he's the one who they've all been following, and learning from. Maybe's he's been a poor role model, but experience has given him a different take on what it means to be honest, to trust, and to respect. Just because something makes you safer, doesn't mean it's worth the sacrifice, or the risk. Conversely, sometimes it's taking the risk and crossing lines that pays off. Not everything is black and white, as much as the MC might like it to be.

Or maybe he's just full of shit, and all of the ways he's been badly used have left him bitter and mean. Maybe a lot of the pain his kids have been feeling is Trace's fault, if you clear away the dust, blood, and tears. All that's left underneath is bad choices and pain.

But that place, Diadem, has been their home and playground. It brought them all together, and gave them each a family after having none to count on in ways that matter. But Trace is certain things will be changing, whether they like it or not.

Ah, well. It is what it is, ain't it?

He's pulled his hair back, but left off the bandana and chose a nicer outfit than he'd ever be caught in outside of a funeral. It's his best attempt at a compromise—looking nice without looking like someone he shouldn't. Usually, his attire consists of t-shirts, tight jeans, leather belts, and motorcycle boots. Today, he's in tailored, dark pants, and a dark button-down shirt. He tries to remember what he looked like last time he was face-to-face with Gray, comparing it to the present, and can only laugh. Oh, but the years have taken their toll.

The door opens with barely any warning. Trace stands, cloaked in stubborn shadow.

"Well, shit," he chuckles, grinning widely.

Screw the years. Screw how old I feel, or how old I look.

Trace meets Gray halfway, seeing only his lapis lazuli hued eyes and that reluctant, composed smile which haunted him for so long. The smile breaks into soft laughter. The sound of that laugh is an instant victory for Trace, knowing how hard he worked to get Gray to feel comfortable enough with him to do so, letting down some of the guardedness that keeps him mysteriously distant, constantly.

Gray offers a hand, but doesn't seem surprised when Trace comes in closer for a hug instead. Clapping Gray on the back, feeling the firmness of broad back muscles beneath his impeccable suit, Trace gets high, instantly, off of the scent of him. It's full of memories and takes him out from under the low place he's been stamped down into. The formality in all of their communications over a decade of time, the distance of miles separating them, the supreme carefulness that comes with the way Gray lives his life, out of necessity and choice—none of it matters. Not when it feels this good to be close again, even if it's while playing vastly different roles than they have before. With a sigh, they both seem to let it all go, transforming into the younger men they used to be, temporarily free of current responsibilities.

Though Trace technically initiates the kiss, as soon as it begins Gray takes control. It becomes *his* kiss. He owns it. The easy way Gray slips into that role makes Trace chuckle again against Gray's lips. His hand hooks around Gray's jaw, admiring the close shave making the skin so smooth. Trace marvels that the taste of him is the same as it always was as he opens wider for his demanding former lover, savoring the patient, slow attack in the way Gray kisses and uses his tongue. There's nothing nervous about him, never was. Not even a little bit. Gray's confidence, skill, and willingness make Trace's cock just as hard as it always did.

Trace knows too, in the way Gray comes at him with renewed vigor, biting down on Trace's lower lip; he's still trying to outmatch Trace. But, as Trace has always told his old flame, it's the *trying* that holds him back. Gray will always give a little more of a shit than Trace ever could, simply because of who he is as a man. He's burdened by rules and duties while Trace is down in the dirt, wild and independent. Trace is a snake. Gray is the hawk. The snake can always slip down lower, through the cracks, hiding out, no matter how sharp the hawk's sight might be.

When they break apart, noting how goddamned handsome Gray still is, Trace licks at the small cut on his lip from the bite, saying, "Missed you, bright eyes."

Gray walks away, beginning to pace, folding his arms. He looks everywhere, mapping the room, catching each detail and filing the information away for further analysis. God, but it makes Trace tired. He goes back to his seat.

Without asking, he guesses at all of the research Gray must have done in the past few days, learning as much about Trace's people as is humanly possible while a continent and an ocean away. More than knowing names and relationships, Gray likely also knows who each of them are, their more public faults and indiscretions, and their reputations. Trace doesn't know how much Gray is already aware of, but he's sure he's likely to find out, fast.

"Like I need your rogue shit, Tracey," Gray says.

Opening a case filled with a neat row of cigars, Trace selects one. After trimming off the end, he lights it up. The sour haze of smoke begins to gather, but the hawk's sight is too sharp. It pierces right through, questioning without voicing the question, analyzing without permission.

Trace just sucks on the end of the cigar and squints up wearily. There's no point in being cagey. Not anymore.

The lingering effects of Trace's admissions to Gabriel and the others are too hard to shake off. Everything those boys have been through, the amassed horror of it all—it's too big. Too mean. Trace tells himself it's the smoke as his eyes tear up, thinking of all of those boys being raped, being hurt in ways that won't ever heal, by the same people who were supposed to protect and watch out for them, no matter what.

Because it's Gray, who was there when Trace's psychological wounds from whoring were still raw, when there was no hiding any of that either, he doesn't even try to hide things he could never begin to show to his newfound family. What Trace tries to spare Micah, Gabriel, Ben, and Darrek and Kyle most of all, he leaves right out in the open for Gray. Staring up at him, not blinking, letting Gray look his fill and analyze whatever the fuck he wants to, Trace practices his own sort of patience.

"Damn tired of my kids being hurt," he answers, finally, in a worn-down, tear-choked, angry voice.

There's a tight nod. A glimmer of understanding. Trace places the cigar between his teeth and lowers his gaze.

"I know the feeling," Gray says, not unkindly. Changing the subject, for the moment at least, he asks, "How is Yasha? Any word?"

"He's out of the game."

Yasha Lachinov, who so recently permanently deleted his only means of contacting Trace, has been one of Trace's most reliable contacts within The Company, and one of the people who enabled Trace to supply useful intelligence to Gray for so long. With Yasha, it was a business relationship, but one with more than enough import to form a bond that has run deeper than need may have called for.

"Trouble?" Gray asks, an eyebrow rising.

"Nah. Expecting a kid, believe it or not."

"Oh," Gray said with surprise. "Good for him."

"Yeah," Trace agrees wholeheartedly. Whenever someone manages to grab hold of a second chance at life, he can't help but be happy for them, especially someone like Yasha who has been through so much and gone out of his way to selflessly help others. "So. What've we got here, then? You brought Jack and Jan, who I can't *wait* to meet by the way. I'm assuming we're gonna just let that all play out as it will, within reason."

He gives Gray a sly look that Gray bears admirably.

"You've got your hands full... I've got my hands full... See what life does to ya?" Trace grins, blowing out smoke. "How long are you here?"

"A week."

"You got my message with Micah's address?" Trace asks. "He's got quite a place. Not nearly as nice as yours, but not many people have a place as nice as yours, do they? Should serve your needs, though. And it's better than a hotel."

"Mm. Is Micah being hurt, too? Or do his troubles have solely to do with Moira?"

Those remembered screams fill Trace's head, there and gone, as bracing as a blast of arctic wind.

"God, you're an asshole sometimes," Trace sighs. "I know you're not this stupid, but don't fucking mention her name. To anyone. He loved the hell outta that little girl. Losing her ripped his whole life apart. All of them... in pieces. *All* my damn kids."

The room blurs. The cigar is taken out of his hand. He feels Gray there, crouched down and staring.

"I really thought this shit would get easier once the whoring stopped," Trace confesses quietly, feeling beaten down.

A hand caresses the side of his neck. Trace leans in to the touch, overlaying the fingers with his own.

Gray asks, "Who hit you?"

"My boy, Gabe."

"Because of Harry?"

"Yep. I had it coming. Been telling him for a decade I'd see to it Harry would die. He was pissed off I followed through. Never wanted me to fight his battles for him. Bet you know how that goes.

Stay with us for the week," Trace beseeches, letting Gray hear the need there, and the tiredness.

"Okay," Gray agrees. "We'll make it enjoyable. Hmm? Introduce the kids. Yours and mine."

"Oh Jesus," Trace groans. "Don't we have enough trouble already? You really sure about this?"

Gray laughs at that, standing. "Yes. I'm sure. Let us help. A distraction at least."

"Hell of a distraction," he murmurs with a raised eyebrow of his own.

Gray laughs again, sounding like he's needed it. It's Trace's cue, his opening, and he knows it.

"Okay," he says, sitting back, arms folded, attention piqued. "Lay it on me. What'cha got?"

Chapter 16
Introductions

Gabriel and Darrek arrive early at Micah's place, but stay in the Discovery rather than go inside. Darrek watches Trace lean in the front doorway, watching them in return. The odd emotions swirling in Darrek's heart have had a strange effect on things. There is so much relief, but it's hollow. You shouldn't feel relieved one of your parents has died. No matter how demented the circumstances, there should be grief. Darrek's grief though, is more full-bodied and all-encompassing. It does start with Jerry, but reaches outward, sweeping up many people in its wake. Mostly, he finds himself staring out into space, trying to convince himself what's true is true.

The worst part is probably how okay with it all he feels. He's okay with Jerry being gone forever. That's not something Darrek thinks he'll ever lament, for any reason. He's better off. His mother is better off. His brother and his brother's son are better off. The world in general is better off.

Of course, the same is true of Harry, but the astonishing fact that Trace initiated Harry's murder makes Darrek's head spin.

Darrek turns to look at Gabriel. He's in the driver's seat, leaned back, eyes staring. Gabriel's body is relaxed, settled into its place. Darrek says, "Maybe we should have bought bigger cups of coffee."

Gabriel glances down at the small, eight ounce paper cup in his hand and replies, "I have no idea how to play this. Coffee can't help with this level of shit. I mean, these guys, they sound *intense*."

"You're pretty intense, too, by the way," Darrek tells him. "So are you all really doing the video thing right away?"

"Sounds like it," Gabriel answers, shaking his empty cup like he was hoping for one last drop to drink.

Trace had called, explaining more about the help Gabriel will need to give Gray. Everything Trace told Gabriel, Darrek heard as well, since secrets are now officially against the rules in their relationship, no matter what they may be. The deal is that a video with sexual content of Jack, underage, has been posted online without his consent. The IP address is local. Gray needs Gabriel's help in tracking it down, so they can make sure it's taken down.

Darrek tries to imagine it from Gray's point of view. It would be like if there was a video of Darrek and Kyle together, from their teenage years, on the web for anyone to access. Something like that would absolutely make him go insane. Darrek can't fathom having to deal with it. He would do anything to put a stop to it, and make the videos disappear, so he is wholeheartedly supportive of Gabriel helping out.

"You're not going to leave me alone with them, are you?" Darrek asks a little fearfully.

Gabriel actually smiles at that.

"I'm serious."

"I know," Gabriel chuckles. "I'm not going to make you do anything you aren't comfortable with, okay? My first responsibility — always — is to take care of *you*."

"Yes, Sir," Darrek answers, reaching up to touch the collar around his neck. He takes a deep inhale in order to feel the leather constricting his air, wanting to feel the band tight against his skin. The key to the collar's lock sparkles on the fine silver chain around Gabriel's neck.

Gabriel seems to notice Darrek's gaze. He reaches for the key and unfastens the chain.

"What are you doing?" Darrek blurts. "Sir? Gabe?"

"Gray is a Master Dom. Jack is a Master Sub. This is high level shit, like I said. I think we need to try to keep things as informal as possible so we don't get in deeper trouble than we need to. Understood?"

"Yes, Sir," Darrek murmurs, though his heart rate has increased. Nervousness kicks in, strongly. He leans forward, turning in his seat as Gabriel uses the key to unlock and remove Darrek's collar. "You will still act as my sub. You will be respectful. You will stand by my side. You will speak when spoken to, and will interact with them freely. I'll be right next to you, the whole time, until I have to lend my help with the videos, but by then we'll have a better idea of what's going on. Micah and Lily will be there, because, well, it's their house. Ben and Kyle are sitting this one out. That was Trace's call. He knows things are still difficult there."

"Okay," Darrek sighs, taking a deliberately deep, calming breath, inhaling through his nose, blowing it out through his lips. "Um, Trace is wearing a suit. It's freaking me out a little."

Gabriel gestures widely at his own attire—jeans and a dark grey t-shirt with black leather boots. He's also wearing a knit hat pulled down over his dark hair, as he hadn't had any interest in styling it that morning.

"Yeah, I know," Darrek allows, glancing down at his big, muscle-bound body clad in cargos and blue shirt, paired with work boots. His long, light hair hangs loose about his shoulders. Maybe he should have pulled it back. Trace has pulled his hair back. For half of a second, Darrek considers asking Trace for a hair tie, then realizes Hell would probably freeze over before Darrek ever mustered the bravery necessary to ask such a stupid thing of someone who intimidates him so much. Then he considers asking Gabriel to ask Trace for a hair tie, and promptly decides he's not fit in any sort of way to be introduced to new people and should just stay in the SUV and spare himself the embarrassment.

"They're not gonna spank you for being underdressed. Unless I give them permission to, of course," Gabriel grins, grabbing the door handle. "Come on. Move your ass."

Darrek groans, knowing Gabriel would totally do such a thing, and opens his door to follow, as ordered.

—◻︎—◻︎—◻︎—

Darrek and Gabriel have been together for over two years. When you're in a relationship that long, day in and day out, you tend to gradually overlook, more and more, things that may be blazingly obvious to everyone else.

Like the size difference between them. Darrek is six foot six inches tall. Gabriel is over six foot himself, so he's not short by any means, but in comparison—measuring muscle mass as well as height—he can seem almost half Darrek's size. Gabriel is slighter, slimmer, shorter by many inches and, to put it plainly, *prettier* than Darrek. Dressed as casually as they are, both of them slightly shell-shocked by the news of their fathers' deaths, there is no way an outsider would be able to tell that Gabriel is the powerful Dominant to Darrek's obedient, meek submissive.

And, of course, Darrek never considers this. He's too close to see it. Usually.

Standing around in Micah's large, formal sitting room off the main hall, with Trace, Micah, and Lilianna bustling around getting the house in order in anticipation of guests, Darrek's previous numbness is chewed away, bit by bit, by building anxiousness. He's not sure how much these newcomers know, how they will react or treat the strange, possibly uncouth Americans in their midst.

All Darrek wants, as a sleek black Mercedes pulls up in the driveway, is to be home with Sierra, playing catch in the yard. No part of him wants to be in that sitting room. He wishes Gabriel had gone without him, then scolds himself for wanting to foist such stress upon his Master, abandoning him in his time of need.

Frowning at his predicament, Darrek tries to hide his panic as best he can. He stands up straighter, hands fitted into the pockets on his hips, and pushes down, hard, on all of the uneasy feelings making him want to puke on his shoes.

Three men, all with dark hair, all with blatantly, widely different ways of carrying themselves, emerge from the Mercedes and walk up to the house. One looks like a gentleman, one a badass, one a normal guy.

"Oh my god," Darrek whines under his breath, gazing up at the ceiling as his composure slips, his breath coming faster.

"You're fine. Breathe. They're not gonna bite," Gabriel murmurs to him.

"I don't wanna do this," Darrek moans in a whisper on a sigh. "At all."

With his eyes on the trio who are getting closer by the second, Gabriel says, "No choice. Man up. It'll be over soon."

"Christ, this is as bad as when I met you! I felt like I was coming *apart. Look* at them! Tell me they're not intimidating," Darrek challenges.

"They're not intimidating," Gabriel says with a slight smirk, glancing sweetly up at Darrek just as Trace, Gray, Jack, and Jan enter the room.

Gray is identifiable right away, mainly because of his sleek, expensive-looking suit and the suave, seductive, don't-even-think-about-fucking-with-me vibe he gives off. He's older than Gabriel, but younger than Trace, maybe somewhere around Ben's age. Not that Darrek knows Ben's age. He realizes he's never asked.

Jack has jet black hair and grey eyes. Darrek marks him instantly as a blue-collar guy, and not just because of his t-shirt and jeans. He looks ready and able to kick ass if he needs to or, hell, if he just wants to.

Jan is much less bristly. With brown hair and brown eyes, he's dressed in a nice pair of dress pants and a button-down shirt. He looks as unsure about all of this as Darrek feels, which causes Darrek to instantly feel a connection with him.

Tensing up with the strong whiff of threat in the air, feeling outmanned, to compensate Darrek flexes his arms and his chest, just to comfort himself. Focusing on his physicality helps distract from the mental games at play. He stands straighter, composing his expression, making direct eye contact with those who look his way. Meanwhile, from the corner of his eye, Darrek sees Gabriel bow his head, hands in his pockets as he grows contemplative and melancholy. Concern for Gabriel, thinking maybe his emotions are catching up with him, overwhelming him, Darrek feels a flush of protectiveness for him. Taking a half step in front of Gabriel, Darrek uses his sizeable body to shield his partner somewhat from the new players in the room until Gabriel is able to recover.

"Okay boys. Here we are," Trace says easily, gesturing in a wide circle at all of them as they gather in the same room and Lilianna closes the door out in the hall. "This is Darrek and Gabe. And Gray, Jack, and Jan."

Forgive Us

Micah shakes hands with Gray. They're speaking to each other too quietly for Darrek to hear what's said, but he's more distracted by the way Jan and Jack are looking at him and Gabe.

Shit. Oh shit.

There's a quick, cursory appraisal of each of them as Darrek shifts a little more in front of Gabriel. It would be awful if their first impression of Gabriel was to see him weakened and upset, even though he has just cause to feel that way given all they're going through. Then Jan crosses to Darrek, hand extended to offer a shake. The instinct to look over and down at Gabriel for permission is strong, and he almost gives in, but his gaze catches on Jack first, because Jack is *moving*. Jack comes right for Darrek and grabs Jan by his outstretched wrist. With a displeased sneer, Jack yanks the hand back, away from Darrek. Darrek is given a cold, measuring, head-to-toe glance from Jack, like Darrek has done something wrong, broken some unspoken rule already.

How could I have broken a rule already? I haven't done anything!

All of the sadness, all of the mental stressors from dealing with the news of Harry and Jerry, all of the additional stress from being thrust in the midst of these confident, professional, mysterious acquaintances of the man who scares Darrek more than anybody—it compounds faster than he can process.

That yanked-away hand feels like a slap across the face. Darrek bows his head slightly, chewing on his lip as his lungs burn from the strain of trying not to cry, trying more than anything not to cry. His right hand slips out of his pocket and moves over to Gabriel's side as Gabriel steps forward. Not confidently, just needing, his fingers brush Gabriel's hand.

Darrek knows, without a doubt, what to do next as soon as he hears Gabriel say softly, in a breath of a command, "Kneel." Though he's not looking at Darrek, he knows when his Master has commanded him, so Darrek goes instantly to his knees, bowing his head more. Some of the fear is pushed back when he feels Gabriel's hand on the back of his head, petting his hair.

A hesitant glance up through strands fallen over his eyes shows Darrek the hard-as-iron look on Gabriel's face. Blood rushes instantly to Darrek's cock at the sight of Gabriel in full Dominant mode.

Jan looks angry, but with Jack, not Darrek or Gabriel. He pulls his wrist free of Jack's hold as Jack snaps at Jan in warning, "No one fucking touches you without my permission."

"It's just a handshake," Jan says under his breath to a seething, intensely jealous Jack. "You've insulted my slave," Gabriel says in a low growl, instantly drawing Jack and Jan's attention. "And I don't recall giving *you* permission to get that close to him, either."

Gabriel isn't riled at all. He's just focused on Jack, determined and clearly pushed over some line drawn in the sand by the perceived insult. As Darrek's cock gets even harder at the display of Gabriel's power, he marvels at the strength in Gabriel's soft, gruff voice. It's not loud. It doesn't need to be.

Gabriel takes a step forward, away from Darrek's side, closer to Jack. He steps up in Jack's face and Darrek detects his Master's amusement as Jack and Jan—but mostly Jack, seem to once again take the measure of their sizes, his confusion momentarily overriding his jealous, protective instincts regarding Jan. Darrek is so much larger; of course they would incorrectly assume he was Master, especially given his stance, shielding Gabriel. There's no fucking question now, though. Jack can't seem to stop staring with wonder at Gabriel, looking closer at his eyes when further scans of his body don't tell him what he wants to know. As seemingly nonsensical as Jack's jealousy in those circumstances is, Darrek can easily relate given how he'd been likewise preoccupied with Gabriel. Maybe for Jack, safeguarding Jan always comes first, just like how with Darrek, Gabriel does. When he chances a look, Darrek sees the others aren't getting involved in what's happening. In fact, Micah and Lilianna are barely in the room. Trace and Gray are standing together. Trace has a cocky smirk on his face, looking with pride at Gabriel. Gray, on the other hand, is so precisely focused on the dynamics of the scene unfolding before them it sends a chill down Darrek's spine. There's capability behind that cool measuring, more capability than Darrek can imagine.

That's the man who murdered Harry. He's British intelligence and a Master Dom. Gray could be capable of anything. With a weapon or a whip, he could lash out at any one of us, if provoked.

Jan glances back at Gray, his self-consciousness and a hint of guilt apparent for just a moment. That's when Darrek remembers how Jan isn't in the lifestyle. Following the rules and protocol isn't second nature for him, so he has to be wondering if he's in the wrong, even if Jack behaved badly in stepping between Jan and Darrek.

Trying to be very still, very quiet, and only do as his Master instructs, Darrek watches Gabriel stand inches from Jack, who is strung tight, ready to fight. Gabriel's strength is not physical, though it's unquestionable when it's right in your face, with a devil's patience and the willingness to back up everything hinted at by that razor-sharp edge in his hushed voice.

"You've insulted Jan," Gabriel continues, reading the situation more clearly than Jack had, even if he'd been initially preoccupied when they'd entered. "And you've insulted your Master by not seeking his knowledge before walking into this room and making assumptions about who you think we are, because you clearly have no idea. You owe them each an apology. Now."

Darrek catches Jan's eye, seeing his bewilderment, pleased but also amazed by Gabriel's reaction. Darrek tries to apologize to Jan too, with just a look, sensing maybe he's been swept up in this all the same way Darrek has, with just as little knowledge of how to handle it.

When Jack's gaze drifts from Gabriel's eyes to his lips, Darrek has to repress a smile, knowing from one look things have shifted, just like that.

Gabriel slowly licks his lower lip wet, then says with deadly softness, like a knife moving in the dark, "Apologize to Darrek."

"Sorry about that, Darrek," Jack answers a moment later, seeming to struggle with the effort of shifting his gaze from Gabriel's lips to Darrek's face.

"Dare, stand up and shake Jack's hand," Gabriel tells Darrek, still not looking his way. Not needing to.

After getting to his feet, Darrek extends a hand and they shake. Jack continues to visually measure them, and it makes Darrek's lips curl in a crooked grin. "Hi. Nice to meet you," he says politely.

Jan takes the opportunity, moving in to take Darrek's hand next, claiming the handshake he was previously denied.

"Good to meet you," Jan says with an honest smile.

"You too," Darrek smiles back.

Jack is back to trying to stare down Gabriel. Gabriel holds his ground, though, and Darrek's smile only grows when he sees Jack go back to looking at Gabriel's mouth.

"Sorry for being rude, Jan," Jack says.

"I'm waiting," Gabriel says, like he's bored, as there's hesitation before Jack turns his attention to Gray. He takes a step closer to Jack, into his personal space, like he wants to make Jack back off.

Jack glances back over his shoulder at Gray without moving an inch. After sharing a complicated look with him, Jack says, "My apologies."

Then he turns back to Gabriel, eye-to-eye, giving him one last head-to-toe look, and takes a step back, laughing softly. Seemingly unable to take his eyes off Gabriel, Jack chuckles, "Well, fuck me. David brought Goliath to his knees."

Chapter 17
Access Points

There had been a call from Trace early that morning. Trace did most of the talking, since Gabriel wasn't in an entirely forgiving or chatty mood.

"These guys eat, breathe, and shit protocol," Trace had warned. "It ain't like it is with us. It's about rules, hierarchy, and respect, all the time, but especially when gettin' your first sniff of a new ass. You might feel like you need to watch out for Gray the most, since he's the leader of the pack and all, but it's really Jack you need to tiptoe around. You're a Dom. He's a sub. That's what it comes down to, no matter what kind of extra supreme deluxe sub he thinks he is. He's probably bigger than you, and meaner than you, and able to kick your ass around the room with all of that karate shit Gray warned me about, so you keep your goddamned eye on him, you hear me, baby boy?"

"Yeah, sure," Gabriel had sighed. "I get the picture."

"If he pulls any kind of shit with you and Dare, you have every right to put him back in his place. You get me?"

"Yep. Got it."

"You sure you don't wanna hit me again? Fuckin' hate that you're mad at me like this."

"Maybe later. But, you know, I have a feeling if you were some kind of hooker for ten bleeding years the last thing you need is someone hitting you, even if you do deserve it."

"Love you, sweetheart."

"Yeah yeah."

Thanks to that phone call, Gabriel was ready for it when things went sideways, right away, when Gray, Jack, and Jan arrived. Gabriel had seen plenty of men in his life going off half-cocked, wound tight as a coiled spring. That was Jack, and there was only one way to handle it. So, he didn't give Jack a fucking inch, and he didn't raise his voice or feed that temper, he just let Jack see, without a motherfucking doubt, who was boss.

Yeah, so maybe Gabriel saw it coming, that he might not be instantly pegged as the Dom to Darrek's sub, and maybe he did find it kind of hilarious when Jack tucked his tail back between his legs, his striking grey eyes lowered and fixed on Gabriel's lips.

Maybe more than anyone else Gabriel has ever met, Jack is someone who needs taming, a gilded cage made of actual bars or maybe just very special kinds of rules to bounce himself off of when things go south and all of that bottled energy comes spilling out. Personally, Gabriel's never been a fan of cages, though. There are other ways to make someone feel safe and cherished than to beat them into submission — lots of other ways.

Gabriel can feel Darrek's desire for his collar merely through the way he's holding Gabriel's hand. It's like an ear-splitting scream, setting Gabriel's nerves on edge, so he keeps telling him softly, "It's okay, baby. I've got you. You're okay."

Jan is watching them, and listening. All of Gabriel's senses are cranked up to eleven, taking it all in, so he feels Jan's attention as much as Darrek's need. Gray is watching, too. As is Jack, though Jack is watching many things at once, looking restless and ill at ease.

Trace and Gray share a look. Trace says under his breath to Gray, "Should we do this, then? Get it out of the way?"

Gray nods. Trace waves Micah and Lilianna over, saying to them, "Keep an eye on Dare for a few minutes. Get Jack and Jan settled in their room."

Gray excuses himself to go check out the second floor, but Gabriel hardly notices because Darrek pulls on his hand, hissing into Gabriel's ear, "Don't leave me."

"Hey," Gabriel tells him, turning to hold his gaze. Gabriel's iron will is perfectly displayed and undeniable. "You're mine. No one touches you. Got it? They all know it, now. You're safe. I'll be nearby. I'm not leaving you. Micah and Lily will stay with you. It's fine. *It's fine.*"

"Love you," Darrek whispers, barely a breath of sound, but it feels loud in the room. Many sets of eyes are still on them.

Gabriel pulls him down for a brief, light kiss. "Love you too," he replies, almost smiling. "You'll be okay."

Darrek nods, looking slightly more confident, at least until they let their attention drift from each other and realize that Gray is standing right next to them, waiting. Then, Darrek's hand clamps tightly around Gabriel's once again.

"Gabriel, Darrek. It's nice to meet both of you," Gray says politely. "Thank you for being here despite the circumstances with your fathers."

Gray holds out a hand and for a second Gabriel just stares at it, part of him drifting off, imagining some terrible scene with this man standing before him and the monster who made Gabriel's life hell. Then, Gabriel doesn't feel so very strong after all, but there's no helping it. He takes Gray's hand, unable to reply but willing to shake with him. When Gray turns to Darrek, Darrek first looks for permission from Gabriel. After a nod, he shakes with Gray, putting on a brave smile, too. Gabriel is proud of him for it.

From a few steps behind Gray, Jack stares at his Master when Gray asks Gabriel quietly, "Would you be so kind as to help me with something?"

"Yeah," Gabriel relinquishes. "Why not?"

The force of Gray's presence, the capability in him, is dizzying. It's the same kind of way Trace intimidates people, even the people in his self-made family, but stranger, more inexplicable. With Trace, you know exactly what he might do just from the wicked smile on his lips and the gleam in his eye, but Gray gives nothing away. Gabriel has a feeling that Gray keeps things to himself, accruing facts, plans, and intentions until the exact moment when he needs to act. It's eerie and a little off-putting; making the hairs on the back of Gabriel's neck stand up the longer he stands that close to the man.

Letting go of Darrek's hand, Gabriel gives him an encouraging nod, leaving his side and following Gray to the hall where Trace joins them. The urge to glance back at Darrek is strong but somehow Gabriel manages to resist.

―⎓―⎓―⎓―

With Gray occupied somewhere in the house with Trace and Gabriel, and Jack busy taking his measure of their sleeping quarters, Jan is left in the hallway outside of a series of bedrooms. Everyone seems to be distracted with some task or other, so it gives him a chance to observe quietly in order to get a better sense of who's who and what's what. The whirlwind of introductions left him with some immediate impressions from people's size, stance, and general temperament. Something as simple as a handshake or eye contact provides helpful information whether you're in the boardroom or lingering outside of a relative stranger's guest bedroom.

There were a few things about Trace that set Jan slightly on edge. His age, for one, places him more in line with a father figure type than a friend or lover. Jan hasn't had too many pleasant experiences with much older men, as his father has always been a sore subject. Jan's experience with the man who wanted to replace Jan's father in their family dynamic was just as rosy, meaning not in the slightest. But there was something there between Trace and Gray which Jan did not expect at all. It'll warrant further scrutiny, though. He can't quite put his finger on it yet.

Gabriel's handling of Jack's rude behavior was impressive, so Jan credits him for that. The way he carries himself, the way he speaks, and his focus all mark him as a Dom. His relationship and choice of partner in Darrek is certainly interesting. Jan runs through the others in his head, while watching Micah and Lilianna—their hosts—putter about in the bedrooms, ensuring everything needed is there and ready. Jan has noticed their wedding bands, and the comfortable way they interact, but they've given off the cues of being in the lifestyle as well, and very comfortable in their appointed roles. Darrek is the odd man out. He lingers in the hallway with Jan, looking awkward and unsure. Jan still has no idea how Jack assumed Darrek was the Master in the relationship with Gabriel, even given how big Darrek is. He seems a gentle giant in every way. It's more than that, though. He doesn't behave like a typical submissive. He just seems like an everyman with as much of a limited understanding of the complex dynamics at play between all of these Masters and slaves as Jan does.

"Gray wants this room," Lilianna is telling Micah from a spot near the top of the steps. She indicates the first bedroom. Moving past the door to the next room, she says, "I've already put Jack and Jan in this one."

"Why? Did he say?" Micah asks her.

"Something about access points," she murmurs.

"Bloody typical," Jack comments from just inside their bedroom doorway. He's pulling open drawer after drawer in the bureau. They're all empty, but he continues to check them anyway.

"The room's great," Jan says to Lilianna. "Thanks."

"No problem," she replies with a friendly, genuine smile. "If you need anything at all, just let us know."

In the bedroom to the left of where Jan and Darrek are standing, Jack walks in a circuit around the whole room, checking everything out. When he goes into the adjoining bathroom and they hear the water begin to run in the sink, Darrek immediately averts his gaze like he's intruding. Micah is investigating some of the other rooms nearby. Lilianna is gathering fresh towels from a closet. Jan stays by Darrek's side, giving Jack his space while he makes himself more comfortable with their allotted sanctuary. He suspects he's making Darrek feel reluctant to leave but it's clear Darrek doesn't know what to say.

"Sorry about all of that," Jan tells him, gesturing to the downstairs and turning his attention more fully to Darrek.

"No problem," Darrek says with a crooked little smile. "It's just been a tough couple of days. Really, uh… stressful. So you're Jan, huh?"

"And you're Darrek. What do you do, if you don't mind me asking?"

Darrek seems to take a moment to look Jan over, from his tousled brown hair and casual dress attire to his easy-going smile. Interestingly, Darrek's gaze fixes longest on Jan's hands of all things. But then Jan sees how Darrek's hands are calloused, the nails uneven or banged up, the skin marred with small cuts. As he works in finance with no real labor intensive hobbies, Jan's hands bear no sign of manual labor.

With audible reluctance, Darrek admits, "I'm a carpenter. Used to work with a construction crew, but lately I've just been doing custom pieces, made to order. And I help Gabe out with his business. He's a photographer. How about you?"

"Financial consultant," Jan says, liking Darrek more with every subsequent sign that—for the time being at least—he's not playing by anyone's rulebook, but just trying to get by, moment-to-moment. "That was incredible by the way, how Gabe handled Jack and put you at ease. I can tell he really cares about you. How long have you been his submissive?"

"Oh, uh...." Darrek glances around a little nervously. There's no one else around, though. Micah is waiting but keeps his distance, supervising like a Master with the humble respect of a submissive. Jack is still in the bathroom washing his hands, and that's just part of the OCD, as the organizing and inspection of the room is as well. Pushing his long hair behind an ear, Darrek says, "Not that long, really, I guess. Two and half years? Before that I was engaged to be married to my high school sweetheart, Sara, actually, but she ran off with my brother, Steven. That was kind of the end of that. Meeting Gabe and him being a guy and all... it was kind of a fluke, but once he had me, I didn't really want to be anything else but his. God, that sounds corny, doesn't it?"

"You're bi?" Jan says with surprise.

"Yeah."

"Did you always know?"

"No, it's kind of complicated, but there haven't really been many guys I've been into. It's pretty much a case-by-case deal."

"You sub with anyone before Gabe?"

"Not really," Darrek says, somewhat bashfully, hands in his pockets, head bowed.

"Sorry about all of the questions, this is just really fascinating," Jan explains. Each revelation from Darrek only spurs more curiosity. "I've never subbed at all, and I've never had the chance to ask someone who hasn't been in the lifestyle forever how they got there or why they like it. With Jack, the reason why he likes it is pretty clear, but you seem like more of a regular guy, y'know?"

"I guess I've never really thought about it," Darrek admits. "Not since I first met Gabe, at least. I was freaked out at first about thinking a man was hot, to the point where I was asking my dog, Sierra, for advice. Pretty pathetic, huh? But I mean, he was a *guy* and we went really far the first time I subbed for him."

"Sex?"

"Yeah," he admits, glancing up at Jan's eyes. The more sincere interest Jan shows in him, the more at ease Darrek seems. Jan wonders if it's really been that long since Darrek has had a conversation with someone who doesn't already know his whole life story. "Gabe kind of took my virginity. It was… sudden."

Jan chuckles, smiling widely.

After a pause, Darrek smiles and laughs with him, saying, "And I guess I kind of took his virginity too, so it was a pretty big deal for both of us."

That piques Jan's interest, fast. "What do you mean, took his virginity?"

"Oh, Gabe never had sex with his subs before me. I'm the only sub, who he, uh…." Darrek leaves the sentence hanging for Jan to fill in the blanks.

"Ever?"

"Yeah."

"Fucking hell," Jan murmurs, trying to imagine it. "So it was just you and him, at Diadem, in a scene and it ended with sex?"

"Not exactly," Darrek says bashfully. He glances around again, but Micah is still hanging back. Lilianna has vanished. Jack is out of the bathroom, but isn't paying any attention to those standing in the hall.

Darrek continues with, "Trace was there, too, assisting Gabe. Gabe was instructing Trace as to what to do to me. I've always been sort of intimidated by Trace ever since. Gabe was the one to help me relax and feel safe, but Trace was the one who was actually *doing* everything, until the end when Gabe took over and, well. You know.

Is this too much information?"

"No," Jan says. Inching a little closer, Jan softens his voice, biting his bottom lip as he looks Darrek over. "Not at all. Why Gabe though? Out of everyone?"

"I don't know," Darrek sighs, thinking about it. "He's... beautiful, and gentle, and strong. He's proud of me for being able to handle whatever he throws at me. We've both been through a lot, and we each have our own baggage, but when I'm with him, submitting to him, I can stop worrying about it all and just focus on what he wants. It just feels good to let him take control. It helps everything make sense. It's pretty much the *only* time everything makes sense, because he loves me. He takes really good care of me. Having him, someone who cares so much about me, keep me safe — it's all I've ever wanted."

They're standing fairly close by then, their voices hushed.

"How about you?" Darrek asks, his gaze roaming over Jan's face, down briefly over his body, but always coming back to his eyes. "Why Jack, out of everyone?"

Jan glances back to Jack beside the nightstand and says it as simply as he can. "He's complicated. Yet in the same breath, that all unravels when it comes to how he loves."

"Yeah, I hear that," Darrek agrees. "And Gray?"

"He and Jack have serious history. Gray was there and he wasn't going anywhere, and, well... you kind of just become lost in him. What kind of dog did you say you have?"

"Oh, uh, she's a golden retriever. She's my best friend."

Still smiling, Jan tells him, softly, "I'd love to meet her."

Suddenly, Jack emerges from the bedroom. Right away, he seems to tune in to how cozy Jan and Darrek are, walking right up between them as he demands, "Just fucking peachy. What's this shit?"

"Darrek has a dog," Jan tells him, being deliberately vague to get a rise out of Jack.

"Where?" Jack frowns, looking around everywhere, up and down the hall, behind Darrek's back.

"Not *here*," Jan says with a chuckle, shaking his head for Darrek's benefit from over Jack's shoulder. "How's the room?"

"Good. Room's good," Jack answers, looping an arm behind Jan's back and drawing him closer, away from Darrek. "Not that you'd know anything about it, you're so busy talking about dogs."

"We're not just talking about dogs."

"No? What else?"

"Sex."

"Sex?"

Jan gives Darrek a quick, amused glance that only makes Jack frown and tense up again.

"It's not what you think," Darrek starts, trying to explain before Jack can overreact or misinterpret. "Jan asked how I started subbing for Gabe since I used to be straight, and sex was pretty vanilla for me before him."

That gets Jack's attention. Arm still looped possessively around Jan, he turns his sights on Darrek and gives him a new sort of measuring, appraising look.

"Yeah? You been with anyone else? Sub for anyone else?"

Darrek doesn't respond right away. It's curious, since they're fairly straightforward questions. "Not like that," he winds up saying. "Trace was there once, but I never had sex with him, and there used to be another guy — a sub, Kyle — but Gabe is the only one."

Jan and Jack share a look.

"What?" Darrek asks.

Jack asks, "That your choice or your Master's? He doesn't want anyone else touching you?"

"I, uh," Darrek flounders. "I don't know. I guess it's my choice. Or, maybe it's his choice. He's not super into monogamy, but maybe I shouldn't be telling you that. I guess it's never come up. There was an issue a couple months ago with another submissive. Kyle. So I don't think Gabe would let me be with another sub like that, and all of the Doms we know are friends, so it would be weird. What?"

They're both still smiling at Darrek's obliviousness. Little does Darrek know his small circle of Dom friends has just gotten a hell of a lot broader, as Diadem's rogue status with the Master's Circle is likely a thing of the past.

"Nothing," Jack says. "You're just this big, soft-ass, submissive giant."

Uncertainly, Darrek replies, "Um, thanks?"

"Let's let these guys get settled," Micah says, stepping forward finally and putting a hand on Darrek's arm. To Jack and Jan he says, "Come on downstairs for something to eat or drink whenever you're ready, okay? Kitchen's toward the back of the house. That's where we'll be."

"Will do. Thanks," Jack replies, winking at Darrek before dragging Jan into the bedroom by the front of his shirt and slamming the door shut.

Chapter 18
New Threats, Old Instincts

The weirdest thing about being alone in an office with Gray and Trace is trying not to imagine them screwing around with each other or figuring out the dynamics of how that must have played out. Gabriel keeps looking at each of them, erasing the wear and tear of the years which have passed in the meantime, and puzzling out the possibilities.

Of course, once Gray's attention turns more fully onto Gabriel, some of the distractions become a non-issue. He boots up Micah's computer, admiring the state-of-the-art setup and becomes hyper-aware of Gray's presence at his side, in the chair beside Gabriel's. Trace hovers nearby, waiting for a way to be useful.

Gray asks, "How are things with Daring Angel?"

Gabriel tenses slightly at the question, trying not to look over at Gray, wondering just how much research the man has done and how much he knows, since he obviously knows about Gabriel's business, at least.

"Fine. Things are fine," he answers. "It keeps me busy."

"Do you miss working at Diadem?"

"Hey, there any coffee in this place?" Gabriel asks Trace, tiredly.

"Yep, you'll be okay if I...?"

"Yeah."

Trace leaves. After taking a deep breath, Gabriel turns to Gray, bearing his scrutiny. "If there's something you want to ask me, I'd appreciate it if you'd just ask."

"Oh, I will."

"Jesus," Gabriel sighs, rubbing his head as a headache begins to form. "Do you know the week I've had? What the past two days alone have been like? I *just* found out you—this guy I don't even *know*, but who somehow knows Trace a hell of a lot better than I do—*killed* my step-father. You killed a human being, because of some personal favor nonsense, and that's not even all! You would have also killed my partner's father if he hadn't croaked already! But he did and now you're here, when things haven't even calmed down yet, looking at Trace like you know all of this shit I don't, and you know what? I'm not even sure I want to know what those looks you two share are about. I don't fucking want to know. I have been doing *everything I can* to keep Darrek from losing his fucking mind, since his family has been trying to call because, surprise! Jerry's dead. And we've both been so on edge, I can't even...." He finishes with a low growl of frustration.

"Yes, the news about Harry must take some adjusting, as well as the news about Trace, and our arrival. And meanwhile, Darrek is relying on you quite heavily as his main support system in the wake of Jerry's death. It's understandable the Grealeys would try so persistently to contact Darrek, what with the sequence of events surrounding his stroke. You won't be able to avoid them forever. The funeral is tomorrow. They'll wonder why Darrek hasn't answered their calls and it's probable they'll continue to try to make contact until they know he's received their messages."

Gabriel can only laugh, shaking his head, muttering, "Fucking hell. You know all of that, huh? Wonderful."

It all makes him feel like the walls are closing in, and he has no way out. The tension in his body notches up, but there's nothing he can do to escape the pressure. He has duties to perform and responsibilities to live up to. There's no time to bitch and moan about things he can't change.

"There are plenty of people here willing to lend support if you or Darrek need it," Gray tells him.

"I can handle Darrek," Gabriel argues reflexively. Even if he can't handle anything else, Gabriel knows he needs to handle Darrek, and put his own problems aside until he knows Darrek is okay.

"Alone? Even with all of the stress you're under? Is that wise?"

The computer has finally booted up. Gabriel gratefully turns his full attention to it. All of the information he needs has been written on a sheet of Micah's notepad paper by Gray and is sitting by Gabriel's right hand. Ignoring Gray's question, Gabriel focuses on analyzing the video link and the user information connected to it. After handling all of the video uploading for Diadem for years, and now with his own videography business to monitor, it doesn't take him long to dig into the code and get some answers.

Trace comes back into the office with two cups of coffee, passing one to Gray and one to Gabriel.

"So," Gabriel tells Gray, "the signal isn't coming from the U.S. at all. It's bounced from Corsica, of all places. See that?" He points to a single line of data on the screen. "That means there was a delay with the upload. The video was posted four months ago with an encryption code that delayed it, so it didn't update the porn sites until a week ago."

The stern look on Gray's face makes Gabriel glad the man's attention is no longer on him. Chancing a glance over at Trace, Gabriel waits for Gray to digest the news.

"I don't see anything else here that would tell us anything worth knowing. Is it enough? Does it help?" Gabriel asks Gray.

"Yes. It does. Thank you, Gabriel."

"Is there anything else you need?"

Gray lets out a breath, his focus turned inward now. "No."

"You sure?" Trace asks.

"Yes."

Just like that, Gray gets up and walks out of the room. Staying where he is, in front of the computer, Gabriel stares at the screen.

"I don't want to see it, do I?" he asks Trace. "The video."

"Probably not," Trace murmurs, coming over to sit on the desk's edge.

Maybe it's the weight of it all loaded onto his shoulders, but part of Gabriel craves the way Trace can take care of him. When Trace is in charge, things fall in order. Chaos is tamed.

Gabriel sips his coffee, wishing Trace would lock the door and put him in his place. It would be nice to have a few moments of forgetting all of the stress and just be able to react to immediate stimulation.

"Jack was a teenager," Trace says. "Some meathead, skinhead thug took some up close and personal video while taking Jack's ass for a ride, cutting him up a little, too, showing the camera how hard Jack's dick was while he yelled and fought. And that? You don't need to see that, baby boy."

Sitting back in the rolling desk chair, trying not to imagine it, being overwhelmed by it all, Gabriel doesn't move much when Trace knocks the chair with the toe of his boot, turning Gabriel to face him instead of the screen.

"It was posted *everywhere*," Gabriel says in a hollow voice. "I keep thinking, what if Harry did the same to me? What if he'd—"

"Stop. Stop it," Trace says abruptly, cutting him off, cutting the thought off. Planting his hands on the chair's armrests, he gets in Gabriel's face, stern as fuck all. As much as he'd like to put up a fight for Daddy, Gabriel can't manage it. All of his energy reserves are depleted.

"*I* was a teenager. I was sixteen," Gabriel whispers. "And fifteen. And fourteen—"

"Stop it, baby boy," Trace growls. "He's fuckin' *dead*."

"My goddamned life wasn't twisted enough for you, was it?" he seethes. "Daddy killed Harry. What do ya think about that, boys and girls? I traded in a pedophile for a *fucking murderer*."

As vicious as the words are, Gabriel still tilts his head as Trace's mouth comes in for his throat, baring it for him. Breathing harshly through his nose, he feels the fight in Trace's body, and tenses up, waiting to see what kind of response he's provoked. Trace's breath is hot on Gabriel's neck, the scruff of his neatly trimmed beard dragging over the skin, the tip of his nose nudging. The suit is quite a turn-on. Gabriel has rarely if ever seen Trace wear one before. It makes him look less the biker sex god, and more a gangster.

Any other day, Gabriel would be hitting out at Trace, giving him a real fight to go with his words, not backing down an inch. But today, Gabriel has nothing left to fight with. Gray was right; he can't even handle himself let alone Darrek, too. And realizing it hurts more than anything else.

When one of Gabriel's tears dampens Trace's cheek, he backs

off a hair, looking into Gabriel's bloodshot eyes. Trace palms the side of Gabriel's face. Gabriel closes his eyes, leaning into Trace's touch.

"Who takes care of you?" Trace demands.

"You do," Gabriel answers. He chokes a little on the words, which come out gruff and thick.

"And who am I?"

"Daddy."

"Who loves the hell out of you and would do fucking anything to make sure you're safe?"

"You, Daddy."

"And don't you forget it. I'm driving you home."

Shaking his head, Gabriel argues. "You can't leave. You have guests. And Darrek... I won't make him watch that. Not today."

"Then you'll stay here, in one of the bedrooms, until I say you can come out. Should I call Benny?"

"Ben's got Kyle," Gabriel manages, hoarsely, his eyes watery, his body jittery.

"Lily can go babysit," Trace tells him, looking down his nose at Gabriel's weakness, like he wants to fuck it out of him.

"That's not fair to her or to Kyle."

"Oh, are we still playing this game? Who is fucking in charge here?"

Letting his head fall back on his shoulders, Gabriel hisses, "Shit."

Trace grabs him by the jaw and gives him a hard kiss, tonguing him deeply, making Gabriel moan. Just as his hips tilt up off the chair, Trace sinks a knee onto the seat between Gabriel's legs and grabs a handful of his crotch. Choking off a cry, neck aching as Trace renews his attack on Gabriel's mouth, Gabriel's senses clamor, worry forgotten, every care gone, given over freely.

"Tracey," Gabriel hears from the direction of the door, not understanding right away.

"Yeah, bright eyes," Trace answers. He breaks the kiss but doesn't let go of Gabriel's genitals. Only then does Gabriel glimpse Gray in the doorway, watching.

"Fuck," Gabriel groans, writhing when Trace doesn't let up at all, not wanting Gray to see him in such a submissive state.

"Everything okay in here?"

Watching Gabriel closely, Trace cocks his head to the side a little and asks, "What do you think, beautiful? Everything okay?"

The fingers locked around his balls twist and Gabriel can't hold in the cry. Is comes out louder than he would have liked. Then the room falls away entirely, burned out of existence by blinding sensation. For a few long seconds, he can't speak and only gasps.

"Answer him," Trace orders.

But Gabriel can't. Humming through the pain, he hears Trace ask, "Who takes care of you?"

"You, Daddy," he answers automatically. It's a thin rasp of words, but words all the same.

"See? I knew you could speak if you wanted to. Now, Gray here is worried about you, and ain't that sweet? Tell him what you want right now. You want more or less?"

"M-more," Gabriel croaks. "Please."

The fingers twist more sharply and Gabriel yells, head thrown back. The pain draws out until he has to push at Trace with both hands, gripping him by the arm and the throat.

"Stop it!" Gabriel roars.

Trace lets go, smiling. "Now that's more like it. Go upstairs, to the bedroom at the end of the hall to your right. Take your fucking clothes off, kneel on the bed and wait for me. Do you need Benny or not?"

All Gabriel is aware of, past the throbbing in his groin, is Gray's eyes on him, judging, measuring. Trace has just told the man he'll be dominating and fucking Gabriel right in the damn house. He's basically stopped short of giving him an engraved invitation to come watch the show.

"No, Sir," Gabriel says quietly.

Trace nods. "Go then. Get!" He points to the door.

Head bowed, he hurries past Gray and down the hall to the stairs.

–⎔–⎔–⎔–

Forgive Us

"Stop fuckin' looking at me like that," Trace scolds over the rim of his coffee mug. "How old are you anyway? I thought by now you'd have gotten over using the silent treatment to get people to spill their guts, for fuck's sake."

"How long are you going to make him wait?" Gray asks, leaning against the center island in the kitchen.

"Oh, so you *are* concerned about him then?" Trace takes a sip and sighs. "That fucking video, man. He's scared for Jack, scared for himself... feels like that tortured kid again, not like the man he is. I don't think it would have gotten to him that much if it wasn't for everything else, with Harry, with Jerry. And that's *my* fault. My problem to correct. He needs to feel safe again. He ain't gonna survive without his fight instinct alive and kickin'. That kid he used to be couldn't fight *anything*. He can't help Dare and he can't help himself if he's giving up. *You* used to remind me what it meant to take for yourself, instead of following along blindly. Gabe needs that, now. Ain't no one else gonna give it to him."

"Tell him I'm making sure Jack is safe."

The sound of voices and footsteps in the hall alert them to the approach of Jack and Jan, who appear in the doorway. They're both somewhat flushed, kiss-bitten, and smiley. Trace rolls his eyes and finishes his coffee, figuring he can guess what they've been up to in the meantime.

"Found something to suck on, Jack? Hasn't spoiled your appetite, has it?" Gray asks.

After a sharp look at Trace, Jack tells Gray, "Nah, you know me."

Gray gestures at the platter full of cold sandwiches on the counter. Jack and Jan take two of the stools and have a seat in front of the food.

"Been trying to figure out why you didn't mention the virgin Dom," Jack says, still eyeing Gray. "Jan here got the story from Dare when they got all cozy talking about sex and subbing in the hall."

"You didn't exactly ask, did you?" Gray replies.

"Gabe's got his reasons why he doesn't fuck his subs," Trace says, taking his mug to the sink. "Maybe you should respect them."

"Yeah, bet Gabe didn't learn how to not fuck subs from watching you, did he, old man?" Jack says to Trace.

There's no way he'd know how much that comment would make Trace bristle, but Trace contains the reaction with effort. "Sure didn't, kid," Trace grins. "Why, you want a go? Have a chat with Gray here, and see if he lets ya. I'm game to take you on, show you how someone with *real* experience moves."

"Right," Jack replies, looking Trace up and down.

"Go on, Tracey. We'll be fine," Gray tells Trace from over a shoulder. Trace knows Micah and Lilianna are with Darrek out on the porch, eating lunch out in the fresh air. Everyone's as settled and occupied as they're going to get.

Crossing behind Gray, Trace lets a hand rest on Gray's shoulder, giving it a squeeze. Jack's gaze, burning hot with jealousy, snaps right to the contact, especially when Gray reaches up and briefly overlays Trace's fingers with his own.

"Don't sweat it, kid," Trace says to Jack tiredly. "We're old news. He's all yours."

"If you need anything," Gray starts, nodding to the second floor.

"I can take care of my boy, bright eyes."

"Didn't say you couldn't."

"Oh, so you think *I've* got my hands full, then? Ain't *that* the pot calling the kettle black?"

"Didn't say that either."

Trace laughs coolly, giving Jack and Jan another look, trying to get past the wonder of having Gray there, in the same room. And not only is he there, sticking his nose in everyone's business, like always, but now he's nosing around Trace's kids, too. He knew it was coming, though. That's what's been making him so nervous about this long-awaited visit—once you start something, and let people in, there ain't no shutting them back out.

He realizes his hand is still on Gray's shoulder, and pulls it back because Jack is nearly on his feet. His eyebrows are drawn so closely together, he looks like he's going to strain something.

"Remember what I said," Gray tells Trace. "About distraction."

Knowing Gray well enough to read between his lines, maybe more than anyone else does, even Jack and Jan, Trace marvels at how Gray is trying to slip in to things. A favor here, a favor there. Trust is formed. Lust and desire are conjured. Curiosity opens the door and suddenly you find yourself stepping into a world full of old rules and massive power, only there's no exit, no turning back.

Just from a few words and the way he suddenly appeared when Trace was with Gabriel, when Gray should have been busy enough handling the information about the video upload to care, tells Trace a lot. Gray wants to get his hands on Gabriel. For what purpose, Trace has no idea, only it seems nothing is off the table. Because if Gray wants Gabriel, that means he has to offer something in exchange, and what else is there to give but Jack or Jan? Not that Trace would ever really expect Gray to bargain with either of the two people Gray guards with just as much fierce love and attention. Jack might let his mouth get him in trouble now and then, but he and Jan seem off-limits for such a trade. But, maybe not. Maybe there is enough trust left between Trace and Gray to allow it to happen. But Gabriel is the last thing Trace would ever give up, willingly. No one gets Gabriel without Trace's say so. Darrek might be Gabriel's partner, but Darrek doesn't know Gray like Trace does. Even if Darrek gave the go ahead, Trace is more than ready to step in and put a stop to anything that doesn't feel right.

"How could I forget?" Trace chuckles. "Gonna be a hell of a week, folks. Hell of a week."

On his way out of the kitchen, Trace sees Jack go around to Gray, whispering questions in his ear, looking concerned, not possessive anymore. Gray's face is like a mask, though, hiding everything behind a composed, controlled façade. It makes Trace feel sorry for Jack, that he's faced with the mask rather than the man. But that's all about survival, and knowing firsthand all about that, Trace can't fault Gray for it. Sometimes there's just a certain way you have to play your hand, or else the whole game goes up in smoke.

Chapter 19
Gabriel's Submission

"Dare gave the go ahead," Trace tells Gabriel as soon as he walks into the bedroom at the far end of the hallway. Gabriel is kneeling on the bed, facing the headboard and turned away from Trace. He's naked, his posture lax. No one else is on the second floor. When there's the sound of the front door opening and closing below, Trace wonders if it was someone coming in, or people going out, and whom.

Gabriel doesn't react.

"You want the door locked?"

Gabriel shakes his head.

"You want the door *closed*?"

He shakes his head again.

"You know what you're agreeing to by making those choices, right? Just so as we're clear?"

"Yeah, I know," Gabriel says softly, sounding resigned.

"Is it 'cause Gray and I were together? Don't trust him on my account."

Gabriel gives Trace a grave look from over his shoulder and that's his answer in its entirety.

"Shit," Trace sighs, holding the door's edge. "Okay."

With a deep breath, Trace finds his focus, letting everything fall away but what his submissive needs from him. There's still not an ounce of fight in Gabriel's form, so Trace knows he has to play this a different way than before. Pain got him close to wanting to fight for himself, but it hasn't lasted long.

"You know the Master's Circle is big into security and surveillance. Is that what you need, darlin'? You need people watching your ass on a shining screen night and day? Watching you fuck and get fucked? You really want that shit in your life? You'd be safe as can be, but it comes at a steep price. Once you trade in your privacy, there ain't no getting it back."

"Tell that to Jack, why don't you?" Gabriel says softly. "I'm sure he'd love you for it."

Three quick strides and Trace is at the bed. He grabs Gabriel by the balls and pulls back, forcing Gabriel to fold forward to lessen the strain. Curling around himself, Gabriel gasps and folds his hands over his head.

"You testing me, boy?" Trace asks with plenty of warning in his voice.

But Gabriel's only answer is to cry out into the bedding, letting the fabric absorb the sound. Increasing the grip of his fingers around Gabriel's testicles, Trace keeps the skin pulled tight and, when he gets no coherent answer, says, "Tell me, right now, what your safeword is."

"Discovery," Gabriel says quite clearly.

"You little bitch," Trace laughs. "I expect a fucking answer as clear as that every goddamned time I ask you a question. Do you understand?"

"Yes, Sir."

"Are you testing me?"

"Yes, Sir."

"Why? You wanna hurt? You want me to fuck your ass that much harder?"

"Yes, Sir."

Trace releases Gabriel's balls. Gabriel sags instantly, gasping for air. He makes quite a picture there, ass up, legs spread, head down. There's a reason Trace didn't train Gabriel to be a submissive, and instead made him a Dom. He hates seeing Gabriel as submissive as he is in that moment, purely needing another man to hurt and fuck him over. It feels like a failure on all counts, especially because Trace knows he's going to give in and go along with it. It's near impossible to deny the needs of someone he loves so much.

"Don't you move a muscle. You keep your hands right there,

on your head, and you don't shift those knees unless you want me to call the whole gang in here to hold you down while you take my cock. Understand?"

"Yes, Sir."

The supplies Trace needs are nearby, in Micah and Lilianna's bedroom across the hall. He brings condoms, lube, a gag, and rope back to Gabriel. Slowly, diligently, Trace begins to wind the rope around Gabriel's nude form, circling his wrists, leading the ends around his torso to go around and around his chest, over each shoulder and under again, down to his drawn-up legs to wind around each knee. Once Trace is done, Gabriel is totally immobilized, breathing heavily but evenly, his eyes closed and body relaxed within its bonds.

Gabriel chose to submit, to yield, so Trace wants him to own it, to realize the position he's put himself in.

But with the past having rushed back in to Trace's life, quite literally, he can't help but take a wider view of his circumstances. Standing over Gabriel, bound and begging for it, Trace has a lot of regrets. Both sides of his personality—Patrick and Trace—are at war with each other. Trace screams while Patrick gives in. His hand slides in a caress over the back of his boy's head, through his soft hair and it feels like a fist wringing the life out of his heart. The act of touching, fucking, has always come so easily to Patrick. It's the answer to every problem. But not with Trace. Not like this.

"Damn you Gabriel, for putting me here," Trace whispers in accusation.

Gabriel breaks, instantly, cringing, and hiding his face in the soft bedding below it as he sobs.

"I'm so sorry," Gabriel cries.

"Of *all* of the things in my life I have done, that you ask me to hurt you, like *this*, when I love you, *so much*...."

The words hit Gabriel harder than any whip could. Stripping out of his clothes, Trace climbs onto the bed behind Gabriel, and curls his body around Gabriel's form as if using himself as a human shield for Gabriel's benefit. A moment after their bodies touch, Gabriel shivers, moaning softly.

"But if you need me to protect you, this closely, I will, for as long as I live," Trace swears, picking up the gag—a strip of black fabric.

"Please," Gabriel begs. "Need you."

"I know, baby. I know," Trace hushes to him as he fits the fabric between Gabriel's teeth, pulls it tight and knots it behind his head.

After rolling on the condom without moving away from Gabriel, wanting to keep him feeling secure and not alone, Trace pushes lube into Gabriel with two fingers which reach as deeply as he can, to the last knuckle. Gabriel cries out, his eyes shooting open, all breath leaving him.

The fingers pull out, replaced instantly with the head of Trace's cock. As it pushes against Gabriel's unprepared opening, Gabriel half-sobs, half-moans. His eyes roll up with pleasure and goosebumps rise over his skin from head to toe.

By the time Trace is fully seated, the urge to thrust and move inside the snug, hot vessel of Gabriel's lithe body is so intense it makes him dizzy. Even though it's not the first time they've had sex, the novelty has not worn off for Trace. It's not entirely for Gabriel's benefit that Trace hesitates, sheathed in his boy, whose sweat-slick body is wound in rope, completely at his mercy. Being with Gabriel is different than every other sexual encounter Trace has experienced, and his pairings seem infinite when he bothers to look back on them all. Being with Gabriel makes Trace feel like a bad person—a man who failed to save someone lost and desperate, who takes advantage of that which cannot protect itself.

Breathing in the scent of Gabriel's sweat and musk, wanting to move but unable to move, feeling the thrumming of Gabriel's pleasure, Trace witnesses his boy's intoxication at being allowed to submit to someone so very trusted. But Trace still can't move.

"I'm so sorry," Trace apologizes, for everything, for not being nearly enough, and kisses his boy's head. "It's not your fault. It's mine. All of it. Every bit. I should have done more, tried to keep you out of this kind of life instead of throwing you in."

"He doesn't need your apologies. He needs you to make him feel *safe*."

Gray. Trace doesn't look up, but sees him in his peripheral vision, wondering how much he heard. Gray's hand moves over Gabriel's head, caressing through his hair.

"Isn't that right, slave?" Gray asks.

Gabriel moans.

"Move. Now," Gray commands, so Trace draws back, presses back in, and Gabriel gasps harshly. Tensed from head to toe, straining against the ropes, he doesn't even breathe as Trace begins to fuck him with deep strokes. "Breathe, slave."

Shuddering, but breathing, drawing air through his nose, Gabriel bears it as Trace's movements get harder, driving into him.

"You're safe. Your Master loves you. Do you trust him?" Gray asks, still caressing Gabriel's head.

Gabriel nuzzles against his touch, and nods, grunting, biting on the gag. For long minutes, as Trace takes Gabriel, making it last, making him moan, Gray doesn't leave or move from his spot. Gabriel's blush suffuses his entire body by the time Trace climaxes, not meeting his old lover's eyes as he pulls out and goes to get rid of the condom.

When Trace walks back to the bed, he sees Gray inspecting the knots and technique used to bind Gabriel. Then Gray is looking right at Trace, plenty of accusation in his expression.

"What does your slave need?" Gray asks, leadingly.

Trace rolls his eyes and retrieves a plug from the other room.

Gray holds out a hand for it. He begins coating it with lube while Trace goes back to the bed and begins to stroke Gabriel's cock, drawing it down to point back between his legs. In response, Gabriel tries to lift his hips up farther, but can't because of the ropes, and groans with discomfort and embarrassment. Going slow and keeping the friction light, Trace keeps his free hand braced on the back of Gabriel's thigh and watches Gabriel's reaction when the lubricated plug touches the flushed knot of his asshole.

A broken cry erupts from his chest and his cock pulses pre-come as Gray works it gently into him.

"Breathe," Gray says soothingly when Gabriel chokes and stops drawing air.

Gasping, he comes in a flood over Trace's fingers before the plug is even all the way inside him. A few calculated tugs at the ends of the fabric tied behind Gabriel's head and the gag falls out of his mouth, allowing them to better hear his every moan and whimper while Gray, with torturous slowness, works the plug the rest of the way in. When it's nestled in place, Gray rubs over Gabriel's rim and Trace pulls at a strategic place on the rope. It all comes loose, but Gabriel doesn't move. His hands stay clasped behind his back, his ass pushed out, and head bowed.

"Thank you, Master Gray," Gabriel says softly.

"You're welcome," Gray answers, giving Trace a sharp, steady look. It takes all of Trace's will not to smack Gray's hand away from Gabriel where his fingers continue to touch. Gray pushes at the base of the plug and Trace can tell Gabriel feels it, like a promise.

For Gabriel, the simple act of Gray touching him where no one outside of his family — self-made or otherwise — has touched him has a strange grounding effect. It takes him out of his head completely. It makes it not about who Gabriel is or who he was or the shitty circumstances or how cruel and unfair life can be to just about everybody — it's about submitting and a Dom taking care of his sub. That core must be preserved, and Gabriel realizes how they've let the lines blur to the point where they don't even see those lines anymore as they step over them time and time again.

But Gray lives strictly between the lines. Even when he appears to cross them, like with bumping off Harry, it's done officially, formally. It's business, not a grudge.

The key, Gabriel realizes, is to redraw the lines and pay attention to them this time around. It started with Darrek and Kyle. Drawing those boundary lines has allowed both men safety and comfort as they have healed from old wounds and learned to carry on. It can't end with them, though. It has to go all the way. It has to be the way they live, from that moment forward.

This is what Gray shows Gabriel, with just a touch.

If Gabriel is going to submit to Trace, or Ben, it has to be within the lines. Gabriel should have respected Trace's inability to perform up to his standards under the current extremely stressful conditions, just as Trace never should have said what he said. He only said it, though, because they were already so far over the lines, the rules had already been obliterated.

There's still pressure against the base of the plug. That's Gray. It's like an anchor. When Gray's hand moves, caressing over the curve of Gabriel's ass to his lower back before falling away, that's dismissal.

"Gabriel, do you need help getting up?" Gray asks.

"No thanks," Gabriel answers, ready, knowing exactly what he needs to do.

First he straightens to his knees, letting the muscles adjust and as blood begins to flow back into his limbs. He breathes and stretches. When he's ready, he backs off the bed and stands.

Gray and Trace are both silent, the air thick with unspoken accusation, but Gabriel still has the key, the way to fix everything. Taking it with him, he faces Trace, with that black and blue eye and wearing an expression both sour with guilt and bitter with anger. Gabriel funnels all of the joy of his revelation into his right hand. He balls it up into a fist and targets Trace's jaw.

The punch never connects, but Gabriel didn't expect it to. If there's anything that tells Trace they're back where they both belong, it's Gabriel lashing out at someone he knows will have no problem containing the fight.

Trace catches Gabriel's fist, laughing, his sour bitterness gone in an instant. Gabriel's left fist comes around and Trace catches that too, pinning Gabriel's arms together in front of his chest, holding them there without showing the slightest bit of strain.

"There's my boy," Trace grins happily. "Where you been hiding?"

"Fuck you for saying that to me," Gabriel spits. "Truly. Fuck you."

Still smiling—not heartbroken or overwhelmed at all, Gabriel delightedly notices—Trace says, soft and deadly as sin, "Get on your goddamned knees. Now. Don't you make me say it twice."

The act of directing all of what he had left in him at Trace leaves Gabriel vibrating, skin tingling, muscles aching, mind racing. Trying to control his erratic breathing, he takes his time getting to his knees in front of Trace, their gazes locked. In a funny way, it's the plug up his ass, put there by Gray, which enables Gabriel to do it. It feels like plenty enough defiance against Daddy to put Gabriel back in a safe zone.

"You know I went easy on you. I barely touched you. It won't be that way next time. That's your only warning. Now, what do you say?"

"Yes, Daddy," Gabriel says on the exhale, his chest rising and falling heavily.

"Leave us," Gray says, only after walking over to Trace, looking him dead in the eye.

Something tightens in the center of Gabriel's body and his next breath cuts off abruptly. Trace notices and says, "It's okay, beautiful. I'll be right next door."

Trace walks out of the room. Lilianna is in the bedroom across the hall. She makes eye contact with Trace, beckoning to him with a tilt of her head.

Then the door closes behind Trace, leaving Gabriel and Gray alone together. The silence draws out.

Gray cups Gabriel's chin, tilting his head up. Gabriel's eyes stay lowered and he hates the soft sound he unwittingly makes in the back of his throat for causing him to seem so weak in front of such a man. He feels Gray looking, measuring, and the longer it goes on, the stiffer Gabriel's cock gets. When he's fully erect, Gray's thumb slides in a gentle arc over the ridge of Gabriel's jaw, like another dismissal.

"You may speak freely," Gray tells him.

"How long were you there?"

"You heard the door? That was Jack and Jan going outside. I came up here instead."

"So the whole damn time, then. Fantastic."

"I'm here on behalf of the Master's Circle. I will be monitoring all of the activity, personally." After a torturous moment, Gabriel manages to lift his gaze to Gray's face, which is unreadable but alert, as always. "He should not have said that to you. Your abuse is a trigger for you, and blaming you for any part of it during a scene is a *serious* offense."

Worry, stark and nauseating, washes over Gabriel. At first he can't even find his voice.

"He didn't mean it! It's not his fault. He didn't know you were listening—"

"It doesn't *matter* if I was listening—"

"And I shouldn't have initiated this or agreed to it. Not with everything going on. Not now."

"He didn't have to take part," Gray points out, arguing against Trace, who is the heart of Diadem. If the MC is out to knock down Trace, they're out to dismantle Diadem completely. This is just the first step.

"He was just reacting to what I said downstairs, about Jack's video and Harry," Gabriel says, and Gray doesn't blink, he just looks like he knew about that too. Gray was listening then, as well. "Look, I'm the one who asked him to fill this role. I don't call him *Master*, as you heard. He's *not* my Master."

"He's Daddy," Gray finishes. "Which makes it even more crucial he behave appropriately during a scene."

"It was one mistake, okay?" Gabriel pleads, too aware of his position, on his knees, begging, baring the plug that Gray gave him, to have as a reminder.

"Something tells me this is not Tracey's first mistake," Gray counters. "Just because you care about him doesn't mean you're safe with him."

"He's the *only* one I've ever felt this safe with," Gabriel says through gritted teeth, angrily turning his face away when tears begin to slip down his cheeks. "I've made mistakes too. Punish me, not him."

"Stand up," Gray says softly.

Gabriel obeys instantly, without even thinking about it.

"Look at me and say that again," Gray invites.

When Gabriel can't, chewing on his lip, it makes him feel like he's doing no good at all by throwing himself against the Master Dom's cool steadiness.

"You've known me for a day. Hours. You're not trying to punch *me*, are you?"

"No offense," Gabriel replies. "But you're not my Daddy."

"Fair enough." Gray says, stepping back, "I'll be watching."

"Yeah, I know." Gray opens the door. Gabriel sees him knock on the other door. It opens a crack. Trace is standing there in nothing but a towel. "Take care of your boy," Gray tells him sharply.

"Sure thing," Trace answers without inflection. Holding the door open, standing aside, he waves Gabriel through, saying, "C'mere, babydoll. Let's get you cleaned up."

Chapter 20
First Impressions

Gabriel doesn't waste any time. As soon as he's out on the front porch, needing to get out of there and recover both mentally and physically at home, he fishes his keys out of his pocket, touches the unlock button on the fob and says, "Dare, let's hit it. Come on."

In the driveway, Gabriel's hulking, black Discovery beeps. Its lights flash.

Micah, Jack, Jan, Darrek—all of them are there, and it feels like they're staring at him, waiting for some kind of explanation for why they were veritably chased from the house by both Trace and Gray, but Gabriel doesn't give an inch. When Darrek doesn't react immediately, Gabriel glances over at him, and sees him standing with Jan, both of them with their phones out and talking quietly together.

"Oh, for Christ's sake," Gabriel sighs, rolling his head on his shoulder to work out some of the stiffness.

"Quite a ride you got there," Jack says. He gets up from the Adirondack chair on the porch overlooking a green, sprawling lawn, lined with tall trees and thick shrubbery, and makes his way over to Gabriel. Jack looks good, Gabriel can't deny that. The guy is sexy as fuck but his personality puts Gabriel on edge. He's like a combination of Kyle's wanton willingness and Ben's inability to rein in his shit or filter any of it on the way out. It's a hellishly dangerous mix. Gabriel can see why Jack not only needs sweet Jan but hard-ass Gray, too, to tame him.

When they're eye to eye, it seems like Jack is reading between Gabriel's newly drawn lines, discovering secrets in the margins. He's freshly showered, but his damp hair is hidden under the hat.

Any other giveaways would be more subtle, but maybe Jack can handle subtle when he wants to.

"Yeah, tell me about it," Gabriel murmurs in agreement, with a sly look over his shoulder and back where he left Trace and Gray.

"What ride are you talking about?"

"What ride are *you* talking about?"

"The beast in the drive or the beast in the bedroom."

"Exactly," Gabriel agrees without agreeing.

"So you and Trace?" Jack says leadingly.

"It's business."

"Business, eh?" Jack asks with raised eyebrows. "Don't suppose you're still taking orders?"

Unable to help it, Gabriel laughs. "Slick," he grins.

"Jack, give up," Jan calls.

"Fuck you, Richards. Don't think I haven't noticed you trying to play Truth or Lick Dare. He's too tall; you'll need a step ladder. Let it go," Jack replies.

"Are you ready yet?" Gabriel asks Darrek impatiently.

"Yeah! Yeah," Darrek says, still doing something on his phone, hunched a little over the tiny screen. "Jan gave me his cell number, and I gave him mine."

With another heavy sigh, Gabriel gazes up at the porch's roof.

"He wants to meet Sierra, so I thought we could get together for brunch in the morning, bring her along, and go for a walk through town."

Jan comes over to Jack and Jack asks him under his breath, "Sierra's a girlfriend on the side or something?"

"The dog," Jan tells him with a crooked grin. "Should I make you a spreadsheet with all the names and relations to keep 'em straight?"

"Taking the piss?" Jack asks with a wary squint, biting at his lip.

Darrek is smiling happily at them, watching as Jan gives Jack a kiss while chuckling against his lips. Gabriel takes Darrek's hand and says, "Okay, kids. Not staying for the show. Been a long damn day."

They walk out to the Discovery. Jack and Jan follow, maybe just for an excuse to get off the damn porch and away from the drama brewing inside the house. Gabriel wouldn't blame them. It's the same thing driving him to get in the car and go.

"Nice to meet you, Jan," Gabriel says, shaking with him.

"Morning, then?" Jan says, glancing up at Darrek.

"Yeah, call me," Darrek agrees eagerly, shaking Jan's hand like he wants to do more than shake his hand.

"Christ's sake," Gabriel mutters. He goes to circle around to the driver's side but Jack steps in his way.

"I meant it, you know. How about we borrow that bike, blow off some steam?" Jack—hot, dangerous and willing as ever—nods back in the direction of where Trace's Harley is parked around the side of the house. The sly look in his stark, grey eyes and the careless tousle of his nearly-black hair, makes Gabriel want to find a way to get such a bare-knuckle fighter to the ground, held and tamed. It would be empowering and sexy as hell. "I'll take the Discovery. These Land Rovers have all sorts of cooling issues, y'know. They overheat because of bad water pumps or head gaskets. Be a shame if it overheated out there on one of those deserted dirt roads, with you on that Harley coming up on me, unawares. We could do a little carjack role play."

The worst part is as soon as Jack suggests it Gabriel starts to see it play out in vivid color, with obscene, imagined sounds filling his head. Finding Jack off the road, stranded, threatening him with some kind of weapon, getting him over the hood and taking him for that ride he seems to want to take as much as Gabriel suddenly realizes he wants to give.

Gabriel's hesitation in answering only makes Jack's eyes light up brighter as he bites his lip again and starts watching Gabriel's mouth for the word go.

"Give it up, Jack!" Jan calls again.

"Richards, working here!" Jack shouts back, momentarily distracted. "It's not only Gray testing these lot out."

It's enough of an out that Gabriel has to take it; he slips past Jack, opens the car door, and starts to get in.

"Oh, come on!" Jack says with frustration.

"Lovely meeting you, Jack," Gabriel says with a hint of dark sarcasm barely disguising the sexually charged power behind the words. They lock eyes for another moment, just long enough for Gabriel to make it clear he doesn't need the framework of a role play scenario, permission from Gray or anything else should he decide he wants to take what Jack has to give.

Darrek gets in the Discovery too. Rolling down the windows, starting the engine, Gabriel calls, "Hey Jack!"

"Yeah?"

"Is it true what I've always heard about Brits?"

"What's that?"

With a deadpan expression, only the barest hint of a smirk in the curl of his lips, Gabriel shouts, "They really *suck*."

He only gets the briefest glimpse of Jan laughing and Jack's wicked smile in response before they're around the bend in the road and out of sight.

When they're a few blocks away, Gabriel sees Darrek's smile has lingered, though it fades more the closer they get to home.

"It's good for you," he tells Darrek. "Really good."

Embarrassed, caught daydreaming about Gabriel-knows-who, Darrek scoffs and ducks his head so that his hair falls, obscuring his features. "It's nothing, I was just—"

"I know what you were," Gabriel says gently. "Jan's great. And, bonus, he has nothing to do with any of the baggage with the lifestyle, but he lives it every day anyway."

"He lives in England, Gabe," Darrek says, with almost no smile left. "It's not like he's about to be my new best friend."

"He doesn't have to be. It's just good to see you happy again."

They're nearly at the house. Darrek hesitates, but asks, "So what's with you and Jack?"

"Lemme guess," Gabriel smirks, "You're asking that one first, the question about Gray second, and the one about Trace last."

"Something like that," Darrek admits, looking too damned sad again, even though a ghost of the smile remains.

"I warned you they were gonna be intense. Jack *is* a sub, in an intense way. Gray *is* a Dom, also in an intense way. I saw it coming from a mile off. I'll admit, I'd have had a hell of a good time if I got the chance to dominate Jack way back when, but times have changed. I'm a new Dom to him, so he's just checking me out. Fuckin' feisty, though," he chuckles. "But we threw 'em both for a loop, didn't we?"

"They really thought I was your Dom," Darrek says with awe.

"Well, you are enormous."

"I've never had any complaints."

They pull up into their driveway. The Discovery's engine is turned off. Laughing, Gabriel leans over and waits for Darrek to meet him halfway for a kiss.

After they separate again, Gabriel asks, "Can we do this inside?"

"Just tell me, please," Darrek pleads with heartbreaking sincerity. It makes Gabriel want to kiss him again and again. "I need to know what happened."

"I helped Gray get what he needed, but that video... it's of Jack, underage, being worked over by some sick motherfucker, and it was posted to the goddamned *internet*, all of those porn sites, for anyone to see. Thinking about that, adding it to everything else going on in my head right now, and sitting there with Gray — the guy who fucking did the damn deed, murdering Harry — it got to me. So, Trace helped me relax."

"So that's why you wanted to sub for him."

"Yeah," Gabriel nods, gazing at his hands in his lap. The engine makes soft noises as it cools off, the world quiet except for an occasional gust of wind whistling around the Discovery's windows. "But it wasn't the right time. We should have waited, cooled down first. Trace was upset, too, and — "

"Did he hurt you?" Darrek demands, sharply.

"No. No, it wasn't like that. He just said something that kind of made me feel bad about it — needing to sub for him." When he can tell, without even looking, that Darrek is upset, Gabriel continues, "But like I said, it was on both of us for not waiting. Trace apologized. He felt like shit after saying it. But, uh, Gray was there the whole time."

"What?"

"*Observing*, he called it. I didn't know he was there until he stepped in, literally, and took control of the scene. I mean, I know how it sounds, this guy we hardly know listening in, walking in while Trace is fucking me, starting to give orders and all, but... I don't know, Dare. It felt a lot better after Gray was in charge. Everything he said or did was for my safety, and I found myself trusting him. It made me realize maybe we've been going about everything wrong. The rules are there for a reason. They keep us safe. We've been breaking them too often. The submissive's safety needs to come before everything, even the Dom's emotions. Trace, Benny, me, we all need to learn that. I think that's part of why Gray is here—to get the Doms of Diadem back in line, and I think it's a really good thing, for all of us."

Softly, Darrek asks, "He touched you?"

"Yeah," Gabriel nods.

"Was it weird?"

"Not like I expected," he says, looking sideways at Darrek. "Gray's a professional. You can tell. *I* could tell. How are you? I know the past two days have just been crazy."

"A little overwhelmed, I guess, but okay," Darrek shrugs. After bearing Gabriel's worried glance for a few long moments, he adds, "I know I need to deal with my family."

"You have lots of options, baby. I know you've said you want to be the one to handle this, but I'll do anything I can to help. You can write a letter, you can make a quick call with a script in front of you, you can even change our number to avoid them a little longer if that's what you want."

"But they'll still know where we live, and they'll wonder."

"Yeah. They will." Taking Darrek's hand, Gabriel tells him, confidently, "I'm with you. We can do this. But first I need your help with something *very* important."

When Darrek only raises an eyebrow with confusion, Gabriel nods to the house. "Come on."

Because Darrek's adorably perplexed expression lasts all the way upstairs, into the bedroom, right up to the edge of the bed, Gabriel can't stop grinning, though he bites at his lips to try to hide it.

"C'mere," he coaxes, drawing Darrek down with a hand for a longer, slower kiss. "Take my pants off."

"Yes, Sir," Darrek says automatically, seriously, which makes

Gabriel chuckle. He twists off his shirt and tosses his knit hat, but lets Darrek do the rest, toeing off his boots when needed. Once he's completely naked, Gabriel sees Darrek is still confused.

"What?" Darrek asks, as Gabriel laughs again, smiling wider.

"You're adorable."

"Thank you?"

"I have an order for you, slave," Gabriel says, trying for a serious tone and not completely succeeding. "Make love to me."

He guides Darrek's arms to wind around him, and after some caressing while Gabriel tries to kiss away Darrek's lingering, faint frown, he sees Darrek's eyebrows jump in revelation. "*Oh,*" Darrek murmurs against Gabriel's lips, his fingers finding the plug at last.

"Have I told you you're adorable?"

"Yes, Sir," Darrek smiles. "Recently."

"Think you can take care of that for me, slave?"

"Yes, Sir," Darrek says solemnly, smiling just as much as Gabriel, now. "I'll do my best."

―○―○―○―

"My room. Now," Gray says to Trace. Lilianna has gone outside with everyone else. It's just Trace and Gray in the house. Gray goes into his bedroom by the top of the stairs. Trace follows him in.

"Couldn't help noticing the lack of a collar on Jack," Trace comments, needing to get a jab of his own in before Gray really fucks him over. "How is it a Master Dom takes a sub like Jacky boy for… how many years has it been? And no collar?"

Ignoring the jabs, or maybe just getting madder because of them, Gray switches on an mp3 player and turns the volume up. Then he closes the door behind Trace and locks it. Trace can figure out the rest. No doubt Gray has combed the room from floorboards to ceiling to ensure it's secure.

"Where the fuck is your head?" Gray seethes in a quiet growl, more visibly angry than Trace has seen him in a long time. It makes him feel a little proud for being able to so easily get under Gray's skin. He gestures up and down Trace's body. "This? Not a bloody improvement. Not when I know where you come from. *Kneel,* slave."

Trace sighs, letting go of himself. The identity he's wrapped himself in for over ten years falls away. Then, Patrick kneels at the feet of the Master Dom. The pose is familiar, comforting, as the wooden boards dig into his kneecaps and he clasps his hands behind his back, head bowed. It's like he's back there, at headquarters, with the whole line of the Master Dom and Domme's seated in front of him, passing judgment. That might even be an improvement from where he finds himself, faced with only riled Gray.

"*Selfish* fucking prat," Gray says, still angry. Patrick sighs.

"Now who's letting emotions cloud judgment?" Patrick glances upward without moving a muscle, and he smiles, knowing he's going to pay for that one with the skin off his back. "Sir," he adds. "Or maybe you're going to give me a refresher on the consequences of fucking people who've been deemed off limits? That'd be *truly* fucking ironic, Master Gray."

Unable to stop smiling at how he's managed to irritate his former flame, Patrick watches as Gray self-corrects instantly, cooling off, redistributing all of his fury into fuel for formal, warranted punishment later.

"You know better," the newly composed Gray replies. "Have I ever called you a whore during a scene?"

God, that hurts, because he's right. Just like always, he's absolutely fucking right. Gray had always been mindful, once he knew about Patrick's history, to always make sure he was treated with respect and care. And Trace couldn't do the same for Gabriel. When it mattered most, Trace put his own feelings ahead of the welfare of his submissive. Lowering his gaze, trying to push all of the new regret for hurting Gabriel into a place that can be purged with his eventual punishment at Gray's hands, Patrick answers, "No, Master Gray."

"Get yourself together. You're endangering *all of them* by behaving the way you are."

Patrick laughs without raising his head and says, with more of his accent slipping back in, "Split personality here, Sir. Trace protects Patrick. Hell, he protects everyone. Gotta keep both halves apart for safety. You know about safety, don't you, Master Gray?"

"That doesn't mean you don't have to abide by the rules. *You* need to set the example they model themselves after."

"I know I fucked up," Patrick says defensively. "I'm sorry, Master Gray. Won't happen again."

"Oh, I intend to make sure of that," Gray replies, the threat conveyed loud and clear.

Chapter 21
Patrick, Master's Sub

17 Years Earlier, London

It was hard to stay in any one place long. It felt unnatural. And when he was at headquarters, it was even worse. Surveillance was an issue. They were always watching through the CCTV feed and from security posts throughout the building. For Patrick, it was a blessing and a curse. There were people out there who would have loved to shut him up, permanently. He'd become a problem that needed addressing. The Master's Circle was the only thing standing between him and the bad guys. So, he needed their damned oasis of control. He had a room there to live in temporarily, to which only he and Nicholai had a key, not that security couldn't get inside in a heartbeat if they wanted to.

But he got out when he could, as much as he could. Finishing off a five mile run around the property, he headed to the gym and made straight for the boxing bag.

By the time he'd spent most of his restless energy — which told him to get his ass moving, to dodge and weave and stay light on his feet — he was dripping sweat and breathing hard.

Patrick was bare-chested, wearing exercise shorts and sneakers, his short, black hair tousled but his chin shaved smooth. He'd always been diligent about hygiene and grooming, and had never been able to stand having facial hair. As nice as it was to get some exercise, he needed a shower as badly as he needed to breathe, so he walked through the hall connecting the gym to the elevators, heading home. On the way, he waved to those he recognized, giving everyone his most charming smile. He'd learned long ago, as long as you could fake a good, convincing smile, you could get away with murder. Mastering the ability to have a pleasant expression even when he was at his most upset was a skill he'd come to depend on.

When the elevator stopped at his floor, he got out and walked down to his door. His key was on a chain around his neck, around which was also fastened his collar, which never came off except for showers and sleep. Pulling the chain off and running a hand back through his damp hair, he worked to unlock the door and went inside.

The room itself was plain, with only the bare essentials—a bed, a small table and chairs, a bureau, nightstand and a few strategically placed bolts in the ceiling, walls, and floor. There was also a cabinet for which he didn't have a key, in which Nicholai stored all of his toys and gear. The only personal touch he'd made were some automotive magazine photos, taped to the wall beside the bed. He was a big fan of American engineering, and couldn't wait to get a few project cars to refurbish, once he was back in the states. There was no timeline, though. Nothing, yet, was certain, which only added to his restlessness.

Luckily, there was also a large adjoining bathroom for his private use. Without even bothering to toe off his sneakers, just dropping his key on the bureau, Patrick went into the bathroom and turned on the water in the shower to let it heat up. Standing in the bathroom doorway, feeling the old listlessness come back, strong, he stared blankly at the private balcony which overlooked the beautifully landscaped grounds below. There were large, glass-paned doors leading out to them. The glass was bulletproof. The doors were locked. That was so he couldn't go out there and jump off. He was about five floors above ground level. The shitty part was it wasn't even standard procedure to lock those doors. That had been done just for him, after he'd met with the MC psychologist and she wasn't able to rule out suicidal tendencies.

He heard the room's door open and winced. Glancing away, he saw the bathroom mirror wasn't fogged over. Had the hot water not kicked in? Or had he been standing there, staring at the balcony for longer than he thought he had?

Nicholai walked in, pocketing his key, closing and locking the door behind him. He looked good, as always, with his solid build, light brown hair, strong jaw, blue eyes, and broad shoulders. They were the same age, but Nicholai was ex-military, so he automatically had more badass points than Patrick.

The deal was they never had set appointments to meet. It was part of Patrick's contract, as well as the fact that no one else besides Nicholai, in the MC or outside of it, was allowed to touch him. Appointments were a trigger for him, since it made submitting feel too much like servicing johns. But, sometimes it sucked to not be able to anticipate and prepare himself, physically or otherwise.

Immediately, Patrick's hand came up to rub over his collar. There was a love bite hidden beneath it, so he was real fucking glad he hadn't taken it off for the shower yet. Nicholai hadn't yet found proof Patrick had taken a lover, but he knew. Sure, he knew.

"Slave, aren't you listening to me?" Nicholai asked, his voice butter smooth. He was standing right in front of Patrick, in the doorway of the bathroom. Patrick hadn't noticed him walk over.

"Absolutely, gorgeous, what can I do for ya?" Patrick grinned, biting his lip and taking a step into Nicholai's personal space.

"High protocol, slave," Nicholai said with a slightly pained sigh that made Patrick instantly realize he'd done something wrong. "Show me you know what that means."

Nicholai was doing that thing where he kept hands off, full eye contact, and it was like an itch under Patrick's skin. It was easier to be touched, to close eyes and get swept up. It was so much harder to meet Nicholai's gaze and bear his scrutiny.

"Course I know what that means," Patrick laughed softly, grin still in place, like a mask. He toed off his shoes and socks, shucked out of his shorts. Instinct overrode logic for a bunch of different reasons, none of which had to do with the particular man standing before him. Patrick closed his eyes, humming, and moved to stroke himself, to put on a show for his audience and keep things in the safe, familiar realm of sex. He knew he looked good, with sweat trickling down through the cut of his hips, the thick muscle of his thighs, the planes of his abs, and the swell of his chest muscles.

When Nicholai moved, immobilizing him, he pinned Patrick's

arms behind his back, sweeping his feet, causing him to sail forward into the bathroom counter, the edge of which caught him at hip level. Groaning through the pain, knowing he was going to have bruises there later, he laughed it off as the cuffs were snapped around his wrists.

By his ear, Nicholai said in quiet threat, "If you don't start obeying me, I will have no choice but to isolate you again. Forced seclusion, forced chastity."

"Sorry, Master," Patrick murmured, looking at nothing, trying not to feel, think, or hurt.

Nicholai took hold of Patrick's dick, guiding it upright so it was pinned between his hips and the counter's edge, forcing him to keep from leaning against it. Then a chain was clipped to a ring on the front of his collar, pulled tight so he was forced to stay bent sharply over, facing the mirror.

There was something in Nicholai's hand, but Patrick didn't want to look at what it was. He didn't want to see anything. He just wanted to go inward, where it was safe, and where no one could touch him.

"Do you trust me, Patrick?" It was asked with gentle affection and sincere worry, which hurt more than any yell, any physical pain. All he ever wanted was to be loved, to be cared about in a real way. He had that with Nicholai. To think he was betraying one of the few people who actually loved him was the biggest reality check he could get.

"Yes, Sir," Patrick answered, filling the words with regret.

"Then look at me."

"Can't," he said through gritted teeth, feeling tears course down his cheeks, willing to suffer any pain to avoid seeing them on his face.

The bamboo cane whistled through the air, connecting with the thickest part of his ass, biting through skin, into muscle. Blowing air out through his nose, swallowing his scream, bearing down and tensing up as the pain spread outward, he fought, and felt something inside loosen.

He raised his eyes. The cane cut through air again and, seeing it coming, he chased forward to escape but only wound up crushing his dick. Crying out, pulling on the cuffs, the chain around his neck, feet slipping over the tile, he was lost in the agony.

"Manners, slave. You maintain eye contact. You show respect."

There was blood dripping down the curve of his ass. The wounds were hot, burning lines, crisscrossing the skin. He locked his eyes on Nicholai and tried to control his breathing.

"Better. It's your choice, slave. Reward or punishment."

"Yes, Sir."

"I am not someone you flirt with. I am your Master. You show me respect."

"Yes, Sir."

"Now, answer truthfully. Have you been letting him fuck you?"

It took a hell of a lot of effort, but he didn't look away. He didn't even blink.

"Yes, Sir."

"Five lashes as punishment. Maintain eye contact or it's going to be ten lashes instead."

"Yes, Sir."

His screams rang off the tile, and his blood flowed more freely, but not once did he look away. His tears dried up. Panting, trying not to collapse forward and further injure himself, eyes rolling deliriously, Patrick fought to regain control of himself.

A hand caressed through his hair, lovingly. A hard body pressed up against him from behind, welcome and wonderful.

"Why, Patrick?" Nicholai asked softly. "Why would you allow him to hurt you that way?"

"He loves me," Patrick whispered, knowing he sounded naive, hoping the words were true, and not just a secret wish. Even if Gray wouldn't say the words, that he loved Patrick, it was still possible he did, deep down. Fresh tears began to fall, and Nicholai looked like he wanted Gray racked and whipped for days on end, until he felt a fraction of the pain he was bringing down upon the man he so carelessly had sex with.

"If he loved you, he wouldn't treat you this way. Don't you see that?" Nicholai pleaded.

Patrick breathed out a laugh, sniffling, having no pride left to gather.

"Yes, Sir."

Sighing, Nicholai caressed him. The urge to close his eyes was strong, the touch felt so good.

"Have I been obedient for you, Master?"

Nicholai hesitated. Then, freeing himself from his pants, slicking himself with lube, he lined up with Patrick's body and began to press inside. It was a slow, gradual process. By the time he managed to squeeze his cockhead through Patrick's unprepped rim, Patrick was fully erect and moaning. Staying relaxed, holding the position, he begged softly for more, mouth fallen open in ecstasy as Nicholai claimed him more fully, sheathing himself to the root.

The pleasure overlaid the pain perfectly, and Patrick wanted to draw the moment out forever, to always be there, claimed so utterly by such a devoted man.

But, the restlessness came back only a few hours later.

Then, Patrick descended to the ground floor, found his bike and took off. Technically, he'd been ordered to stay on the property by the MC, so they knew his bike and would follow. He knew how to lose a tail, though. It wasn't exactly brain surgery, even when you were dealing with professionals.

Eventually, he pulled up to Gray's home. He was shown in to the study, and it felt exactly like he was going to service a john. All of the freedom he found with Nicholai, and the mental release that helped him stop reflexively filling a role he no longer needed to fill, was ground down by that wait, pacing around the study. It was why Nicholai tried so hard to convince Patrick not to see his new lover. He understood the damage it was doing to him.

But it was more important to Patrick to try to find something real, and was just his, too precious to be bought and sold. He wanted, above all else, to belong to someone who cared.

Gray appeared, at last, and Patrick went to hug him, even if Gray didn't want to be hugged. Gray smiled cooly and Patrick embraced him, tucking his chin over Patrick's shoulder and clapping him on the back.

"Hey, bright eyes."

"I assume you weren't followed—" Gray started to say, his hands caressing lower. But when he casually rubbed over the seat of Patrick's pants, Patrick's sharp hiss abruptly halted the sentence. The wounds had been tended, but they were still raw. Trying to hide his grimace and the dying light in his smile, Patrick avoided eye contact and tried to pull away. Gray held him there, taking his face in hand, looking him over with a keen eye.

"Nicholai," Gray said quietly, angrily.

"Don't sweat it, okay?" Patrick said quickly. "I can take it."

He could feel all of it, all of the progress, all of the control coming unraveled. It made him sad and it was harder than ever to keep the smile on his face. So, he leaned in and kissed Gray to hide the signs of hurt. When Gray kissed him back, there was power and passion there, more than there should have been. He pushed Patrick back against a wall, his hands everywhere, unfastening Patrick's pants, catching his mouth with his lips, and it was so easy to get lost there, in Gray's need for him. That was why he kept coming back, and chose to disobey, even if it meant he got hurt.

Nothing was more important than chasing the possibility Gray might love him enough to keep him; not even taking care of himself.

Chapter 22
Observations

Sitting in Micah's office, Trace opens his laptop, taken from the room's small vault where he's been locking it up, just in case. He boots it up and opens his browser to access email. One by one, he goes through his mental list, typing up a new message that's almost identical each time he saves a draft in a new email account. He's sending his new phone number for a disposal cellphone he's never used. It might be a risk to give it out that way, but he has to take it, and give them a chance to call him if they need to.

Because something is wrong.

He can feel it. Yasha said he was getting out of the game because of the baby his wife is expecting, but that doesn't account for all of the silence from Patrick's many contacts. He's sent out inquiries, asking for people to report back, even just to say everything is status quo.

There's been nothing. The silence is eerie and implies, in his opinion, everyone suspects there's someone listening in who shouldn't be.

The last account he checks, as usual, is Nicholai's. It makes him feel better just to type a message. This one is different than the others, more honest, and heartfelt. Even if it never gets read, he's glad to be able to compose it, a little message in a bottle he can float out there, hoping for a reply.

He's not really surprised when he sees from the corner of his eye as someone enters the room.

"Hey, bright eyes," Trace says instinctively.

"Something's worrying you," Gray observes. He walks over to

the desk, standing on the other side of it, scrutinizing his prey.

"What *isn't* worrying me?" Trace counters with a smile. Sighing, he adds, "It's too quiet. Something's off. Bad vibes, kid. Tons of 'em."

There are plenty of contacts who will talk to Trace, but won't talk to someone like Gray. Some people have simply been through too much to partake in any useful exchange of information with MI5. Trust isn't easy to come by if you've been in The Company, like it is with those in the MC. Trace's soft touch yields more reward than Gray's hard-fucked style, which is why Trace has been useful to Gray for so long.

"Why are you doing this to yourself, Patrick?"

"Don't," Trace says sharply, glancing toward the open door.

"You're falling apart. I've *seen* you fall apart. I know what it looks like," Gray reminds him. "Why haven't you introduced yourself to Micah, at least? Don't trust him?"

"Nah, I trust him," Trace murmurs, thinking of Nicholai. He'd always sworn to himself and others he trusted Nicholai, but did he? Patrick had never let himself fall completely for his Master. Bone-deep guardedness always kept them a breath away, even in their closest moments. It was enough emotional space to let the doubt seep through, clouding the waters. Was he doing the same thing with Micah? Were Patrick's fortified walls keeping out the one man who might be his long-sought true love? It was a terrible thought to consider. "You know, I've kept all of this, this entire part of who I am, away from all of my kids. Even when I have to make a call, and I can't be Trace for a while, I have to… I don't know. Get away. I get far away. There's a ritual I go through each time, to leave Trace behind, just in case."

"It's too late for games," Gray says. "You were better as a submissive. It suited you."

"Trace doesn't submit to anyone."

"Fine. Leaves one option then."

"Fuck, kid. You're killing me," Trace groans, swiping a hand over his face. "Hate this fuckin' beard still, you know. Fuckin' sick of all the lying. How can I expect them to trust me if I'm not trusting *them*?"

"Sounds like you know what to do." Gray holds his gaze, like he used to when it was too hard for Patrick to see people seeing him, and Gray was brave enough to try to help him bear it. "After the party, we'll address this with Micah. Privately. Leave Trace behind."

"Yes, Sir," Trace says with a sad smile. There's no choice anymore. No more hiding. No more lying.

―⊂⊃―⊂⊃―⊂⊃―

"Any observations to report so far?" Gray asks Jack. It's late. They've retired to the bedroom Jack and Jan are sharing. Gray sits in a chair in a corner of the room, with a good view of the door and the adjoining bathroom where Jan is showering.

"You mean other than how cozy you and Tracey are?" For Jack, it wasn't just the casual touches but the way Gray and Trace looked at each other that set off internal fireworks of jealousy. They burned like hell, in spectacular colors, and all he can see now is the afterimage, seared into his brain. He's never seen Gray look at someone the way he looks at Trace. Gray's always been good about being professional at all times, but his interactions with Trace are different. So what if Trace is an ex? Everyone's got history. Gray's not going to be an exception. But it's the way it doesn't seem like the spark between them is history that keeps shooting off those bottle rockets filled with resentment.

"Yes, other than that."

"Pegged Dare wrong, didn't I? But hell, look at him! A fuckin' mountain of a submissive. Totally harmless."

"You think so?" Gray asks with a cocked eyebrow.

"Why, you don't?" Jack retorts, wary of Gray's doubt.

"I didn't say that, did I? How about the others?"

Gabriel is the next one to come to mind. He's a puzzle, and the more pieces of Gabriel Jack has to work with, the less they seem to fit together. Average height, slim build, pretty face, and virgin Dom with a physically intimidating sub, who's got a thing on the side with Gray's ex. "Not sure what to make of Gabe yet. Tracey's got a soft spot for him, doesn't he? The two of them snuck off earlier while the rest of us were conveniently out of the house."

"I was there to monitor the scene," Gray admits.

"Yeah, what's that supposed to mean?"

"Mean's I'm keeping my eye on both of them, and I step in when needed to keep everyone safe."

"You had to step in?" Jack says with surprise. "The ex got out of line, then?"

"It was handled. It's fine."

"So you don't trust him. Trace."

"That's not what I said," Gray says seriously. "We arrived at a complicated time for all of them. The dust needs to settle before I can get a clearer picture of what's going on."

"So there's a lot more *monitoring* to do," Jack provides, leaning heavily on Gray's clinical term for watching and participating in any and all action happening while they're there. "If you need any help with that…."

"You're volunteering, then? Good."

Jack isn't quite sure he likes the coyness of Gray's look, but answers, "Depends on the situation of course."

"Oh, of course," Gray agrees, but still with the fucking coy look.

"You're gonna have to get him a dog, you know."

"Mm," Jack grunts in agreement. He and Gabriel are seated on a bench in a public park that's a short walk from the café where they'd had brunch. For most of the meal, Jan and Darrek chatted away excitedly, though quietly, while Gabriel and Jack gave each other complicated glances over the small table, drinking their coffee and trying to wake up. Now, Darrek and Jan are playing catch with Sierra, seemingly without a care in the world. "It's likely he always fancied one, growing up. So, you like to watch?"

"How do you mean?" Gabriel asks, playing dumb. He has a pretty good idea what Jack means, as they'd all discussed their various jobs over their meal. Jan definitely came across as the white collar businessman of the group, though with something like Darrek's penchant for attracting chaos and danger, no matter how pure his intentions may be. How else do you explain Jan winding up with Jack and Gray, of all people?

Jack went on and on about mechanics, talking about running a shop, rebuilding engines, and dealing with random breakdowns that get towed in, like Jan—it was how they met. Most of it went right over Gabriel's head. Back when he used to live with Trace, he would be regularly dragged out to the garage as Trace tried to teach him some basics of vehicle maintenance, some appreciation for the craft. Not much of it stuck. Gabriel would nod, grunting in reply to pretend he was listening when he was actually busy fantasizing about taking proper advantage of all of the grease, chains, and tools and take some lucky submissive apart, or maybe just letting Trace wrestle him over the hood or to the dirty floor for some angry hand release or a slow, deliciously torturous blowjob while bound to Trace's beloved bike. It was the same with Jack. Gabriel pretended to give a shit about the specifics, when really he was just figuring out the details of how that carjacking scenario might play out, or trying to picture Jack dirty, sweaty, and wearing nothing but a pair of coveralls pulled down and bunched around his thighs, arms bound in chains, body tense with fight.

Another thing they learned was Jack and Darrek share an interest in tools, so to speak. So, they had that in common. When prodded by Jack to explain how he spends his days, Darrek got more into the particulars of slaving away in the garage over carpentry projects. Gabriel could only smile when he noticed the same sort of glazed expression on Jan's face the more Darrek explained specifics, figuring he was happily lost in the fantasy, just like Gabriel had been with Jack. Plus, Gabriel can't deny how sexy Darrek looks when he's flushed, sweaty, covered in dirt and sawdust, and just begging for a good, hard fuck over the side of his workbench.

"You're a photographer," Jack says, with a raised eyebrow and a leading expression. "Professionally speaking. And, you know, there's the whole virgin Dom thing."

"Why am I not surprised you heard about that?" Gabriel asks no one in particular as a tennis ball rolls his way. Sierra bounds over to him. Picking up the yellow ball, Gabriel scratches behind the golden retriever's ears before tossing it back to Jan. As soon as the ball is in flight, Sierra barks excitedly and sprints after it.

"So," Jack murmurs, when Sierra is gone. "You like to watch."

Really, Gabriel has never given it much thought, or has had to explain what he likes, or why. Working at Diadem, it was always about what the client was after, or sneaking off for some screwing around with his co-workers. The particulars of Gabriel's desires stayed safely locked away and largely un-scrutinized. But, looking back over his time with Darrek, and the way the dynamics of their play has always skewed, Gabriel would have to admit it does appear he likes to watch. How else would you explain Gabriel's constant, intense enjoyment of seeing Darrek's newly chiseled body being wracked with pleasure and pain, brought to its limits, tested, tried, and fucked? He doesn't let himself consider Kyle, or at least not for long, though his time as Kyle's Dom would fit the pattern.

Without meeting Jack's gaze, Gabriel remarks, "I'm gonna go way out on a limb and guess you've had a little experience with voyeurism. You know, being *Gray's* sub and all."

"Why'd you say that?"

"Oh, just a *wild* guess," Gabriel says sarcastically. It seems sarcasm is an international language, though, because Jack picks up on it right away. The energy from Gabriel's right side, on which Jack is seated, cranks up. "Seems he's here in a supervisory capacity for the MC. I found out firsthand, yesterday."

"With you and Tracey," Jack acknowledges, giving Gabriel a sideways glance.

"Mm," Gabriel hums in agreement. "So, *Jack*, it's gotta be a two-way street, right? Why would you sub for a Master voyeur if *you* weren't an exhibitionist?"

"You wanna give it a go, if you know so much about it?" Jack shoots back more than a little defensively.

"Well, I don't think I'd get bored watching you," Gabriel admits softly. "Far fucking from it."

He wonders if Jack knows anything about Harry, either, or Gray's part in it all. Gabriel would bet a fortune he doesn't. In fact, Gabriel would bet there's a whole world of revelations concerning Gray Jack doesn't know about.

"Look, I appreciate you guys coming out today to do this," Gabriel says sincerely. "Dare's been in a bad place, mentally, and this is helping. So thanks. Just seeing him laugh like that is incredible."

Gabriel watches Jan try to keep the tennis ball out of Sierra's reach, though she jumps for it, trying to climb him like a tree while Darrek laughs his ass off, arms up, waving for Jan to throw. Though he feels Jack's eyes on him, Gabriel waits a while before turning to face his scrutiny, not giving an inch but letting Jack look as long as he likes. The more Jack begins to realize he won't learn anything about Gabriel so easily, the more it seems to drive him to try harder, liking the challenge.

"So *just* him, huh?" Jack says, gesturing to Darrek. "He's the only sub you've had sex with?"

Gabriel can only chuckle, leaning forward with his elbows braced on his knees.

"Why him, though, out of everybody?"

With a glance back, up and down Jack's body, Gabriel slowly, subtly licks his lower lip wet, the smile lingering, before turning back to watch Darrek try to outrace Sierra.

"Wouldn't you like to know," Gabriel grins.

"Yeah! I would!"

And Gabriel just laughs.

Chapter 23
Life of the Party

Kyle is most definitely in the mood for celebration. The bad guys have been defeated. Good has triumphed over evil. There should be food, drink, and merrymaking, or so he's been telling Ben nonstop until the poor bastard snapped and agreed to go to the party—with certain, specific conditions for Kyle, just so he could get a break from the incessant shameless pleading.

And really, Ben doesn't have a valid reason not to go, anyway, even if Darrek is going to be there, and even if Ben hates the shit out of Gray without even knowing the guy. For a solid twenty-four hours, Kyle tries to puzzle out the reasons why Ben is so angry about the whole thing, if it's because Gray took out Harry without Ben knowing a thing about it, or if the whole bitch fit is really about Trace trusting someone else other than Ben with something so big. And, of course, there's all of the lying involved. The whole laundry list of things Trace never bothered to mention about his past is like a knife in Ben's back, making him want to lash out at everyone involved in the perceived betrayal.

But, whatever. Kyle doesn't really give a shit. So what if Trace used to be a hooker? Or spent time in England learning the secrets of the most skilled and powerful Masters in the world? So what if he used to care about other people besides them? Everyone has a past, and Kyle is just glad they haven't had to deal with Trace's baggage all of these years. He's had the decency to keep it all to himself and spare them the drama.

As soon as they get to Micah and Lilianna's place, Kyle is ushered directly to the staircase. Ben slaps a paper sign to the wall at the bottom, taping it down, then another halfway up and a third at the top. Leading the way, not caring one bit about the stupid signs, Kyle finds Micah walking down the hall.

"Hey," Kyle says brightly. "Thanks for the invite! I'm not allowed downstairs."

"Yes, I know." Micah says with a slight, discomfited sigh. "You can hang out in the study. It's through there. There's food, drinks, a stereo, lube, and condoms in case of emergency."

"A *stereo*, you say, huh?" Kyle grins.

From directly behind him, Ben groans and says, "I knew this was a bad idea. Hey, Mic."

"Hey, Benny. Oh, uh, might I put in a request for some fair warning if you're looking to give Trace another black eye?"

"Not worth it," Ben grumbles.

"Ben's upset Trace has other friends," Kyle tells Micah.

Seeing Ben's overtly grumpy expression, Micah appears to think things over, then suggests. "Maybe a dance battle, then? Winner fucks the loser in a gingham dress to the cheers and applause of the rest of the houseguests?"

"The loser wears the gingham dress or the winner?"

Micah shrugs, "Coin toss."

"I vote for the dance battle," Kyle chimes in.

Lilianna hurries past with an armful of things, saying cheerfully, "Hey guys! Welcome!"

"Hey, Lily! I'm not allowed downstairs," Kyle calls back.

"You gave him an order to say that to everyone, didn't you, Ben?" she asks, getting quickly farther away.

"Maybe," Ben allows as she disappears into a bedroom, shaking her head. Holding up his stack of signs, he tells Micah, "I'm gonna go hang the rest of these up. I guess someone should introduce our new playmates, if they're in residence and all. Are Hunter and Grealey here yet?"

"Not yet," Micah answers. "Follow me. Kyle, make yourself comfy. Lil's gonna hang with you. She'll be right in."

"Groping privileges?"

"*Full* groping privileges."

"Awesome."

"You don't even like girls!" Ben argues, already headed downstairs.

"Ben, it's a party! We're celebrating! It's all on the table!"

All Kyle catches of Ben's grumbled reply is, "Put you on the fucking table," before the rest gets lost as Kyle leaves to go investigate the party possibilities of the study.

A little while later, Kyle has Lilianna helping him mix drinks. Kyle's mp3 player is plugged into the stereo. Loud dubstep thumps from the speakers, making them have to shout over the music. He's busy getting the inside info on Lilianna's female lover, Saoirse, and halfway through drinking a concoction Lilianna says is named Adios Muthafucka when Trace and a hot stranger appear in the doorway.

Guessing by the age and expression of the guy to Trace's left, Kyle figures out who it is before Trace even gets the chance to say, "Kyle, this is Gray."

Lilianna goes to turn down the volume on the stereo.

"Howdy," Kyle says in greeting. "I'm not allowed downstairs. What's proper etiquette in these situations, anyway? Curtsey? A deep bow? Kiss some sacred ring? Let's go with curtsey."

He pretends to lift the sides of an invisible skirt and does a deep curtsey, bowing his head and staying low as he says seriously, "It's an honor, your majesty."

"The fuck are you giving him to drink, Lil?" Trace asks as Kyle straightens and takes another sip of his drink.

"Oh, he's just happy," she says. "Give him a break."

"It's called *Adios Muthafucka*," Kyle explains. "Want one? We can all drink to the passing of those evil shits, let they land like ripe turds in the deepest pit of hell and float there for all eternity."

"Yes, the signs make a lot of sense now," Gray says to Trace.

"See? There's no such thing as overkill with this one," Trace replies. "Benny takes good care of him. Doesn't he, slave?"

"Ben's my hero," Kyle answers with an astonishing level of honesty. So much so, it seems to catch them all off guard.

Good, he thinks. *Let it.*

"See?" Lilianna scolds, putting her arm around Kyle. She smells like spiced apples and cinnamon and, in his slightly intoxicated state, Kyle feels a brief, tangible desire to lick the side of her neck to see if she tastes just as good. "He's fine."

"On your knees, slave," Trace commands gently.

As Lilianna takes the drink from Kyle's hands, he can feel her aggravation on his behalf, and appreciates it. Right away, he goes to his knees, head bowed, hands clasped behind his back, and stays silent.

Gray walks over. Kyle stays very still.

Gray reaches down and lifts the new silver tag dangling from the collar wrapping Kyle's neck, reading the inscription. Then, with the side of a finger, lifts Kyle's chin. Keeping his eyes downcast, Kyle invites the Master Dom's judgment. For a long moment, the man's attention feels like many fingers crawling over Kyle's body, but it's nothing Kyle would ever be worried about. The only thing he has to be concerned about is probably downstairs, wearing a similar collar, maybe bound and kneeling by his Master's side, and even that isn't really a concern, but more a constant, distracting tugging at Kyle's heart.

"Do you plan to ever go back to working at Diadem, Kyle?" Gray asks.

"Maybe if the situation was right, Sir. Right now, Ben's enough for me."

He's seen your videos, a voice whispers, making the hairs at the back of his neck rise at the thought of this Master Dom seeing him in such a state, seeing everything Diadem's Doms did to him over the years.

Briefly, Kyle thinks of the slightly weird emails he's been getting to his account through Diadem. He'd used a fake name in the credits to all of his videos, and it's the fake name that's on the email account, one set up for him automatically as a promotional tool through the website. Most of what Kyle gets in that account is spam or fan mail. Lately, though, he's gotten a few messages that have been addressed in the text to Kyle, not the fake name.

He hasn't told anyone. He doesn't want them to worry when it's probably one of Kyle's many random hookups from before he was with Ben. They probably just recognized him despite the masks and blindfolds, and are out to rile him a little. The messages themselves are normal enough, saying which videos they liked him in the most.

He knows it's stupid and harmless, so he pushes it out of his mind.

"What if you were working as a sub, but *not* at Diadem?" Gray asks.

For the first time all day, Kyle's heart begins to beat harder with wonder, dread and curiosity as to what Gray could have in mind.

Would I sub for another Dom? Someone who wasn't Ben or Gabe, Trace or Micah? Someone I didn't know as well as the back of my hand?

It's a somewhat terrifying thought, to be put at the mercy of someone he doesn't know, and couldn't play to his advantage. The more he thinks about it, the more nervous he becomes, until Gray's thumb slides over his jaw in a soothing manner. Kyle realizes he has closed his eyes, begun to frown.

"Would you consider it?" Gray asks quietly.

"Yes, Sir," Kyle answers, though almost everything in him screams in protest.

"Even though it scares you?"

He can feel his chest rising and falling with each breath. Gray's hand slides back along the side of Kyle's jaw, and Kyle tilts his head, bowing it but tipped to the side so his neck is offered to Gray. It feels like Gray already has him strung up, naked, and spread.

"Yes, Sir."

"Stand."

No sooner has Kyle found his feet, hands still held behind his back, than Gray, inches away, says, "Eyes on me."

The moment Kyle looks directly into Gray's eyes, he feels his touch, gentle, at Kyle's groin, through his pants. His breath catching, Kyle tries and fails to swallow a soft groan, forcing himself to hold Gray's stare, though it takes concerted effort.

"Your Master doesn't have you caged," Gray observes, as Kyle feels Trace and Lilianna watching, listening. "Why?"

"He doesn't need to cage me. He trusts me. I didn't want a cage tonight, Sir."

Gray would cage me, Kyle sees, from the man's expression alone. *Cock cage, anal lock, hood, shackles – the whole shebang.*

With a subtle nod, Kyle is dismissed. Gray turns and leaves with Trace.

Part of Kyle wants to leave, too, and flee to the safety of his own home where only Ben is Kyle's Master. At first he can't move, barely blinks, but then he feels Lilianna wind her arm through his. Her hand is on his chest, feeling his pulse race.

"You okay?" she asks, her breath warm against his cheek.

Am I okay? It takes him a moment to decide.

"Yeah," he nods, relaxing finally.

She passes him his drink and he takes a gulp.

"Dance with me," she asks. "No more drama. We'll just have fun. What do you think?"

"Sure," Kyle grins, gratefully.

―◇―◇―◇―

The evening draws on. Eventually, Micah comes upstairs to check on his wife and lets her, along with Kyle, tempt him into dancing with them. The music pounds with a heavy beat, pulsing under Kyle's skin, filling his head, lungs, muscles, and everything else. Buzzing from the strength of his drink, Kyle easily gets lost in the rhythm. With his thigh fitted between Lilianna's legs and his hand on her ass, they rock, dip and grind against each other. Her arms are slung loosely around his neck. His lips are brushing against hers as Micah enters the room. Rather than stop what they're doing, Kyle simply pauses, waiting.

He doesn't have to wait long. Micah comes right up behind them, fitting himself against Kyle's back. Taking Kyle by the hip, Micah nudges them back into movement with the tempo of the song. His crotch grinds against Kyle's ass and Kyle presses against Lilianna.

When Kyle pants, "Hot," Lilianna draws his shirt off, taking it up over his head. He keeps his arms up even when it's off, twisting a little with the dance, undulating as Micah reaches around to palm Kyle's cock through his jeans and Lilianna pets his now-bare chest.

"Ben says you're fair game, tonight," Micah whispers by Kyle's ear.

"I'm *totally* fair game," Kyle agrees. "Don't worry. I know the rules."

"Bet you do," Lilianna smirks, pulling him down into a kiss as Micah pops open the button on Kyle's fly, slipping a hand inside from behind as they continue dancing. Micah's palm closes up in a gentle squeeze around Kyle's dick and he gasps a little into Lilianna's mouth.

"Easy," she hushes. "We're just dancing, right?"

Micah squeezes harder. Kyle thrusts reflexively into the touch, which hurts but in a wonderful way. Gripping his ass through his jeans and sucking on his lips, Lilianna responds to Micah's touches as much as Kyle does, getting turned on fast just from watching.

Tangling one hand in her long, dark, silken hair, he gasps, his lips brushing over her cheek as Micah pumps him, sometimes hard enough to make him cry out. But they keep dancing. He realizes only after a long while they're not alone, and maybe they haven't been alone for quite some time.

Micah lets go then, turning Kyle to face him. Lilianna goes to the wet bar for another drink, then takes it to the couch only a foot or two away to sit and watch. Still buzzing on the alcohol, and now completely, aching hard, Kyle tries to care that there are now two ridiculously hot, dark-haired guys, whom he doesn't know, standing in the room. One of them goes to sit with Lilianna. The other one, with darker hair, and a dangerously intent look on his face, comes over to Kyle and Micah.

One of Micah's hands cups Kyle's jaw, keeping their eyes on one another as they move back into the dance, swaying and rocking. His other hand, though, gets Kyle's fly open the rest of the way, inching his jeans down. His cock is exposed, jutting up, reddened and stiff between them as Micah thrusts against it, making Kyle grit his teeth because at the same time, the newcomer moves up against Kyle's back, dancing with them, finding the rhythm right away. His hands are on Kyle's bare hip and the back of his shoulder.

"Hey, I'm Kyle," Kyle says breathlessly. "I'm not allowed downstairs."

"You been bad, Kyle?" he's asked. The British accent makes him smile.

"Fuck, that's hot," he moans. To answer the question the only way he knows how, Kyle says, "My Master protects me."

"Look at me," Micah orders.

As soon as he has Kyle's gaze, Micah rocks firmly against his bare erection, hard enough to make Kyle whine. The newcomer tugs on Kyle's collar. Lips skate over the side of his neck.

"Who's your Master?" the British one asks.

"Ben."

"Ben says you're fair game, right, Kyle?" Micah says he guides Kyle's cock completely free of his pants and the British one slides Kyle's jeans down farther in back to bare his ass, too.

"Yes, Sir. Fuck yes." As the dark-haired, grey-eyed newcomer gropes Kyle's ass and Micah pulls a condom from his pocket, Kyle says, "Just dancing right?"

"Right, baby," Lilianna giggles. While watching the action closely, she's also in low conversation with the other one, with brown eyes and a less threatening look about him.

"You calling the shots, here? Tracey know about that?" the British one asks.

"He does, and I am, isn't that right, Kyle?"

"Yes, Sir," Kyle sighs as Micah starts to roll the condom onto Kyle.

"Safeword?"

"Varese," Kyle answers.

The British one slides a finger through the crack of Kyle's ass, making a sound of appreciation when Kyle makes a nervous half-moan, half-purr.

"Fuck," Kyle breathes, letting the British one take control of their dancing, moving Kyle with him as Micah slides down to kneel in front of Kyle's groin. "Fuck me. Fuck...."

Micah swallows Kyle's dick and the British one rocks, hard, against his ass. Fingers fondle at Kyle's nipples, scratching lightly over his chest. They keep Kyle's hips rolling in time to the beat of the music, even though he's buried in Micah's throat and gasping, clutching the back of Micah's head, clawing at his dark hair.

"Please," Kyle begs.

The new one rubs Kyle's ass again, pulling his cheeks apart

Forgive Us

with a hand, fingering his hole. When Kyle hums, two fingers enter him. Micah sucks him harder.

"Fuck," Kyle moans, knowing they're coming right up against the rules, knowing, too, what he needs to do next. He draws in a deep breath, then yells as loud as he can, "*Ben!* Micah's sucking my dick and one of the cute British ones is here too—"

"I'm Jack," he hears from the one fingering his ass.

"Jack! Jack is here!" Kyle yells. "And he's really fucking hot and can I come?! BEN! Ben, can I come?!"

Lilianna and the one on the couch—who must be Jan—are snickering. If Kyle expected Micah and Jack to slow down or ease off until Ben has replied, they don't. When Kyle hears footsteps pounding up the stairs and coming down the hall, he's breathing hard, dizzy, and closer to orgasm by the second.

"What the holy fuck is going on in here?" Ben demands as he walks into the room.

"I thought he was pretty descriptive, actually," Jack says, moving his two fingers in slow, long strokes that trigger Kyle's gland every time, making him quiver and writhe.

Ben takes a look around the room, his gaze sweeping over Kyle appraisingly. Then he shrugs, "Yeah, you're good. Permission granted."

"Sweet. Thanks, Ben!" Kyle calls, reaching back for a handful of Jack's hair as Jack chuckles beside his ear.

A moment later, Ben has left the room, but Kyle glimpses another form in the darkened hallway, keeping their distance but watching.

"Hmm, Ben left," Lilianna observes. "Guess that means he's not in charge, now, doesn't it? So, what do you think, Kyle? Should Micah let you come? I feel like you'd owe us if he did."

But Kyle doesn't even care, he rides Micah's tongue, thrusting faster, getting off on having all of their attention on him. Jack slips another finger in and Kyle just widens his stance, pushed closer to the edge, willing to do anything to cross over.

"Please," Kyle moans.

"Jan," Jack beckons. "Don't miss out on the fun."

"I'm good here, thanks," Jan replies.

"Yeah? Could be better than good, though. A *lot* better."

Micah pulls off and Kyle sees him look up, past Kyle at Jack.

"Master Micah, how's about we give innocent ol' vanilla Jan there a taste of what he's missing?"

"Sure. I like the sound of that," Micah smiles, standing. "What do you have in mind, Jack?"

"Jack," Jan argues. "Gray said—"

"Just a kiss, Jan," Jack coaxes. He rubs over Kyle's prostate again, making him thrust against air and gasp, frowning. "Kyle's harmless, see?"

"I just don't think—" Jan starts.

"Stop *thinking*, Jan," Jack sighs. When Micah stands aside, Jack removes his fingers and guides Kyle forward. Kyle lets himself be moved up to the couch, so he's standing astride Jan's legs. Jack tugs Kyle's pants down the rest of the way and waits for Kyle to step out of them. Naked, he feels a hand wrap his hip from behind and another flatten itself on his back, guiding him forward again.

"Jack," Jan groans, but doesn't say anything else, just stares at Kyle's body, groping it with his eyes as Jack manhandles him onto Jan's lap. A little reluctantly, Jan reaches up to touch Kyle's jaw. Frowning, closing his eyes, Kyle responds to the touch with more goosebumps and a shiver.

"Kiss him, slave," Jack says, then slips his fingers back up Kyle's ass, provoking a small cry.

Leaning slightly forward, bowing his back as Jack's touches bombard Kyle with stimulation, Kyle holds on to Jan's shoulders. They're lips brush together. Kyle chases in for more, getting off on Jan's tentativeness. Jack's hand is in Kyle and on his back, so he's startled when someone else wraps their fist around his dick and begins to stroke. Moaning into Jan's mouth, Kyle figures out it's him and thrusts.

Jan's other hand caresses over Kyle's throat, down his sternum, down his abs. Caught between them, riding Jack's hand and Jan's as well, Kyle moves, rocking forward and back, making soft cries and gasping. Moments later, he climaxes, coming into the condom with a shudder. Jan tongues him deeper and Jack feeds a third finger into his ass, understanding where this is all headed. The thought just makes his hips twitch harder, fucking Jan's hand on the comedown.

"Damn, that's sweet," Jack says by Kyle's ear.

Kyle knows who it must be, out there in the hall. He's not stupid. So, when Jack pulls Kyle to lean back a little and Micah is there, getting the condom off and wiping him down with a cloth that Lilianna passes to him, Kyle only surrenders to whatever comes next.

"Lay him down on the couch, ass over the edge," Micah says to Jack and Jan.

In a blur of hands moving him, guiding him, he finds himself lying down on his back, with his bottom up and hanging over the edge of the couch's arm. Micah hands Jack something.

"B-ben," Kyle gasps, remembering as Micah pulls Kyle's legs back with both hands, exposing his ass to Jack who's rolling on a condom. "Need permission. Ben!"

"It's okay. He's here," Micah tells Kyle. Kyle glances to the doorway, and Ben is there. Gray is still there too, farther back.

"Jan, you in?" Jack asks. Kyle sees Jan glance to the hallway, like he needs his own permission.

"Yeah. I'm in," Jan agrees taking another condom from Lilianna.

"Breathe," Micah instructs, as Kyle's breathing gets out of control. Lilianna turns up the volume on the stereo and that makes it easier. It lets his sharp cry get washed out as Jack enters him. There are only two people in the whole world who have had Kyle the way Jack is having him, but maybe it's better to let it be less sacred. Kyle realizes the safeword isn't even a temptation as Jack's cock slides deeper. Kyle just wants *more*. Jack is the one holding Kyle's legs now, pushing them back as he claims his ass. But that's not all. Jan is settling on his knees on the couch by Kyle's head.

Kyle opens wide and reaches back to hold Jan's hip when Jan moves to take Kyle's mouth. Keeping his head tilted back, letting Jan slide into his throat as Jack thrusts farther up Kyle's ass, Kyle can't deny how good it feels to give himself over to them, even if they aren't from their trusted little circle. Ben is there. And Gray is there. Kyle feels safe. Jack tugs back, pushes in and Jan does the same. Kyle purrs and Jan moans as the sound vibrates up his shaft.

"That's it," Micah says, watching on, still the one giving the orders. "Don't hold him down. He's not going anywhere. You okay, slave?"

Kyle whimpers sharply on the next firm thrust from Jack who pushes his legs back farther and rides his ass with steady, rapid movements, where Jan goes slower, but deeper. Kyle gives Micah a thumbs up sign, his cock trying to stiffen again already.

"Dancing, my ass," Ben mutters. Kyle just barely hears him under the blasting music, meant to drown out his cries, most likely to spare Darrek, downstairs, from having to hear them. As soon as the thought of Darrek occurs to him, Kyle lets it go, lets him go, all over again, wishing only that they could talk later, maybe, about all of this and laugh. It would be like old times.

Instead, Kyle grips Jan's hip, pushes down into Jack's thrusts and basks in the decadence of total, tantalizing, wonderful submission.

-⭕-⭕-⭕-

Kyle lies on the couch with his head in Ben's lap. Jan is dancing with Lilianna. Jack has vanished for the moment. First, he'd gone into the bathroom across the hall, but Kyle saw him slip out, going in the direction of the stairs. He hasn't been back yet.

"Not to slam your powers of seduction or anything, but I think Jack did it—or, well, did *you*—to piss off Gray," Ben says quietly to Kyle. "The whole thing with getting Jan involved, letting it go as far as it did…."

"Yeah, I kind of figured. I could see him out in the hall—Gray."

"And he was *pissed*," Ben says slyly from the side of his mouth, stressing the last word. "It's one of the reasons I came in here. Wanted to get you clear should the prick explode or something."

"You still don't like him, huh?" Kyle asks, looking up at Ben.

Ben shrugs, gives a non-committal quirk of his lips, too. "I don't know. He's really… British. The stiff-upper-lippy, God Save the Queen kind. There's just something about him. I mean, we talked. The dude knew way more about me than I was comfortable with and the whole thing felt like a test, like there was a clear right way and wrong way to say everything. Plus, he *kills* people. The whole thing rubs me the wrong way. Seeing him with Trace, how cozy they are when they talk, makes me want to do something to piss them both off."

"So I guess that's why you let Jack and Jan fuck me?"

"One of many reasons. You didn't seem to hate it."

"Yeah. God, that was awful," Kyle jokes. Taking a deep inhale, letting it out slowly, he stretches his legs and says with a yawn, "Now I just want a nap."

"Kitty's all worn out," Ben smiles, stroking Kyle's hair. "Go ahead. Gives me a reason to avoid the cockfight that's likely happening downstairs."

"You really think Gray would do something if he decided he doesn't like us?"

Ben thinks it over, then answers, "Let's just hope he decides he likes us, shall we?"

Chapter 24
Darrek, Collared

"Good, here he is," Gabriel sighs, closing the door behind Ben as he walks into the office on the first floor of Micah and Lilianna's place. Voices echo down the hall from the kitchen where everyone seems to be hanging out. Darrek hadn't gotten a very good look around when they'd come inside through the back door, since he's collared and under a very strict set of behavioral guidelines — the major ones being to speak only when spoken to, eyes down, and address all Doms with the utmost respect. He's heard many voices he recognizes and senses a lot of people around him but mostly he stays focused on the tops of his sneakers and the feel of Gabriel's hand on his back. "Dare, you can speak freely now."

"Thank you, Sir," he murmurs, tracking Ben's movements from his seat behind the desk. Gabriel and Ben are standing over him and it makes Darrek's instinct to kneel kick in, hard, but Gabriel ordered him to sit, so he'll sit.

"What's up?" Ben asks, folding his arms, giving nothing away.

Darrek glances over at Gabriel one more time, just to be sure, but Gabriel only gestures to Ben expectantly, saying, "It's okay."

"Okay," Darrek starts, drawing in a deep breath. He asks Ben, "How is he? How's he dealing with… you know?"

Ben doesn't answer right away. He seems to take inventory of the fact that they're in a closed room, apart from the party, of Darrek's collar, the look on his face, and the tone of his voice. But that's just Darrek's best guess. He's never asked Ben directly about Kyle's well-being before, but there's a first for everything, especially with Jerry's lifeless body lying somewhere, stinking of embalming fluid.

That's the part Darrek wishes he could see, the proof his father is really gone. The rest of it he has no interest in. He imagines it'll be a big parade of make-believe as nearly everyone who knew Jerry Grealey talks about him fondly, as if he was one of the good guys, a good dad, and a good man.

The longer Ben delays, the more awkwardly Darrek stares up at him, feeling outmanned, outmatched in a house full of men who would love to tie him down and test his limits. He scratches at the arm of the chair, swiveling slightly, wondering about some of the broken picture frames around the office.

"Well, I guess he's kind of being a little shit about it all, actually," Ben says, finally. "He's acting like it's great and no big deal, but he was shaken up by the news. In my humble opinion, it's left him feeling adrift or something, like he doesn't have anything to tie all of his worries to anymore. Jerry was one of the biggest factors in his life for a long fucking time, and now... It means Kyle doesn't have to worry about your safety as much anymore. That might be the worst part for him."

"So what are you gonna do?"

"Keep him focused on moving forward. You should do the same."

"But he's—" the words stick in his throat. "He's okay?"

He can't look at Ben. He hears footsteps, feels a hand land heavily on his shoulder.

"Breathe, slave," Gabriel commands. Darrek blows out all of his air and takes another breath.

"He's okay," Ben tells him, giving Darrek's shoulder a squeeze. "Are *you* okay?"

"Tell him," Gabriel urges, his expression hard and unyielding. He's been in full Dominant mode most of the time ever since their new friends from overseas showed up, leaving Darrek feeling constantly turned on, and happily in a completely submissive mindset. Running around in the park with Jan and Sierra had been amazing, reminding him how life could still be good, how he can still laugh and have a great time, despite everything else. Darrek had made up his mind about what he needed to do shortly after they'd said goodbye to Jan and Jack, though he only spoke up once they'd gotten to the party and he was suddenly surrounded by the most fearsome, confident, capable people Darrek has ever known.

Gabriel doesn't like it, though. That doesn't mean he'll stop Darrek. He'll just use it as even more reason to keep Darrek on a short leash, mentally, physically, and emotionally, but Darrek is absolutely fine with that. Gabriel, he can handle. It's the rest that worries him.

Ben is still next to him, towering over him, the hand on his shoulder keeping his ass firmly planted in the chair's seat.

"I want to call my mom, and tell her to stop trying to contact me."

"What, *now*?" Ben blurts.

"Th-they've been calling. They won't stop. I'm worried they'll come up here and track me down. A while back, I made Gabe promise to not get involved so I could try to do this for myself. If I just tell her to back off, I feel like I'll finally be able to relax. I want to be able to relax and stop being so afraid. It sucks. It's been poisoning everything and I'm sick of it."

He can sense Gabriel and Ben communicating without words, over Darrek's head, but it doesn't matter. They can't stop him if he wants to call.

"You think someone from your family's been trying to get in your house to see you?" Ben asks.

"I-I don't know. Maybe? The police said it was probably a false alarm, since nothing was stolen and there was no sign of forced entry. Kyle was with me last time I called home, which is why I wanted you here, instead," he tells Ben. "I refuse to do this at our house. And I can't ask Gabriel to be the only one supporting me, because he's stressed too. I feel safe here. Everyone I care about is here. If I'm gonna do this, it has to be now."

"Breathe, slave," Gabriel says sternly, as Darrek starts to feel jittery, panicked. Ben starts to gently massage Darrek's shoulders and it feels really nice. Darrek tries to blow out the stress, to calm his mind.

"Sit over here, so he can see you," Ben tells Gabriel. After Gabriel rolls a chair closer, and Ben turns Darrek's chair to face where Gabriel sits in his, Ben says, "Give him the phone. You know the number?"

"Yeah," Gabriel frowns, picking up the receiver for Micah's desk phone, then punching the buttons in sequence. Ben keeps kneading the muscles of Darrek's neck and shoulders. It's pleasant and distracting enough to stave off a tidal wave of anxiety, making Darrek feel intensely grateful for Ben's presence. After Gabriel hands Darrek the receiver, he keeps his hand close, resting on the desk's edge like he's ready to yank the phone away from Darrek and take over if this goes badly. His eyes lock onto Darrek's. "Short and simple. Direct. Confident. *No apologies*. Got it?"

Darrek nods, hearing the ringing, wondering if she'll pick up or not.

"Hello?" A female voice answers.

Darrek sits up straighter. Gabriel puts his left hand on Darrek's thigh.

"It's Darrek, Mom."

"Oh my Lord!" she exclaims. "I can't believe it! Do you know how hard we've been trying to reach you?! Do you have any idea—"

"Mom," he cuts in, keeping his tone of voice firm, giving no leeway. "I know Jerry's dead—"

"*Jerry*? He was your father!"

"Listen to me. Please. I have something to say and I need you to let me say it without interrupting or questioning me." He lets it breathe, and she doesn't say anything else, so he continues. "I won't be there for the funeral, or the wake, or any of it. I need everyone to stop calling me. Don't come looking for me. Don't try to contact me in any way. I'm asking this of you and Steven and everyone else in the family. I'm dealing with this in my own way. Gabriel is helping me through it, and I'm seeing a therapist, so you have no reason to worry. I'm not ready to talk to you about what happened between me and Jerry, and if I ever get to the point where I am ready, I'll contact *you*. Please respect my decision. That's all."

"Darrek," his mother gasps, speechless.

"Goodbye, Mom. Love you."

He hands the phone to Gabriel, who ends the call.

You're going to prove your sin and show God that you are indeed a deviant and a pervert and a homosexual. Take your penance or prove your sin.

Ben is holding Darrek up. Darrek feels like he's sinking through the floor, though, and can't see, can't speak another word. The pressure builds in his lungs until they burn as much as his eyes. It's all a wash. He can feel them—Ben and Gabriel—but he's gone. He's somewhere else.

I can hold your hand, right here, and make it so that you are unable to touch Kyle with these fingers in unclean ways. Temptation will be removed, praise Jesus. Or, you can perform your filthy acts, there on that bed, and choose to let God Himself be your judge.

Hands hold his face. Another set of hands brace his chest, holding him to the chair.

Submit yourselves for the Lord's sake!

I'm hurting him, Daddy!

"Breathe in through your nose. Now. Good," Gabriel commands.

It's okay, Dare. I know you have to.

"Blow it out through your mouth. All of it. Hold. Hold it."

God! I chose God!

Prove it, then. Take off his pants.

"Okay, in through your nose again. You're safe. Nothing is going to happen to you, do you hear me? Answer."

Darrek nods, manages a tear-choked, "Yes."

A small, breaking voice whispers, *It's okay, Dare. I know you have to.*

With awful, pained whines, he clutches the chair's arms as Gabriel grips the sides of his face.

"Look at me, Dare," he urges. "Look at my eyes. Look at where you are. You're safe. We love you. You're okay. It's done."

Ben is massaging his shoulders again. His fingers scratch up Darrek's neck to his scalp. Combing through Darrek's long hair, he massages his head, then rubs back down to his shoulders again.

The voices fade back. The longer he looks into Gabriel's eyes, the quieter it gets until all that's left is the here and now.

"That's it. Keep taking deep breaths. You did it, baby. It's done. Just breathe."

Gabriel puts a tissue in his hand, and Darrek uses it to dry his nose and eyes.

With a ferocious breed of determination, looking like he'd take on the world just to keep Darrek protected, Gabriel demands, "Who takes care of you?"

"You do." It sounds weak and sort of pathetic. He can't believe how good Ben is at massage, though. And the improbability of enjoying that, in that moment, makes Darrek want to smile, and that's good. His eyes roll up as Ben goes back to massaging his scalp. Breathing gets easier.

"Feels nice, doesn't it?" Gabriel asks.

"Yes, Sir," Darrek grunts, trying not to moan with both relief and pleasure. Ben's fingers make small circles at Darrek's temples. They stroke along the edge of his jaw, back down the sides of his neck, over his shoulders and down his arms. Focusing on the touches, anchoring to them, to how nice they feel, Darrek begins to calm down.

"Who do you trust?"

"You."

"Who's in charge?"

"You."

"What's the *only* thing you have to do?"

"Trust. Respect. Obey."

Gabriel's mouth is on him then, kissing deeply, passionately, slowly.

When they break, the hair at the back of Darrek's head is pulled sharply, forcing his head back. Then Ben is kissing him, just as deeply, almost angrily, and Darrek can't hold in the moan any longer. Kissing Ben back, letting him take as much as he wants, it zaps the rest of Darrek's fear, and the rest of his fight, too. It's forgiveness and permission, love and absolution. It's everything Darrek has wanted and everything he needs.

No sooner is his mouth released, than Gabriel is giving more commands.

"On your knees, slave. Do it."

He slips to the wooden floor, his kneecaps connecting.

"Take his shirt off," Gabriel tells Ben. "You bring it?"

"Yeah. It's right here."

Ben passes Gabriel something. Then Ben is pulling Darrek's long-sleeved shirt up and over his head, leaving him bare-chested.

"The shoes and socks, too," Gabriel says as he ties a blindfold onto Darrek. The black cloth blocks his sight completely.

"You had your favor, slave," Gabriel warns. "Now you're gonna pay me back. We're going to rejoin the party now, but you'll be chained. Whether you get to keep your clothes on or not is up to me. Whether anyone touches you, *where* they touch you, *how* they touch you, is all up to me. What's your safeword?"

"Tundra," Darrek answers. A hand grabs tight hold of his crotch through the jeans, and he has no idea if it's Ben or Gabriel, but whoever it is, they can feel that he's hard. He grunts, face flushing hot, body thrumming.

"You want it?"

"Fuck yes, Sir. Please."

There's a tug on his collar. After he feels tension, he figures out it's a leash that's been clipped to it.

"Good. Now *crawl*."

Chapter 25
At the Mercy of the Masters

Ever since he was sitting at his computer, knowing what he was about to do to himself psychologically by watching the old videos of Moira, life for Micah has been surreal. Trace's tender, devoted side—something he rarely if ever shows anyone else—has come out in full force, replacing for Micah much of the love lost in other facets of his life. In as many ways as he's been abandoned, it doesn't seem to matter anymore, because Trace isn't leaving. He's a constant. In contrast, Micah has also become more aware of the distance that's always there, between himself and his wife. Back when Lilianna was seducing their babysitters, it all seemed so exciting and enchanting. He loved the open honesty of his sex life in his marriage. Now that he's hurt her by secretly submitting to someone besides her, someone Lilianna thought was only a friend with benefits, it's the honesty of his sex life that's causing the biggest problems. Now they have official representatives from the Master's Circle, dissecting Diadem and its employees, examining in detail all of the ways they've all fucked up. Every relationship within their circle is being scrutinized, but Trace's relationships most of all. Sometimes, when Gray or Jack is watching him, Micah feels like a specimen pinned to a board—not a human, just a case study. It's all like some weird dream caused by the tranquilizer Trace injected him with. Maybe he's still lying there, on the bed in the downstairs guest suite, waiting to wake up.

In the meantime, Darrek is shackled to a D bolt in a rafter of the kitchen, over by the far wall in the eating area. There's a clear view of that spot from the rest of the kitchen, but no view from outside, through the windows lining the wall. The bolt had been installed for Micah and used by Lilianna, then Trace, to keep Micah restrained while allowing them to dine or prepare food. Because the kitchen is so vast and open, it was always a heady experience to be helpless there, in the heart of the house.

Of course, Darrek has been wearing a blindfold since he crawled in, so he can't see all of the people lingering nearby, watching him squirm. He's another one of Diadem's case studies, too, helpless to the poking and prodding. Micah is sure Gray will be stroking all of Darrek's vulnerabilities before long. He can't even hear them, because Gabriel has put a set of headphones over Darrek's ears, connected wirelessly to an mp3 player. The music drowns out the low voices in conversation around him. Micah would bet Darrek can sense everyone, though. It's probably a prickling over his skin, a tingle at the back of his neck, creeping down his spine, causing his balls to draw up protectively. As someone who knows the highs that come from submitting to exposure and stimulation, Micah knows that what Darrek is feeling must be incredible.

Darrek is much taller than Micah, so the chain his wrists are shackled to doesn't pull his arms up as much as it usually does Micah's. Darrek's arms are bent, held together in front of him. The only piece of clothing on him is his jeans, and even those are unfastened, hanging from his hips. Trace is there, with his hand inside Darrek's opened jeans, tugging at a steady pace. Gabriel is behind Darrek, his fingers lightly stroking along the center of his back or playing in his hair, letting his slave know there is, without question, more than one person attending him.

It's clear Darrek isn't used to situations like this, but that only seems to be drawing the Doms in that much closer as they catch the scent of their willing, weakened, anxious prey. Darrek's nervousness is palpable from across the room in the way he draws up on his toes when the stimulation draws to a peak, or when Trace's hand twists just so. Then Darrek's head rolls on his shoulders, forward to hide his face behind hair, back to let out a deep groan. Glistening with sweat, breathless, wanting, his muscle-bound form is absolutely captivating to behold. Micah would switch places with him in a heartbeat, to be that cared for, and so delirious with pleasure.

Master Dom Gray is there, only a few steps away. Micah has been constantly hyperaware of Gray's presence at all times since he arrived. He's not only Trace's ex, he's the man who finished what they started with Harry, in addition to being the representative of the Master's Circle, a man with such connections, wealth and access, Micah can't really fathom it all. It's not quite jealousy, per se, that he feels toward Gray. Micah can't put his finger on it. He just knows it feels right to focus on making Gray, and Gray's companions, comfortable, as well as to treat him with the utmost respect and to keep a very close eye on him. It's been a little exhausting, being constantly ready for anything. It's been going okay so far, but just over the past day or so, Gray's tension has ratcheted up. He's unhappy, on edge. Some of that is because of things which have happened, in private, between Trace and Gray. Some of it isn't. Micah's greatest fear is that Gray will be pushed too far and lash out at Trace, the one out of all of them who's supposed to be in charge of things. Or maybe that was Gray's plan all along—to come see what they've been up to without the MC's supervision, and to crack the whip to get them all in line, or to make an example of Trace so the rest of them know not to go out of bounds again.

The whole situation makes Micah restless, quiet, and more comfortable playing the part of Trace's submissive than stepping up as one of Diadem's Doms for hire. He'd slipped, once, upstairs with Kyle, being seduced by Ben's permission and Kyle's willingness. Now, Micah thinks it was a mistake, because Jack and Jan were involved. Now Gray seems angrier than ever.

Chancing a glance at the man from his seat at a stool along the counter, Micah asks, "Can I get you anything?"

Gray approaches and brings Jack along with him. Gray takes the stool next to Micah, but only after handcuffing Jack to one of the legs. Jack kneels there, the silver on his wrists gleaming, his eyes focused like a hawk on Gabriel and what Gabriel is currently orchestrating with Darrek on the other side of the room. He doesn't talk back to Gray, or fight him. He's passive. Micah wonders what happened in the interval between when Gray saw Jack with Kyle, and when Gray brought Jack downstairs to be Gray's pet for the rest of the night. They had slipped off into one of the other rooms together, that much Micah knows. But that's all.

"No, thank you, Micah," Gray says, sitting by Micah's side, looking him over. There's plenty of food set out for everyone to help themselves to, and a bar set up for drinks, should anyone be inclined. There's also music playing, though of a softer sort than what's still playing in Kyle's sanctuary upstairs.

It's odd to have a moment alone with Gray. Though there are plenty of others around, none of them are paying Micah or Gray any mind at the moment. Darrek is the show.

"There are a few things I've wanted to say to you," Micah starts.

"Is that so?" Gray asks, sipping coffee.

Another glance around the room shows Gabriel passing something to Trace in a closed fist. With a wicked grin, Trace examines what he has, then steps closer to Darrek. Soon after, Trace's hand and the mystery object, vanish inside Darrek's gaping jeans, Darrek cries out, his knees bending, arms straining as they take his weight. A muscle in Jack's jaw flexes and he shifts slightly, pulling at the cuffs, coming up onto his knees. Gray keeps him anchored, though. He's not going anywhere.

"I won't pretend to know what goes on between you and Trace," Micah says quietly. "But I can tell the way it's been going. Clearly, you're aware of the facts behind what you walked into here. You're a man who does his research. But do you truly understand? *Can* you understand? *He saved my life.*" Micah remembers the pain, so all-encompassing, so final, and Trace pulling him out of it, with no selfish motivation at all. "More than once. He takes care of Lily when I can't. He's a damn good man."

"You think I don't know?" Gray asks from behind the rim of his cup.

That's when Micah begins to suspect maybe there is nothing he can say which will make any difference. Maybe it's all futile.

With a feeling like surrender, a sagging in his shoulders and his hopes, Micah asks, "What was he like, before?"

There's always been an air around Trace like life has scraped away all of the extra layers to his identity, and what's left behind is pure, undiluted, and brazen. There's no sign of masks, or lies, and no hidden intentions. He just is. Micah loves that about him, admiring the honesty so much, all he can do is put himself at the mercy of it, over and over again.

But after meeting Gray, Micah has begun to suspect Trace used to be different, that it was a process which made him who he is, and a painful one at that.

"He smiled less," is the first thing Gray says, gazing over at the man with his silver-streaked hair, the sound of his deep, throaty chuckle temporarily filling the room. Darrek gasps harshly, then whines, but Gabriel's hands are on him then, one wrapped around his chest, the other tucked down between their bodies where he's pressed to Darrek's back, and Darrek moans. Micah begins to suspect that's all Gray will say, until he adds, "He was... wilder. More wary, even though he was a hell of a lot younger. And yet, he was much more disciplined."

Micah sees it then, in Gray's eyes. Gray still loves Trace, in his own way, though he may never admit it. And Micah can't decide if it's good or bad that there are feelings behind Gray's actions. After all, love is the most brutal force in the whole world.

"Whatever you're intending," Micah begins, searching for the right words, "it has to count for something that we're all closer than family, thanks to him. *He* made us family. He *earned* our loyalty, and trust. He saved us. All of us. Sure, he's made mistakes. So have I. So have you. We *all* do. But he knows when he's wrong, and owns up to it. Everything he does is with love. What more do you want? How could you expect more than that?"

Gray just stares at Micah, giving nothing away.

"I would do *anything* for him," Micah whispers, meaning it entirely, holding Gray's gaze until he understands.

With a nod, letting his gaze drift to Darrek, Gray says, "Good."

When Gabriel and Ben take over the handling of Darrek, Trace goes outside for a smoke and Micah is able to slip out through the front door, undetected. He circles around the house to find Trace. Over by a towering oak in the backyard, just one of many shadows, moving in the dark, Trace draws Micah in and pushes him up against the thick trunk, kissing him breathless. Their moans slip away on the wind. The tree is between them and the house, but the absence of light in that corner of the yard conceals them as well.

"Think he's still watching us somehow, right now?" Micah asks.

"He's always watching, love."

"You don't mind?"

"Got used to people watching a long time ago. At least he's got good intentions, and sees clearly," Trace replies in a whisper, lips skimming over Micah's mouth. "How'd Kyle taste?"

"Young," Micah smiles.

Trace laughs softly.

"Cocky," Micah adds.

Trace laughs harder.

"How's Darrek?"

"Wet as fuck," Trace says in a low growl, nipping at Micah's lip. "Just makes me wanna get my hands on you, though."

"Even if we won't have privacy?"

"*Especially* because we won't have privacy," Trace says with a wicked chuckle. "I know you, love. You get off hard on submitting while intimidated. Tell me it ain't true."

"It ain't true," Micah tells him, doing his best to sound convincing and sincere, but breaking into a chuckle, fast, when Trace starts laughing again. "Hey, just because I like to do the whole cop/criminal rape role play thing with you doesn't mean—*ahh!*"

"Shh," Trace chuckles, pressing his fingers to Micah's lips to quiet him. The hand grabbing Micah by the balls loosens its grip. "I got my gear in the truck, y'know," Trace tempts in a whisper, trailing the tip of his tongue over the edge of Micah's earlobe. "You could try to cuff me again, read me my rights, and we'll see where the billy club ends up."

"You fucker. I *know* where it'll end up." Micah shakes his head and Trace kisses his helpless smile away until he moans.

"You want it, don't you?" Trace whispers by the shell of Micah's ear. "Spread 'em wide, lemme slip my fat club up your tight, virgin, cop ass. I'll work it loose for ya, before I fuck it hard, then I'll call my partner in, and let him take a turn ridin' you, too."

"Fuck yeah," Micah pants, rocking against Trace's steadily kneading hand, his dick so hard he aches. "You're killin' me."

"Just a little longer. It'll be worth the wait," Trace promises.

"You always are," Micah tells him, pulling him in for one more kiss.

They only have a few minutes. Micah knows he's needed back in the house to help ensure everything and everyone is taken care of, but there's also the issue of Lilianna. She's been mostly keeping upstairs but, now and then, she comes looking for Micah, like she suspects he's off doing exactly what he is in sneaking off with Trace, right under her nose. She's an intelligent person, one of the smartest Micah knows, actually, and he knows she hates to be made a fool of.

Micah had probably been in the wrong when he'd embarrassed her in front of Trace by telling her about his collaring the way he had, but there was so much resentment built up in him by then, he knew something had been bound to happen.

Trace growls and rips open Micah's fly, almost splitting the seams as he forces the fabric out of the way and pulls Micah's stiffened cock and heavy balls free. Gasping, wincing as Trace momentarily keeps the tension on his genitals at its limit, giving Micah the gift of pain to drown himself in while they kiss, Micah's thoughts roam.

He loves Lilianna. He's just angry with her choices and the way things have been working between them. Being angry doesn't mean he wants to end their marriage. The thought of losing her for real, forever, terrifies Micah. It makes him feel like someone's just shoved him out of a plane and he's falling through thin air with no parachute.

Trace strokes Micah's cock with one hand, yanking down, hard, on his balls with the other. Micah's knees threaten to give out. Grunting, eyes rolling up, he feels the urge to thrust get lost in the ache from the tension and pressure on his balls.

"I don't want Gray to hurt you," Micah rasps, chasing a fear, reacting to instinct.

Trace lets go to caress him everywhere, and it's intoxicatingly un-careful, his hands kneading, scratching, rubbing over Micah's chest, down his side, over his ass, along his upper thigh. Trace's hand wraps behind Micah's right thigh, tugging his leg up, kissing him with an angry scowl. Moaning, when Trace releases Micah's lips and bites at the ridge of his jaw, the side of his neck, all Micah wants is more, or to keep going farther into the dark, where no one else can find them.

"Don't want Lily to hurt *you*," Trace counters, eyes blazing. He grinds against Micah's bare cock, and Micah groans through clenched teeth at how hard Trace's dick is. Gripping a handful of Trace's hair, Micah pulls him in closer, trying to keep him there.

"I deserve it, though," Micah confesses.

"So do I, love," Trace sighs, and Micah could swear he hears a hint of a British accent, but that has to be his imagination taking over.

"I want you," Micah begs, when Trace's passion seems to wane, his gaze roaming over to the house beyond them.

Trace pulls Micah's pants back up, tucking him away again and closing his fly, frowning in concentration. "Look, whatever ends up happening in there," he says, nodding to the house, "I'm *with you*. Ain't going anywhere. You trust me?"

"Yes, Sir," Micah nods, caressing Trace's neck, combing his fingers through his thick beard. "More than I trust Lily. That's the bitch of it."

"Ain't that the truth," Trace murmurs. "No matter what happens from here on out, Mic, it doesn't change how I feel about you, or how much you mean to me. Okay?"

The words don't sound like the Trace he knows at all, and that terrifies Micah, chilling him to the bone. The look on Trace's face is even worse, portending doom.

"All I need in this world is family. *You're* my family, Micah, and I love you," Trace whispers, kissing him gently, tenderly.

Micah sighs, tearing up. Trace wipes the tears away before they can fall.

"We'll be okay," Trace promises, sounding so different, it hurts worse than anything Micah has felt yet. It's a sign that maybe Trace hasn't been as honest as Micah thought he was being. But if he can't trust Trace, who can he trust? "Come on."

Trace goes in through the back. His thoughts and emotions in chaos, Micah circles back around to the front again, taking his time. When he opens the front door, Lilianna is there, at the bottom of the steps, waiting for him. She walks over, wearing a chilly smile and says, "Can't you even have the decency to wait until I'm done trying to entertain *your* guests, before sneaking off to suck his cock and laugh at me together?"

"Well, you know all about sneaking off, don't you, Lil?" Micah retorts quietly, through the sting of accusation and anger. He's too upset about Trace's implications to be as careful as he should with Lilianna.

With a pained laugh, she shakes her head, glances away.

"I have *always* been honest about Saoirse. I *always* asked for your consent first. I have *always* put you first, before *everyone* else. They all know, don't they? All of Diadem knows how stupid I've been, thinking you were just a *Dom* to them."

He doesn't reply. He can't.

"Jesus," she breathes, looking so wounded, all he wants is to hold her and apologize, but she already feels so far away.

"Lily," he starts, not knowing what he could ever say to her now.

"No, don't worry," she says, turning from him and heading back toward the stairs. "I'll be out of your hair soon."

Gabriel knows Jack has been paying attention to every single move he's made for nearly an hour now, ever since Gray brought him down like the well-trained sub Gabriel knows he is. The scrutiny keeps Gabriel on his toes.

The blindfold, the headphones, the positioning and control of every single thing Darrek is aware of has been carefully orchestrated by Gabriel. Darrek hasn't seen Ben's signs about Kyle, bearing his photo and a stark warning that if Kyle is seen downstairs to alert Ben, Trace, or Micah instantly. He hasn't heard Kyle's moans and cries from upstairs. Darrek doesn't even know for certain that Kyle is in the building, though maybe he can guess.

Together but separate, both Darrek and Kyle have gotten to enjoy the party without needless stress about confronting each other. Kyle, for damn sure, has been enjoying himself. And now Darrek is too. Gabriel can see it in the slacked nature of his mouth, the way the sweat trickles over his body, the way he tilts his hips into every little touch he's given, making soft, pleading noises he can't even hear himself make—Darrek is one stroke away from orgasm, riding the knife's edge. Gabriel intends to make it last for *hours*.

Ben and Kyle are upstairs, as is Lilianna, who Gabriel suspects is getting a little stressed out over the whole hosting ordeal, especially when she's hosting a houseful of men with all sorts of devious intentions for each other. There's something in the way she interacts with Micah and Trace that causes Gabriel to suspect that maybe something's off there, causing additional strain.

Jan wandered down once, to check on Jack and Gray. When he saw Darrek, Jan seemed dumbstruck and lingered to watch for a few minutes at Gray's side before retreating upstairs again with some food and a flushed face.

The two female members of Diadem's staff—Sam and Alyssa—are there, seated at the table with Trace and chatting like there's nothing odd about having a mostly-naked sub chained behind them. Every once in a while Trace will reach over to Darrek and grip the cloth around his groin, where a number of tiny clamps are attached to sensitive areas of his genitals, twisting them, squeezing flesh, and Darrek will fight a little and strain, making pleading sounds without the ability to hear himself and be embarrassed. It's all a head game, and Gabriel knows Darrek is getting off on it so hard there's not a single brain cell free in his head to worry about the call to his mother. One of the more interesting moments was when Alyssa began to touch and work her particular magic on Darrek. Even though that had been Darrek's initial intention all along—to go to Diadem to be with a Dominatrix, it's the first time he's actually been with one. Gabriel could see it in Darrek's expression when he noticed the difference in her touch and her smaller, softer fingers. Darrek liked it so much Trace had to give Darrek's balls a good squeeze to calm him back down.

As the night draws on, Gabriel knows what he needs to do. Stepping away from Darrek, leaving him in Trace's capable hands, Gabriel goes to Gray.

Jack is there, at Gabriel's feet, and Gabriel feels it like a caress, the urgency of Jack's want, the way he would do anything to get to play for a while in Gabriel's care. But Jack is Gray's. It's a line Gabriel won't cross without permission.

"Will you help me with him?" Gabriel asks Gray, directly. He starts to speak as soon as he has Gray's attention, speaking quickly to get the words out before he can stumble or doubt the decision he's made. "And be there for a scene with me and Darrek at Diadem? He knows I've had sex with Trace and Ben. Dare has only ever been with me. Before, it was just women. If you were there to show him what it is to submit to a male Dom who has no other responsibilities to him, and go as far with him as I have, I feel like it'd do wonders for him. Darrek responds well to submitting. It gives him peace, and happiness. I want that for him, now more than ever. So, even if this means I'll owe you, I'm asking, will you do it?"

It's a trial just to keep from looking down at Jack, who seems to be literally fighting himself to keep from speaking up. With a straight face, total control, Gabriel waits for Gray's answer as Gray considers him, and Darrek too.

"I'll have a few conditions of my own."

"That's fine," Gabriel tells him, feeling hopeful, pleading inwardly, and trying to play it cool outwardly. Gabriel knows that should Darrek be at Gray's mercy, on that level, at Diadem, it would take him so far away from his past and all of its problems, there would be no looking back. Darrek would be rooted firmly in the future, and Gabriel with him. They would be connected to Gray, and the world of the MC outside of their little town. Gabriel wants it so badly, he can taste it.

"When were you thinking? Tomorrow?"

"Um, yes. Sure. Tomorrow. He's ready for it if you are."

Running his tongue over his teeth, looking thoughtfully at Gabriel, Gray seems to consider all of the factors. Gabriel doesn't know what it is that gives Gray pause, but something surely does.

"Okay," Gray says, finally.

"Okay? Really?" Gabriel asks, smiling despite himself, and despite the fact that he's just asked this intimidating man, who has done the unthinkable, to fuck his lover.

"Yes. I'm in. I'll arrange things on my end tonight. We'll meet first thing in the morning at Diadem and arrange the rest there before beginning, to make sure everyone's on the same page."

"Okay. Thank you."

"Glad to help," Gray says with a nod. Then he glances over at Darrek with evident hunger, and just as much obvious pleasure that Gabriel evidently trusts him so much.

I'm doing it for Darrek, Gabriel reminds himself. *He deserves to feel safe, and happy.*

Briefly, despite his best efforts to avoid it, Gabriel catches Jack's gaze. They lock eyes and Gabriel feels it like electricity. Heat rises under his skin. The look Jack gives him is like a wild animal, barely tamed, ready and waiting to pounce. As much as Jack seems to want to challenge Gabriel, baring his fangs, threatening to bite, Gabriel wants just as much to be the one holding Jack's leash and feel the heady power which would come with taking such a dangerous man. It would be better than any drug, any other high life could offer. Though fleeting, Gabriel would savor it, then come home to Darrek where they could just look at each other and know they're each stronger for whom they've faced in the dungeon, when their hearts are already so completely possessed.

The sadness of the past few weeks lifts, like clouds parting for the sun. Infused with new energy, Gabriel swells with gladness for what's yet to come.

Chapter 26
Helpless Surrender

"Oh God, *please*," Darrek begs shamelessly. Time has no meaning. He hasn't the faintest idea how long he's been chained up in Micah's kitchen. Darrek knows he's in the kitchen because of the way they'd had him crawl, down the hallway and into a room where the acoustics hinted at a bigger space. Plus, the kitchen smells of wine, cheeses, fruit, and those weird little pâté things Darrek wasn't brave enough to try earlier when he had the chance. He's pretty sure the kitchen just smells like *him* now, to everyone else at least. Sweat runs down his body in rivers, dampening his hair, making his pants cling tightly where they still cover him. Pheromones, energy, sex and heat exude from him, filling the air until he feels like he's choking on it, anchored in the dizzying fog of his own making.

He can't see a thing, thanks to the blindfold, and can only hear things distantly, through the pounding music playing in the headphones clamped to his ears. They've been playing with him, keeping him on edge for too long. He's been touched, teased, fondled, and stroked and he can almost always tell it's not Gabriel doing it. But Gabriel is there. Darrek can sense him, above the sexual intoxication and body heat, like they're connected on another plane far up above everything else. Sometimes it's a woman's hand touching him, slipping into his jeans, and it's been causing wildly unexpected reactions in him. That it's Gabriel, allowing this, orchestrating this whole scene, having Alyssa—it's probably Alyssa, or maybe it's Lilianna—coax him along the knife's edge of that sensation right before orgasm makes Darrek crazy. The simple matter of having a woman touch his cock is amazing in and of itself. Thankfully, he can't hear himself over the music blasting in his ears, because that would be awfully embarrassing, maybe even enough so he'd want to use his safeword. But, since he has been able to hide in the noise, he's protected from having to worry about how he's crying out, how desperate he may seem, and the things being said around him, *about* him.

It's glorious.

He's gotten so close, so many times. Then another hand — which has to be Trace, no one else is as much of a bastard as him, unless it's Ben, it could be Ben — grabs him by the balls, using one of those damned clips or just their fingers to make him hurt. The ache skates right past light pain into full-blast screaming before it eases back farther, farther, until Darrek knows he's moaning, begging for more, not caring who hears or who responds, as long as they do.

But he can't take it anymore.

Let them fuck him in the safety of his cocoon of blindness and deafness, a show for the whole party. They can all have at him for all he cares, just as long as they let him come. All he wants is to be allowed to come.

You wouldn't really be okay with that, would you? A voice in his head inquires.

He can almost see them — a line of Doms and possibly the Dominatrixes too, wearing harnesses to accommodate him, waiting their turn at taking Darrek's ass for a hard ride. Sex in which he's on the receiving end is something Darrek has only given Gabriel. Maybe that's not fair, or right. He can't think of anyone else who has saved themselves the way he has.

A hand caresses over his dripping back, the muscles knotted tightly in his fight to hold on and keep from coming apart. He can't tell who it is, or even if it's male or female anymore. They brush over his shoulder blades, down his spine, even lower, lower…

The hand pivots and pushes inside his jeans and he almost wishes he wasn't wearing them anymore, just so Gabriel could see, since at the very least Darrek knows it's not Gabriel touching him. Not now.

Two fingers rub firmly through his crack and he even has a half-second to get mad at himself, thinking, *You're not really going to be this much of a whore, are you? Yeah, I want it, but do I want it this much?*

But it seems he does, in fact, want it that much because he tilts his hips slightly, offering his ass, and pushes back on the digits when they pause against his opening. His whole body quivers slightly, head bowed, mouth gasping as the fingers push into his body and god but he's glad he can't hear anything.

"*Please,*" he begs, for anything, for everything.

A finger tilts his chin up. The hair is cleared from his face, then tied behind his head.

He knows he's cursing, making wanton, terrible sounds as the fingers pump and slide deeper. His feet spread as far as he can get them.

He can feel them all staring, at his body, his reactions, at the hand on his hip, steadying him as he's finger-fucked. His cock weeps pre-come and now he's growling, teeth gritted against the building pleasure, the feeling of being so displayed, so closely watched and by who knows how many people.

The jeans are pushed down, exposing his body completely, and what's being done to it. The fingers slide and he has relaxed into it, riding them counter to each thrust. Someone tenderly touches his face, and it's Gabriel, Darrek knows instantly. Moaning his name, pleading for him, he's kissed, lightly, on the lips. The fingers slide in one push all the way up inside him, a hand strokes his cock, and he comes, all defenses down, no way to hold back.

It feels like fireworks under his skin, exploding it and leaving only the pulsing glow of supreme satisfaction. Everything drains from him. His muscles go lax.

They unhook the chain. His jeans are pulled back up so he can walk, led by his linked hands to the nearest bathroom, back down the hall he'd come from, if his senses are still at all intact, which they might not be.

When the headphones are taken off, the blindfold removed, he can hear, instantaneously, how hard he's breathing, how each exhale twists with a slight sound of ache and need on the end. Right away, he clamps his lips shut.

Gabriel caresses his cheek, smiling, looking as gorgeous and immaculate as ever. "Don't. Don't hold back. You're exquisite, Dare."

Darrek's mind feels jumbled, like it's having trouble processing words after having to deal only with sensation for so long. He doesn't even think about what he wants, he just moves, turning toward the sink, positioning himself in front of where Gabriel stands, and slips the jeans back down over his hips.

"Please, Master. Want you. Need— *fuck*!"

Gabriel is in him with one push and Darrek's mouth works around an unvoiced cry.

"What did I say, slave?"

So, Darrek lets it out, crying out with how full, how possessed, how wonderful it feels to be Gabriel's. The sound ricochets off the tile walls. Gabriel takes him hard. Darrek would reach back to hold him, to feel the muscles flexing, but his hands are still bound, so he just takes the ride, trying to make it as good for his Master as he can.

When it's done, and his body is quaking again, this time from exhaustion mostly, he moans, "Love you."

"Love you too, baby," Gabriel grins. "Now, let's get you showered."

He doesn't even have to ask. As soon as he's under the blast of the invigorating spray of the showerhead, he sees Gabriel peeling off his clothes to join in.

They don't speak at first. Darrek rinses his mouth, cools his skin, and can't help but groan with joy as Gabriel scrubs his body clean.

When he's drying off, looking doubtfully at his sweat- and come-stained clothing, Darrek says, "Thanks for that."

"You're welcome. You needed it."

"Yeah, I guess I did."

Gabriel sees Darrek's curled-lipped expression and says, "Micah's half the size of you and your thighs would never squeeze into Trace's tight-ass jeans. You're stuck with those 'til we get home. Sorry baby."

"'S'okay. At least I have a dry shirt."

"You could always just wear the towel, you know," Gabriel suggests. "If it slips off, they've seen it all already."

"Oh my god," Darrek groans slightly, but without feeling, just a dull sort of realization. "I guess they have, huh?"

They leave the safety and seclusion of the bathroom, with Darrek indeed wearing the towel rather than the sweaty, come-stained pants. He finds his shirt and pulls it on. When they reenter the kitchen, Darrek catches the gaze of multiple people, but it's Jack he sees first, kneeling beside Gray and looking utterly submissive.

"Oh my god," Darrek laments softly, taking a tally of who's there and matching up identities to what he felt. Jack was there. Hell, he could have been participating for all Darrek knows. Jack's gaze drags up and down Darrek's body in a way that makes Darrek's face go red, especially because after Jack has taken stock of the delirious, sated submissive, he stares hard at Gabriel next. For Darrek, there's no doubt at all the sentiment behind the look Jack is giving Gabriel.

Gabriel walks over to the kitchen table, but Darrek would much prefer a couch, so he turns his head to look down the other hall, in the direction of the living room. "I don't suppose we could—?"

"No. Come here and sit," Gabriel says sharply, in command.

But it's too late. Darrek sees the paper sign taped to the wall a few feet from the doorway. He walks over to it as Gabriel sighs, "Shit."

It's a printout with Kyle's face in the center and in bold type around it: 'This is Kyle. He's not allowed downstairs. If seen downstairs, tell Ben, Trace, or Micah immediately.'

"Are you fucking kidding me?" Darrek asks, anger seeping into his voice. "These look like *wanted posters*. Kyle hasn't done anything wrong! Why would you bring him here only to treat him like a criminal?!"

"Hey," Trace says sharply from his seat, drawn abruptly out of a conversation with Sam. "Is that how you speak to your Master?"

"I'm not just talking to him!" Darrek argues. It feels like a fist is squeezing something vital in the center of his chest, making tears spring to his eyes. "Kyle doesn't deserve this! He's *upset* and *scared*, like me, and—"

"Hey, baby, hey, look at me," Gabriel urges gently, stepping right up to Darrek and holding his face in both hands. "Breathe. It's okay. Kyle's okay. He's been having a hell of a time. He's thrown his own party upstairs and he's had plenty of visitors. This was Ben's idea to keep both you and Kyle feeling safe and happy, so you could enjoy yourselves without dragging the rest into it. Kyle knows you're down here. He's in on it. Hell, he's wearing a little silver dog collar—or cat collar, I guess—that says to return him to his Master if lost, with Ben's cell number. It's fucking engraved and everything. You know him. I know you do. Kyle keeps his damn eyes opened, even when it's not good for him. I decided it was better if you didn't know about the whole Kyle thing. You had enough on your mind with the call and everything else."

Darrek hates the tears streaming from his eyes. He angrily wipes them as soon as they fall, but they won't stop and everyone is still watching him, even Jack. Especially Jack.

With regret and sadness, Gabriel sighs, "You want to see him, don't you?"

Darrek nods, stealing glances in the direction of the stairs, feeling the pull like there's a hook lodged in his midsection, drawing him away.

"Benny's gonna shit a brick," Trace warns.

Gabriel takes Darrek's hand and they start to walk. "Yeah, well, I'm not responsible for him, am I?"

Ripping down each of the signs they pass, gathering them up in a crumpled ball in his hands, Darrek feels the tightness in him loosen a little with every paper he removes. Not saying a word, Gabriel leads Darrek upstairs. The music is loud and thumping, getting more raucous with every step. They get to the second floor, and a few steps later they're at a door to a study with low lighting and a number of the missing guests, including Ben and Kyle. Gabriel takes the balled up collection of paper from Darrek and tosses it into a nearby trash can.

Kyle sees them standing there in the doorway after a pause, before Ben. Kyle has been lying with his head pillowed in Ben's lap, but upon seeing Darrek, Kyle springs upright and points at him.

"This is totally against the rules and it's not my fault," Kyle blurts. "I had *nothing* to do with this. I was here the whole time, minding my own business, not setting *one foot* downstairs."

Still crying, still hating it, Darrek feels the tightness come back,

Forgive Us

strong. His vision swims and the tears hit him like a fist. When he starts to sob, he loses track of everything. Then Gabriel hugs him, holding the back of his head, clasping Darrek's enormous body to him to help him feel better.

"Jesus Christ," Ben groans. "Why are you up here? Why is *he* up here? The fuck is this, Hunter?"

"Enough, Ben," Gabriel snaps. "It's enough."

Darrek has to ask. He won't be able to breathe until he does, so, sobbing, he turns to Kyle, letting go of Gabriel, and says in a hitching, tear-choked voice, "Are you okay?"

It flips a switch in Kyle, who had been fine, or seemed to be. When they walked up to the room, Kyle had been relaxed, smiling, but just like that's he's crying too and he turns to punch Ben in the shoulder.

Kyle gets to his feet and looks around the room, at Jan and Lilianna sitting together, drinks in hand, at Ben, at Gabriel.

"Fuck you. Really," he says to Ben, shaking his head. Turning to Gabriel, he adds, "And fuck you, too."

Then Kyle crosses directly to Darrek and wraps his arms around him in a hug. Darrek folds Kyle up in the embrace and the walls staving off an emotional meltdown, keeping Darrek together after exhaustion sets in, come tumbling down. The trial of enduring the endless ringing of the phone, the remembered, shrill screech of the house alarm, the cops filing through the place, the news about Jerry and Harry, the news about Trace, lingering worry about Kyle, simple tiredness from the scene they'd just finished downstairs—all of it compounds until Darrek feels psychologically trampled. Clinging to Kyle, crying into his blond, shining hair which smells like home and everything familiar, Darrek feels Kyle's hands clawing at him, gripping with strength and determination and maybe some fear that they have only moments before they're separated again. He's crying as hard as Darrek, but soon surpasses him. Kyle's grief and pain pushes Darrek to get control, and he does, smoothing Kyle's hair, keeping him held as long as he needs it.

Ben and Gabriel are both waiting there, inches away, like they're about to pry them apart, which seems to make Kyle just hold on tighter.

But, for a long time, they stand like that. Ben and Gabriel don't step in. Jan and Lilianna excuse themselves, giving the foursome their privacy. Gradually, Kyle stops crying and calms down. Kyle's body feels hollower and thinner in Darrek's grasp as Kyle asks, "Are you okay?"

"I asked you first," Darrek counters.

Kyle sniffs, drying his face on Darrek's shirt. The dampness touches Darrek's skin and he can't help but smile a little at being used as Kyle's personal handkerchief. It doesn't mean anything, or imply anything. It's just nice to be near him again, and to know for the time being he doesn't have to wonder and worry. Just to get to talk to Kyle makes him feel so much better.

"Yeah, I'm okay," Kyle allows.

"I'm calling bullshit."

"You're the one that came up here crying and fucking pantsless," Kyle retorts.

Darrek snorts, laughing. "Long story."

"What kind of party are you even having downstairs that you lost your pants?"

"What kind of party are you having up *here*? What is this, house music? Are you having a rave?"

Kyle laughs helplessly, burying his face in Darrek's chest, then recovering slightly and stepping back, letting him go.

"I missed you," Kyle whispers, the tears coming back hard and fast, scaring Ben enough to make him step forward. "Don't," Kyle warns. "I'm fine."

"I missed you too," Darrek admits. "And when I saw the signs taped up everywhere… you shouldn't be punished like this. Locked away in some room, because of me. I would never have come here if I knew it meant this for you."

Kyle gazes raptly up at Darrek, not saying a word.

"You're incredible, you know," Kyle says with a small, yet honest, smile. "I almost forgot what a good friend you are."

He seems to realize it was the wrong thing to say when Darrek has to chew his lip and bow his head to hide the torrent of shame which engulfs him.

"No," Kyle says sternly, "Screw that! You are! You're my *best friend*, Darrek. You will always be that, even if you're not here."

"You're my best friend, too," Darrek manages, feeling swept away and simultaneously right where he needs to be. It looks like he's scaring Ben, but Darrek doesn't stop even though maybe he should, and says, "I love you and I'm so sorry for the way everything has turned out. It just… *sucks*. I've been so worried about you, with everything that's happened, with Jerry."

"That's enough," Ben says.

"Shut up, Ben," Kyle says. To Darrek he asks, "You never answered my question. Are you okay?"

"No. Not really. But, I mean, it helps to be able to ask you how you are." He takes a deep breath and lets it out.

Gabriel passes them tissues and hands Darrek a glass of water. "You look pale. Come sit down."

Ben seems ready to usher Darrek right back downstairs where he came from, but Gabriel steers him to the couch instead. It does feel good to sit and he sips the water.

"What the hell did you do to him down there? Where did his pants go?" Kyle demands of Gabriel.

"Ben distracted you. I distracted Dare," Gabriel says coolly.

The words seem to process gradually. Darrek sees it happen in Kyle's face. Their eyes meet and Kyle appears to get confirmation of his suspicions. He's smiling but then it twists into a sneer and Ben catches him right as he surges for Gabriel.

"Hey! Calm it the fuck down!" Ben yells.

With awe, Darrek gazes upon Kyle's fury for him, for what he's imagining Gabriel has offered Darrek up to endure.

"Calm it, slave!" Ben roars.

"Kyle," Darrek says, drawing his attention away from Gabriel. Feeling his face flush as Kyle looks right at him, jittery with anger on Darrek's behalf, he says, "I liked it, okay? That's not why I'm upset, and you know it. You're not the only one who had safety precautions imposed. You were up here with the music blasting. I was down there blindfolded and with headphones on so I didn't know about you, about *this*, until after. So relax, okay? You know what it's like, to get off on distraction. It's not something to get angry at Gabriel about. Gabriel takes good care of me, just like Ben takes care of you."

Kyle sits beside Darrek, giving Gabriel the stink eye.

"Hey," Darrek murmurs with raised eyebrows. "You don't see me getting all up in Ben's face, do you?"

"Maybe that's because you know I can handle myself," Kyle growls.

"Enough," Ben seethes.

"Fuck you," Kyle retorts, sitting back, looking like he's not going anywhere soon.

Chapter 27
Supervised Visitation

"So," Kyle says slowly, hands folded, glancing over and up at Darrek. The music is off. The room is too quiet. "What's up?"

Darrek shrugs, feeling hugely uncomfortable with the way Gabriel and Ben are silently staring at them, seated side-by-side in a pair of chairs placed directly in front of the couch on which he and Kyle are sitting.

"I don't know. What's up with you?"

"Mom and Dad over there don't look super keen on this whole supervised visitation thing."

"You're Mom," Ben tells Gabriel, leaning over slightly, arms folded.

"Gee, thanks, Knox," Gabriel replies, not amused at all.

"You're welcome."

"How's, uh, Sierra?" Kyle asks, sounding like he's fumbling for any safe discussion topic, no matter how random, just to keep them talking.

"Good, I hope. Haven't seen her much. We've been staying at a hotel," Darrek says.

"Why?"

Gabriel and Darrek look at each other. Thinking of all of the things they've been actively avoiding — and it's a long list — Darrek answers for them, saying, "I really needed the rest. I haven't been exactly comfortable in our place lately. We left Sierra with a dog sitter. I mean, honestly, we've barely been home this week at all, even just to check the mail. But this has been going on since before Trace laid the whole bombshell on us. For weeks now, I've tried to be out as much as possible."

"You can't avoid your own house forever," Ben says.

"I know," Darrek sighs, feeling frustrated with himself. He's used to feeling that way, though. His frustrations with his circumstances stretch way back, years and years.

"I cancelled our phone service," Gabriel says. "The landline doesn't even work anymore. We've got the new security system on the house, all the wiring has been replaced so we don't have those weird false alarms anymore. I mean, I'm not exactly thrilled by the cigarette butts the workers left everywhere, but... whatever. The call to certain people has been made. We've done everything possible to correct the problem. It's time to try to get back to normal. With Gray, Jack and Jan being here, I've barely been able to get in to the office and get any work done."

"I know. Now I just have to get over it in my own head," Darrek grumbles. "It's like a mental wall or something. Something feels off to me. I've been talking with our therapist about it."

"If we have to move, we'll move," Gabriel concludes.

"I don't want to move, though," Darrek says with regret. He suspects it might be the only answer.

"Is this my fault at all?" Kyle asks.

"No," Gabriel, Darrek and Ben answer at once, in unison.

"Jeez. Okay, just asking," Kyle chuckles, hands raised in surrender. "So, what have you been working on?"

"Oh, and I've been making a lot of rocking chairs. Custom orders."

"Your chairs do rock," Kyle says, nodding with approval.

"Thanks. Yeah, I got an order for a table and chairs set," Darrek tells him. "I'm gonna dovetail the joints, make it out of English oak, I think. It's a lot of work, though, especially with everything else I've got in progress. And also since I haven't been in my shop in a while."

"I can help if you want," Kyle offers, glancing over at Ben as he says it. "If you give me the specs, I'll do whatever you need and I won't cut into your commission. I'll do it for free. It's good to be busy, be making things."

Darrek bites his lip, hangs his head. "That would be—" His

voice catches. He takes a breath, hisses, "*Fuck.*"

Bouncing his leg, clearing his throat and glancing around the room, Darrek tries to compose himself, determined to do the right thing and safeguard Kyle no matter what his own preferences might be.

"Shit," Kyle groans. "I'm sorry. I shouldn't have—"

"I would like that," Darrek cuts in, battling with his emotions and succeeding a little more, moment by moment. "But it might not be a good idea."

In what appears to be an attempt to soothe, Gabriel leans forward and says gently, "We'll talk about it."

Kyle starts, "No, I shouldn't have thought—"

"We'll talk about it," Gabriel repeats. With a slightly tired sigh, glancing longingly back at the room's door and the rest of the house beyond it, Gabriel says, "Well, this is has been a barrel of laughs. How long are we doing this?" "Now now, sweetcheeks," Ben *tsks* with a smarmy grin. "Let the kids play a little longer. They're all tuckered out from their long day. Once they get this out of their systems they'll sleep better tonight."

"That's disturbing," Gabriel tells Ben, not smiling at all.

"But not inaccurate," Ben counters with a raised finger. His smile grows and he leans in. With a whisper, he coaxes, "Give Daddy some sugar."

"One step too far," Gabriel deadpans, even as Ben begins to slide a hand up the inside of Gabriel's thigh.

"Oh, come on," Ben says softly against the shell of Gabriel's ear. The hand creeps farther and Gabriel isn't pulling away. Ben's thumb strokes over the swell of Gabriel's groin and he says, "I can literally see this shit turning you on right now."

"Gross," Darrek says, willing them with all his might to knock it off. "Seriously."

"See?" Ben smirks at Gabriel. "Totally accurate."

"What else is new?" Kyle asks Darrek, luring him back into the conversation. Ben gives up his pawing at Gabriel with a resigned sigh so they can keep monitoring the chat.

"Well, I called Mom. My, uh, actual mom. Like, an hour or three ago, I guess. What time is it anyway?" He glances around for a clock or a watch.

"It must have sucked to call."

"It did. Hence the distraction." He gestures at the towel he's wearing.

"Why did you? To tell her to fuck off?"

"Something like that."

"Good."

"How about you?"

Kyle shifts to sit back and smooths out his pants. "Got fucked by both of the hot British ones an hour or two ago. The Js. What time is it again? Did we decide?"

"I don't know. There aren't clocks in here," Darrek says, looking around again. Then he sits back and tries to gauge Kyle's expression, or read into what may have happened. "Jack and Jan? No shit?"

"No shit," Kyle smiles proudly. "There was an attentive audience and everything. Micah was the Dom slash ringleader. *Sickeningly* hot."

Ben clears his throat, loudly, scowling at Kyle.

"Lay off, Dad," Kyle says dismissively.

"Huh," Darrek grunts, piecing some things together. "That must be why Jack looked so whipped downstairs. Guess Gray wasn't happy."

"Eh, fuck 'im," Kyle scoffs. "Dude's such a tight-ass, and not in a fun way."

Smiling at Kyle, just looking at him there, by Darrek's side, the both of them talking about stupid, normal things, it feels like old times. It feels like better times. It warms his heart, filling up the empty places that have formed since Darrek had to let go of his oldest, dearest friend. But as good as it is, it scares him, too, because what if this is all they'll have? What if they only get this one night to feel normal again before it all goes back to the way it has been for months? The idea makes Darrek anxious, like he needs to squeeze in every word, every thought in case this is just another, prolonged goodbye. So, just so Kyle knows, just in case he needs to hear it as much as Darrek needs to say it, he tells Kyle urgently, with feeling, his eyes misting over again, "I really missed this."

Seeming to prove Darrek's worst fears, that he and Kyle are still too linked, too close, too able to sense things in each other that maybe they shouldn't be able to, Kyle reacts like he hears all of the implications of Darrek's words. He hears Darrek's pain, feels his fear, and wipes angrily at his eyes, hissing, "Stop, for fuck's sake."

Darrek knows then, like it's been spelled out in the tears drying on the backs of Kyle's hands. Kyle can't go through another goodbye. He can't keep saying goodbye to Darrek. There's no choice left for them but to act like everything is normal in ways it will never be normal. Not for them.

And Darrek doesn't know why it is Kyle won't cry for Ben, and grieve in front of Ben, but cries too easily for Darrek. That's a puzzle Darrek doesn't even want to try to figure out.

"So," Darrek begins, trying to find their way back to normalcy. "How about Trace being a hooker?"

"Oh, I totally called it," Kyle says, blowing out a breath, raking his fingers through his hair, then settling into the couch again. "He was always talking about having lots of practice, right? And he's never been capable of being shy. And he'll fuck anything. *Anything.*"

"How much do you think he charged?" Darrek murmurs, wondering.

Kyle's eyes widen and he shakes his head at the idea. "Not enough, that's for damned sure."

"So, can I ask you a question?" Darrek ventures. He gives it a moment before continuing, and takes the time to look around at each of them in turn—Kyle, Ben, and Gabriel. "You guys have both been up here for a while now, right?"

Ben clears his throat again, intentionally, loudly, and gives Kyle a hard stare like he's trying to speak telepathically to him. Kyle doesn't take the bait, though.

"Yeah, but Ben went down for food once. What?"

Unbelievable, Darrek thinks. He stares right at Ben. Ben returns Darrek's stare and his lips slowly curl up in a knowing smile. It's subtle, but it's there.

"What?" Kyle repeats, oblivious.

Darrek sighs, looking between Gabriel and Ben. "I don't want to know, do I?"

Ben just keeps smiling. He licks his bottom lip wet and seems to urge Darrek to ask, just so Ben can confirm his suspicions that it was him who had his fingers working away inside Darrek's ass not so long ago, making Darrek come so hard, he's still recovering from it. Darrek feels Ben's stare like it's fingernails trailing over his skin, down his chest and lower, to places only the towel conceals from view.

"How long was he downstairs?" Darrek asks Kyle directly, wondering exactly how much of the touching was Ben.

"Don't answer that," Gabriel says abruptly.

Kyle laughs, agape. "Did you just give me an *order*?"

"*Don't answer that*," Gabriel repeats, stern as ever.

"Wow," Kyle says with amazement. To Ben, he inquires, "What did you do?"

"Don't answer that either," Gabriel tells Ben.

Kyle says, "Does this have anything to do with the lack of pants? It does, doesn't it? No wonder no one's shocked the Brits fucked me. Y'all are preoccupied with the kinky shit happening downstairs."

"I was chained in the kitchen," Darrek tells Kyle. "There was… *touching*, but I was blindfolded and couldn't hear anything so I didn't know who was touching me."

Kyle sits forward and smacks Ben's leg with a loud *thwack*.

"Ow!" Ben frowns.

"Pussy," Kyle sneers. "Did you even go down there to get food?"

"I totally brought back food!" Ben protests. "You ate some!"

"That's not what I meant."

Looking levelly at Kyle, Ben says with a cocky grin, "What can I say? Being a Dom has its privileges."

―――◻―◻―◻―――

There is no hug goodbye. They don't even *say* goodbye, unless "later" counts as goodbye. But judging from the fierce determination in Kyle's eyes, Darrek is left certain it wasn't a onetime thing. Maybe, as long as Ben and Gabriel are there with them, it would be okay to see each other now and then to work on carpentry projects together.

Wearily, Darrek leaves the house. Gabriel takes his hand and leads him to the Discovery after saying a brief goodbye to those left at the party. Gray, Jack, and Jan have retired to their rooms. Sam and Alyssa have left. It's just Trace, Micah, and Lilianna there to thank them for coming and say goodnight. It's mostly a blur for Darrek. The emotional toll is setting in, leaving him spent and craving the forgetfulness of sleep. He wants to be in his own house, with the sanctuary of his workspace in the garage, and the personalized dungeon upstairs and Sierra waiting eagerly for a scratch behind the ears before seeing them up to bed where Darrek can lie with Gabriel and drift off. But that's not where they're headed. They'll be going back to the hotel they've been staying in, rather than going home.

The temptation to mentally replay the phone call with his mother is great. The temptation to try to figure out who had their hands on him, when, and how, is equally strong, as is the desire to try to guess what Kyle may not have said but implied in their conversation, not to mention imagining what went on with Jack and Jan.

"Look at me," Gabriel says. It's an order. It's clear from his tone. They're in the Discovery, the engine idling, the radio off. It's dark out, with the half moon and countless stars well concealed behind thick clouds.

When Darrek meets Gabriel's gaze, he sees mostly his Master's iron will and not an ounce of apology or regret for anything which has transpired that night. It's strangely calming, to be faced with such confidence.

"There's something you need to know," Gabriel continues, with the same edge to his voice, the one that makes Darrek hard just from anticipation alone. "You have an appointment at Diadem tomorrow."

"What?" Darrek blurts.

"With me. Gray agreed to help me in a scene with you there."

Dread is like fingers caressing in the dark, not bothering to ask permission before they reach between your legs, slipping into places you never asked to be touched.

"What does that mean, help you?"

"You will submit to him," Gabriel tells Darrek. "Completely."

The question echoes, unanswered but unvoiced, *what does that mean?*

Gray is a Master Dom. He's intimidating in ways even Trace isn't intimidating. He's skilled and capable and liable to do things Darrek is in no way prepared for. He imagines being naked, bound, submissive, and helpless in the presence of such a man and instantly squirms in his seat.

Gabriel's hand falls on Darrek's leg. He's wearing the soiled jeans for the drive home and they just add to his discomfort, remembering the way Gray had looked at him, how just being near him had made Darrek's instincts drive him to want to beg for mercy, for attention, for pleasure, for pain. Gray is the unknown. He's not family, like the other men from Diadem have become. Gray owes him nothing. If anything, Darrek owes Gray for the services he has rendered. Maybe that's what this is. Maybe Darrek is payment.

Almost swallowing the word, he murmurs, "Okay."

"Okay?" Gabriel repeats, his eyebrows raised.

Darrek nods, exhaling heavily. "Yes, Sir."

Seeming pleased, Gabriel says, "Good. Tonight, what happened to you in there, what you felt, was your warm up. Tomorrow is the real deal."

He feels it then. It's all on the table. The ghosts of those fingers, on him, in him, make him close his legs, curling forward in his seat to brace his elbows on his knees, covering his mouth with his hands.

Gabriel's fingers tangle in Darrek's hair, making him shiver and all he can say, all he can do is groan, "Fuck."

Chapter 28
Knowing Trace

Micah hangs from his outstretched arms, his wrists in shackles affixed to chains that stretch to either side of the bedroom. His ankles are shackled to rings embedded in the floor, keeping him spread, but they're mostly unnecessary. The next lash of the whip falls around the middle of his back and he bites back the throaty yell which bubbles up instantly, tensing against the pain, even though he knows it does no good. Trace will wait until he's relaxed again before striking. He'll wait for hours, if need be.

But, to be honest, the wait is the best part.

With the party finally over, Micah, at last, has Trace's attention all for himself, until their official MC supervision arrives. When they'd first come upstairs to the bedroom together, Trace had sat Micah down in the light to get a good look at his face, judging whether he was able to endure any more that evening after such a draining day.

"You up for this, old man? Not too tired are ya?" Trace asked.

"Oh, Jesus. If *I'm* the old man, you must be fucking *ancient*," Micah said seriously, making Trace laugh again, his eyes lighting up. It always felt so good when he was able to make Trace smile, taking him away from his many worries for a little while.

"Well, after this week, the rest of this black might go real damn fast," Trace admitted, running his hand back over his salt-and-pepper hair. "I'll just be your silver fox." Trace gave him a sly, sexy look that had Micah dragging him in for a kiss, chuckling against his lips.

"You'll always be my silver fox, *Tracey*," Micah teased.

"Nope. Not gonna happen," Trace warned. "I might let them British fuckers get away with that, but *you* I can quite fuckin' easily bend over my knee to spank your ass red in punishment. It ain't my damn name. But if you need proof I ain't a girl, I'll happily fuck you dizzy with it."

"Oh, I know you can," Micah assured him, loving him more by the minute.

The teasing worked better than Micah had hoped, bringing out Trace's hard-assed, surly, aggressive side.

Now, Micah's ass throbs around the obscenely large plug Trace fed into him, slowly, after trussing him up. With his back to the door and no music playing to mask his screams, it's only a matter of time before company joins them. The spectacle of Micah impaled, whipped, and pathetic, his body thrumming with need for pain and the promise—no matter how distant—of release, feeds his greatest pleasure. Humiliation has always been the most direct route to Micah's most spectacular orgasms. It has ever since he was a teenager, too smart for his own good and definitely too inquisitive.

An incredibly bright young man, he began college at age sixteen and studied far away from home. His roommate had been gay and quite insatiable as well. Prone to bringing home other young men when he thought Micah was gone, that particular roommate was quite a big factor in helping Micah's repressed younger self tap into buried, misunderstood desires. Micah had never seen two men sucking each other's cocks before, so he'd snooped from the shadows, and gotten caught. He'd been humiliated by the size of his erection when they groped at it, as well as how much he liked it when one of them sucked him off, too, just to make him guilty of the same act, lest he be tempted to start talking and spread gossip.

It all spiraled from there. They didn't care if he was underage, just that he begged for it and acted so incredibly nervous when they informed him how they were going to fuck his virgin ass, taking turns until no one would ever suspect it didn't regularly get taken for rides.

He'd told Trace the whole story, in graphic detail, long ago. It had been used as fodder for their own role-play too many times to count, how Micah had been such a horny, timid twink, letting his male roommates fuck him dizzy while he was simultaneously already dating Lilianna. She'd been clueless at first. He wound up telling her the truth, fearing she'd walk in on them before he could confess. That's when he discovered her fondness for voyeurism and making out with hot girls at parties when societal rules grew lax. They were a match made in heaven.

But now Lilianna is gone. Once Gabriel, Darrek, Sam, Alyssa, Ben, and Kyle had left, she'd told them she had no interest in sleeping in the house that evening. Nursing her hurt feelings after catching Micah slipping away to have a moment alone with Trace, she said she would rather put her feet up and rest somewhere quieter where she didn't have to worry about playing hostess for a few hours. Micah couldn't blame her for wanting some sanctuary and space. She was more introverted than he was by nature, and wasn't used to having so many people around twenty-four seven, so it had to be making her crazy. Trace offered his place, but she just gave him a polite smile Micah was well familiar with and declined.

Micah knows Lilianna's quest for quiet is sincere, but it's the tension with Micah pushing her into Saoirse's arms. Feeling guilty for the part he's knowingly playing in creating even more distance between himself and his best friend, Micah invites the pain Trace gives him with the whip. Micah knows he's being a bastard to his sweet, overwhelmed wife. Trace is right. They need to talk and stop hurting each other. First, though, comes direly needed, complete submission.

He wonders if Gray is already watching, or if maybe he's got his hands full with his own pair of horny troublemakers.

The whip falls, catching Micah by surprise. It slices in a hot line across his ass, making him scream brightly. He draws up on his toes as the fire spreads, going down into the muscle, radiating outward.

"What'cha thinkin' about?"

"Horny troublemakers," Micah says in a thin rasp, grimacing.

"Oh, good," Trace says happily.

They've been at this for an hour. Though Micah's thoughts keep turning in circles, they haven't strayed into territory too dangerous. Trace keeps him there, keeps him grounded.

"May I?" Micah hears, and all he knows at first is it's not Trace's voice.

It takes him a few seconds to realize it's Gray speaking, and by then Trace must have given over the whip, because it falls again, and with so much more force than Trace was using, it blindsides Micah. All of his thoughts are erased in a scorching, merciless white heat that obliterates all of his senses, everything lost in the pain from the lash across the thickest part of his ass, right where Trace had just stricken him.

It's so much worse. Micah fights the chains, something he rarely if ever does, sobbing, trying to get it together.

From directly behind him, though he hadn't heard Gray approach, Micah hears, "I thought you should have a taste of how it feels when *I* wield the whip, before...." It's soft, a whisper, and Micah whines, fearing more pain, but a hand moves in a caress over his lower back, then down to barely graze over the wound from the whip. He shudders but calms a little, head hanging, hiding his face. Gray's other hand takes firm hold of the base of the plug.

Micah moans.

"Steady," Gray hushes, drawing Micah's hips back as far as they'll go, then begins to draw out the plug.

It's worked out of him with such patience, by the time it's most of the way out, Micah isn't cognizant of how he's gasping, mouth opened, knees quivering, cock hard as steel.

Gray draws it completely out and says, "That's better, isn't it?"

The shackles on his ankles are unhooked from the floor. His wrists are unchained as well. Confused, Micah stands there limply as Gray guides Micah's arms down around behind his back, clipping the cuffs together.

"Thank you, Sir," he mumbles, throbbing, every muscle throughout the entirety of his body feeling the effect of the last lash, the pain not receding at all.

"Easy now," Gray says, so softly, inserting something new in the plug's place. It fills Micah's ass so swiftly, he cries out a little. It starts to vibrate.

Gasping, feeling the stimulation to his prostate right away, he's lax as hands turn him, walking him a few paces away.

"Sit on it, not your legs," he's instructed. His shoulders are pushed down and he sits with his ass flush to the floorboards, setting his whole weight against the vibrator.

Moaning, cock straining upward between his legs, Micah revels in the humiliation of it all, so close to release, it makes him want to cry tears of joy.

Then Gray leaves him, and things start to happen which Micah doesn't know how to process or interpret.

"Chains?" Gray asks Trace, whose expression is as inscrutable as stone. "No?"

Seemingly in response to the slightest incline of Gray's head, Trace walks over to the St. Andrews cross. Facing it, he grabs hold of the beams; his arms stretched wide, legs spread. He's naked as well, but Gray is fully dressed as he wields the leather whip, standing back and admiring his target before striking.

The whip leaves a red, perfectly horizontal line across Trace's ass. He grunts thickly, physically struggling with what Micah knows must be unbelievable agony. But then he takes a few deep breaths and becomes steady once more.

Another lash, striking the same place exactly and the scream almost breaks free. Micah honestly doesn't know how Trace contains it.

One glance at Gray's face and Micah looks instantly away, lest he draw the man's wrath on him instead. Whatever is happening isn't about Micah at all. That much, at least, is clear. This is an old struggle which may have been paused for a decade's time, but carries on now like it was minutes rather than years.

Micah stops counting the strikes as Trace's stifled yells ring in his ears, music he's never known.

Trace sways slightly. It's not much but it seems to be enough for Gray, who sets the whip aside and approaches the man on the cross.

"He doesn't know you, does he?"

"No, Sir," Trace says in a stranger's voice, a strained and cracked one, with tones wholly different than any he's heard before from Trace's lips.

"He *should* know you, don't you think?"

A terrible look passes between them; one Micah has no desire to witness. His body sings with stimulation, with pleasure, and he doesn't want it. He wants to be out of there, to not have to witness this. Trace has always been the strong one, unmovable, steady. It's the rest of them that have been allowed to fall apart. What's to become of them if Trace is unmade by this Master Dom from his past?

They would be lost without him.

But then Trace moves, shifting his grip, his stance. He bends himself slightly over at the waist, arching his back, sticking out his ass in invitation.

"No!" Micah says sharply. "Trace—"

"He's right," Trace grimaces, not looking at Micah, looking only at the floor. "As usual."

Something happens, a great shift and peeling back of gauzy layers, one after the other, but at first Micah doesn't see it. He's blinded by a flare of righteous protective love for his strong, beautiful Master made weak and vulnerable for this man, this stranger come to haunt them all. Micah resents Gray's presence so much in that moment; it consumes him, much as thoughts of his dearly departed consume him when he allows them to. It makes him want to scream and break things, to lash out and purge the violence brewing in his heart.

A few more insubstantial wisps melt away from the facades of these tough, rigid men, capable of terrible and wonderful things.

Micah realizes, a moment at a time, how Trace's expression has changed. There is no reflection of pain from the whipping there any longer. He's still bracing himself, but in a more physical way, against the wood crossbeams. His arms and back are tensed as Gray rocks against the junction of Trace's spread legs. Touching Trace gently, caressing his sides, then down the fronts of his thighs, around to his erection, Gray is like a man whose mask has been knocked askew. There's true passion there, Micah sees, old affection which can't be mimicked for convenience's sake. He touches Trace as if he needs to, has no choice but to indulge, though logic and rationality might tell him otherwise. It's an inner battle as Gray fights only himself and Trace stands there, open and ready, just waiting, enjoying every point of contact, each small proof of Gray's care.

"Oh my god," Micah gasps softly.

He has never seen Trace like this, so submissive, yielding so completely. It makes Micah's skin feel too tight, too hot, and too cold at the same time. A shiver of lust from the vibrator shoots up his spine and out through every nerve ending.

Trace—who has been the most powerful, fearsome man Micah has ever known—is practically unrecognizable, but maybe it's just to Micah he's become a stranger. Maybe this is who Gray has been waiting patiently to see since he arrived. Perhaps this is the Trace who worked for ten years for an organization that farmed him out like a prize piece of meat, not a person with a soul, just something to be had for the right price. Micah has been trying not to think about it, because it's easier to not think about it, how beaten down and used up Trace must have been after that ordeal. But, then, that's the precise moment in his life when Trace met Gray. Trace admitted as much.

Gray pushes two lube-slicked fingers through Trace's opening, and Micah sees Trace's mouth work against the unspeakable pleasure of that sensation. Reaching up, Gray gently pulls the tie from Trace's long hair, freeing it. It spills over his neck and shoulders. Combing through it, scratching Trace's scalp with one hand while fingering him loose with the other, Gray plays Trace like an expert, and Trace reacts beautifully. Fingers rub the back of Trace's neck, down his spine as Trace undulates and moans. His skin is flushed, his eyes dark, chest heaving.

It's intoxicating to watch, but then Micah glances over at Gray and sees how wild and intent his eyes are, locked to Trace. Every reaction, each small cry, each contraction of muscle is specifically produced by Gray's hands, his will. Nothing is unexpected. It's like a dance they may have been doing together for years, with no one to witness it but each other. And Gray is absolutely determined to complete it.

"Micah," Gray beckons.

At first Micah is afraid and doesn't move. He isn't sure he can willingly put himself in the middle of that, to be played as Trace is played. Not that he would ever admit it to Trace, should he ask, but it's mainly the sight of Gray's fingers buried to the hilt inside him that draws Micah. It's so forbidden, so tantalizing, he can't resist, even with warning alarms sounding in his brain. Is that what Gray is experiencing, too? A surrender to the animal, denial of the practical?

It's difficult to stand, unaided, with his legs crossed in front of him and his arms bound behind. He shifts to his knees before he's able to get one foot under him, then the other. Padding barefoot over the floorboards, he crosses to them with his head slightly bowed, bracing against the unknown, moving hesitantly.

Gray takes hold of Micah with his free hand, guiding him to stand between them.

"You don't use condoms with each other, correct?"

"Yes, Sir. That's correct," Micah murmurs. Heart racing, he's barely able to hear himself over the pounding in his chest and the roaring of blood in his ears. Gray is at his back, a warm, simultaneously threatening and reassuring presence. Micah is pressed tightly against from behind, brought up against Trace. With his arm wound around Micah's right hip, Gray takes hold of Micah's cock and strokes it slowly. Blood rushes there, swelling the organ painfully, making Micah moan.

"He trusts you in ways he hasn't trusted anyone else, even me. You should know that. You should know him. He forgets how it used to be, but I don't. I can't."

Micah feels it then, and stares down the length of his body as Gray fits Micah's cock against Trace's hole. The fingers withdraw, spreading the ring of muscle and pushing Micah to fill the gap.

"Oh fuck," Micah groans through gritted teeth, head thrown back as Gray pushes him from behind, making him take of Trace. A loud moan shatters the stillness of the room's air and Micah doesn't initially know it's not him who has cried out, but Trace. Gray steadies Micah's member, working it farther into Trace with little pushes, his hips rocking now against Micah, driving him forward into Trace.

If Micah was expecting anything, it wasn't this. Gazing at Trace, whose eyes are closed now, focused on the sensations, only, Micah sees his pleasure in the softness of his mouth, the faintest of smiles playing at the corners of his lips. Trace's body reacts to each push by bracing for the force of it, pushing back into it then drawing forward to do it again. When Micah's body demands he go harder, faster, Gray holds him back, measures the pace, keeps control. Trembling, breathing hard, Micah is the farthest gone of all three of them.

"Should I let him come?" Gray asks Trace quietly, with a smile hidden in the words.

"Please," Trace gasps, made wanton and shameless.

Gray's lips are at Micah's ear. Micah tilts his head ever so slightly to accommodate him, offering his neck. Gently enough to make Micah twitch and thrust with need, Gray's silken lips skim over the shell of his ear and he whispers, "He loves it hard and rough. Give it to him."

Micah's body responds instantly, the cradle of his hips beating Trace's whipped buttocks as he thrusts inward with speed and force, chasing his climax. With a whimpered exclamation, he tenses from head to toe, shooting his load into Trace with the mind-blowing rush of a spectacular orgasm to fry his senses. Stars explode in front of his eyes. He drinks down air while his cock tugs slowly back, then presses in, over and over, decadently, as aftershocks buffet him. Gray's hands caress Trace attentively until Micah is spent.

Gray pulls Micah carefully free of Trace and unfastens the cuffs on his wrists. For just a moment Gray is gone. Then he's back with a towel, drying Micah's face. With that done, he wraps the towel around Micah's waist and asks, "I need a moment with him."

Micah hears himself saying, "Okay," and lets Gray guide him to the door. Before Micah can truly think about what's happening, he's standing in the hall and the door closes, locking behind him.

Chapter 29
At Long Last

The more things change, the more they stay the same, Gray thinks. There he is, Patrick, the bruised soul so used to giving and pleasing, he's lost most of himself in the process. He's given so much to his new family; he's been left in tatters. But, when things are simplified, and it's just warm bodies in the dark, the exchange of pleasure and pain, the man who now calls himself Trace becomes who he has always been. Gray happily takes him back there, to when they met, when at first all Patrick knew was surrender.

In his mind's eye, Gray sees him back there, in a suite at headquarters. He was standing by the sheer curtains of a set of doors which should have opened up to the balcony, but didn't. Those doors were a symbol of the confines of Patrick's existence, always allowing him to look out upon the world around him, never permitting him to take the chance of being part of it and connect with others in a meaningful, straightforward way. It was one of the reasons why Gray was compelled to break him free of his careful cage, built by Nicholai.

Patrick's body was golden in the morning light. He looked around as soon as Gray's presence was detected, the suite's door left unlocked so he was able to enter. With bowed head and an exquisitely submissive posture, this man, who was not Trace at all, was nothing but devoted to fulfilling Gray's every desire, no matter what it may be — as any good whore should.

That's when it happened, when Gray knew. It was that moment by those delicate, white curtains, with all hope for himself extinguished in those haunted eyes. That was when Gray felt with his whole heart that this man, standing in offering before him, deserved so much more than he'd ever gotten from anyone else.

And Gray silently resolved to give it to him. He would give him everything, no matter what he needed to do to make it happen.

Yes, the years have passed, as they are wont to do. There are now more wrinkles crinkling the soft skin by Trace's eyes. His body and spirit have changed along with many other facets of his identity. But part of him is still that bruised soul by the gauzy curtains, hollowed out and nothing to fill himself back up with. Part of Trace is still trying to fill the empty places. He's just going about it in new ways.

Perhaps it's fear that has kept Trace from confiding in Micah as he should. More than anyone, Gray understands the nature of his fear. So, he gives Trace permission to expose the misguided, badly-used boy he used to be, and miraculously, pieces of trepidation tumble away. Trace radiates gratitude, but there are other side effects to how Gray opens his former lover. Once Trace has been opened, the most vulnerable parts of himself are exposed. Intoxicated by that vulnerability in the same ways he used to be, so many years ago, unable to resist, Gray orders Trace to bed.

As Trace climbs onto the bed, lying face down, legs spread wide, Gray follows him down, the condom already on. It's so familiar, an old rhythm they both know how to follow instinctively. Trace tilts his hips, his back bowed, accepting Gray's cock like he needs it, can't continue on without it.

"Still so beautiful," Gray murmurs, sheathing himself completely. He moans an old, forsaken name. "*Patrick.*"

"Please," Trace begs on a gasp, bitten off as it begins to sharpen to a hard edge.

What's it a plea for? Salvation? Forgiveness? Love? A chance to do it all over again, differently?

Gray draws back, presses in. Trace pushes back to meet him, hiding his face with some of the old shame which left him so frequently unable to look at those who would be with him.

"Give them this," Gray urges. "Give *Micah* this. You've been hiding too much away."

"I can't," Trace begs, broken. Broken already. Or has he been broken all of this time, ever since Gray cast him out, too afraid to give his whole heart when things got too difficult between them? Gray drives in harder, holding Trace down, making him feel, taking him apart and scattering the pieces.

"He won't leave you if you make yourself weak for him. And if he does, he never deserved you," Gray whispers, conveying in the only way he can that he has loved Patrick, all this time, even after trying not to. It's an admission and apology too long in coming.

Seemingly understanding Gray's intent, Trace quakes, trembling with the onslaught. He's spread wider, taken deeper, split open until there's no going back to what was, and Gray moans, "*Patrick…*"

—◦—◦—◦—

Trace is drowning in Gray, swept up in a cascade of tenderness, regret, and hope. Nicholai was always fighting for sanity, for control and calm. That's what he wanted to give his beloved submissive. Gray was rebellion and chaos, wild passion, rough sex, and the promise of maybe finding something real, to call his own.

It occurs to Trace then, as Gray makes love to him the way he's done so many times before, of what's been given despite the improbability of it, or how hard Patrick once fought for it, futilely.

Gray does love him. Trace feels it in every whisper of his old name, every touch and thrust as Gray drives to claim and possess, for a moment, what will never be his anymore.

Breathing out a laugh, his heart mending in the most torturous way, Trace opens himself to that gift. Reaching back, holding on, giving over, he says softly, "Love you, bright eyes. Always have. Always will."

"I'm sorry. For all of it. But I wouldn't take it back. Not for anything," Gray promises.

They kiss over Trace's shoulder as Gray drives the breath from him, going harder, worshipping him the only way he can. It feels like forgiveness, and completion. So many years of searching, and it was there all along.

"He's better for you than I was," Gray says against Trace's lips.

Trace moans, holding on, trying to make it last, knowing it won't.

He tenses with orgasm, gasping as Gray thrusts hard one more time, holding there as he comes.

"If Jack runs to you, don't send him away, all right?" Trace tells him, needing him to understand. "Please? As a favor for me?"

Gray just looks at him, seeing him the way no one else can or could, and it feels good. To be known like that is its own reward.

Gray holds on a moment longer.

"Micah will take care of me."

"Will he?"

"He needs me as much as I need him. It's what I've been looking for. He's my family."

Trace sees then Gray doesn't want to leave. It's another piece of beautiful completion, and it makes Trace glad, makes him strong.

With an honest smile, Trace says, "Time to try this a new way, right? Learn from our mistakes?"

Gray nods.

"Thank you for sticking with me," Trace tells him, caressing Gray while he can. "You never really let go, and it's meant a lot. But I need Micah now."

Gray exhales heavily. Trace savors the feel of him, inside and out. Then, he lets him go.

It's time to move on.

Micah stands there, staring at the doorknob in disbelief.

He's just been locked out of his own bedroom, from his own lover.

There's a bathroom right across the hall, and he needs a shower, but can't move an inch. There's no question. He can't leave Trace. He *won't*. So he sinks to the floor again, sitting beside the doorway, ear turned to catch every sound.

There's movement from within the bedroom. The bedsprings squeak. He hears whispering, gasping, grunting, the sounds of passion and what must be two bodies intertwined.

Micah tries to listen harder, to figure out what's being said. The sounds continue. Flesh moves against flesh, sliding, slapping along with labored breaths and swallowed moans that make all of the hairs on Micah's body stand on end.

He hears a voice that isn't Trace—Gray—moaning with pleasure, so much so, it won't be silenced. It occurs to Micah that words are being whispered, and he can't quite catch them. Ear pressed to the wall, he hears Gray moan, "*Patrick.*"

Micah shivers, his skin prickling.

Though he cannot see them, he knows what he hears. It's the sound of Gray fucking Trace, and Trace surrendering to it. Micah lays a hand on the wall, wishing he was in there, instead of stuck on the outside.

Soon, the room falls silent.

Faintly, there's more whispering. The bed creaks. Footsteps move across the room and the sound of water in the adjoining bathroom helps Micah track what's happening.

When the door does finally unlock and open, it's just Gray standing there, slightly tousled, his shirt undone, though otherwise faultless. Scrambling to his feet, Micah has something set into his hand. He doesn't bother to look at it; he's too distracted by Gray.

"What did you—?"

"He needs you," Gray interjects. "Not me." He grips Micah's shoulder; jaw flexing as he struggles to master his expression and rebuild all of those layers which had hidden what was buried beneath. Maybe there is pain and longing in Gray's eyes. The longer Micah looks for it, the harder it is to find.

Gray moves past him, down to hall to seek out his own room.

Micah hurries into the bedroom, dropping the small bottle of ointment in his hand when he sees what had previously been hidden from view.

It's Trace, lying sprawled on the bed, naked and boneless. His eyes stare, unblinking, unseeing. Wetness glistens at the junction of his legs and the red, angry stripes of welts from the whip are screaming at Micah for treatment and care, but the worst of all, by far, are the silent tears leaking from Trace's eyes.

"No no no. Hey," Micah scrambles, darting to the bed, crouching beside it and pushing the hair back from Trace's face. "I'm right here. Trace? Look at me, okay? Please? What's wrong?"

His fingers tangle in Trace's hair. His thumb strokes over the soft skin under Trace's eyes with their vacant stare, clearing teardrops away. Trace reaches out, folding their hands together, drawing Micah in.

"I love you," Micah whispers fiercely. "I love you *so much*."

Maybe it's enough, because Trace's gaze sharpens. He glances over at Micah, kneeling there, leaning in closely, silently urging Trace to come back. But it doesn't look like Trace at all and it scares Micah profoundly.

I did this to him, he thinks, suddenly. *With Moira, with Lily. I scared him like this, too.*

"I love you, too, Mic. More than you know," Trace says, his voice softer, sweeter than Micah's ever heard it before. Micah's vision blurs with tears. He blinks them clear.

Trace's right hand comes up, gripping Micah behind the ear, pulling him in closer. Their foreheads touch and Micah can breathe.

He gets the sheet and covers Trace with it. He finds the ointment and sets it on the nightstand, in reach. Then Micah removes the towel and climbs into bed, letting Trace draw him into his embrace.

Held in Trace's arms, Micah hears him ask, "Don't leave, okay? Don't shut me out, even if I screw up. Love me enough to trust me and talk to me about whatever's wrong. That's all I ask. I'm yours."

Right away, he knows. That's what this was, what it always was, for the man Trace used to be. He was left. Trust was broken. *Everyone* left him. Gray, maybe most of all, would leave and he just did it again, but it's no longer Gray's job to care for Trace. It's Micah's. Gray knows it. That's what the ointment signified. Gray needs Micah to do for Trace what he can't, and that's be there, patiently, to help put him back together, so that he can be strong, and happy.

That's not all, though. Trace is also asking Micah not to repeat the mistakes he's making with Lilianna with him, should things ever go wrong between them. For so long, Micah has unthinkingly shutting out his wife instead of talking through their problems. He's causing the destruction of his marriage by doing so. And Trace is afraid, in time, Micah might do the same thing to him.

"I'll never leave," Micah swears. "I'm yours, too. No matter what. I don't give my heart lightly. And I know I've screwed up with Lily. I'm going to make it right with her. She deserves more respect than I've been giving her. I've been wrong. I admit it, okay? I'll learn from my mistakes. I'm pretty good at that."

"I know," Trace sighs, with what sounds like relief. "Thank you, love. Humility goes a long way with me, for what it's worth. There's nothing more attractive than a man who can admit he's wrong once in a while."

Trace's arm draws more tightly around him, keeping him there, and Micah feels him take a deep breath, calming down.

"We'll protect each other, okay?" Micah says.

"Deal," Trace murmurs.

"It was amazing to have you like that. Thank you for trusting me that much."

"Hell, you're worth it. Shouldn't have waited so long," Trace confesses. "Then again, Gray always did figure things out before me. He even figured out *us*."

"Remind me to thank him when I'm less mad at him," Micah replies. Trace laughs and Micah turns in his arms to see him better, and to kiss him until nothing else exists but them.

Chapter 30
The Old and the New

The lighter is giving him trouble. He finally gets the flame to catch and lights the cigar, sticking it between his teeth. The house is dead quiet, so the footsteps are clear enough from down the hall. It could be any of them, but for some reason Trace thinks it's Jack whom he has pegged as the most restless of the bunch. Maybe he's checking that damned photo again—a rare candid picture of Gray.

Trace has caught him at it a few times now, picking it up, dropping it to the nightstand, then waiting as if the photo was going to sprout legs and walk off. Sometimes he reaches out to straighten it, aligning it perfectly to the edge of the tabletop. Sometimes he doesn't. It's the damnedest thing, part of the OCD that has him carefully sorting his clothes by color and type in the drawers of the guest room, not that Trace would admit to checking.

Jack is in Trace's head more than anyone that morning. Part of the reason is because of Gray and what went down the previous night. There've been so many loose ends between them for so many years, the way Gray swiftly tied them all up in a neat bow—apologizing, confessing, and rebuilding at the same time—leaves Trace dizzy. The whole world seems new that morning. Many important questions, like whether Gray really did care, have been answered. It makes it so much easier to look ahead rather than back. And ahead, for Gray, is Jack. He's the reincarnation of so many things that plagued Gray before, only much more capable of soundly kicking Gray's ass. It makes Trace chuckle, pitying the poor bastard for having his hands so full. It also makes Trace feel grateful to have Micah, whose complications Trace can more than handle, even on a bad day.

Jack is one of the primary people having to deal with Gray's shit on a daily basis these days. Trace feels sorry for the kid, being stuck with that. Like life wasn't hard enough on the kid without Gray's drama chiming in on top of everything else. Sure, it's been a mutually beneficial arrangement, from what Trace has determined, but still, just the fact that Jan is a part of their relationship shows Trace that Gray isn't delivering everything Jack needs in a partner. There's no softness there, not enough given back. Or maybe that's the old resentment talking. Who knows anymore?

You're in my shoes, kid, Trace thinks as footsteps, which might be Jack's, creak and groan. *They might be work boots instead of motorcycle boots, different style, different color, but they're the same inside. Good fuckin' luck to ya.*

The cigar is good. It helps clear his thoughts, settle his nerves. It's going to be a difficult, weird morning after an equally twisted night, so he needs every bit of coherency he can muster. Trace is going to have Jack on his hands for quite a while, all by his lonesome. He could see it in Gray's face, how he was looking for any excuse to call it off, anything to keep Jack away from Trace. Jack is Gray's treasure. Trace gets it. Still, Trace didn't shit a brick when Gray started touching Gabriel, or Micah.

Micah.

Trace chances a backward glance from where he's sitting hunched over on the side of the bed, facing the curtained window. Micah is reclined on the pillows, frowning at his phone as he dials once again.

Shaking his head, turning away, Trace mutters, "Give it up, love. She ain't answerin' this time neither."

"Pessimist," Micah grumbles, putting the phone to his ear as it rings.

"Why do you think she left here?" Trace asks, rhetorically, gesturing around the room with the hand holding his cigar. Tendrils of smoke outline the various pieces of bondage furniture. "Let her be gone if she's gonna go. When she's got her head in a better place, she'll come back."

"She's still my wife," Micah sighs, hanging up when voicemail picks up again.

"For how long?"

He catches Micah's eye over a shoulder and gets hit with *the look*. Exhaling heavily, he faces the window once more, showing Micah his back, laced with faint old scars and fresh new wounds.

"Are we going to talk about this?" Micah asks softly. "And whatever the fuck that was with you and Gray?"

"It was a test," Trace shrugs. "And the end of a long, ongoing conversation. After he caught me at the exact wrong time with Gabey, he flipped his shit. Totally warranted though. I should have known better than to take my hurt out on my boy. Just shows how sloppy I've gotten, and that needs to change. But anyway... Yeah. *Gray*." Standing, pacing a little, Trace does his best, patented Gray impression and says, "*Like I need your rogue shit, Tracey*. All he's doing is trying to get me back in line, nice and obedient, ready to ask 'how high?' when the MC says jump."

"The accent's hot on you," Micah comments.

Trace rolls his eyes. "He broke so many goddamned rules to get me in his bed, and he's a damn hypocrite for faulting me trying to do things my way rather than *theirs*. For some godforsaken reason he's got his sights set on Gabey and agreed to the scene with Dare this morning. And Gray wants Jacky boy to be there, but not in the room, which means Jacky's with *me*. And Gray *hates* that Jacky's gonna be with me. He's got his panties in a twist, doing everything he can to find an excuse, some tiny fault to pick at and use to get out of the deal." He shakes his head again, blowing out smoke. "*That's* what that was. He comes on all hard, then gets soft on me, finally finding the balls to own up to shit he should have handled long ago, but all of it is about the end goal. Always is with him these days. He's just trying to see if I'm cracked or not. Don't get me wrong, I love the bastard just as much as I ever have, but there's gotta be an expiration date on how long someone is allowed to be a pain in your ass. Fucking egomaniacal, control freak, pantywaist fucking Gray."

Micah nods solemnly, then asks, "What's a pantywaist?"

Trace flaps a hand at him, rolling the cigar between his teeth.

"Have you always slipped into a British accent when you get riled up, and I just haven't noticed, or is that new? I mean, you rarely if ever get this way, so maybe I just haven't noticed."

They stare at each other for a long moment, neither budging nor backing down.

"You scared the hell out of me, you know," Micah says angrily, but softly. "He *whipped you*, had you submitting to him so easily when you never submit to *anyone*. He *fucked* you. He called you—"

Micah stops abruptly at a sharp look from Trace.

"You heard that?" Trace asks in a deadly, soft whisper, squinting through the haze.

"Yes, I fucking heard that. And that wasn't even the worst part! When I came in here, and saw you… like *that*…."

The way Micah is looking at him, with wet eyes and protective fury in the clench of his jaw, it's so novel, Trace doesn't quite know how to respond.

"We're all different on the inside, aren't we? I ain't made of stone. Never have been. Just because I don't get that way around people—"

"I'm not people," Micah says sharply.

"I know," Trace sighs. "I know you're not, love. But what you saw last night? That mess that I was… a pathetic, miserable sap… *that's* why he left me. That's why I can't…."

"I would *never* leave you for not being able to be strong sometimes. How hypocritical of me would that be? And also, I'm *not* Gray."

"Yeah, and I ain't *him* anymore," Trace murmurs, sucking on the cigar. "It's just bad dreams. It ain't real. Bad, bad fuckin' dreams."

He walks to the dresser and finds a hair tie. Gathering his hair in one hand, he wraps the tie around.

"We need to talk about this," Micah insists, still holding the damned phone, like he's going to keep calling, though Lilianna's never going to pick up. God, it makes him mad. All of it. It makes him want to fix things that have been broken for too long.

"Not this morning. But we will."

"I hate that he knows you better than me."

Trace finds a pair of pants, softens a little and says, "The past don't mean *anything*, love."

"It does to me."

Clothes in hand, Trace bears the itching, crawling, creeping dread of his old life and his new bleeding together, changing everything irrevocably. Then, nodding once, he goes into the bathroom and closes the door behind him.

―◻―◻―◻―

"God, you're young. I'm old enough to be your father, you know. Both of ya. Feel like I'm fuckin' babysitting."

Jack just stares with lowered brow, his light eyes burning, his body tensed and looking absolutely capable of the swift, blinding attack he wants to happen but won't. Not with those cuffs on, chaining his wrists to his ankles, though Trace is pretty sure he could pick the lock quickly enough. It's the protocol more than physical restraints that are keeping Jacky boy in check, plus curiosity about what the fuck Gray and Gabriel are up to in the other room.

"Gonna keep me chained in here all day, then?"

"You want me to?" Trace asks with a faint smile. "You noticed the ten year pattern of his, right? I skew ten years older, you're ten younger. Kind of funny."

"Yeah, fuckin' peachy," Jack murmurs, staring at the closed door.

"It bothers you, doesn't it? All of these little things about him you didn't know before. All of that need-to-know-basis shit always drove me nuts, though I bet it wasn't as bad then as it is now. Always have to remind myself not to take it personal. Wouldn't be able to live with it, though. Not every day."

Jack shifts, rolling his shoulders and his head as if to keep limber, stay loose. He's on edge already and they haven't even started yet.

Darrek is there, too, hogtied on his stomach in jeans and a t-shirt but barefoot, blindfolded, earbuds blasting music to keep him from hearing much. It had been his choice to come, though Gabriel had warned him they were getting there bright and early, to set things up. Trace supposes it's easier to wait in literal chains, close by, than in figurative ones from afar, especially when you've got something this scary coming your way.

Trace is glad he'll be here, watching, when Gray and Gabriel start to work the kid over. Gabriel has no idea what Gray is capable of, but Trace does. Trace has a real good idea of Gray's spectrum, so it's better, safer, for Darrek to have Trace on the lookout, as one more safety measure.

Gabriel and Gray are setting up the camera downstairs in the dungeon and the video screen in the east recovery room, checking the angle and the feed. In the meantime, Trace has been left in charge of the youngsters in one of the other recovery rooms next door.

"He tell you what this is? What he's doing?" Trace asks.

Jack doesn't answer.

"Did you *ask*?"

The door opens. Jan leans in and says to Trace, "They're ready. Just bringing up some supplies. They'll come get Dare first and then you two can go in."

"Thanks, kid," Trace grins.

Jack catches Jan's eye, holding him there a moment longer. It bothers Jack, Trace sees, that Jan has been allowed to oversee everything, learning, taking it all in, while Jack is stuck where he is, with Gray's ex about to act the part of Dom while Gray does god knows what downstairs with Gabriel and Darrek in the less-than-state-of-the-art BDSM club. But Jan is too curious not to take advantage of it all. Trace wonders if it's because Darrek is the one who's going to be submitting that swayed Jan's decision at all. The two of them have been cozy enough, becoming friends. Trace's guess is it's not friendship Jan is looking to see once ripped, golden, fucktoy Darrek is naked and spread, bending to the will of two powerful Dominants.

Even once Jan has slipped back out, Jack keeps gazing longingly at the door.

A minute or two later, Gabriel and Gray walk in, throwing the door open wide. The air and energy changes instantly. Darrek senses it even with the blindfold and the music to distract him, lifting his head and turning toward the movement. While Gabriel goes to Darrek, gripping the chains and unlocking the ankle cuffs, Gray goes to Jack. With one caress of the side of Jack's neck, Gray draws all of Jack's focus. Tuning in to Gray, anticipating, Jack's eyes slip closed at the touch and his posture speaks of Jack's need for Gray to stay with him, to include him rather than lock him away. But then Gabriel is helping Darrek get to his feet, testing them and making sure they haven't gone completely numb from the pose he's been in.

"You know where we'll be," Gabriel says to Trace.

"Likewise, beautiful," Trace grins.

Gabriel leads Darrek slowly from the room, guiding every step. Left with Gray and Jack, Trace says, "You'll hear him just fine with the acoustics in this place, especially if the doors are left open." The lack of a security team drives Gray nuts, a fact of which Trace is fully aware. "I know what I'm doin', bright eyes. We'll get along great, I know it."

Gray's attention drifts from Trace to Jack. "Obey him as you'd obey me." The hand on Jack's neck drags in a gentle arc. Jack tilts his head, offering his neck, head bowed. Then Gray lets him go, steps back and Trace comes forward.

With a smile lingering at the corner of his mouth, turning it up on one end, Trace hooks a finger under Jack's chin, tilting it up. His thumb skims over Jack's bottom lip and Jack tenses, looking angry as hell. Still smiling, Trace moves fast, grabbing Jack by his dark hair, right at the back of his head and yanking, forcing Jack's head back and making his light grey eyes go wide with surprise. Trace runs the back of a finger lightly down Jack's exposed throat.

"Easy," Trace hushes. "I ain't gonna do anything you don't like, trust me."

Wary, alert, Jack studies him. The tension of Trace's hand in his hair countered by the sweetness of his tone is like Trace's calling card. He gives Jack a chance to read it thoroughly. Swiftly, Trace unlocks the chain connected to Jack's ankles and draws him up, hand locked around the back of Jack's neck. Jack's arms are still bound behind his back, the chain dangling down from them. Taking up the slack, winding the chain around his fist, Trace keeps tight hold of his captive, pulling hard on the chain so Jack feels he's going nowhere. He grips the back of Jack's neck and pushes him somewhat roughly out of the room. He might not be so rough with other subs when first starting out with them, but knows Jack is different. Jack will be mentally comparing Trace to all of the nasty fuckers back at the Master's Circle who he's danced with in the past. If Trace doesn't intimidate Jack into falling in line, Jack won't fall in line. It's as simple as that.

"Let's get this show on the road, darlin', shall we?"

Gray exits behind Trace, giving him a look of clear warning as Trace moves Jack to the room that has been specially set up for him. Jack doesn't notice, he's too busy taking in the sight of the adjustable metal table and the wheeled cart filled with supplies, draped with a white towel to hide what's beneath, in the center of the sparse room. There's a sink on one wall with disinfecting supplies lining the edge. Sunlight creeps in through the slats of the closed blinds. A screen stands on top of a cabinet at the foot of the bed, but the power is off, the picture black. Keeping Jack's back to the door, where Trace knows Gray is lingering, watching, he manhandles Jack up to the side of the table. By his ear, in a controlled growl, he says, "Lay down. Let's make you comfortable."

"Looks real comfortable," Jack murmurs. The recently scrubbed metal gleams in the light. The scent of industrial strength soap lingers in the air, tickling Trace's nostrils. Trace quickly unfastens the cuffs, setting them aside. Just as swiftly, while Jack is still scrutinizing the set-up, Trace takes hold of the hem of Jack's shirt, getting it over his head and off of him in a fluid movement.

"Get on the damn table. Now."

Jack's gaze lifts, his lips nearly drawing up in a wicked grin. "Yes, Sir," he answers, sounding like a smartass, looking like he's not likely to do anything of the sort, short of Trace body-slamming him onto the damned table. For a long moment, it's a standoff. Trace's smile has died, and there seems to be something about his lack of amusement that gets Jack to act.

As soon as Jack begins to shift onto the surface, lying on his back, Trace pulls him down firmly by both wrists, rapidly fastening the leather cuffs around one wrist, then the other, buckling them tightly shut. They bind Jack's arms with his hands up near the sides of his head, his elbows bent. The table is flat, but just for the time being. Once the show gets started, Trace will make sure the audience has a good view.

Testing the cuffs, gaze narrowing, Jack grunts, "Fucking hell."

Trace runs a hand down the center of Jack's chest, taking his time. He strokes lightly over the front of Jack's jeans before grabbing hold of his scrotum through the thick fabric, squeezing and yanking once. As Jack's hips tilt up instinctively, his jaw clenching with a grunt of discomfort, Trace smiles down at him. "You're not going anywhere, princess. These pants, though? These are coming off."

Jack's chest expands as he draws in a deeper breath, then blows it out. Trace flips open the button of Jack's fly with his free hand, not easing up on Jack's balls at all, and Jack glances back at the doorway, opened but empty.

Laughing darkly, Trace tells him, "Just the two of us, now. Gray's… well, he's got his hands full with someone else, but you won't be left out. Your boy, Jan, is down there, too. Front row seat."

Jan's name prompts a swift flare of anger from Jack, just as Trace finishes drawing down Jack's zipper. Grey eyes blazing, teeth bared in a snarl, Jack tests the cuffs on his wrists, curling forward to snap at Trace.

"Yeah, I know you're real protective of him. I ain't touchin' him, though, am I? I'm touching *you*."

The jeans come off with one hard tug, while Trace is standing by Jack's bare feet at the end of the table. Trace fastens another set of leather cuffs around Jack's ankles, keeping them spread to either end of the table's edges. With that done, he clicks the button to turn on the TV. A view of the dungeon from above comes up, center screen. It's zoomed in fairly tight on another metal table, but this one is vastly different from the one Jack is bound to. The one in the dungeon is much, much shorter, with moveable, adjustable arms at the base and sides, as well as a cradle for the head. It's bathed in a pool of light from an overhead lamp. In shadows around it, the shapes of Gabriel and Darrek come into view. A moment later, Gray is there as well.

Jack's breathing becomes more uneven, his gaze glued to the screen. The sink is just below and to the side of the TV. Going to it, Trace washes his hands, using plenty of soap. Once finished, he dries them with a paper towel that gets tossed in the bin. Moving around the table, Trace folds Jack's genitals up in a freshly cleaned hand, gripping the flesh of his sac and shaft gently. Jack's gaze doesn't waver from the screen but his breath catches.

"Gonna make sure you enjoy yourself, Jack," Trace whispers, kneading, feeling Jack get hard, slowly. "Let me hear your safeword."

"Mercedes."

Hooking the junction of his index finger and thumb of his left hand around the root of Jack's sac, wrapping the fingers around, he pulls, stretching the skin to its limit, then constricts, adding plenty of pressure. With his right hand, Trace grips Jack's shaft, swiping his thumb back and forth over the tip. Trace sees Jack's gaze drift up to the ceiling, forsaking the screen.

"Don't let me distract you, now," Trace says. "The screen's there for you, not me." The edge of Trace's thumbnail finds Jack's slit. He works it in, prying gently at the edge. "Gonna stuff you, slave," Trace warns, his voice quiet, "Everywhere I *can* stuff you. Make you yell. Give Gray down there something real sweet to listen to while he's busy taking Dare's tight, near-virgin ass for the ride of his life. And don't worry. I know all about you. Unlike you, slave, I ask questions. I do my homework."

The nail digs in. Balls in the vise of Trace's fingers, Jack groans.

"Goddamn, we're gonna have fun," Trace chuckles.

He feels Jack shiver, hissing, "Fuck. Fuck. *Fuck.*"

Chapter 31
Master Gabe, Master Gray

"Strip."

Darrek thought the dungeon would be chilly, but they must have the heat cranking. It's hot enough that he doesn't mind losing the clothes; in theory at least. He's been in that place, with Gabriel, more than once, but never like this. Gray is there, shirtless and intimidating as fuck. Jan is there, too, which is somehow just as bad. Sitting on the far side of the room, on a chair, leaned forward with his elbows on his knees like he's eager to see the spectacle Darrek is about to make of himself, Jan stares and Darrek shivers.

There's a camera, too, behind and above Darrek, capturing everything. Gabriel is standing behind Darrek, as well, giving orders but letting Darrek see only Gray and Jan.

He hasn't tried to figure out what they're going to do to him. Every time he begins to speculate, his mind shuts down. It's nervous anxiety but also desire for the unknown, for a greater challenge than anything he's ever faced before in a scene. The promise of what might happen had him wanting to masturbate in the shower last night and this morning, though he knew Gabriel would catch him or be able to tell, and be displeased. Now though, he's turned on and terrified in equal measure.

"I said, strip!" Gabriel barks.

"Yes, Sir," Darrek fumbles. He gets hold of his shirt and pulls it off. Tossing it on an empty wheeled cart nearby, he hesitates before moving to unfasten his jeans. They're all looking at him, and his body. His nipples stiffen and his skin flushes with the heat and the attention. Breathing out a low hum of pure anxiousness, like steam from a teapot about to boil, he feels too big, too loud, and too awkward when the rest of them are composed and silent.

He does it quickly, undoing his pants, hooking his thumbs in the waist of both jeans and underwear and pulling them down. After stepping from the legs, he sets the clothes aside on the cart, too. Then he's naked, being ogled, and shuts his eyes so he doesn't have to see them looking.

"Hands behind your head! Legs apart! Chin up! And I didn't give you permission to close your eyes, slave."

Responding to the commands is mostly reflex. It's easy. But being in the position is not, especially seeing everything. To his left is the contraption he knows they intend him to get into and he tries not to look at it, but stare straight ahead, at a spot on the wall.

There had been paperwork for him to sign that morning. Gabriel had sat with him, explaining, going over the checklist slowly, item by item. He'd had to select things that were triggers for him, and note what he didn't want. There hadn't been much he had checked off, as Gabriel had asked him to really consider each one from a fresh perspective, knowing his preferences and tastes had adjusted after being a submissive for so long. Now, just like the first time he encountered Gabriel in the dungeon, as Master and slave, he's reciting the list in his head again, wondering why he didn't check off more than he had, and realizing how much they could do to him.

Gray had come in when Darrek was ready to sign, looking it all over, then signing as well as Gabriel. The official nature of the ritual also set Darrek on edge rather than serving to help calm him down.

Fingers brush the underside of his cock, making him let out a startled little noise. The touching continues, and he knows it's Gabriel, so it's easy to bear. The light, tickling contact makes him begin to get hard, though, and all he can do is stand there, fingers woven behind his head, palms braced against his hair, and breathe as he's fondled.

It goes on and on, until the attention and the stiffness of his dick is all he knows. It's his whole world. He can hear himself breathing, can feel how hard his heart is beating and the prickling of the air at his bare skin.

There's a warm presence at his right side. That's Gabriel. Darrek keeps himself from looking, but feels him there. From by his right ear, he hears, "Tell us your safeword."

"Tundra."

"You're safe here," Gabriel tells him gently. The reassurance only stokes the fire of his nervous energy, though. If Gabriel is trying to keep him calm, it means something major is coming his way. "You can trust us to take care of you, okay?"

"Yes, Sir," Darrek grunts. It's challenging to answer questions while being played with in front of the others. It occurs to him just how much he had been relying on the blindfold as a comfort mechanism the night before. Gabriel's fingers stroke lightly up to his tip, drawing circles around it. Face hot, body tense, cock responding exactly as Gabriel wants it to, Darrek fights not to close his eyes.

Then Gray moves forward a step or two and begins to open his pants, his eyes still locked on Darrek.

A low whimper of dread begins to sound from back in Darrek's throat. It draws out, sharpening as Gray guides his pants down, wearing no underwear beneath, and steps out of the legs.

"Breathe," Gabriel whispers, caressing. "Don't over-think this. Focus on what you feel and what you see, not what you think may or may not happen."

There's only one reason why Gray would be undressed.

"Oh my god," Darrek moans, frowning, head tilted back to give himself a different view.

"Eyes forward, slave," Gabriel scolds.

The presence at his side drifts away. His hands are gripped, held where they are behind his head. Gray walks up to him, his cock heavy, dark, and hard. A tremor begins in Darrek's body, shaking him from his core outward as Gray reaches out to touch him. Fingers trail over the side of his abdomen, down the ridge of his hipbone, and the low whimper begins again in his throat. He hates it, but can't stop it as the fear grips tightly.

"Breathe in… and out," Gabriel hushes. Gray's fingers brush up over Darrek's navel, following a line up the center of his body and over to his left nipple which is then flicked, pinched and twisted sharply. Darrek's eyes roll and his breath leaves him with a grunt.

Grinding his teeth together, he bears down on the hurt which doesn't let up as Gray doesn't let go or ease the twist. Darrek's cock weeps pre-come and Gray's other hand moves to stroke his own shaft. The tremor gets worse because Darrek can't not watch Gray stroking himself, like a promise, showing Darrek what he's about to get.

Gabriel's hand brushes Darrek's back. Eyelids fluttering, Darrek mentally latches on to the contact. Gray lets go of Darrek's nipple, rubbing firmly over the pectoral muscle and the sore, throbbing nub. Then he grips it again and twists even harder. Darrek bites off a hard shout, his arms quivering.

Gray lets go again, rubbing back and forth over Darrek's areola, rolling the nipple which beats with his pulse as blood surges there.

"Again," Gray says softly, pulling the nipple out and down, stretching skin as far as it will go. Darrek's elbows come forward as he blows out breath through the pain but Gabriel just takes his elbows and draws them back where they were.

"Ahh, fuck," Darrek whines.

Gray keeps stroking himself, gazing up and down Darrek's body while he does.

"You like that? The pain?" Gray asks.

Darrek struggles to speak, his mouth working as Gray pulls harder. Gabriel passes him a small pair of medical clamps.

"Mm... yes, Sir. Shit. Fuck. *Fuck.*"

Gray attaches the clamps to the nipple, leaving them to hang there, stretching the flesh, keeping it compressed. Gingerly lifting the handle, Gray watches with what looks like dull curiosity as Darrek gasps, mouth fallen open when the clamps are pressed completely upright, toward the ceiling.

"What are you thinking about?"

"How much it hurts, Sir," Darrek growls.

"Anything else?"

"Your, uh... your cock, Sir."

"More specific, please," Gray coaxes, pressing the clamps to one side, then the other. Darrek has to blink his eyes clear as tears begin to pool.

"I like your cock, Sir," Darrek says more gruffly with a pair of tears spilling over his cheeks. Gabriel's hand moves on his back, and that's good. It makes it easier.

"You *like* it? Do you *want* my cock, slave?"

"Yes, Sir," Darrek murmurs, quietly, grunting roughly as he pushes down on the pain and the humiliation.

"Say it. Loudly."

"I want your cock, Sir!"

"Good. Ask me and maybe I'll give it to you."

It's an order, not a request.

"Walk forward now."

Gabriel guides him with gentle pressure between his shoulder blades. They move him up to the strange metal table, tilted at a slight angle with the narrow, jointed metal beams sticking out to hold arms and legs. He feels the camera's eye on him, senses Jan there, beyond the circle of fear, pleasure and pain, seeing everything.

"Have a seat," Gabriel says, manhandling him into the right position on the table, getting him lower than he initially puts himself, having him scoot down once he has laid back so his ass hangs off the end. His head is set in the cradle, his arms on beams stretching out perpendicular from the table at his sides. Leather bands wrap his arms and Gabriel binds one, then the other. Pulled tight are bands wrapping his wrists, below his elbows and a third set, farther up at the top of his biceps. Once his arms are completely immobilized, a strap is wound over his forehead, keeping his head still. Gray pulls on a pair of latex gloves. A tray is wheeled closer but kept out of his line of sight.

Practicing his breathing exercises, he tries to keep from watching or panicking as his legs are set on the folding arms with stirrups and strapped in just as tightly, by his ankles and under his knees. They adjust the angle so his legs are spread apart as far as is comfortable but also bent back sharply. They're locked in place with a loud click from each side. He's completely spread, his ass presented, his genitals exposed, his nipple screaming with pain that he knows will only worsen once the clamp comes off. Then Gray reaches for lube.

"Can I please have a blindfold?" Darrek blurts out.

"No," Gabriel answers.

"*Please*," he begs, voice wavering. Gray turns toward him and swiftly inserts two hooked fingers into Darrek's anus. "Please! No, fuck. Oh fuck. Oh *god*."

Pivoting his wrist, rotating the fingers while pumping them, Gray pries at Darrek's asshole.

"Calm down," Gabriel says sternly. "It's just fingers. Can you handle this or not, slave?"

Darrek sucks in air through his nose, then blows it out his mouth. He does it again. Gray closes Darrek's reddened erection in a loose fist and strokes while the fingers work diligently to spread lube and open his ass.

"I can handle it," Darrek says.

"Prove it. You have been fucked before?" Gabriel asks.

"Yes, Sir."

"You do like getting fucked?"

"Yes, Sir," Darrek says, less confidently.

"Do you want Master Gray to fuck you, slave?"

Darrek moans and closes his eyes, beginning to get delirious from how good Gray's ministrations feel. He really feels it then, getting a little beyond the panic to realize he is enjoying the way it feels.

"Good. That's good," Gabriel praises, brushing the hair back from Darrek's face. "Answer the question. Do you want Master Gray to fuck you?"

"Yes, Sir."

"Then what do you say?"

"Oh god," Darrek moans. Gray spreads his fingers as wide as they'll go, adds a third. Darrek's whole body reacts, undulating on the table. His cock drips pre come. It's shiny wet with it. "Please fuck my ass, Master Gray. Please fuck me."

Out of the corner of his eye, Darrek sees Gabriel nod to Gray. His heart skips a beat. From the cart by his side, Gray produces a dildo and coats it with more lube. Reaching between Darrek's spread thighs, Gabriel palms Darrek's ass and, digging the fingers in, yanks his cheeks apart. He's held opened like that while Gray lines up the phallus and slides it in with a firm push, burying it in one stroke.

"No! Fuck!" Darrek lets out a throaty yell, his whole body throbbing around the toy sheathed in his rectum. Gray holds it there and strokes Darrek's cock, root to tip, through the slippery, clear fluid soaking it.

"That's what you asked for, slave," Gabriel tells him, matter-of-factly. "If you changed your mind, we can always take it out."

Just like that, Gray begins to slowly withdraw the long, thick object. When it's completely out, Gabriel lets go of Darrek's cheeks and goes to the cart. He comes back with a bottle of fluid and a cotton swab, walking with it around to the side of the table, Darrek's left side.

"What is that? What are you doing?" he blurts.

Gabriel looks darkly at him, saying nothing.

"Uh… Sir. Sir, please, may I ask what you're doing?" The last word lilts up as Gray stuffs Darrek full of three fingers and triggers his prostate.

"Fuck," Darrek whines, cock twitching, straining up to his belly as he writhes on the fingers. His hips chase up from the table and he cries out as Gray taps his gland, shuddering, humping air. Meanwhile, Gabriel pulls off the clamp and swipes cool fluid over Darrek's sore nipple. He barely notices. Gray takes hold of Darrek's balls, drawn up tight and ready to shoot, yanking on them, pressing up inside him to get at his gland while drawing his hips back down with tension on his testicles.

"I'm piercing your nipple," Darrek hears just a fraction of a second before feeling pressure and a sharp, specific point of pain. Glancing down at his chest, he sees Gabriel holding a thin, long spike of a needle which is now speared through his left nipple.

"Oh my god. *Oh my god*," he gasps, shocked. The hurt blooms from the spot and he's unable to look away from the metal spike through his pink, swollen flesh. Then Gray massages his balls. He strokes up Darrek's shaft once, fingers stuffing his ass full, massaging his gland. Darrek comes with a choked, devastated moan, shooting up the length of his torso. Gray strokes him through it, pulling his fingers out, replacing them with the phallus and fucking Darrek with it in long, slow movements in and out of his ass. His whole body clenches up around the orgasm, eyes rolling back, everything funneled down between his legs and purged from the tip of his cock.

"Good, baby," Gabriel praises tenderly, caressing Darrek's face. "Just feel it. Feels good?"

"Yes," Darrek gasps, breathless. A tear slips from each of his eyes and he sobs softly. Gabriel's lips touch Darrek's in a brief, light kiss and he shudders with the heady force of how indescribably good it does feel, especially knowing they've barely started. They aren't nearly done with him.

Chapter 32
Darrek's Submission

Darrek knows exactly why Gabriel is doing what he is, having Darrek submit to Master Dom Gray, challenging his boundaries as much as he ever has. He's trying to correct the balance in their relationship and in Darrek, himself. Ever since the phone started ringing Darrek has sunk into a dark place where the regret and painful remorse of what transpired with Kyle lingers at the edges of everything, keeping him from a good night's sleep, from being able to concentrate on work, from being able to surrender completely when he's submitting to Gabriel, and even just in existing, moment to moment. It's a weight, dragging him down. It hasn't really sunk in that Jerry is gone, that it's truly *over*. So much of it all, from the shrill chiming of the phone, to the call he made to his mother the night before, seems unreal, a delusion he's suffering from while his younger self is still trapped in his old bedroom, waiting to be hurt or to be forced to hurt someone he loves.

What Gabriel is trying to do is slam Darrek back into reality, the here and now, utterly and completely, in every sense. Pain is a link to his past, though. It's familiar. Darrek knows he can handle it, no matter how bad it is. As long as he's the one suffering, that means everyone else is okay.

So, Gabriel doesn't use pain. He shocks Darrek's system in other ways. The piercing is a mental challenge, scarier in concept than it is in reality. Staring down at the needle impaling his nipple, feeling the flesh throb with the beat of his heart, he doesn't fear it now that it's happened. If anything, he fears Gabriel will just take the needle out and leave it alone, letting the wound heal like it never happened. Darrek has more than enough old, scarred wounds. He doesn't want any more.

A cool cloth is used on his face, brushing the sweat and tears away, drawing him back out of his head, into full alertness. His orgasm makes him sleepy, relaxed. The temptation is there to sink back into the dark, to let go. Even bound as he is, legs spread, arms spread, head strapped in, bathed in searing light from above, he feels comfortable enough to drift off.

But then Gray moves the plastic cock up Darrek's ass, pumping it in and out, fucking him like he wants Darrek to really feel it, to be unable to ignore it. Darrek moans, low and long. Gray's other hand is on Darrek's spent cock, fondling the shaft and the head. It makes Darrek squirm restlessly on the table, wanting the touches to stop until he's recovered, suspecting they won't.

He wants to see Gabriel but can't, since Gabriel is staying behind him, letting Gray and the dungeon itself fill Darrek's view. From far away, echoing, he hears a rough yell and it distracts him from the uncomfortable stroking of his oversensitive cock and the pounding of his ass.

That's Jack, he realizes. *Jack with Trace. They're watching me. They can see me, right now.*

The yell comes again, sounding angrily tormented in a way very similar to the way Darrek feels.

From just beside and a little behind him, he detects movement. Gabriel beckons to the shadows. It doesn't make sense—his crooked finger, his hushed, "C'mere. Come closer."

Then he remembers Jan.

"No," Darrek says in a rush. "Don't. Please. Please?"

The phallus is withdrawn from his body, then set aside on the tray. Gray rolls on a condom and Darrek strangles on a big, thick blanket of terror smothering him. It begins to feel like he's above himself, watching it all happen as parts of his mind disconnect from the rest. Jan moves closer for a better view. Gabriel is playing on Darrek's typical reactions to humiliation, one of his greatest weaknesses. The only greater weakness of Darrek's is the fact that he has never been fucked by any other man than Gabriel. He's taken multiple partners, but not been taken. Before he met Gabriel, he had fooled himself into believing he was straight. Being committed to Gabriel has been a comfort to Darrek. It's safe. But Gabriel has been with Trace, and Ben, out of necessity rather than choice. Darrek has taken Kyle and wears that shame as part of his lingering, constant torment. Of course Gabriel would arrange this. If he makes sex less sacred for Darrek, the mental pressures can vent.

That's just logic talking, though. As Darrek watches Gray move up between his spread thighs, his fully erect cock in hand, pushing it down to align with Darrek's opening, Darrek begins to make a tight, scared humming sound, behind tightly sealed lips. Breathing hard through his nose, but shallowly, he tries to stop making that awful sound. It only causes the noise to break into a whimper, which feels worse. His body clenches with anxiety and he wants Gabriel's hand, needs to feel him there and can't do this without reassurance. It feels like betrayal. It feels like too much.

Jittery and tense, feeling many sets of eyes upon him, trembling, hands in fists, feet flexed, he feels the blunt end of Gray's cock press at him.

"Gabriel?" he gasps tightly, around the lump in his throat.

"I'm here," Gabriel says, laying a hand on the side of Darrek's face.

He hasn't been this scared in a long, long time.

Staring down the length of his body at Gray, muscle-bound and more intimidating than Gabriel has ever been, more than anyone, save Jerry, has ever been, Darrek sees, *feels*, Gray enter him with a firm thrust.

There's another of those faraway roars from upstairs but it gets lost in Darrek's sobs. He tries to hold them in, push them down but then he can't breathe. His lungs refuse to work. He can feel Gray inside him but can't see anything, can't feel anything else. His chest burns the longer he goes without inhaling.

"He all right?" Jan asks nervously from a few feet away.

"Dare, baby, breathe," Gabriel coaxes with a hand on Darrek's chest and another cupping his jaw, the fingers tenderly brushing his skin.

"I'm so sorry," Darrek weeps. "Tundra."

It happens so fast, he can't keep track. Suddenly he's not

strapped down at all, but sitting up. Someone puts a glass of water in his hand. Glancing up, he sees Gabriel with the towel. He uses it to dry Darrek's face, looking back into his eyes with profound concern.

"What do you need?" Gray asks. "Do you need to stop?"

"I just...." he glances around at the three of them, still so focused on him. "I just need a minute."

"Why did you apologize?" Gabriel asks softly. "What's wrong? This doesn't mean you don't love me, you know."

Hanging his head, letting loose the ties holding him together, he cries into the towel. Gabriel moves into his arms, wrapping him in an embrace, setting his chin on Darrek's shoulder and rubbing his back. When they part, Gabriel examines the needle in Darrek's flesh, pressing gingerly beside the area, then dabbing with a cotton ball Gray passes him to clean away blood.

"Should I take this out?"

"Don't, please," he blurts in answer. Embarrassed, he bites his lip and chances a quick glance over at Jan before asking Gabriel, "You don't have any, um... jewelry for it, do you? I want to... I want to keep it."

"Yeah," Gabriel says with a faint smile, breathing easier, too. "No problem. Should I do both?"

Darrek nods, as a blush heats his skin.

"Are we stopping?" Gray asks.

He shakes his head again. "No, Sir."

"Do you want this?" Gabriel asks seriously, and he's not talking about the piercing.

"Yes. I do. I'm just—" He lets out a shaky exhale and sips from the glass of water. Gabriel's hand is on his knee and on his shoulder, steadying him.

"I want this for you," Gabriel says. "I want you to enjoy it. That's all. There's no trick, okay? I know you haven't felt safe in a long time and I want you to feel safe here. What do you need?"

"No restraints."

"No restraints?" Gabriel echoes, searching Darrek's face. "That's all?"

"If I'm going to do this, I want to feel like I'm choosing it and doing it willingly. Does that make sense?"

"Yeah," Gabriel smiles.

"And I want—" the confession sticks, snagging on a barb of self-protection before ripping free. "I want to hold your hand, if that's okay."

Gabriel's mouth is on him then, kissing gently, his lips on Darrek's lips. His breath is warm, his touch so tender it makes Darrek smile.

"Love you," Gabriel whispers.

"Love you, too."

When Darrek is ready, he lies back down, taking a deep, cleansing breath.

"Is Jack okay? He's been… loud."

"Jack's riled, is all. It's expected," Gray grins. "He doesn't like not having control."

"Yeah, don't pay him any attention," Jan smirks. Darrek sees Jan's gaze drift down his body, especially when he folds his legs and brings them up to brace against the adjustable footrests. Then Jan notices that Darrek sees him looking and gets flustered, going pink in the face and running a hand through his hair. "So, you're okay then?"

"Yep. I'm good," Darrek smiles, amused at the effect he's having, as well as a little proud. "I'm not boring you, am I?"

"Nah, not boring at all. Very informative," Jan says, too fast, still trying not to stare at Darrek's groin and the wet, stretched, loosened hole his lover is about to sheath himself in for the second time.

"You guys aren't recording this, are you?" Darrek asks, curious.

"Yeah, that'd be awful," Jan murmurs sarcastically.

Darrek chuckles and Gray says, clipped and stern, "Enough. No more chatting. You want to be here, you're silent." That's directed to Jan. He turns to Darrek next and approaches the table.

"How are we, slave?" he asks Darrek.

"Fine, Sir. Thank you."

Gray caresses up the inside of Darrek's thigh, his touch skating feather light over Darrek's balls and shaft, then up over his abdomen to his pierced nipple. With his latex-covered fingers he tugs slightly at the needle, then rubs gently over the speared flesh, making Darrek suck in air with a groan.

"Clamps," Gray says to Gabriel with a quick upward glance, taking Darrek's untouched right nipple between two fingers and twisting until he cries out. Gabriel hands over the clamps and swabs disinfectant over the area.

"Oh my god," Darrek moans, then gasps harshly as first the clamps are snapped on, then three of Gray's fingers wedge themselves up his ass. "*Fuck*."

"Say please," Gabriel teases.

"Please, Master. Want it."

Gray pulls on the clamps, rotating them, bending them this way and that as Darrek wriggles on his hand. His cock slowly begins to stiffen once more. Grabbing the sides of the table with both hands, Darrek feels the urge to push down against Gray's fingers and watches avidly as Gabriel gets the other needle ready. It shimmers brightly in the overhead light, wet with disinfectant, sharp as hell.

"You want this?" Gabriel asks with raised eyebrows, lifting the needle.

"Yeah. Yes, Sir."

"Why? Because it hurts? Fucking pain slut."

Gray rubs over Darrek's gland, making him whimper and thrust. Letting go of the clamps, he uses his freed hand to stroke Darrek's cock instead.

"Want you to mark me, Sir. I wanna remember this."

"Good," Gabriel says with approval. "But first you're going to cooperate with Master Gray. Understood?"

"Yes, Sir."

He draws his legs up, holding them behind the knees.

"Ankles, slave. I want your ass out all the way. No being shy today."

"Yes, Sir."

Shifting his grip, he takes hold of his ankles instead.

"P-please fuck me, Master Gray. Want your cock, Sir."

"Mm, very polite," Gray smiles. He doesn't waste time. A second later he's breached Darrek's outer ring and pushing hard to go balls deep. Darrek shouts, fingers gripping, pulling at his legs.

Gray's hands are on his hips, his ass, spreading him as he works deeper. It feels so good, Darrek forgets everything—where he is, what's happening, what he's been worried about.

"Fuck," Jan murmurs from nearby—very nearby. He sounds closer than ever. Upstairs, the roar of frustration comes again, and Darrek has to laugh. It quickly turns into a hard moan because Gray is fully seated; splitting him open, so far inside, Darrek sees stars. Arms quivering, he feels his ankles grabbed by Gray instead, and lets go.

"Nice and still now. Hold it right there," Gabriel instructs, standing right by Darrek's side with the needle pinched between his fingers.

"Jesus Christ. Oh my god," Darrek groans, unable not to look as Gabriel lifts the clamp, aligns the needle and jabs.

It's through before Darrek can react. He stops holding his breath and breathes through the small, sharp pain, laughing again, breathlessly.

"Yeah, I can tell you really hate that, huh? Fucking pain in my ass," Gabriel complains with a crooked grin. "How's it feel?"

"Fucking good, Sir," Darrek answers, trying not to look at Gray or where their bodies meet.

"Ready to behave? Be a good girl for us?"

"Yes, Sir."

The headrest moves. Gabriel lowers it a few notches until Darrek's head is back, his neck elongated in a straight line. Darrek suspects where this is going and his breath catches again.

"Easy. Easy. Close your eyes if you need to, okay?"

"Yes, Sir," Darrek answers, but it's gruff, tense. Gray draws back, pushes all the way back in and it feels like dying. Darrek's mouth works around an unvoiced cry. Then he feels it, latex-sheathed flesh against his lips. A hard shudder works through his body.

Mouthing at the head of Gabriel's cock, he hears him say, "Good, show us you want it. Ready to obey your Masters, slave?"

"Yes, Sir. Please," he begs. Opening wider, he invites Gabriel to take his mouth.

"Just your tongue and lips right now. That's it. You want to please us, don't you? You want us to both give you our cocks?"

"Fuck yes," Darrek moans. He licks the tip, tasting latex, wishing he was only tasting Gabriel. When he gets more contact, he drags open-mouthed kisses as Gabriel keeps just within reach. Meanwhile, Gray withdraws again, torturously slow, until he's out. He rubs over Darrek's rim, letting go of one of Darrek's legs. Darrek grabs it, holding it back for him.

He feels intense pressure, then, as Gray feeds him four fingers at once. Darrek's rim stretches tight and smooth around the digits and he cries out, a throaty, rough sound.

"Open wide, slave," Gabriel commands. Darrek obeys and gets fed Gabriel's cock. It passes through his lips and goes back into his throat. The whole length lodges there and Darrek struggles to take it. Gabriel caresses his throat, his chest, holding where he is, then drawing back, pushing in again. Eyes watering, gasping for air when Gabriel's cock withdraws from his windpipe, Darrek revels in it.

The fingers in his ass pull out, replaced once more by Gray's dick and they both begin to move in him with long, slow strokes. Gray has both of Darrek's ankles again, pushing them way back, so Darrek is free to grab the table and take one of Gabriel's hands with the other.

"Good," Gabriel sighs. "Just relax. So good, Dare."

Gabriel's thumb brushes the back of Darrek's hand and he focuses on that as they use him, taking him at both ends while his spectators look on. He doesn't let himself think about it and is glad he can't see Gray or Jan. It's enough to feel them, to obey and surrender.

When Gray quickens his pace, it becomes difficult for Darrek to breathe and stay relaxed for Gabriel. Gagging on him, he's grateful when Gabriel pulls out to give him a break, but then Gray goes harder than ever. Beating Darrek's ass with his hips, Gray fucks him at a brutal pace until Darrek is shouting, grabbing Gabriel's hand and the table so hard his hands ache. The friction in his ass makes it feel raw, sore and he gulps air. Gray pushes Darrek's legs even more sharply back, folding him in half, going so deep, so hard that Darrek's eyes roll back, a low, unending moan coming from the back of his throat where he can still feel Gabriel.

"What do you say, slave? Remember your manners," Gabriel says sternly.

"T-thank you, Master Gray. Please fuck me harder."

He didn't think it was even possible, but somehow Gray does go harder. All Darrek can do is gasp and shout. Gabriel grips his hand, caresses his face. Darrek's cock is so hard it hurts, begging for relief, for one touch, one stroke. That's all he needs to go over the edge.

"Please, Master," he beseeches shamelessly. "Please let me come. Oh *god*."

"How's that cock feel, slave?"

"So fucking good," he moans. "Shit…"

Gabriel strokes him, root to tip, corkscrewing up then down and Darrek's whole body locks up, clenching up around his second orgasm. Gray moans and Darrek gets woozy as he shoots, his entire body sizzling, tingling. He's gasping, gulping air. Gray's hips snap and Darrek knows he's coming, filling the condom. It makes him feel proud, makes him smile through the wash of exhaustion.

"Hold his legs," Gray tells Gabriel, who pulls them back. The cock withdraws from him, leaving him too empty. A moment later, there's a loud crack and a bright red line of pain cutting across Darrek's ass as the leather strap strikes it hard. It takes Darrek's breath from him even as the pain intensifies the aftershocks of pleasure. Shuddering, still coming, he begs, "Please more. Please."

The strap falls again, and again, and again.

Someone else takes his legs. He's filled again, but it's different. He's too tired to look, though. But as they begin to move inside him, taking of him yet again even as his body sings with glorious pain-laced-pleasure, he knows it's Gabriel.

"Thank you, Master," he cries, the tears streaming now. "Thank you. Please more. Oh fuck…."

Chapter 33
Dominating Jack

"What's your pleasure, Jacky boy?"

Holding the 5mm urethral sound where Jack can see it, swiping disinfectant along it, Trace lifts his eyebrows, waiting expectantly.

"Darrek there's got a raging pain kink," Trace continues. "I got to play with that way back when. Don't know if you'll find this out today or not, since they've got special plans for him, but that kid's fuckin' *loud* if you hurt him the right way. And Kyle... you met Kyle, didn't you?"

Trace smiles, watching Jack's reaction. He's been quiet, closed off. There is a lot to take in, though. Trace'll give him that. Thanks to the TV, Jack is watching Gray play with Darrek's cock and get inside an ass that's been sole property of its owner thus far. In addition, Jack is catching glimpses of Jan at the edges of the screen and sneaking glances regularly at Trace as he goes through an overly thorough cleaning ritual with the gear he plans to use. Plus, Jack is bound, naked, to a metal table with no one watching on security cameras, no team of men waiting in the wings to rush in should things go wrong. That's why Trace goes through the cleaning, to put Jack at ease, to show he knows enough about Jack's triggers so Jack will have a little less to worry about.

At the mention of Kyle, Jack's focus shifts. Trace can tell he's remembering, perhaps trying to figure out if Trace resents what Jack took part in with Kyle at the party.

"Or your dick met Kyle, at least," Trace continues. "Anyway, he's got a thing about taking a cock."

Setting down the sound on a sterile cloth, Trace selects a thick, smooth black phallus and begins to clean it, wringing it with large swabs soaked in disinfectant, his hand twisting up and down its huge length. Tossing the swabs, squirting some lube onto his hand from a large pump, Trace takes a step, crossing from the cart to the table. He reaches between Jack's spread, bound legs and inserts his middle finger up Jack's ass, pushing the slick deep. While the finger pumps, Trace says coolly, "Kyle's ass used to be clamped shut *real* tight. Now, he's letting just about anyone have at it if they're pretty enough."

His finger draws out. He coats the large silicone phallus with plenty of lube and brings it down between Jack's legs. Aligning the end with Jack's hole, holding it there firmly, but not pressing hard enough to begin parting the muscle, Trace asks with a grin, "Ain't he, Jack? So, how about you? What turns your knob?"

With the fingers of his left hand, Trace pulls Jack's cheeks apart, spreading him to expose more of his hole, and adds pressure to the base of the toy. The wet, rounded tip pushes at him. Trace spreads him more, increases pressure again, and Jack cries out roughly. The wide head of the toy passes through Jack's sphincter. Trace lets go of the toy, leaving it there, just barely inside his slave, most of the phallus resting on the table, extending from him. Jack shudders slightly, his eyes closing for a long moment as he grunts, tensed up. Hands planted on the table, Trace studies Jack, showing him that he's not in a hurry. He could do this all day.

From the cart, Trace selects another, smaller phallus and starts cleaning that one as well. Jack struggles on the table, still watching both the screen and Trace, his eyes flicking back and forth. Trace can tell Jack doesn't like the look of that second, flesh-colored dildo; not when he barely has the first up his ass. So, Trace lets Jack see his amusement, his patience. Once the toy is clean, Trace moves to stand by Jack's middle.

"You gonna open up for me or should I get a gag?"

Jack seems to think it over, chest heaving, looking everywhere but mostly at the TV screen, murmuring quietly, "Fuck. Fuckin' fuck." Then he opens his mouth wide.

"Mm, maybe I'll use the gag anyway," Trace says conversationally, reconsidering.

"My fuckin' mouth is open, Sir," Jack argues.

"Yeah, but it's more fun for me this way."

Trace cleans the gag first, too, letting Jack watch. Then he fits it between his jaws and fastens the strap tightly behind his head. The stainless steel dual O-ring keeps Jack's mouth open very wide. The black leather straps looks pretty against Jack's tan skin. His pink tongue rests on top of the second ring. The gag makes Jack's breathing quicken before he starts to get it back under control.

Bringing the smaller, flesh-toned dildo to Jack's mouth, Trace eases it through the steel rings, over his tongue and back into Jack's throat. At the same time, he grabs hold of the black phallus and presses it farther into Jack's rectum. Entered at both ends, Jack moans, loudly. The TV screen is forgotten. Trace moves both toys shallowly, going deeper with every push, and is pleased to see Jack's dick stand up and take an interest.

"See, that's what I thought," Trace says, enjoying the sounds of Jack's throat working around one cock as his ass struggles to accept the other. "Nothin' wrong with needing some nice, big, hard cocks stuffing you full at both ends. Not at all. But that's why you've got two boyfriends, don't ya, slave? One for each hole."

He gets the black toy all the way up Jack's ass and leaves it there. He slides the smaller, flesh-colored toy all the way through the gag until the plastic balls rest there, preventing it from going farther and returns to the cart.

Jack moans thunderously, shivering, eyes closed, his dick a dark, reddish purple and straining.

When Trace returns to his side with the sound, Jack's cries get lower, louder, and more fervent. Pre-come weeps from his slit. His eyes open slightly, fixed on the screen, though he looks dazed, flushed and more than distracted by his own body. He doesn't appear to watch Trace align the narrow end of the long chrome-plated, stainless steel sound with Jack's urethra, but as soon as there's the slightest bit of pressure to the small hole in the end of Jack's cock, a throaty shout erupts from him, voiced around the dildo stuffing his throat.

"Easy, princess. I know you like it."

Trace lets the sound drop slowly into Jack's opening, which

parts readily around it. Jack gasps harshly. When a few inches are inside, Trace holds the sound still and reaches up to Jack's mouth to slide the cock out of it.

Gasping for air, unable to close his mouth, Jack breathes through the pleasure and the pain.

"Say please," Trace teases in a mocking, sing-songy voice. "And remember those fuckin' manners."

Jack tries to say the word, but it's difficult to manage with the gag. The table has been slightly raised on one end, so Jack can see the screen clearly. A glance up shows Gray sliding an object up Darrek's ass. Trace relaxes his hold on the sound, letting it drop farther into Jack. At the same time, he reaches for the thick toy in Jack's ass and begins to fuck him with it, with deep, slow strokes. The sound goes deeper by the moment; the movement in his ass is constant. Jack is riveted to the screen. He shouts his torment, goosebumps raising over his skin. His eyes roll and it takes him a moment to find the TV again.

The sound goes as deep as Jack's body will let it. Trace fills Jack's ass with the toy, then lets go. With both hands, he steadies Jack's reddened, swollen cock and holds the sound pinched between two fingers.

"How's that feel, princess?"

Jack gasps roughly, toes flexing, fingers splayed, and Trace begins to draw the sound back out.

"Now, myself," Trace says conversationally. "I like variety. I ain't picky. But I don't like to be bored. Gray was always good about that, but I guess I don't have to tell you, do I? He can be *real* fuckin' creative, especially with a switch."

Jack's gaze snaps immediately to Trace. He mumbles some words that sound something like, "What the fuck? You're a switch?"

"You know, I think I like you more when your mouth is busy with something other than talking."

He slides the cock back down Jack's throat to silence him. Then he returns to slowly moving the sound in and out of Jack's urethra.

"You don't ask too many fuckin' questions, do ya, slave?" Trace chuckles. "Even when you *can* talk. You really think I was with Gray as long as I was without going for a spin as his submissive? Why would I *not* give that a shot? I've been where you are. We aren't that dissimilar, age difference or no."

Trace gets the sound fully seated, steadying Jack's cock with a hand, then reaches for one of the pre-cleaned tuning forks on the cart. Striking it against the side of the table, he touches the vibrating object to the sound buried in Jack's penis. Jack arches on the table, his back bowing. A long, low moan of pleasure purrs from him. His hips twitch up, fucking air.

"Told you I'd take care of you, didn't I, Jacky boy?" Trace grins.

—◯—◯—◯—

The table served its purpose, but going into the scene, Trace's hope was always to lose the table at a certain point.

When Trace sees, via video feed, Darrek getting back on his own table without restraints, ready to get fucked, Trace knows it's time. He gives Jack the choice. The sound is taken out, the black phallus, too.

"Your choice, slave," Trace offers, making sure it sounds like he doesn't give a shit either way. "You can get off the table, no shackles, and get fucked. You'll get off, just like Darrek's about to get off for... shit, I've lost count. The second time? The third? Damn, but Gray's good at gettin' that boy to shoot his load. Or, you know, you can lie there and let me help you skate the edge a while longer."

Jack, possibly wanting to have the other cock taken out of his mouth, hesitates but Trace can see him thinking the offer over.

"Nod if you want up."

Meeting Trace's eyes, Jack nods, slowly but deliberately. Trace unfastens the shackles. When all four are loose, Jack sits up, sliding his legs over the side of the table. A bullwhip sits inches from Trace's hand, ready and waiting. But Jack only slides to the floor.

Trace points to a spot on the floor, at the head of the table, facing the screen.

"There," he instructs. "Right there. Don't make no difference to me, sweetheart, but if you want my cock, that's where you stand. Once Gray gets back up here, will he let you come? I'm thinkin' no.

I would, though."

Head bowed but gaze locked on Trace, Jack moves around to the indicated position. He plants his hands on the table in front of him, and sticks out his ass, stretched and wet from the toy. Taking his time, Trace walks over to the sink, opens his jeans and pulls out his cock, stroking it, letting Jack watch. He turns, washing his hands again at the sink. Just for giggles, he soaps his dick, too, and chuckles at the sound of Jack's faint moan. Then he rinses and dries off, giving Jack's nude body a long, appreciative look. He finds a condom from the tray and holds it up for Jack to see before opening the wrapper and fisting it onto his cock as he moves around behind Jack.

"Watch," Trace whispers by Jack's ear, taking him by the hip, moving closer as Jack shifts his stance wider, arching his back slightly. On the screen, Gray, standing between Darrek's legs, guides his erection to Darrek's ass and enters him just as Trace enters Jack.

Jack's startled cry is nothing but exquisite, ball-busting pleasure. Trace sinks in deep, and doesn't even have to draw Jack's tight, hot ass back onto him, Jack pushes back to receive. After Trace gives him a few slow, long thrusts, they see Gabriel get ready to take Darrek's mouth. Jack's moan is even sharper when Trace finds the base of the toy nestled in Jack's mouth and moves it in and out at the same pace that Gabriel fucks Darrek.

"Can you feel him?" Trace asks in a whisper. "How's he taste, Jack?"

Jack's eyes close. He forces them open and back to the screen. Trace moves inside him with Jack helping out more than enough, fucking himself back onto Trace's cock in time with Gray's movements inside Darrek. Reaching around to find Jack's erection, Trace strokes him lightly, giving him an extra squeeze around the tip. Jack shouts, shudders, and comes. Trace pulls the toy out of Jack's mouth, sets it aside and focuses on working him through the orgasm, drawing it out. Once he's past it, Trace unfastens the strap of the gag, removing it and setting that aside, too.

Jack works the stiffness out of his jaw, flexing it, then renews his focus, getting back into position, pushing his ass back onto Trace. On the screen, Gray is really giving it to Darrek, pounding his ass.

Trace takes hold of Jack by the hips with both hands and starts giving it to him just as hard.

"*Fuck* yeah," Jack moans.

―⚬―⚬―⚬―

The room next door has an adjoining bathroom, complete with shower. Trace ushers Jack in, holding his arm, and guides him to the bed, dressed with fresh, white sheets.

"Shower, soap, towels, all in there," Trace tells him, pointing. "But first I make sure you're okay."

Jack's gaze lingers on the door. He might not have even heard Trace at all.

"He's coming, lover boy." Trace pushes him back to lie down when Jack hesitates, but lets Trace move him easily enough. With a satisfied, albeit tired groan, he gets comfortable as Trace hands him a bottled water, then begins examining him for injury.

After all of the little signs, one after another after another over the course of the long day, of Gray's lack of faith in Trace's ability to properly, respectfully handle Jack, Trace's mood sours. He comes crashing down, hard, from the high he'd been on. The sharp looks of warning, the careful scrutiny, the patronizing reminders—it all hits just a little too close to home.

All of the healing that had happened the night before seems like a fool's dream when faced with the very real ways Gray's trust in Trace is lacking. Resentful of having his direly needed, fleeting sense of closure doused with a cold dose of reality, all Trace wants is to get out of there and go find Micah. With Micah, everything feels balanced in ways it never has with Gray. But Trace knows he can't go. He has a role to play and responsibilities he can't ignore. There's not much Trace can do, when faced with the judgment of a Master Dom, especially one who's acting on behalf of the Master's Circle. What he *can* do, though, is keep being honest, even as he toes the line and nurses resentment he would wish away if he could.

Too many secrets, too many undisclosed intentions and mind games.

"Must say, you're not what I thought you'd be," Jack admits, reacting only very slightly to Trace's poking and prodding.

"Yeah, well, something Gray likely failed to tell you is my endearing propensity to give a shit about people."

"Are you implying I don't?" they hear from the doorway. Trace glances back to see Gray standing there, flushed but immaculate as ever, watching them with vibrantly blue eyes which hide more than Jack will ever know.

"I think this is a case of people hearing what they want to hear," Trace replies. "It wouldn't kill you, you know, to say important words out loud now and then. My two cents."

At first Trace can't look away. There's too much left over from the night before. The part of him that's Trace wants to punch Gray in the teeth for pretending not to care, way back when, then caring anyway, and also for invading Trace's family only to shake them all up in permanent ways. The rest of him that's Patrick is still there, flat to the bed, just taking, taking it all and trying to hold on to make it last just a little longer.

Funny how the two, warring sides of his personality mostly just leave him there, drifting, uncertain what to do about almost everything. The only thing that bleeds through is the ways Trace hates Patrick's weakness, which turns into resentment aimed squarely at Gray for dragging all of this shit up when it had been mostly, blessedly buried.

When he turns back to Jack, Jack is watching Trace's expression intently. Maybe too intently.

"The fuck is he talking about?" Jack asks. "What is this?"

"Nothin', kid," Trace sighs, standing. "It's just Gray making sure we know who's on top." Before Jack can counter that or get a word in, even as he tries to, Trace adds, "Don't worry, bright eyes, I treated him at least as good as you do. I assume you'll take over from here."

A muscle in Gray's jaw twitches.

The whole mess of it is there, in the doubt in Gray's expression. Gray didn't really trust Trace with Jack, not completely, just like he didn't trust Trace with his heart, just like he doesn't trust Trace to run Diadem, just like he doesn't trust Trace to know who he is or what he needs.

"*The fuck did you expect?*" Trace accuses hoarsely, his voice suddenly filled with too much emotion, too fast. His body shakes with the anger, so big it feels like it's eating him from the inside out. Gray waits patiently, bearing it without a word, but not looking away. He doesn't even blink.

When he's a little more composed, Trace gives Jack one last hard look and asks Jack, "You okay here? We good?"

Looking confused, slightly worn out, and overwhelmed, Jack has no response at first. Then he nods, tightly. "Yes, Sir."

"Good." Trace nods, too. "'Scuse me."

Gray steps out of the way to let him pass, but Trace can feel it in the air around him as he comes close enough to brush shoulders with the man. It's not over. Not by a long shot.

Chapter 34
Just a Kiss

The sun is bright in the recovery room, the building quiet except for the low murmur of voices somewhere in the building nearby. The silver studs had been put in Darrek's nipples before they left the dungeon and he was mostly out of it for that part, as well as the slow, shuffling walk upstairs. He kind of resents being put in bed to rest, but knows it's important. He's still got a long way to go in coming down and feeling strong enough to be up and on his feet. Gabriel has been at his side constantly, watching, offering water, checking his pulse and temperature.

"You've gotta keep those really clean," Gabriel reminds him again. "Make sure they don't get infected and heal properly."

"I *know*," Darrek replies, again. "I got it. Relax."

"You're telling *me* to relax? You used your damn safeword. Do you know how much that scares me?"

"It worked out fine. I'm fine."

"Look at me, Dare."

He meets Gabriel's grey-blue eyes, holding their scrutinizing glare. After a moment, when the tension in Gabriel's expression doesn't ease up, Darrek extends a hand, palm up, for Gabriel to take. He's lying back in the bed, propped up on pillows, shirtless but wearing pants. His ass aches like it hasn't in a long time and he knows it's going to take a while for him to recover.

Gabriel lays his hand on top of Darrek's, folding their fingers together.

"I'm sorry I scared you," Darrek tells him.

"Stop apologizing. You didn't do anything wrong."

"How's Jack?"

"Peachy," Jan answers, before Gabriel can. Jan has just appeared in the doorway and leans against it, hands in his pockets, looking casually handsome in all the right ways. Beyond him is Gray who nods at the room, clearly gesturing to Jan for him to go in.

"Go on," Gray urges when Jan hesitates, as Jan looks at him from over a shoulder.

Something makes Jan pause a moment longer, but then, head bowed, he walks to Darrek's narrow bed. Gabriel lets go of Darrek's hand and stands, moving back to give them space. Sitting on the edge of the bed by Darrek's side, Jan asks, "You okay? That was bloody intense."

When Jan's gaze drifts down to the piercings, it makes Darrek's lips curl in a shy sort of smile. Butterflies of the sort he hasn't felt in a long time begin knocking around in his stomach.

"Yeah, I guess I just don't know what to say," Darrek says. "I mean, after everything you *saw*...."

Jan looks up at Gabriel, who nods in the same strange sort of way Gray did. It makes Darrek wonder what he's missed. They all seem to know something he doesn't.

Quietly, almost so much so that Darrek misses it, Jan murmurs, "Liked what I saw," and lays a hand on Darrek's chest. Jan's fingers caress and wrap around Darrek's side, under his pectoral muscle. Jan's thumb extends up beside the new piercing.

The skin-on-skin contact causes Darrek's heart to leap up into his throat. His face grows hot. Slowly, he begins to catch on but he's still not ready for it when Jan leans in, shifting closer, and his other hand gently clasping the side of Darrek's neck.

Then Jan's mouth is on his, feeling him out, tasting so strange and new. Darrek frowns heavily, holding back at first. Fear leftover as instinct from the ways he has felt attraction to friends in the past, and how wrong it was, how it something to pull away from, leaves Darrek confused and floundering. But maybe Jan knows this about him, too, because he doesn't let Darrek shy away. He presses in harder whenever Darrek begins to draw back. Their heads tilt to the side and Jan's tongue teases over Darrek's lower lip. Opening for him, Darrek moans softly as Jan's tongue enters his mouth, searching. Darrek tangles his fingers in the back of Jan's short hair. Jan's thumb rolls over Darrek's tender left nipple, making him gasp and frown even more heavily.

Eventually, Jan pulls back. He sucks briefly on Darrek's lip.

Darrek can't let him go. Not yet, not with what he fears will come next, so he holds Jan there. Nuzzling the side of Jan's face, a tear slips from each eye.

"It's okay," Jan assures him. He pulls back farther and gives Darrek a smile.

Gabriel is watching. Gray is watching. So, he sees with surprise, is Jack, lingering by Gray's side. Then they all drift away, before his eyes. Gray and Jack vanish down the hall. Gabriel excuses himself and leaves the room.

"It's okay," Jan repeats, still smiling slightly, touching their foreheads together.

Wiping hurriedly at his eyes, Darrek tries to pull himself together. Jan passes him a tissue from a box beside the bed.

"Thanks."

"You're really something, you know," Jan tells him.

"So are you."

When Jan kisses him again, it's slower, more drawn out, and Darrek feels it all the way down to his toes. As exhausted as Darrek is, Jan's mouth, his fingers brushing sore, newly pierced flesh—it turns Darrek on hard. He realizes the others were there to give permission, to ease them in to this.

Darrek breaks the kiss, studying Jan but unable to puzzle out everything in his expression. There's determination and attraction, definitely, but subtler things as well.

It's another part of the lesson Gabriel brought Darrek to Diadem to learn, Darrek realizes suddenly. Sex has been made less sacred, less stressful, thanks to Gray. And now here's Jan, helping in his own way to get Darrek past his mental stumbling blocks, showing him how he doesn't have to see himself the way his father wanted him to see himself. If Darrek wants to be with someone, and Gabriel agrees with it, it can happen. In fact, if Gabriel wants it to happen, it more than likely will. Darrek can take his pleasure, or his pain, then return to the man he loves, his Gabriel, when it's through.

The dynamics at play with Kyle don't have to apply to everything, every scenario. Darrek knows himself now. There's no reason to be afraid.

There's *no reason* to be afraid.

With Darrek off in his head, his gaze slipping over Jan's eyelashes, the shape of his mouth, the line of his jaw, Jan seems to get tired of waiting. He pulls Darrek close again, claiming his mouth, kissing it so deep, Darrek moans.

When Jan is done with him, Darrek is breathless, sighing, "Jesus," with a little laugh and sinks back into the pillows behind him.

Jan gets up, smiling wickedly at Darrek, taking one last long look down the length of him before turning to check the door. Gabriel appears there and shares a small, pleased smile with Jan which Darrek can only marvel at.

"Close your eyes," Gabriel urges his patient, lying dazed and thoroughly kissed in the bed. "Take a nap. You could use it. I promised you that you were safe here, and you are."

"Okay," Darrek agrees. After Gabriel comes over to kiss Darrek's temple, Darrek lets out a sigh and takes a fresh look at his life. The weight he's been carrying feels miraculously gone. Is it true? Can it be? Have all of the things he used to fear truly left? It feels, in that moment, that it all has shifted on him, putting him on an entirely new course where only good, hopeful things can flourish. "You make me feel so damn lucky," he whispers to Gabriel, pouring his whole heart into the words.

"Likewise, gorgeous," Gabriel smiles, beaming from within, tenderly brushing the hair back over Darrek's ear. "Now, take a nap."

"Yes, Sir," Darrek grins.

———⛓———

With the taste of Darrek on his lips and tongue, Jan lingers in the hall by Jack's door. Focused on putting on his boots in the shadowy room on the wrong side of the building to catch the sun, Jack is gorgeous as ever. Enjoying the view and the sight of Jack slightly more at ease than he'd been thanks to Trace and whatever happened between them, Jan replays memories from watching Darrek, and watching Gray and Gabriel attending to him.

Jan understands Darrek's curiosity about dominating and submitting, as well as his reluctance to lose himself completely in the role of being a slave. The way Darrek seemed to save himself for the right person, the right *man*, is similar to the way Jan saved himself for Rob, the lover who never claimed him in actuality, just privately, for ten long years. In moving past that part of his life, Jan has realized how much he missed out on while he was Rob's secret. Now, Darrek is taking the same type of journey, learning how to let others in.

The memory of Gray fucking Darrek comes back, strong. It makes Jan hard, how Darrek struggled to yield and take it. Echoes of his grunts and moans ring in Jan's ears. Rolling the lingering taste of him over his tongue, his cock swells and stiffens at the pleasure of getting to watch so much. The focus and determination in Gray's eyes, the tension in his body as he moved and rode Darrek's ass, taking what only one other man has ever had, making Darrek shout and gasp....

"There's a barn out back," Jan suggests, inclining his head in that direction. "Fitted with chains and ropes. Want to have a look?"

"Just a *look*?" Jack teases, his gaze roaming down to the bulge of Jan's crotch.

"More than a look," Jan smirks, chewing at the side of his lip.

Jack is up and grabbing for Jan's arm in the blink of an eye. "Well, come on then," he says eagerly and impatiently, pulling him toward the exit.

"It felt fucking sincere," Trace seethes. "Was it? Or was it all part of some grand scheme to fuck me over in every way you could?"

"It *was* sincere," Gray says calmly, though Trace can tell he's managed to push more than a few buttons.

They're standing outside of Diadem. There's no one around. Jack and Jan are in the barn; Gabriel and Darrek are in the main building.

"But it doesn't change anything," Gray adds.

Trace laughs bitterly. "Not for *you* it doesn't. How about for *me*? You come in here, imposing *your* fucking rules on *my* life. You get me to open up to you, make me care about you again in ways I wish I didn't. You make me question who I am...."

"Who else is there to help you get back on track? Hmm? Your kids all look up to you. They trust and love you, but they can't help you. This is bigger than them, so much so, *they can't even see it*. They don't know who you were, so how can they understand who you are? They have no perspective on anything going on with you. They don't see you falling apart. They don't see your mistakes. It's because of how I value you that I'm here to do what I can. I'm not being fucking malicious here, Tracey."

"Their way, the MC way, never worked for me. Why do you think I signed up with The Company? Why do you think I wound up with *you* when I should have been with Nicholai? Why do you think I came here and never went back? Why do you think I'll just roll over and let the MC tell me what to do? *I* control my life," Trace argues, wishing he could care less than he does, just for a little while. It would be so much easier to push all of his feelings behind walls like Gray does.

"It's not just *your* life we're talking about. All of your employees, all of your clients, the family you cherish so much, aren't they reason enough to put ego aside and try to do things differently? All of these decisions you're making—are they for you, or for them? What's most important to you?"

"I know my priorities," Trace growls.

"Do you?"

"Do *you*?" Trace counters.

"You're too smart to fuck this up. Make the hard call. Do it for *them*," Gray says, pointing at the building.

And Trace laughs angrily, wishing, just for once, just one time, that Gray, the bastard, wasn't *always* right.

—◻︎—◻︎—◻︎—

Once Darrek is completely asleep, and has been for a while, Gabriel ventures from the room in search of food. He can smell it wafting in through the window at the rear of the building, half-open to let in cool air to refresh the place. But the open window also lets in snippets of conversation, and the sound of tires rolling, crunching over rocky dirt. Gabriel's plan is to grab something to eat and bring it back to his seat in the recovery room. Darrek will want to see him there when he does wake, whenever that may be.

The building is quiet, deserted except for him and Darrek. Everyone else is outside. He's not sure what he expected to walk in to when he exits through the back door, but whatever it may have been, it isn't what he finds. Gray and Trace are there, heatedly watching each other from across the picnic table. Neither one says a word or glances up when the door closes behind Gabriel, who descends the few steps to the grass.

"Hey, so what the fuck is up with you two?" Gabriel says lightly. "Ooh, pizza."

He lifts the lid and sees nothing but vegetables, hardly a glimpse of cheese or bread.

"Now, see, there's no way you ordered this," Gabriel laughs, looking at Trace.

There's still no reaction. They just eat their food and continue focusing solely on each other.

"Okay. I'll bite. Is it me? It's me, isn't it? Well I ain't staying anyhow. Got some sub-sittin' to do inside."

Taking a plate, he fills it with three slices, just in case Darrek wakes up hungry.

"Where are Jack and Jan?"

"The barn," Gray answers, nodding in that direction. Once he listens for it, Gabriel can indeed hear some of the activity taking place in there. Moans and laughter are carried on the wind across the property.

"That's adorable. They're having a roll in the hay," Gabriel chuckles. "So, is this jealousy, then? There's plenty of room in there. You two can go take the loft or tie someone to the rafters. Don't matter to me who you pick."

Trace finally looks Gabriel's way, giving him a heavy stare, weighted with hidden messages, basically telling him bluntly to get the fuck back inside. No wonder Jack and Jan went to seek more pleasant distractions elsewhere.

"Take my name out of the hat, though. I'm done for the day. All right, you wacky kids, enjoy your lunch."

Plate in hand, he goes back in the way he came, greatly preferring the comforting sight of Darrek's peaceful slumber to the uncomfortable tension at the table.

A while later, after Darrek wakes on his own, the others still occupied with their own business, Gabriel is ready to go. That doesn't necessarily mean he wants to go home. Home has not been the sanctuary of comfort and relaxation it used to be. Whenever he's there, with Darrek, he senses the simmering discomfort, uncertainty, fear and anxiety, all stemming from the stupid phone. Gabriel has since cancelled their landline service entirely. There is no more phone. He's also had the new home security system replaced entirely, to rule out any defect which might have been causing the false alarms. It hasn't helped as much as he would like.

They could always go to Daring Angel and hang out there while Gabriel gets a little bit of work done, but that would leave Darrek with not much to do and without an ideal place to rest.

Undecided, Gabriel helps Darrek get situated and leads the way out to the Discovery parked out front. They leave through the back, since it's closer, and walk around the main building to the front.

"So, we're gonna talk about it, right? I mean we'll probably talk about it. There's, like, a lot. To talk about," Darrek says stiltedly, tripping over the words like he's nervous.

Gabriel can't help but smile up at him. "You're cute, you know that?"

Darrek smiles bashfully, which only adds to his cuteness.

"Talk about what? The kiss? The sex? The nipple studs? I mean, I figured it was all pretty self-explanatory, but we can talk if you want."

"Um, all of the above?" Darrek squints, looking uncertain. "But I guess we can start with the kiss. Not that it was 'a kiss', it was a little more... *prolonged*... than 'a kiss'. But you know that. Probably. Or maybe I should stop talking before I get myself in trouble."

They're almost at the parking lot, and pass beside the somewhat raised front porch.

From nearby, they hear, "You've both been making eyes at each other for days. We thought you might as well stop messing about and get it out of the way."

Darrek glances up abruptly at Jack, looking guilty. Jack is sitting on the front steps, holding a beer, smiling and seeming quite pleased with himself. Jan is there, too. He's been up on the porch, checking out the view but walks down to meet them once he sees who Jack is talking to. He smiles at Darrek in a way that causes the color to rise on Darrek's cheeks, which Gabriel also thinks is quite endearing, to say the least.

Jack adds, "Jan had such a case of blue balls after gettin' an eyeful of you, it would've been cruel not to let him have at it, seeing as how I got to enjoy the show myself. Hell of a show, too."

"Or, you figure if I got my hands on Dare, Gabe might take you down for a go on that cross downstairs?" Jan smirks.

"You know, now that you mention it, Jan—" Jack starts.

"And meanwhile, Gray's had all of us," Gabriel mutters.

"What's that now?" Jack asks, turning to look right at him. Their eyes lock and Gabriel feels it, like a tickle of want, low in the center of his body, how he craves the same thing Jack does. After meeting him, hearing everything he's heard, seeing what little he has seen, Gabriel does want to get the chance to take Jack on, someday. It'd be a hell of a lot of fun, if nothing else.

"You heard me," Gabriel replies, holding Jack's stare, letting enough of his desire seep into his expression to keep Jack interested.

"So, Gray gets a go at you, but I don't?"

"Maybe if you beg," Jan suggests with a crooked grin.

"Yeah, right," Jack scoffs. It's not very convincing. "Oh, come on, beg for me, Jack," Gabriel coaxes seductively. "Please?"

"Don't you start taking the piss, too," Jack warns.

Gabriel reaches up and plucks a stray piece of straw from Jack's black hair, showing it to him before letting it fall from his fingers.

"Busy day?" Gabriel asks.

Looking caught, Jack runs his fingers through his hair, checking for more hay.

"You could say that," Jack admits. When he catches sight of Jan and Darrek, Jack motions for Gabriel to look. They're standing together, watching each other while pretending not to watch each other, heads bowed, smiles barely stifled.

"We'll catch up with you two later. We can head out for drinks or something," Gabriel suggests.

"Yeah," Jan agrees eagerly.

Before he can anticipate it, Gabriel leans in and gives Jack a quick, light kiss, square on the lips. It makes Jack's grey eyes shoot open wide, but Gabriel pulls away before Jack can react more than that.

"Later, Jack," Gabriel winks.

Chapter 35
Micah, Inside and Out

Micah finds his wife in the kitchen, sipping coffee, daydreaming as she gazes through a window above the counter, overlooking the back of the property. The trees beyond the curved driveway fill in the view but some golden light weaves between the branches, shifting with the breeze. Wearing only charcoal gray panties and a smoke-hued silk camisole, the rich, dark waves of her hair spilling over one caramel-colored shoulder, Lilianna is beautiful enough to take his breath away.

It's time for the talk they both knew was coming, but was too difficult and inconvenient to manage before. Micah suspected it might get away from them for yet another day but here she is, waiting for him.

If she hears him approach, she doesn't indicate it, but stays posed where she is, a vision of warm, silky skin, intoxicating curves and very little left to the imagination. She even smells like home when he comes up behind her, empty mug in one hand, and slips his other around her waist, kissing her cheek.

Lilianna hums softly, tipping her head to the side in such a way she's either exposing more of her neck to his lips or pulling away. He can't quite tell.

"You wore this on purpose, didn't you?" he teases. The coffee pot beckons. Crossing to it, he fills his mug.

"Well, you've been such a bitch lately; I figured I should play along," she counters, almost smiling as she glances his way.

Micah takes a look around the room, remembering the party with Darrek strung up, his soft groans an admittedly charming entertainment for the rest of them. The air is full of ghosts, charged energy left behind in the wake of such complicated, needful men. It makes it more of a challenge to have a normal conversation in his own house, with no one there but his wife. It should be cozy but somehow it's not.

Suspecting she can feel it too, that it's part of the spell which has been cast over her, he says, "Christ, the gay testosterone is dripping from the walls these days."

"Tell me about it," she murmurs in agreement, swirling her drink. The dark brew laps at the porcelain, hypnotizing her further. He's having trouble reading her mood, but there's something sad about her, standing there. She looks lost.

"Thank you," he sighs, diving in. There's no point waiting any longer. "For going through with all of this. For putting up with it. I know it's not ideal timing."

"I'm not doing it just for you, you know." He takes a sip, washing down the sting of her cold tone with hot liquid. "Good."

"Who do you love more?" she asks without even bothering to make eye contact, sounding as emotionless as if they were discussing the weather or tonight's dinner menu. "Me or him?"

"Don't do that," Micah scolds gently.

Her smile bitter, she says, "Told you, just playing along."

"You're not a bitch, Lil."

"No? I feel like one, the way I've pushed you away."

Her lip quivers. Her head bows, masking her expression with the curtain of her hair.

God, he thinks, *where did we go wrong? We used to be so happy, so in sync. We used to fit each other so well instead of being the ones who hurt each other the most.*

"You didn't push me," he tells her. "I guess I was just going out of my way to give you reasons to make another choice, other than being near me. I've been so angry about how it's all turned out. I didn't want to turn my anger on you, so I turned it on myself and signed off. That's not on you. It's on me."

He gives her a moment, exhaling a breath, gazing up at the ceiling and leaning back against the counter's edge. When she sniffs and shakes her hair back, he knows it's an invitation to continue, simply because she hasn't bolted from the room or the house, not that she'd want to, wearing next to nothing when it's so cold there's frost on the grass.

"How's Saoirse?" It's a verbal peace offering—a blatant one, maybe obnoxiously so.

She wipes her eyes, laughs and looks his way. "Fuckable as always. But we have *nothing* to talk about."

She laughs again, possibly remembering, and it's richer this time, full of honesty. It's infectious and he chuckles along with her, loving her still, after all these years, as much as he ever has. "Sounds refreshing," he replies, making a face at her.

"If you find awkward silences refreshing, then I guess so," she shrugs, watching her coffee again rather than him. "Maybe it's just part of the process of learning about each other. I forget, sometimes, how long it took us to be really honest." There's a pause, and he braces himself, feeling the meaning behind the silence, that Lilianna is gathering her courage. "Sometimes I think I should move in with her."

They leave it there, in the air between them, and for a long, uncomfortable moment, neither of them touches it. Micah expels a heavy breath.

"Even when I know I shouldn't, I always wind up coming back home to you, Michigan," she smiles, crying and laughing at the same time.

"Oh fuck, don't play that card," he groans, which only feeds her amusement, but that's okay. Anything to stop her crying.

When they were dating in college, Micah was just learning how all-encompassing his personal sexual orientation was. His roommate, Colm—the one Micah liked to spy on—called him Michigan, after Micah's home state. Micah was a small town boy who had never been given the chance to explore his attraction to other boys, other men. Back home, he realized, quickly, no one else around him was attracted to both sexes the way he was, so he closed off, hid his true feelings.

When he started screwing around with Colm, it was like a boulder being pushed over the side of a hill. Ever since, Micah has been unable to stop the building momentum of that force rushing down,

down, down.

He told Lilianna everything. Not at first, but after she began to notice the way Colm touched Micah, whispering in his ear things that made Micah blush and grow instantly silent with guilt. Once he'd confessed to her, Micah felt better. She was angry, though, that there was an element of dubious consent to what had been happening. She told him it was next to rape, it was wrong. No matter how Micah tried to explain it to her, she wouldn't completely believe him.

Maybe that was when it started. That was the seed. Even then, she doubted him. She has ever since, in small ways.

When it came to being with Colm, there was no choice. He couldn't convince Lilianna the sex was harmless, and he couldn't say no to Colm, no matter how conflicted Micah might have felt about what was being done to him.

So, he let her watch.

She was there when Colm fucked Micah for the first time. She was there, too, when Colm brought his friend over again, and they took turns with him, riding him until his cries rang from the walls.

It was the start of everything. But, it's still mortifying to recall. The naive boy he was — with no idea of what awaited him as that boulder gathered speed, tumbling, picking up fetishes and curiosities along the way — was Michigan.

Micah's problems with Lilianna aren't about sex. They never were. They were both equally curious, equally deviant, open to trying anything at least once.

Moira is the problem. Lack of complete trust is the problem. Willingness to hurt each other is the problem. Heartbreak, agonizing and real, is the problem.

Life rushes in. It's not a fantasy. Getting off doesn't soothe the pain of loss. Micah can't make it so that when his wife looks into his eyes, she doesn't see her departed daughter there, in the shape and color. He can't give Lilianna the peace she craves. And he can't stop loving Trace, or needing him as a constant, huge part of his life.

"So, what do we do?" she asks, nearing the end of her rope, dangling over an abyss with no idea what lies below.

"I hate this, Lil. I love you. I always will. But it's not working, is it? You deserve to be happier than I can make you."

She struggles to speak, and can't at first. Looking angry with herself, she grinds her teeth and gazes straight ahead out through the window, beams of sunlight catching in the amber flecks in her eyes and the waves of her hair. "What he did for you the other day... for *us*, getting you out of that damned office, calming you down? That was huge. He's a good man. You should have someone who can take care of you like that."

That day. He has only pieces of it. Parts have been lost to the manic grief, swallowed whole. He can only guess at the extent of what Trace did, for Lilianna and for him.

"He's a keeper, okay?" She looks right in his eyes, not crying, not uncertain. "It's official."

He nods. "I'll always be here for you. If there's ever something I can give you that you need, it would be an honor to be able to do that for you. I feel like I owe you. If I can help you be happy, that would be my greatest wish. I hope Saoirse will make you so very happy, Lily."

"I'll miss you," she whispers, tearing up a little, emotionally kicking herself. He knows she hates failure. She always fought so hard for Moira. When everyone had given up, even the doctors, even Micah and their daughter, Lilianna was still fighting. It had made Micah feel like a terrible father, a bad person, how he'd run out of hope so much sooner than Lilianna had. That's part of Micah's lingering resentment and anger, too, the sense he gets that Lilianna will always be disappointed in him for giving up the fight for Moira. Maybe he couldn't have made a difference in the outcome of her fate, but at least he could have let his wife know she wasn't alone in the battle for their daughter's life.

But it's time to stop. They can't keep blaming each other and themselves for old sins. It's time to concede and take the next steps, alone.

"I'll miss you too."

––⚬–⚬–⚬––

The others return eventually, after Lilianna has gone upstairs to pack some essentials and quietly slipped out, giving Micah a kiss on the cheek before heading to her car. It's good to hear signs of life returning to the house. The space Lilianna has filled in his world, his heart, and his daily existence is like another gaping wound. At least if others are around, and Micah is expected to act as a civilized host, it will keep him tethered, unable to break down the way he would like to.

Micah is curious to see what state his friends, new and old, are in, after all of the activity at Diadem. He'd been told what the plan was, in vague, loosely sketched details. Really it wasn't any of his business anyway. It's never bothered him when Trace takes other subs temporarily, as part of a business arrangement. It's always been very clear he doesn't have that kind of stake in Trace, who is his own man, his own entity entirely. Micah is comfortable letting Trace have of him what he wants. The emotional connection and Trace's commitment to him came after, unexpected.

Sometimes Micah forgets, in just going about his day, doing mundane tasks and losing himself, the extent of his situation with Trace. He'll react, unthinking, as if Trace is still just his employer and a fellow Dom. That particular day, he does this exact thing. He's too mentally preoccupied to be fully self-aware.

With his head full of the finality of the conversation with Lilianna, sitting at his desk, sorting mail and bills, trying not to cry, he notices Trace walk into the office, but only grunts, "Hey. How'd it go?" He sets the electric bill on top of the water bill and tries to remember if he'd left his ledger in the drawer or if it's in the filing cabinet across the room.

A firm hand grabs him by the throat, right under his jaw. Tensing the muscles in his neck, chin tilting up, eyes wide with surprise, Micah becomes very still and lays his hands on the desk.

"Sir?" he chokes out.

Trace yanks the chair back, its wheels rolling over the hardwood floor as he draws Micah away from the desk, turning him around. Another hand grabs Micah by the balls, squeezing hard enough to make his hips lift off the chair's seat.

"Wear your collar," Trace growls. "You, more than anything and anyone else, are mine. They will fucking see who you belong to. Got it?"

"Jesus," Micah gasps, struggling as Trace keeps tight hold of him at both ends. "Okay. Got it. Yes, Sir."

Trace releases him just as roughly as he took him. Gasping, rubbing his throat, closing his legs to protect his balls from further assault, he looks around at Trace.

With some resentment at the rough handling, Micah says, "So, it went that well, huh? Fucking bastard."

He can see how angry Trace is, but it's not anger at him. Micah would bet all of his money he knows perfectly well who Trace is angry with. Something comes over Trace's expression then. It makes Micah shut the hell up, fast. Trace has never been particular about Micah or their exclusivity. Sure, he loves Micah, but they don't typically get all mushy about it, especially in public. But, standing in that office, raging with frustration at their present circumstances and the trials he has endured, Trace looks just about ready to drag Micah off by the hair and stake his claim, violently if necessary, to make it damn fucking clear to everyone present who owns him, who keeps him, and who Micah owes his loyalty to.

He's never seen Trace look so possessive.

After enduring the torture of Lilianna finally letting him go, and sitting alone in their big, empty house, alone in every sense for the first time since he was in his early teens, Trace's sudden determination to make a show of claiming and conquering Micah is an unbelievable shock to his system. He goes from cold to hot so fast, it leaves him dizzy.

Heart thumping, throat aching, Micah knows it's on him to soothe his Master so Trace is calm enough to talk about everything they need to talk about. Dread swells huge, giving him chills, anxious anticipation itching like ants on his skin.

"What do you need?" Micah asks quietly, getting high, fast, off of Trace's evident passion. Nervousness of the sort he hasn't felt since college, when Colm was promising to take his virginity, grounds Micah quite effectively to the here and now.

"Get outside. The yard."

"Shit," Micah hisses, bowing his head. Surrendering, he answers with a meek, "Yes, Sir."

They walk down the hall as Micah leads the way. They pass through the kitchen where Gray is sipping water and exit through the back door. The sense, again, of tumbling downhill in freefall, picking up speed and witnesses, is strong. Down the steps to the driveway, they weave through the parked vehicles to the clipped-short lawn and cross to a spot by the tree line, in the shade.

A thick ring is bolted securely to the hard earth with a long stake. A few feet away, another pair of rings completes the triangle.

"Strip."

"Shit. Shit. Shit," Micah mutters, undressing with shaking hands.

Trace goes to his truck, getting something from inside the cab. As he returns, Micah is barefoot and shirtless, opening his pants. The back door of the house opens and closes twice as people file out.

"*Shit.*"

His heart is beating too fast, making him lightheaded. He stumbles a little, stepping out of his pants and underwear.

"Get in position."

Micah lies down, his arms extended above his head, hands together. It helps him feel a little steadier. Trace snaps on metal cuffs which he links to one of the bolts. Legs spread as wide as they'll go, Micah trembles, face-down, shivering in the cold air, the grass damp and cool under him. Both of his ankles are shackled similarly.

A thick piece of leather is fitted between his teeth. A hand rubs over his head, through his hair, down his neck. He feels keenly watched by multiple sets of eyes. Grunting softly with anxiousness, trying to take deep, slow breaths, he waits for it.

The whip lashes across his shoulder blades and the yell is startled out of him. Biting down harder on the gag, he tries to unclench his muscles as he's struck four more times in succession. Before he's recovered, he feels a weight settle atop him and whimpers sharply.

There are figures by the back door. He can't see who they are, but he doesn't need to. Trapped and bound to the cold earth, he feels his Master's cock nestle between his cheeks, a hot, hard, thick line. Shivering, grunting through the nerves, he closes his eyes and pushes everything into a shout that comes from way down in the core of his body when Trace begins to enter him. There's lube but no prep. He just pins Micah to the ground and drives into him, forcing Micah to take the whole length. "Breathe," Trace says sharply, as Micah fails to inhale and the leather falls from his jaws, opened wide as he gapes, goosebumps pebbling his skin from head to toe.

Trace pushes at him even harder, burrowing in the rest of the way. Micah's rectum parts around him, gripping the invading flesh. Micah shouts roughly after he gulps in some air, then pants. He's given reprieve as Trace waits for the ache to fade back, dragging his teeth along Micah's jaw, provoking more shivers, biting the ridge of bone, biting his neck.

When he manages, gasping, "Thank you, Master. Please fuck me," that's Trace's cue to move. The figures are closer, watching as Micah is fucked in quick, sharp thrusts that have Micah's erection dragging against the cool grass. Trace's pelvis and balls slap against the curve of Micah's ass. Just taking it, enduring it, and trying to breathe through it, the slick slide and intense friction makes his ass throb.

Trace pulls out, shifts off of Micah.

Micah moans, loudly, with an idea of what comes next. He keeps his eyes closed, sensing the others nearby.

Fingers spread him, rubbing an object over his tender hole, through his crease. It goes on and on. His hips come up off the ground, inviting more, and he cries out as it's driven into him—the handle of the whip. Trace moves it in and out, tugging this way and that, corkscrewing it inside, prying him open as it's withdrawn.

Shuddering, toes curling, body aching, gasping loudly, constantly, he cries out, "Thank you, Master!"

A bright yell erupts from him as the handle rakes over his prostate. It happens again and again, his dick soaked with pre-come. He thrusts reflexively into the grass as Trace triggers him.

A hand reaches under his hips, drawing his erection back between his legs, keeping his ass turned up as his cock tries and fails to lift. The handle is worked in and out of him until his body—every inch of him other than his dick, that is—is limp, just taking it. The handle comes out at last. Trace lies down, fills Micah once more with his cock and fucks him slowly until he climaxes with a growl.

"*Mine.*"

"Fuck yes, Sir. Thank you," Micah sighs, lax and drained, tingling everywhere. His body is sore; his wrists and ankles tender from the hard edges of the cuffs.

He's released, lifted, and stood on his feet where he sways. Trace stoops down and slings Micah over a shoulder. As he hangs there, held tightly by Trace's arm as they walk back to the house, Micah hears from a short ways away as Jack asks Gray, "So… my turn next, right?"

―⏾―⏾―⏾―

Kneeling ass-up on the bed, face buried in the downy softness of the bedspread, Micah feels Trace prying him open, flashlight held between his teeth as he swipes on ointment.

"So, I don't know why that just happened, but it seemed really… productive," Micah croaks, his throat raw and voice thin. "Lily was right. She said I've been acting like a bitch and I am *completely* your bitch right now. Did it help?"

"Beautif-ly," Trace grins, chipper as ever now that he's purged his fight.

"Wonderful. Glad to be of service."

A small but hard object is fed though his swollen rim and he complains with a hissed, "Fuck."

Once the plug is in place, Trace says, "Turn over."

Without any energy left, Micah rolls clumsily to his back, legs falling open as Trace climbs on top of him again, this time to kiss him. Trace chuckles happily against Micah's mouth, caressing up and down the side of his relaxed body. The simple affection and passion in the way Trace gently uses his lips, breathing against Micah, is soothing. A hand wraps Micah's shaft. In three strokes he's shuddering, coming with a quiet moan which Trace kisses away.

Pushing his fingers back into Trace's hair, looking into his eyes, Micah says, "I'm still waiting for our talk, you know. When you're ready. While you were gone, Lily and I resolved things, so we should talk about that, too."

"Let's get you showered, first. I'll take you out of here. We'll grab some food; go somewhere there ain't an audience listening at the door."

"Deal," Micah smiles.

Chapter 36
Without a Trace

They get some sandwiches to go. The smell of freshly baked bread, garlic, and pickles fills the cab of the truck. Trace parks in the fields beside Diadem, on the crest of the hill, overlooking houses that sparkle with tiny twinkling lights as the sun sets and darkness falls. The moon is out and brightens moment by moment. The first stars begin to shine.

Windows down, a breeze wafting through, the radio plays with the volume turned down low. It's comfortable. They have their privacy. The night draws the secrets out.

"Here goes," Trace murmurs, watching the horizon rather than Micah, the way Lilianna had done earlier in the day. Micah's a little nervous about what he's about to learn, but just as eager to finally get a glimpse at the bigger picture. If he's going to belong to Trace as completely as Trace wants him to, Micah wants to have some idea who his possessor is. "I was born Patrick Connelly and grew up on the streets of the Big fuckin' Apple. Always got into trouble. I was a little punk, thinkin' I was the shit, that I had it all figured out. There were all of these Irish kids in my neighborhood I ran with. I guess you could say I was a little con artist, so they called me Tricky. Pretty apt nickname. Fit me then, fit me later, too, for different reasons.

"I guess you could call us a gang, but we didn't see it that way. We were just poor fuckin' kids trying to get things we didn't have but felt we should have. Anyway, I knocked up this girl. She was underage. *I* was underage. Her daddy was a mean motherfucker involved in local government. I had no clue, some Republican senator or some shit. Christ, he hated me. The cops got a tip and arrested a bunch of my guys for small charges—theft, breaking and entering, resisting arrest... And me? Well, he had bigger plans for me. He wanted me *gone*. Son of a bitch threatened my mother if I didn't hightail it out of there for good and never contact his daughter again. It's not like he left me any choice."

With a sigh he sinks back into his seat, rubbing his forehead, elbow braced on the door. "The baby was shipped off, given away. I moved to London. That's when I fell in with the Master's Circle. They taught me all kinds of tricks. Felt I was living up to my name," he grins. "God, I was... what? Nineteen? Something like that."

"Patrick," Micah says, trying it out. Trace looks over at him, watching Micah's mouth like he can see the name there. A little shiver races down Micah's spine, thinking of how much Trace lived through before he was even really a man. Imagining what it would have been like to meet the younger version of Trace when Micah was sixteen, instead of Colm, Micah flushes with heat. Sexual confrontation with Patrick would have been overwhelming, in wonderful ways.

"You know me. I got antsy, wanted to get out on my own, away from Nicholai, the Master Dom I trained under, to test my new abilities. So, I hooked up with The Company. The MC didn't trust them, and wanted someone inside to keep an eye on things. They knew I could hold my own, so they didn't fight me when I volunteered. And that was that. Ten fuckin' years. Ten years is longer than it sounds when you're living day to day, moment to moment, appointment to appointment. And it sounds real damn long to begin with."

Their eyes meet again, and Micah can see some of it there in his face, what Trace had to live through, the people he had to service as a whore, a Dom for hire but maybe not *always* as a Dom for hire.

"God, I'm sorry you went through that," Micah says, meaning it with every fiber of his being.

"Me too. I had no clue what I'd signed up for. No fuckin' clue. There's a reason people hire a whore instead of trying to get it for free, especially when there's that much money involved. The twisted, disgusting shit they expect, that they ask for, and keep you there until you provide...." He shakes his head, exhales a heavy breath and licks his lips. "After my time was up, I was drained. It didn't feel like I had much of me left on the inside. I was just a tool, some-

thing more powerful people than me used to get a job done, not a person at all anymore.
"There was nowhere else for me to go, so I went home. London was as miserable as I felt, so it was a good fit. My mentor, my Master, Nicholai, he's the one who told me I needed to ditch the name, my identity, make a clean start for my own safety. He was worried they'd come after me, one of the bastards I used to service. Especially if they found out I was providing intelligence on clients to the right people. His exact words were, 'You need to disappear without a trace.'"
"Oh my god," Micah laughs.
"Yeah. Smartass then, smartass now."
"Trace," Micah repeats.
"Yep. Trace. Grew my hair long, grew the beard...."
"I'm not surprised he calls you Patrick," Micah murmurs, turning to face the window.
"Only when he's inside me, in one way or another," Trace says quietly. "Fucker likes to get inside my head as much as other places. That's when we met, me and Gray. What a love story that was. Goddamn."
"Feelings don't always die easily. You don't need to tell me that," Micah says tenderly.
"God, I hate him. I really do," Trace seethes. "Of all people, it's *him* that knows me the way he does."
"He left you," Micah guesses.
"He left, so I left." With a bitter laugh, he sneers and adds, "But he never really *left*. I knew people through The Company, people MI5 needed more intel on, so he never let me go, not all the way. I came here, met Benny. Shit, how do you meet that kid and not fall for him right away? We started all of this together. Eventually, we met Gabey. Gabey...."
Trace glances over at the main building, probably remembering. "You should've seen him, love. He had nothing to his name but scars but he was so fucking beautiful and *young*. God, he was young."
Clearing his throat, wiping a hand over his face, he says, "You know the rest."

"But the baby—"

"She's better off without me," Trace says immediately.

Shocked, Micah blinks. "You know it's a girl."

"Yeah," Trace grumbles. "She'd be going on thirty-two years old now, for Christ's sake."

"Trace," Micah starts, not knowing how to finish. He sits forward in his seat, feeling driven, feeling like fate has taken hold and given a hard shake.

"You think what you go through," Trace tells him sternly. "What I have to *see you* and Lil go through from losing that baby girl, is hard for me just because I give a shit about you two? I've *told you* how I hate that shit. I *hate* that shit."

Seeing Trace upset instantly makes Micah upset. "You're a *father*," he says urgently, saying it like he needs to convince Trace of the truth of that.

"So are you," Trace counters with a hard, unyielding stare. "Leave it alone."

But she's out there, Micah thinks, desperately, scanning the town below as if he could see her down there, somewhere. *She's out there and she's alive, but she doesn't have you. She doesn't even know you.*

His vision blurs.

Trace takes hold of Micah's chin, wrenching Micah's face around to look at him. He's right there, with all of the strength, power, and easy confidence he's always had and urges, "She's not mine, love. She was *never* mine. Don't kid yourself. Just leave it alone."

"How can you be okay with this?" Micah demands fervently. "How?! She's your *daughter*!"

"Because she's better off without me," Trace repeats.

"You don't know that," Micah argues. "You don't know how amazing you are! She should know you. You should want to know she's okay. You—"

He's silenced with a kiss.

When they break, Trace dries Micah's tears. "She's not Moira. Please, love. This is my choice."

"Damn it, Trace," Micah sighs, calming down.

"You can't tell anyone *any* of this."

He doesn't want to ask, but he has to.

"Are there people looking for you? Is Patrick in trouble? Is that what this is? Is that why Gray hasn't let you go?"

"I don't know, love. I've been around a long time, done a *lot* of shit. I watch my ass."

"I told you I had a talk with Lily today, while all of you were gone. We agreed that it's not working anymore. I mean, obviously it's not, but we said it out loud for the first time. She left, to be with Saoirse, for good. I could feel it, you know, when she packed up and walked out, how real it was. It felt a lot different than the other times she's gone. I could tell she's not mine anymore. It made me feel… frantic. My own damn fault, though. She tried so hard, for all of us…. She said you were a good man. She seemed glad I have you, and won't be alone. Maybe part of her was just waiting for that, for me to have someone else to take care of me, instead of her, so she could say goodbye. Fuck. It was… it was *awful*. It really was. I just feel like I fucked up so much. I had such a good thing with her, and I blew it."

Trace reaches out, takes Micah's hand. Their fingers interlock. Micah gazes down at the sight of it. Leaning in close, Trace kisses Micah's cheek, then stays there, letting him feel the connection.

"I'm sorry you're going through this, but it's a good pain. Healthy. That you can own up to your mistakes, and face them, is a big deal, believe me. You're brave as hell, love. It'll be okay. Promise. We'll get each other through."

"I couldn't do this without you. I'm not strong enough. But with you, maybe I can be. I love how you show me how strong I can be, if I try. And how I can lean on you when I'm weak."

"Likewise, love," Trace smiles. "All my life, I've dreamt about finding a partner I could be myself with. It always seemed so impossible before."

"Thanks, Patrick, for trusting me," Micah murmurs with a small, grateful grin. He doesn't hide his heartache, because he doesn't need to. He doesn't need to hide anything anymore.

"You're welcome, kid," Trace smiles. "Feeling's mutual."

Chapter 37
Just a Letter

Kyle walks to the front door of his house, keys jingling as he searches for the right one. He scoops the day's mail from the mailbox with one hand and finds the key with the other. It slides into the lock. With a turn, the lock releases and he steps inside. Nearby, Kyle Junior meows. The cat's pale, spotted head peeks around the edge of a doorway.

"Hey, kiddo. Miss me?"

The plan is to spend an hour or so with Ben and Gabriel while Kyle and Darrek review Darrek's current work orders and projects-in-progress in his garage, to determine whether they're something Kyle can help out with or not. Gabriel's heading there after he's done work. Kyle just has to wait for Ben to get home from Diadem while Darrek stops by the dog sitter's to get Sierra. Then, they're all due to meet at Gabriel and Darrek's home. Excited to do something so seemingly normal, Kyle lets himself feel happy and hopeful he might be able to safely reclaim some of his forsaken friendship with Darrek.

Kyle flips through the stack of mail—most of which is junk—ready to kick the door shut behind him before the cat can scamper out.

Then he sees it.

It's a letter on which Kyle's name and address have been handwritten. There's no return address, but there doesn't need to be.

He knows that handwriting.

The envelope looks chewed up, like it got caught in the teeth of some sorting machine before it was taped back together in spots. A sticker on the front apologizes on behalf of the postal service.

"No. Fuck. *Fuck!*" he shouts, scaring the cat away.

Before he opens it or does anything else, he remembers what Darrek said at the party about being out of the house and not checking the mail. Instinctively, Kyle knows what he needs to do. The connections have already been made in Kyle's head—one to the next to the next to the next, a chain reaction.

"You sick dead bastard," Kyle sneers. "FUCK!"

He has to get to Darrek's house before Darrek or Gabriel do. That's the only possibility. That's the only way this can go. Kyle will do anything—*anything*—to get there first. His only hope is it takes Darrek longer than expected to fetch Sierra from the dog sitter, and Gabriel gets hung up at work.

Yanking his keys from the door, slamming it closed, he runs, letter in hand, to his car. Hands shaking, feeling cold all over and wanting to vomit, he fumbles for his car key as he pulls the driver's side door open and jumps in behind the wheel.

"Come on, come on, come on," he says, like a mantra, over and over. The key slides in to the ignition. He shifts into reverse.

Maybe it's not what you think. Maybe he wrote to apologize, to repent.

A frightened, disbelieving sort of laugh erupts from him, scaring him even more to hear it.

Those emails I kept getting to my Diadem account.... All of the weird shit happening with Dare and Gabe's house and the phone calls....

Kyle flies down the streets, veering too fast around the turns, gunning the engine on the straight-aways.

"Please, please, please, just don't be there. Please just don't be there yet."

He has to do this. He has to. It's his job, his duty after everything he put Gabriel and Darrek through. All Kyle wants, all he prays for, is the chance to spare them both this one thing.

He turns onto their road. Their house is in sight. Some cars are parked along the road but none of them are Gabriel's or Darrek's.

Hope sparks.

Swerving up onto the grass, leaving the car there, half on the lawn, half on the sidewalk, he throws the door open and sprints to the front door.

The door is locked. He knows there's a spare key hidden somewhere but has no idea where it would be now. Maybe they got rid of it entirely with the suspected break-ins. He could break a window, but he's afraid of climbing over glass shards when he's this manic, so he tries the door first. Some of those cigarette butts Gabriel mentioned are littered over the front stoop, in the mulch beneath the windows, and on the path to the driveway. Gathering up all of his terror, his panic and desperation into a tight ball of energy, letting the endorphins flood his system, he steps back and kicks the door as hard as he can.

It rattles. The connection of his shoe sole and the wood is a boom of sound.

He does it again, thinking of Jerry, and all of those times when he wanted to lash out and couldn't. *Now* is the time to lash out. Now is the time to do what he never could. It's his one chance, and time is running out.

There's another boom and a cracking.

He does it again and again.

Finally, the door bursts open, swinging inward. The alarm on the house begins to shriek but he doesn't even hear it, couldn't care less about what it means.

The letter—*his* letter—is stuffed in the inner pocket of his suit jacket. Running over to the overflowing stack of mail on the sideboard, he sorts haphazardly through the pile, pushing things onto the floor, searching feverishly as fast as he can while the seconds tick by.

He's almost at the bottom and there's nothing. His fright kicks up.

Then he finds it—the same handwriting.

The letter had been stuck to the back of a postcard advertisement for a local lawn service.

Breathing out all of his air in a rush, Kyle prays his thanks and bolts through the house to the kitchen. There's almost no time left. They'll be getting to the house in seconds and the first thing they'll do is try to stop him.

Shaking more than ever, trembling and clumsy, he yanks open

the junk drawer by the sink. Even before he's able to start sifting through the contents, he sees a box of matches set out on the otherwise-bare counter, right in the middle of it. He doesn't know why it would be there, as if waiting for him to use it for this specific purpose, especially when neither Gabriel nor Darrek smoke, but he doesn't care. He pulls the letter from his pocket, rips it open, and drops the envelope into the sink. Striking a match, he gets it lit and drops it onto the envelope. Right away, the paper ignites.

Opening the folded letter, he can already see notations of bible passages written in pencil on the back. When he glimpses the image on the front, he drops the printout into the growing flames.

Bile rises in his throat as the scale of his reaction to it all outpaces his ability to act in his own best interest. He swallows the bile down with effort, trying so hard to look away from the image before him, the edges being licked with flames.

It's a printed screenshot from one of the videos Kyle appeared in for Diadem, showing him in the dungeon, submitting to Ben. He remembers that video. It was the first time he allowed penetration on camera. The screenshot was taken right as he was filled with the phallus, his posture conveying quite clearly his discomfort and anguish.

Pushing the memories back, Kyle drops Darrek's letter, unopened, into the flames. It covers the damned image sent to him by Jerry—his abuser, his tormentor—as a reminder, a message that he had still been watching Kyle after all that time. Years later, Jerry was still watching him yield to the sexual whims of more powerful men, and getting off on it. Trembling violently, Kyle tries to get another match lit. Then he drops that, too, into the growing conflagration in the stainless steel sink.

It can't burn fast enough.

Shrieking. Sirens. Shouting.

"KYLE!?"

He vomits, bent sharply over as his stomach cramps in a pitiful attempt to purge the memories and bad feelings. Everything comes up, all of his celebratory lunch.

"KYLE!"

Eyes watering, his gut constricting painfully to expel the imagined toxins, he hears footsteps running over the wooden floor toward him. He's yanked back from the fire erupting from the sink.

It's Gabriel.

Gabriel looks down into the sink without getting too close. Kyle knows from only the expression on Gabriel's face he sees what's burning in there, and understands why it's burning. Stricken and pale, Gabriel turns, his head swiveling fast as he looks at Kyle.

For a long, awful moment, Gabriel is frozen. Kyle wipes his mouth and considers lighting a third match as the sirens get closer than ever, the house alarm blaring.

Kyle's knees give out before he can decide conclusively about the third match. He crumples down to the floor, bent over, holding himself up by his arms braced on the floor.

Still unmoving, still trying to understand, or maybe trying *not* to understand, Gabriel stands there as the police storm in, guns drawn, yelling, "FREEZE!"

Gabriel raises his hands. Kyle thinks of Jerry beating off to his Diadem videos and retches.

"It's okay!" Gabriel calls. "This is my house! He's a friend!"

Firefighters rush in next. They begin to put out the flames with a fire extinguisher, but the blaze is contained to the sink. It hasn't spread.

"Let it burn!" Kyle cries hoarsely.

The police have holstered their guns but they yell over the shrieking alarm, "Step outside, please."

Gabriel lifts Kyle by the arm, looking him dead in the eye and assuring him, "It's gone, okay? It's gone. There's nothing left but soggy ashes."

Kyle deflates a little, his eyes closing with relief.

An ambulance arrives as Gabriel and Kyle sit on the front stoop; the alarm deactivated at last, the fire department starting to clear out.

"He's in shock," Gabriel explains to the EMT, who wraps Kyle in a blanket and begins to check his vital signs.

Gabriel isn't able to explain much to the police, as he was so late in arriving, so they wait until Kyle is examined before questioning him.

In the interim, Darrek arrives. He's holding Sierra by her leash as the two of them sprint to the house, running up the sidewalk as fast as they can. An officer stops them, but Darrek bellows, "That's my house! That's my partner!" They let him through.

Barking wildly, excited by the activity, Sierra tests the leash's strength but Darrek keeps her near as they cross to Gabriel and Kyle.

Frantic, looking everywhere, Darrek gasps, "What happened?! Are you okay?!"

"We're fine," Gabriel says calmly, probably trying to set Darrek at ease through example. "Like I told the EMT, Kyle's in shock, but I think he's okay. We're okay."

Darrek hugs Gabriel, trying to calm down but looking very confused and concerned.

"Kyle... The fire department... What...."

The EMT finishes looking him over and he draws the blanket closer around him. Gabriel puts his phone to his ear, dials, and says only, "Our place. Get here, *now*," before hanging up.

"Kyle, what happened?" Darrek demands.

"Don't worry about it. It's gone. I got rid of it," Kyle explains.

"Got rid of what? I don't understand!"

"It was a letter, okay?" Kyle begins, sipping a bottle of water someone hands him. "I got a letter in the mail... from Jerry. It must have gotten lost in processing, but it arrived today. It was a crappy printout of a photo of me, at Diadem, from one of the videos. I got here as fast as I could. I burned your letter, Dare. I fucking burned it. There's nothing left. He won't hurt you anymore. I stopped it."

"Who is Jerry?" an officer asks, taking notes.

"My father," Darrek answers. "Jerry is... *was* my father. Jerry Grealey. He's, uh, recently deceased."

"He was abusive," Gabriel explains to the officer. "He abused both of them as kids. He was a sick son of a bitch."

"Your letter got here first, last week probably," Kyle says. "Mine got held up."

"You kicked down the fucking door?" Darrek gapes, staring into the house, still noticing things, still processing his own growing shock. "How... Oh my god. *Oh my god.*"

Darrek goes to Kyle, falling to his knees, wrapping Kyle up in a hug.

Over Darrek's shoulder, Kyle sees Gabriel explaining, quietly, to the officer what he saw of the photo and the other letter, further explaining Kyle's reaction. Kyle tries to tune it out.

"Are you okay?" Darrek asks, holding Kyle's face in his hands, searching him for injury. Police officers mill around the property, going in and out of the house. Kyle tries to watch them, but Darrek pulls Kyle's attention back to him. "Kyle! Are you okay?"

"I didn't want you to know about any of it, but at least you didn't see it," Kyle murmurs. "I didn't want you to know what this means. I wanted—"

"To protect me? It's not your job to protect me," Darrek frowns.

"You protected *me*!" Kyle argues. "You protected me from him for so long and it was my turn, my chance to spare you this. I'm sorry I fucked it up, but at least you didn't open the letter."

"He saw your video."

"I think he saw *all* the videos, Dare. He chose that one to send a message, like he always did. *Everything* had a message. Maybe it was because I took you away from him, and he was angry. Who knows? He's gone now. He's rotting in the ground, just like he should be. I didn't know if you did any videos for Diadem or not, but it doesn't matter. Whatever was in that envelope he sent you was poison."

"I did one," Darrek says softly. "With Gabe."

Kyle winces, covering his head with his hands as he starts to cry. He tries so hard not to imagine it—Jerry watching Darrek's video, too, and deciding things, courses of action based on that. Darrek wraps him back up in a hug, stroking Kyle's hair, murmuring, "It's okay. He's gone. We're okay. You're okay."

After a little while, Kyle calms down. Ben arrives in his truck, pulling up with a squeal of tires, fishtailing slightly in his haste. While he stops and scrambles out from behind the wheel, Darrek keeps talking to Kyle.

"Thank you," Darrek says urgently, holding Kyle's gaze steadily. "Thank you for trying to protect me."

Kyle nods. Ben runs over and Kyle stands. Darrek straightens and steps back. Kyle's blanket falls as he hooks his arms around

Ben's neck and buries his face there while Ben holds him, breathing hard. He feels tensed and ready for a fight, but after Kyle murmurs in his ear, explaining what happened, Ben seems to sag slightly. Kyle understands how frustrated Ben must be by the whole thing, with no one's ass to kick. It's just ghosts and demons, laughing at them from the grave.

―◻―◻―◻―

"Seriously?" Kyle complains. "We just got rid of the cops, and the firemen, and the nosy neighbors. Who called Trace? Did *you* call Trace?"

"He was going to find out anyway," Ben sighs. "He always finds out, trust me."

"But look who he brought! Gray, the fucking hard-ass policeman of all subs everywhere and I just nearly burnt Darrek's house down," Kyle rants. "What do you think *he's* gonna do to me? *Congratulate* me?" Finally accepting the blanket he's been trying to lose, and which the others keep wrapping around him again, he burrows down into it to try and disappear. Trace and Gray climb off the motorcycle they rode over on, taking off their helmets and surveying the scene. Kyle starts to stand, wanting to get out of there, and murmurs, "I'll go look for more nails."

"My ass you will," Ben says. He pushes Kyle back down onto the plastic lawn chair by planting a firm hand on his shoulder.

"I'm the one that busted the lock," Kyle argues. "I should be the one to fix it. I can fix it."

Ben just gives him a no-fucking-way-sweetheart, cocky smile.

Darrek appears from the garage with a large piece of plywood as Gabriel examines the doorframe with a slightly befuddled expression.

"What the great hairy fuck happened here?" Trace demands, his gaze darting from Kyle's car, still parked on the lawn, to the trampled grass, to the busted front door, to the sight of the four of them languishing there, trying to figure out what to do with themselves.

"You said there was a fire," Gray says to Ben, his expression tense, concerned. Both Trace and Gray have a charged, adrenaline-fueled energy about them, and it's a stark contrast to Ben, Kyle, Gabriel, and Darrek's dull quietness. The four share a look as Kyle's guilt flares.

"It's fine. We're handling it," Gabriel says.

"*I* set the fire, okay," Kyle blurts. "I broke in. I set the fire."

"And why the hell would you break in to their house and set a fire?" Trace asks.

Silence descends again.

"Don't do that," Trace says with aggravation. "That's not helping. Someone fucking explain."

"I told you, you shouldn't have called him," Kyle hisses under his breath to Ben.

Ben hesitates, probably unsure of how to put into words what just happened to Kyle, or maybe unwilling to. When his hands come back to rest on Kyle's shoulders, kneading and massaging, Kyle suspects it's the latter.

Gabriel speaks up as he crouches next to the toolbox, eyeing Gray who's examining what he can see of the damage. "Kyle got a letter from Jerry. It was an image from one of his videos sold through Diadem, showing him in a compromising position. There were bible passages written on the back." He takes a breath, sags a little. Darrek concentrates on the plywood, measuring it and marking a line to trim. A moment later, he carries the wood back to the garage to make the cut. "Kyle came here as fast as he could to get Darrek's letter before Dare could find it. He burned both in the sink. Now we're just... cleaning up, I guess."

"How did you know he would have a letter, too?" Trace asks Kyle.

"Lucky guess? Intuition? Conditioning?"

"He was stalking you," Trace says with distaste.

"Cyber stalking at least," Gabriel agrees.

"That sick, dead fuck," Trace sneers. "Wait. If he's dead, how could he send you a letter?"

Gray catches Trace's eye at that, Kyle notices, and wonders what it's about.

"Mine was ripped and taped together like it got lost in the mail or stuck in their sorting machines somewhere," Kyle says. "Darrek's has been sitting in the pile with the rest of the mail from the past week or so."

"Have you noticed anything else out of the ordinary?" Gray asks. "Anything strange?"

"No, it's just the phone calls, really, but we know what that was about now," Gabriel says as the saw whirs in the garage. "We've been avoiding the place. Dare hasn't been comfortable. Maybe this is why. Maybe part of him knew."

Hanging his head, Gabriel hunches there.

"I had some weird emails to my Diadem account, about my videos. There was nothing in them to make me think it was Jerry, but now I'm pretty sure it was him, emailing me," Kyle says, somewhat bashfully.

"Why the fuck didn't you say anything?" Ben demands.

"It was spam or freaky fan mail, not the end of the world," Kyle argues. "A lot of people could have been sending them."

Trace goes to Gabriel, murmuring, "C'mere." When Gabriel is on his feet, Trace looks him over more closely. "What was in Dare's letter?"

"We don't know."

"I fucking burned it!" Kyle snaps. "It doesn't matter. He's a fucking corpse. It was nothing good, not if he was getting his rocks off by watching me get fucked on video."

"Hey," Ben scolds. "Come on; let me get you out of here already."

"No! I want to help. I have to help Dare," Kyle argues. "It's not fair that he has to clean up my mess."

"Fine. Okay. Come on," Ben sighs, surrendering to Kyle's need for inclusion in the process. He gestures for Kyle to lead the way. Leaving the blanket behind, he sees Gray murmur something to Gabriel, then disappear into the house. Trace stays by Gabriel's side. Ben and Kyle walk to the garage.

Darrek is standing there by his workbench with his hands planted on a plywood board. The saw is shut off. He stares blankly ahead as silent tears slip down his cheeks.

"Goddammit," Kyle groans. The instinct is to go forward, go

to Darrek. Feeling Ben's gaze on him, Kyle denies the instinct and stays where he is, arms folded. He takes a deep breath. Darrek snaps out of it a little and notices them. Sniffing, he wipes his face quickly dry and gets himself together.

Kyle starts to say, "Look, I'm sorry—"

"Don't apologize for him," Darrek says sharply, cutting him off. "Don't!"

Turning away from the saw, Darrek pulls his hair tightly back from his face with both hands, the massive muscles of his arms flexing. After taking a calming breath, he continues, "He never let it go. After all of this time... he was *watching you*. How fucking vile is that? And your first thought wasn't for yourself, was it? It was to protect *me*. To spare *me* the hurt. That's *him*. He did that to you, Kyle! Be mad. Please." Darrek faces him, looking desperate. "Be mad about this. Get angry for what he did to you. You don't need to protect me. You're still protecting me!"

"And what is this? What are you doing, Dare," Kyle counters. "Who are the tears for? Are they from imagining what he sent you, now that you'll never know for sure?"

Darrek won't look at him. He looks at Ben instead, and more tears fall.

"Please take him home," Darrek begs. "Please keep him safe. I just—" He chokes on the word, tries again. "I just want him *safe*."

"This isn't your fault," Kyle shouts. "Shit happens, okay? Especially with fucked up people like Jerry. So this was his goodbye present. It doesn't mean anything. It doesn't change *anything*. He's gone. He's done. I'm safe. You're safe. Now, can I please help you patch the fucking door so I don't feel as bad about forgetting where you hide the spare key?"

"You're in shock," Darrek counters. "You should be at home, resting with Ben."

"*You're* in shock," Kyle retorts. "Give me the fucking hammer. Give it! Fucking give it. Give it to me."

"What can I say?" Ben shrugs. "He's a participator. He's not resting until he gets it out of his system, so we might as well let him."

Darrek lets out a growl which comes from deep down, beneath

the frustration and anger. It seems to help. He hands over the hammer.

"Thank you. Jesus, was that so hard?" Kyle scoffs. "Come on. After you."

Lifting the large piece of trimmed plywood, Darrek carries it out of the garage, past Kyle and toward the door. Ben rolls his eyes and follows Kyle as Kyle follows Darrek.

Chapter 38

Contact

He should have checked in by now, Gray thinks. He checks his phone again but there's nothing. No sign.

Something's wrong.

"You look like you've got a stick up your ass," Trace comments. "It started as soon as you heard about the fire, and it's still there. I can see it. Why do you have a stick up your ass, bright eyes?"

Trace and Gray are back at Micah's place, standing in the driveway beside the bike. Gray hasn't moved an inch from the bike's side, mostly because he doesn't think they're done with it yet. As far as they know, Ben and Kyle are still with Gabriel and Darrek at their home. Trace made the decision to leave instead of trying to help at the scene, since he thought it best to give the others their space for the time being. But now Trace is getting a read off of Gray's sense of unease and it's setting him on edge, especially since he can tell it has something to have to do with his boys. If there's something wrong with Trace's boys, Gray knows Trace isn't doing anything else until he finds out what it is.

Gray looks right at him, giving away nothing, saying nothing, even as he tries to weigh the possibilities. If the others are all together, they should be safe. But if they're safe, there's no reason why his contact should be silent about the fire and police activity.

"What the hell were you up to in that kitchen?" Trace demands, getting more riled the longer Gray holds out. "What did you think you were gonna find in the ashes?"

Once glimpse at Trace tells Gray how much his behavior is affecting his ex. They're out in the open, so Trace has it mostly together on the outside, but his eyes tell a different story. His eyes are entirely Patrick, and hardly Trace at all. That's not a big surprise, though, with so much out of their hands. Trace has never been good at letting other people tell him how things are going to be, but Patrick knows sometimes you have to let go and take the ride.

Oh, Tracey, don't you realize? It only gets worse from here. You should stay in the dark, you're safer there.

Pulling his phone out, Gray avoids the questions. He taps a few buttons, checking his connection as there are no recent calls and no unread messages.

"They should have called by now," is all the explanation Gray gives.

"Who?"

"The others are all still at the house, right? No one has left?"

"God, I'm so sick of this shit with you. The sheer fucking lack of a straight answer drives me out of my damn mind," Trace curses as he places a call on his own cell and waits for it to be picked up. "Yeah, hey Benny. You two are still there, right? With Gabe and Dare? Well, why the fuck would he do that? Where the hell are his priorities? No, no. You're probably right. Okay. Keep me posted."

He hangs up and tells Gray, "Gabe left. He drove to his studio to check the mail there, too, just in case. He said it's been a few days since he's been by there."

Fucking hell.

Angry, Gray demands, "He went alone?"

"Yeah, so? He goes to work alone all the time."

"We have to go," Gray says abruptly. "Now."

Gray's phone rings. He looks down at it with heavy sense of foreboding before answering.

"Target's on the move," Gray hears.

"Copy," he replies before hanging up. Urgently, Gray says in command, "Get on the fucking bike, Tracey. Hurry."

"Shit. Now what?" Trace groans as they jump back on and tear down the driveway.

—◻︎—◻︎—◻︎—

When Gabriel gets to Daring Angel Photography, he doesn't turn on any of the lights. There's enough ambient light coming through the front window to see by as he first unlocks the front door, then locks it again behind him before going to the reception desk. It's piled with mail yet to be sorted, though the stack is smaller than the one at the house.

Outside, people mill around on the sidewalk as evening sets in and the sun slowly sets. Tucked away in the shadows, with the deeper, thicker darkness of the rear of the studio stretching out behind him, Gabriel's mind races, trying to get back on track, struggling to think of useful ideas or ways to ensure the safety of both Darrek and Kyle.

He doesn't really think Jerry would have sent something to Gabriel's studio, but you never know. If the guy had done enough research to get him sifting through Diadem's video library when Kyle Roth isn't even credited by name on their website or in the videos themselves, Gabriel isn't putting anything past the man—dead or no. They had always been careful and respectful of Kyle's wish for privacy. They used masks, blindfolds, hoods or camera angles to disguise features and used an assumed name for the credits. Of course, Jerry would know Kyle if he saw him, even if he didn't have a clear view of Kyle's face. Jerry was familiar enough with the rest of Kyle's naked body that he could probably have identified him from his scars, moles, freckles, and coloring. Just the idea of that makes Gabriel sick, of Jerry Grealey sitting at a computer somewhere, avidly scrutinizing the footage until he found just the right frame with the phallus breaching Kyle and real anguish evident in his body language. If Jerry was willing to go that far, maybe he would do his homework on his own son, too, and find out everything on record about one Gabriel Hunter, Darrek's admitted partner, lover, and Master.

Maybe he would cover his bases, and send something equally disturbing to Gabriel's place of business. The only way to know for sure is to check, and there was no way he was bringing Darrek along for the ride. As long as Ben is there, with Darrek and Kyle, Gabriel feels comfortable conducting the search on his own.

He picks up half of the pile, flipping through it piece by piece.

Voices carry softly through the glass of the shop's front windows.

Then he hears something else. Something which sounds like a clink of metal, only it comes from inside the studio, more specifically from the workroom in the back.

"Hello? Anyone there?" he calls out, feeling stupid. For all he knows it could be a mouse, or the heating system kicking on, or something else equally banal.

There's nothing, no response. The noise doesn't come again, but the hairs rise on his arms and all the way up to the back of his neck.

Jerry's dead, he tells himself. *Harry's dead. You're just being paranoid.*

Someone could have broken in, though. Maybe it's a common thief. Maybe it's the same person who knocked over those framed photos.

What're the odds of the studio being broken in to the same day as the house?

Doesn't feel right. It feels off.

Or maybe I'm catching Dare's paranoia, seeing danger where there's nothing but the ordinary.

Shivering, he knows he wants to go look and make sure it's nothing.

"God, don't be that guy," he moans quietly with dread. "Hear a freaky sound; walk into the dark to investigate like a dumbass."

The sound of his own craziness is what convinces him to stop talking in circles, to go look and finish what he came there for so he can leave.

He sets the mail back down and walks through the front room to the doorway leading to his workroom. There are no windows back here, so no ambient light, either, except what slips through the doorway. He glances at the back entrance, a metal door which opens up onto the alleyway behind the building. It's tightly closed.

Eyes adjusting, ears straining to detect the faintest of sounds, Gabriel becomes very still as he listens.

The switch to turn on the lights is to his right. He reaches out for it, sliding in that direction.

He hears movement a fraction of a second before his outstretched arm is grabbed and twisted.

A shout of surprise and fear erupts from him before he clamps his jaws shut as his arm is yanked around behind his back. Metal snaps closed around his wrist tightly enough to cut into the flesh and he struggles, blind and confused. He's not as fast as his attacker who quickly has Gabriel's other wrist as well. The other end of the cuffs is fastened to that wrist, binding both arms behind his back. Breathing hard, Gabriel tries to stay calm, to not get lost to the icy grip of panic. Strange, old survival instincts kick in, helping him stay somewhat rational in the face of imminent danger.

"What do you want?" Gabriel asks. "Who are you?"

"Just wanna *play*, Gabe," a voice says, then laughs.

He's shoved backward by a direct hit to the center of his chest by the man's elbow. Then he's falling, cursing, and lands heavily on his bound arms. Crying out in pain, he tries to keep his bearings and shift position but now the man is at Gabriel's feet. He leans down over Gabriel's prone form. His hands go right for Gabriel's fly.

"No! Please! Just tell me what you want!"

"Told you, Gabe. Just wanna play. Heard how much you like to, how easily you go along…. You let Darrek, that huge fucker, play with you, don't you? Bet he doesn't know what *really* gets you going, does he?"

There's a soft chuckle. Face in shadow, and, from what Gabriel can see in the gloom, with a body average in size and not familiar, the man is a stranger. There's nothing at all familiar about him. That makes it harder to stay calm. At least with Harry, Gabriel always knew what was wanted, and could play along to spare himself as much grief as possible. But how does he know Gabriel's name? How does he know about Darrek?

"Were you in my house?" Gabriel demands.

There's another soft chuckle. "Got a *lot* of nice toys in that spare bedroom, don't you? Tried to come see you when you were home, since I'd have *loved* to try those toys out. But you weren't *there*."

The intruder opens Gabriel's pants and pulls them down to his ankles. Then he sits astride Gabriel's legs, pinning him to the ground.

Strangling on the fear, not knowing what to do with it, how to process it and get back in control, combined with the shock of what he walked into a handful of hours ago at his own home, it clouds his mind, slows every reaction.

Then a flame is ignited.

It's small—a pocket-sized lighter. The flame is lowered to Gabriel's genitals and it's suddenly too much. Heart racing, he's unable to draw breath, unable to move or think. The stranger's hands touch him, lifting Gabriel's penis, bringing the dancing, orange-gold fire down inches away from the skin.

"Please stop! *Please!*"

"It *is* you," the man says happily. "He told me about the scar, how he held the cigarette to you, right here...."

A fingertip strokes the circular mark at the root of Gabriel's penis.

Harry.

"H-he's... he's *dead*," Gabriel grunts, trembling violently, trying to fight past paralyzing horror and keep his wits about him.

"Yeah, he is," the man agrees, pleasantly. The sounds of his words draw together with a hint of a southern accent. "But *I'm* not. Loved all his stories, how you cried when he buggered you, and got so scared but went along with it anyway. I asked him to tell me all about when he burned you. Wanted all the details so I could see it clearly in my mind. Had him tell me how you screamed. It's better when they scream. No way out, is there, boy? We're *all alone.*"

An opened hand slides up the underside of Gabriel's penis and the flame comes closer, enough to feel heat, to want to flinch away.

"Don't!"

"I liked how sometimes you'd answer the phone when I called, and how scared you sounded. Made me hard, thinking about what I was gonna do to you. Sometimes I was watching, you know. I'd peek through the windows, watching you and Darrek get so *scared* together. I'd watch him touch you and think about how soon, he wouldn't be able to touch you that way, not when I got done with ya. Gonna burn the rest off, Gabe, and finish what Harry started... set a few of these short and curlies alight, let the fire chase down to skin... let it spread...." The fire moves even nearer to his groin and Gabriel bucks, trying to throw his attacker off and escape but all the move succeeds in doing is getting the man to hold his tiny, seemingly insignificant flame to the root of Gabriel's penis. Fire licks the skin.

Gabriel screams. His attacker hums with pleasure.

"He always said how pretty you screamed. But he liked knives more than fire. Think of what we could have done, together. Shame he's gone. Won't get to watch me play with you until you're black and crispy...."

The fire lowers to Gabriel's testicles, heat baking sensitive skin, the flame only an inch away, getting closer by the second.

An explosion of sound cracks with violence and volume from the front of the building but all Gabriel can feel, all he knows is that tiny fire as every muscle in his body strains to pull back or fight free, and his own screaming bursting from his lungs as the fire touches skin and his mind threatens to snap.

Shapes stream through the dark.

There's a muffled gunshot—just one.

The man atop Gabriel's legs jolts slightly forward from some invisible hit. The lighter is dropped to the floor. Someone—some other, dark, unknowable shape—runs over, kicking the lighter away. There's a gun in their hand, pointed at Gabriel's attacker. But there are no flashing lights, no sign that these men are police, so Gabriel's mind spins, unable to latch on to anything that makes sense, anything comforting about what's happened.

One of the newcomers—the one who kicked the lighter—kicks the man perched on top of Gabriel. He tumbles off.

Suddenly, Gabriel is free.

Using only his trembling legs, he tries to push himself away, but someone else runs over to him, someone familiar, even in the dark.

"Easy. Easy, beautiful. I've gotcha," they tell him.

"Trace?" Gabriel sobs with relief. "Thank god. Please help. Help me?"

Trace gathers him up, draws him near, and—even though chaos continues to clamor around them, despite pain and terror—after so many times spent alone and afraid in the dark with someone wanting to hurt him, and needing help which never came, Gabriel finally knows what it feels like to be rescued before real hurt can be done.

"I've gotcha," Trace promises. "You're safe."

And for the first time, as his head is cradled in Trace's lap and his body is searched for injury, Gabriel is able to begin to believe that maybe he is, at last, safe.

A balding, pinched-faced, thin-lipped man with a mouth too full of teeth lies curled up on the ground, grinning and clutching the bullet wound in his shoulder. Blood seeps out between his fingers and he laughs as Gray finds the light switch. The room is flooded with searing brightness. Blood and bits of tissue have been sprayed over the man's front, and Gabriel as well, from the bullet fired from Gray's weapon. Gabriel screams again when he gets a better look at the scene, but thankfully Trace has him. He calmly helps to contain Gabriel's fear so Gray can work.

Gray keeps his gun leveled at the target as his contact, also with his weapon drawn and ready, dressed inconspicuously in a dark shirt and dark pants, slips past Gabriel to the workroom, sweeping the space and checking for anyone else in the building.

"I need the keys," Trace barks to Gray. "The cuffs."

"All clear!" Gray's contact yells.

Gray approaches the target, the barrel of his gun aimed for a headshot. He says, "Toss 'em."

The pinch-faced man just laughs.

Gray fires a shot into the man's kneecap. Instantly, the man shrieks, collapsing forward to cover the leg. Gabriel makes a startled, frantic sound from Gray's right.

"Toss the keys to the cuffs. Now," Gray says coolly.

It takes a moment of fumbling with bloodied fingers, but the keys are located in one of his pockets. The pinch-faced man awkwardly tosses them in Trace's direction. Gray kicks them the rest of the way with a foot. As Trace uses the keys to free Gabriel's arms, Gray says, "Can he walk?"

"Yeah, I think so," Trace answers.

"Good. Get him out of here."

"Why?" Gabriel asks, still breathless and clearly in shock as he comes to terms with what's happened, and still happening. "What are you gonna do?"

"Now," Gray says to Trace.

"I want to stay. I want to be here," Gabriel argues. He's rubbing his wrists as Trace helps him draw his pants back up. A moment later, he's trying to stand. Trace helps him over to a chair.

"He's burned," Trace tells Gray heavily. "Looks like the guy was trying to burn his dick off."

Catching the eye of his contact in the front room, watching the front entrance and the street beyond, Gray says, "No one in or out."

"Copy."

To the bloody man on the floor, Gray says, "That true? You tried to burn his dick off? Like you burned Harry's scars off?"

He grabs a metal chair with solid legs from the photography studio's workshop area, and a number of electrical cords as well. While the bleeding, sniveling, chuckling madman hesitates in answering the question with actual words, Gray rips the clothes from him. Dragging him, naked, to the chair, Gray sits him in it. Rapidly, he secures the suspect to it by weaving the cords around his arms and legs, under and behind the chair, drawing his limbs together and using the legs of the chair to keep him from moving an inch. When he's secured, Gray moves one of the umbrella lamps close and switches it on.

Blinded by the flood of bright light, it makes the suspect blink and cringe. Teeth bared, he tries to shift position to ease the strain on the wounds in his shoulder and knee. Saliva drips from his lips as he seethes and spits with anger.

To spur conversation while he works, Gray says, "Harry didn't fight you when you burned him, though, did he?"

"Oh, he fought," the suspect laughs, eyes sparkling with dark delight, "They always fight when their skin begins to boil and bubble."

Scanning the room for useful instruments, Gray sees a portable light on a small, adjustable stand. When he turns it on, the fragile bulb begins to get hot, quickly. He brings it to his suspect and presses the light bulb in between his bound legs, holding it to his exposed genitals, his skinny thighs hugging the bulb's sides.

Staring wide-eyed down at the glass bulb that only gets hotter and hotter, squirming slightly from discomfort, it slowly occurs to the captive man that should he move his legs at all, the shards from the light will splinter into his genitals.

"Even with a dick small as that, it'd still hurt like fuck to get it sliced up with glass. Wouldn't move if I was you." When the man starts to gasp from the increasing temperature of the bulb, Gray says, "You like heat, huh? Let's see *how much* you like it."

The man's gaze roams to Gabriel.

"You look only at me," Gray orders. "You talk to *me*. Harry told you about him?"

"Gabriel," the drooling, bleeding, grinning maniac purrs. "Oh, Harry had *so many* stories. A pervert. Liked little boys. But I liked the story about the burning. Burning them... burning Gabriel, giving him a scar to teach him to behave, and be afraid. Gabriel...."

"But Harry's dead. He's been dead for a while. Why come after Gabriel now?"

The only response is another shrill laugh and a low, "Fuck you."

Leaving the bulb where it is, Gray takes one of the bottles of chemicals lining nearby, used for developing photographs. The bottle labeled as a Kodak Developer is marked with warnings about being a skin and eye irritant. It's just what he's looking for.

Bottle of developer in hand, Gray goes back to the chair. Unscrewing the cap on the developer, he pours some over the open, bleeding bullet wound in the man's kneecap.

An ear-splitting shriek fills the air. Gray stuffs a rag in the man's mouth to muffle the sound. He takes the rag out when the sound begins to die.

"Answer. Why come after Gabriel now?"

Gasping, groaning, the suspect cries, "Been... been watching... waiting to be alone... Had to find him first. Went through Harry's things...."

"Just Gabriel?"

"Just...."

There's hesitation, a grunt of pain, avoidance of eye contact. Gray pours more developer over the wound.

"Just Gabriel! Just Gabriel, yes. Yes. Stop! Fuck!"

"You working with anyone else?"

More hesitation. He pours some of the fluid over the knee wound, then some in the shoulder. While the pungent developer fluid seeps deeper into the wounds, burning the tissue from the inside, he brings the bottle up near the suspect's face, holding his chin to tip his head sharply back.

"Answer the question," Gray says calmly, while holding the opened, tipped bottle directly above the man's eyes. The slightest movement would send the fluid slipping over. "I need names."

Making wild, animalistic sounds, the suspect's eyes grow hugely wide as he growls through the pain. Sweating, bleeding, drooling, gasping, he struggles to speak, but the bottle moves nearer to his eyes and he yells, "No! No one! There's no one! No one else *understands*. No one knows how good it is to make them burn and scream like I can."

There's a crunch of glass as the bulb against his groin is forgotten under all of the agony from the wounds. His shrieking amplifies. Gray's contact appears in the doorway and gives him a nod.

Gray sets down the bottle of developer, sees blood pouring from fresh wounds in the man's inner thigh and scrotum, jagged pieces of the bulb sticking out of flesh. He'd bleed out quickly if left alone, but Gray needs to silence him before they draw unwanted attention, so he grabs hold of the man's head and twists sharply.

The shrieking ends abruptly. The body sags in the bonds.

"We're done here," Gray says.

"I'll call it in," his contact replies. He moves back into the front room. Peering through the blinds of the window overlooking the street, they hear him speak softly, too low to overhear.

Guarding Gabriel, Trace smoothes Gabriel's hair back, kisses his forehead and murmurs, "You're okay. I've got ya, kid."

The dripping of fluids from the body on the chair is overly loud in the relative quiet. Gray nods toward the reception area. Trace catches it, understands, and says to Gabriel, "Come on. You don't need to see any more of this shit. Let's clear out of here so I can make sure you're okay."

Chapter 39
Answers

"I'll call for an ambulance," Trace tells Gabriel.

"I don't need an ambulance," Gabriel argues. "Really, I'm fine. It's nothing I can't treat myself."

They're sitting in the reception area. It's all too quiet inside the photography studio. There are no more cries of pain or defiance, just the quiet as the professionals—people Gabriel doesn't know and never will—clean up the mess. They'd arrived a few minutes after the unnamed man who had arrived with Gray and Trace made his phone call. A team of men and women came in through the rear entrance and got to work without a word. There's a body to dispose of, evidence to scrub away. Once in a while Gabriel glances up at the doorway as people back there go about their work, moving here and there, speaking softly to one another.

Gabriel can't see any blood from where he's sitting, but at the same time, he can still see the blood in his memory. He'd gotten rid of his bloodstained shirt. Trace found a clean one in one of the closets. Trace has Gabriel's wrists held gently in his grasp and he turns them both over, examining the scrapes from the metal handcuffs.

"You're lettin' some damn EMTs look you over. No arguments," Trace says with finality.

Gabriel looks him in the eye, this man who has been more of a father to him than anyone else in his life, whom he's called Daddy for what are probably the wrong reasons, and there's so much gratitude in Gabriel's heart just to have him in his life. Just to be able to call Trace his own.

"I know you're just trying to take care of me, but I'm fine,"

Gabriel tells him tenderly, wanting Trace to believe it so that he'll stop worrying so much. There's a look about Trace at the moment, like he's been shaken up more than Gabriel has ever seen before, in fundamental ways. Like Trace has just walked in on Harry raping Trace's child rather than some random lunatic doing what amounts to minimal harm.

"You're not fine!" Trace growls. "If Gray hadn't been here, if he hadn't known things I didn't know, I wouldn't have known to check on you. It was like that fucker *knew* he had Ben, and Kyle, and Dare, and *me* out of the way so *there would be no rescue* and…. I could have *lost you*, Gabriel. After *everything*, I would have failed you this time. I can't protect you, not like Gray can, no matter *how much* I try."

"But you did save me," Gabriel argues, smiling at Trace's typical stubbornness. "Gray was here because of you. He knew about Harry because of *you*. You brought Gray here. You came and held me and made me feel more safeguarded than I've ever felt in my life. You *do* protect me. You always have. Sure, everyone needs help sometimes. I know that now. You do, too. We're only human, Trace. I love that you want to take care of me, always, but you *can't*. But today? You got here when it counted. And that's a *lot*. It's a miracle."

Trace is shaken. He holds Gabriel's wrists carefully, but seems anchored to the spot. He looks defeated. There's next to nothing in him of the strong, confident man Gabriel is used to seeing.

"Don't you dare think you're a failure," Gabriel tells him, tenderly. "You're the most honorable, steadfast man I've ever know. And no one else besides you could have known to involve someone like Gray in this shit with Harry, even if you had to do it without me knowing. You were right in calling him, okay? I admit it."

Gabriel's phone starts to ring. When he sees it's Darrek calling, there's a sense of vertigo as the rest of the world seems to rush up at him at dizzying speed.

"Fuck," Gabriel murmurs, at a loss. "What do I say to him? I… I can't…."

He answers the call before he gets any farther in his scramble for an idea.

"Hey, baby," he says quickly, "can I call you back in a minute? Kind of in the middle of something. I'm fine. Sorry I haven't called."

There's silence, like he caught Darrek off guard. Then, Darrek says, "O-okay. You're okay? You sound weird."

"I'm okay," Gabriel smiles. "Love you. I'll call back in a minute."

"Okay," Darrek acquiesces. He's still in shock from the letters and the fire. Gabriel can hear it in Darrek's voice, which just makes the dreaded conversation to come that much more daunting. "Love you too."

When the call is ended, Gabriel looks to Trace for an answer, but he quickly realizes that Trace is all out of answers. Trace is shaken, but Gabriel has never seen Trace less than certain of anything.

Maybe Gabriel feels calmer than he should, but seeing someone pay in a visceral way for trying to hurt him has pacified a primal need for vengeance which he never hoped to sate. Resentment falls from his shoulders like a heavy cloak, no longer needed.

Trace's eyes are watery with unshed tears. As soon as Gabriel realizes this, he has to look away. He can't bear to witness Trace crying.

"It was too damn close," Trace says softly. "I just wish it hadn't been so damn *close*, but I'm glad as hell we got here in time, baby boy. All I've ever wanted was to save you."

"I know. And you did," Gabriel smiles. He wraps his arms around Trace, and feels Trace place a gentle kiss to his temple.

"Love you, kid."

"Love you too. And thank you."

"Don't thank me," Trace replies, drawing Gabriel's attention to the figure approaching. "Thank *him*."

"Who are these guys? How did you know? Why are you here?"

They're just the first questions of many, Gray knows. Some he can answer, some he can't. Or won't.

"They're CIA," he tells Gabriel. "I have a... friend... who's been keeping an eye on you. Your attacker's name is Bernard Schultz.

When I took care of Harry, some things were uncovered which raised suspicion. There were Harry's burns, of course, which seemed carefully but crudely applied to remove his scarring, or at least make it unreadable. Anyone who could have done that without killing him had to know what they were doing. There were other signs he was working with a known arsonist. Mr. Schultz fit the profile perfectly, but evidence connecting them was minimal. Not enough to go on. But you were a suspected target, so you've been under surveillance."

"Why didn't you tell me?!" It's asked with more of a tired sort of outrage than any real anger or frustration. Gabriel seems to be recovering from the initial shock more quickly than Trace. His gaze is sharp and clear, his wits intact. That's good to see. "You knew all of that and you didn't warn me?!"

"Nothing was certain," Gray explains. "It was all speculation. The surveillance was only a precautionary measure."

"Surveillance... He was there today, wasn't he? Your CIA buddy. After the fire?"

Gray nods. "When I wasn't contacted immediately after the incident at the house, I suspected there had been complications. Seems I was right. The agent picked up the security alarm's signal at your home at the same time as he was following Mr. Schultz's trail. That's why I hadn't heard from him. He tracked you as quickly as he could, found you here. The lock at the back door had been tampered with. He saw that, circled around the property. Once the agent heard you cry out, he moved to break in through the front. We arrived just before he did."

To Gray, Trace says, "Tell him the rest. He should know."

"We don't know for certain—"

"Tell him!" Trace demands, his voice wavering with emotion. Gabriel is glancing between them, likely as not with no bloody clue what to make of all of this. Gray's gaze fixes on his former lover, amazed by what he sees.

There's more of Patrick in him than Trace now. Look at him. It's all being chipped away.

Gray bites his tongue, looks directly at Gabriel and says, "We suspect all of those phone calls made to your home—most of them, anyway—were Mr. Schultz's way of trying to scare you. Clearly some of the calls were the Grealeys reaching out to Darrek, but not all of them. The phone records have most of the calls coming from one unlisted number. The Grealey's number shows up a few times, but that's all. There were cigarette butts all over your property, though neither you nor Darrek, nor any of your close friends, smoke, which leads me to believe they were left by Bernard, like a calling card. There was also a box of matches on your kitchen counter which has been collected as evidence, though it's doubtful they'll actually find his fingerprints on them. He's been fairly careful to cover his tracks, even as he gave you hints he was watching."

"There were photographs turned facedown in our house after one of the break-ins they assured us was a false alarm," Gabriel says.

"Those were likely Bernard as well, trying to intercept you, alone, and failing."

"He found Dare alone, but I wasn't there. It's *me* he wanted, so he left. He...." Gabriel sighs, putting more of the pieces together. "All of Dare's panic, all of his uneasiness, thinking this was Jerry trying to fuck with his head, but it wasn't Jerry. It was Bernard. *Jesus*. Dare knew. He could feel it. He knew this was coming." Gabriel's brow creases with worry. His gaze is fixed on the doorway leading to the back room when he asks, "Was it like this with Harry? Did you shoot him? Torture him?"

Gray remembers back to that night. He'd tracked Harry back to the abandoned house he'd been holed up in, a bag of scavenged food in hand. Most of his visible skin, almost all of his face, neck and forearms, were riddled with fresh burn scars. A few tufts of white hair sprouted from his head and his eyes held a crazed sort of intensity. But, of course Harry was an intelligent man—a lawyer who'd had a successful career, and who had managed to keep secret the sexual abuse he'd perpetrated on countless little boys. Though Gray intercepted Harry soundlessly, without detection, as soon as Harry realized he was caught and saw the gun in Gray's hand, things took a different turn than Gray had expected.

"I found Harry in a Philadelphia ghetto, living in an abandoned row home. I tracked him there," he explains to Gabriel. "But Harry had already been caught once, by your friends, by Trace, and with terrible consequences."

Harry was like a rat caught in a trap. He scrambled, dropping his half-eaten collection of food pillaged from the dumpsters of restaurants. They were inside the old row home. It was dark, but Gray saw clearly enough as Harry pulled a rusty, dull kitchen knife from a pocket of his overcoat. Harry's intention was evident—not to defend himself, but to avoid further torture. After being cut by Trace, being burned by Bernard, Harry had prepared himself to avoid any more pain at someone else's hands. He sensed what Gray had in store for him. He wasn't stupid enough to be convinced otherwise.

"As soon as he got a look of me, he tried to slit his throat with a knife from his pocket. He didn't succeed. The blade wasn't nearly sharp enough to do enough damage, but the slice he made did make it nearly impossible for him to speak. I tried to get information out of him regarding an accomplice."

Gray shot the knife out of Harry's hand as soon as he'd jabbed it into his throat. It seemed he intended to first dig in, then slice sideways. With his plan foiled, and two fingers and half of his hand blown off from the gunshot, Harry crumpled to the dirty tile floor, bleeding from his neck and his mangled right hand.

The only noise he would make was a gurgling sound as his throat filled with blood from the knife wound. Even though Gray had his own, much sharper, knife, which he used to provide incentive to answer his questions, stabbing into the remains of Harry's right hand—a hand used to destroy the lives of so many innocent children, including Gabriel—there were no names or useful information to be had. There was only screaming and choking as Harry's lungs slowly filled with blood.

"How?" Gabriel asks softly, drawing Gray from his memories, yearning for the gruesome details.

"When I shot the knife from his hand," Gray holds his own right hand up in demonstration, "it took half of it off. I used my own knife to carve away most of what was left, down to the bone. But there was too much blood in his throat. He didn't talk."

"Jesus Christ," Gabriel hisses, gone pale, fast.

"It took him quite a while to die. He was drowning but it was the blood loss and shock that ended him."

"All you did was the hand?" Trace asks, not believing it one bit.

"Fine, I also shot him three times in the groin when he didn't respond to the knife," Gray reluctantly admits. "It was unproductive."

"Oh, I think it was pretty fuckin' productive," Trace says darkly as he soothingly rubs Gabriel's back. Gabriel, seated in his chair, curled forward with his elbows on his knees, covers his mouth with his hands. "You okay, babydoll?"

It takes him a second to respond. When he does, sitting back, staring at Gray, Gabriel says on the exhale, "Yeah. That's... Fuck."

Standing with effort, causing Trace additional worry, no doubt, Gabriel faces Gray. He hesitates, his eyes darting here and there, seeing things which exist now only in his imagination. Then he moves to fold his arms gently around Gray in a hug.

"Thank you," Gabriel says quietly, with heartfelt emotion. Trace stands behind Gabriel, ready to lend a hand should he stumble or fall. When Gabriel ends the hug, looking deeply into Gray's eyes, Gray sees the unspoken commitment in him to repay, somehow, all of what Gray has given.

From the back room, one of the agents gives Gray a signal, then crosses through the front room to wait outside.

"You're welcome," Gray replies.

Gabriel is with the one of the agents, sitting in the backseat of a black, unmarked car, ready to be driven home. Gray insisted on the escort, rather than let Trace drive Gabriel home himself. It was probably a good call. Unable to pretend he's more together than he is, Trace steps aside for just a moment to get some air and calm down before getting in that car and leaving the scene of the crime which almost robbed him of Gabriel for good.

Something truly terrible could have happened here, at the little photography studio Gabriel worked so hard to establish. That business is such a point of pride for Gabriel, as well as Trace, who has only ever wanted the best for his boy. There is so much relief that they were able to get to Daring Angel before Bernard Schultz was able to do irrevocable harm. For over a decade, Trace has had to imagine the attacks perpetrated by Harry upon Gabriel, which Trace would never be able to go back and prevent. But now, at last, Trace was able to stop Gabriel from getting hurt, even if that meant bringing in the big guns with Gray and his friends in the CIA.

It eases a stress and feeling of failure he's had to carry since he first met Gabriel, since Trace felt he could never provide for Gabriel what was needed—a hero to destroy the monsters he lives with constantly.

Now, the monsters are all gone. He can breathe. They all can.

It used to be so much easier. Patrick was without a family for most of his life. It was him against the world. All he needed to do was watch his own back. Sure, he was dying to have people he loved in his life. Having a family was what he wanted most, but he didn't find them for many years.

Now, he's got them. They came from different places, different backgrounds, but now they count on each other when things get tough. And they count on Trace.

It could have gone so wrong. Gabriel could have been tortured for god knows how long before Bernard killed him, or left him to die from his wounds. And Trace would have been home with Micah, none the wiser, while his boy slowly, agonizingly, died at the hands of a madman. Thank god for Gray. Thank god for Patrick and his old, secret life which has enabled Trace to rescue his boy in the way he always dreamed of doing.

Leaning against a building that's dark inside, the place closed up tight, he watches the unremarkable man in a plain suit who is waiting with Gabriel. And he feels Trace slipping through his fingers. Beneath, Patrick is raw and bleeding, scared of Gabriel's close call, of those men in their plain suits, cleaning up the blood and the body, of the past, of the future, of everything. Trace might be strong, but Patrick knows there are things out there in the world worth being scared of. He can't pretend he doesn't. Trace has been Patrick's tool for a long time, a way to convince the world he's healed and ready for anything. Maybe it convinced his kids and his clients, but he doesn't convince himself, or Gray. And that hurts.

When Gray approaches, Patrick tells him, angrily, his voice hitching, "Leave it. You're the big hero, once again. And my boy... My *boy*...."

Gray comes even closer, though, and Patrick can't begin to hide how much it eats him up inside. He used to be filled with pain, which he'd cover over with sex, disobedience, and carelessness. Gray could always see it in him, clearly. Patrick has since filled his life with good people who he's given his whole heart to, but no matter how much he promised to watch out for them, no matter how much trust they gave, it wasn't enough in the end. Danger is still out there.

Jerry got to Kyle and Darrek through Diadem. And Gabriel....

"If I hadn't chased that fucker, Harry, and carved him up, he wouldn't have met Bernard. Bernard wouldn't have known Gabriel. This is my fault. *All of it*," Patrick rasps.

"Look at me, slave," Gray says sternly.

"Not your fuckin' slave—"

"Don't make me repeat myself," Gray says more sharply.

Patrick raises his eyes to Gray's, wishing secretly for Nicholai, and how free he'd felt under his care. Gray is a good alternative, though, because Gray knows. He knows *all of it*.

"Your boy needs you to get it together. He's been through a lot. See him home, and into bed. Put his needs before your own."

"Yessir."

"Recognize your limitations. Confess them to Micah. Allow him to help you the way I know he can. Your pride will be your downfall, otherwise. You need to learn to ask for *help*, Patrick. No more acting out. Trust your family to love you despite your shortcomings. Can you do that?"

He breathes out a laugh, dries his eyes on the back of his arm.

He thinks of how much he does love them, all of them, even Gray, even Jack and Jan, for their humanity and capability to make mistakes. He would never deny them or love them less, just because they fucked up. He needs to give them the same honor. Gray is right.

"Fuckin' hate when you're right, Master Gray," he says. "But I didn't work so damned hard all these years to build all this just so a few evil sons of bitches could tear it all down. My kids are worth the fight."

"They are," Gray agrees. "Make the hard call. It's time."

"Won't it just endanger them more, to know?"

"Not if you keep them close, which I know you will. Take the mask off, Patrick. Let them love you the way I do."

Expelling a heavy breath, he nods, feeling his eyes spill over once more. Gray leans in and gives him a kiss, which makes the hurt and fear fade back a little bit.

"Thanks, bright eyes."

Chapter 40
Talisman

Darrek sits stiffly with Ben in the living room of his and Gabriel's home, the air around them tinged with their worry and fret. The front door has been boarded up for the time being. Kyle is asleep on the armchair, knocked out from too much stress and manual labor. But sleep is a long way off for Darrek.

Gabriel never called back. He left to check the office, then didn't check in or come home for a long time. When Darrek tried calling Gabriel's cell phone, he was brushed off with a promise to talk again soon, but since then there's been nothing. The next time Darrek tried to call, it went right to voicemail. A minute later, he received a text saying that Gabriel was on his way home.

Now, it's a waiting game. Ben looks as concerned as Darrek feels. Ben keeps going to the front window to look for approaching headlights. Darrek keeps checking his watch.

Did Gabriel find something disturbing in the mail? Was there a normal work complication which needed immediate attention? Every possibility Darrek comes up with doesn't fit with the way Gabriel sounded on the phone, or the circumstances.

"Fuck," Ben sighs quietly, pulling back the curtain's edge and peering out into the darkness beyond the house's comforting glow.

"What?" Darrek asks, keeping his voice down so as to not wake Kyle. "What's wrong?"

He stands and sees the cause for Ben's alarm.

A black car which Darrek doesn't recognize has just pulled up to the house. They stare, dumbstruck, as the driver — a man in a suit, wearing a stern expression and a gun holster — gets out, opening the vehicle's back door a moment later. Trace and Gabriel climb out. Gabriel is moving gingerly and Trace is propping him up, though Gabriel tries to wave him off.

"What the hell?" Ben growls. After one look at the impassable front door, Ben jogs to the side door, opening it instead and hitting the button to lift the garage door.

On the chair, Kyle stirs. "What's going on?" he asks, rubbing his eyes.

"No clue," Darrek mutters, his heartbeat quickening, waiting as patiently as he can while Ben clears the way for Gabriel and Trace to make their way inside. The unknown driver gets back in the car, which idles there. "Some guy with a gun drove Gabe home."

"What?!" Kyle wakes up the rest of the way, fast.

At first, alarm freezes Darrek to the spot as Gabriel is helped inside, complaining, "I can walk! I'm fine. Would you just let me—"

"Shut it and let us help you, damn it," Trace snaps.

With no idea what's happening, what to do, what to think, Darrek's fear for Gabriel swallows everything else—every care about the fire, Jerry, Kyle, and anything else on his radar.

"Gabe?" Darrek asks softly, unable to disguise how massively afraid he is.

"Dare," Gabriel sighs with relief, smiling.

Darrek goes to him instantly, gathering him up in a hug.

"Easy with him!" Trace warns.

"I'm not gonna break," Gabriel counters. Strengthening his grip on Darrek, he groans, "God, it's good to see you."

"What happened to you?" Darrek asks, trying to look for changes, for a sign of something wrong. Gabriel does look shaken and pale, but otherwise okay.

"Gabe, get your ass on the couch," Trace orders. "Benny, get him something to eat and some water, would ya?"

After Ben has given Gabriel an apple, a sandwich, and water, and they have all gathered again in the living room, Trace explains what happened. He briefly tells them about Bernard Schultz, the attack, the CIA, the phone calls, and lastly, of Gray. Gabriel keeps his eyes trained on the ground by his feet, his gaze blank like he's reliving it all. Darrek stays focused on Gabriel while he listens, horrified.

"You stayed to watch," Darrek says. "Christ."

"I needed it," Gabriel counters. "I had to be there to see it."

"I know," Darrek sighs, holding Gabriel's hand. Silence has fallen on the room. Trace is as upset as ever on Gabriel's behalf. Ben, Kyle, and Darrek are too stunned to speak at first.

"So, are you okay?" Darrek asks urgently, feeling frantic with the impossible need to protect Gabriel from something that's already happened. "God, I shouldn't have let you go by yourself! I'm so stupid!"

"Hey," Gabriel says sharply, looking Darrek right in the eye. "Do you trust me?"

"Of course. With my life," Darrek frowns, answering with total honesty and devotion, utterly unable to let go of Gabriel's hand.

"Then trust me when I say that I'm fine. Okay? It's done. That bastard is dead as fuck. I saw it happen. And I don't want to ever hear you say that about yourself again, you hear me?"

"Yes, sir," Darrek murmurs, hanging his head, letting Gabriel gather him close with an arm when it becomes too much for him. Gabriel kisses Darrek's cheek and smoothes his hair while he struggles to master his emotions.

"This wasn't your fight. It was mine. I'm grateful you weren't there."

Darrek pulls back, wiping his eyes dry, wishing he could stay by Gabriel's side for the rest of their lives, just so he would never have to worry about him again.

"You need your rest," Trace says adamantly. "You sure you want to sleep here? I'd feel better if you were with us and we could watch over you all. After all of this shit today, you need it. Every one of you."

"I want to sleep in my own bed," Gabriel argues. Darrek hears the iron in his voice. There's no way Gabriel is backing down. "I'm staying."

Ben and Kyle exchange a wordless look with each other. Then Ben says, "We'll stick around for the night if that's okay with you two. Sleep down here. Trace is right, you shouldn't be alone. You're both in shock."

"Thanks Benny," Trace replies, relaxing a little.

"Yeah, that's fine," Gabriel answers.

"You call me if you need anything," Trace tells Gabriel sharply. "You hear?"

"Yes, sir," Gabriel answers dutifully. Trace goes to him, kissing the top of Gabriel's head. Darrek hears him whisper to Trace, "Thank you."

Trace looks hard at him. "Just glad you're all right," he says softly, sounding pained and wholly unlike himself. He doesn't look certain and confident, like he usually does. He just looks like someone he loves, very much, has had a near miss with something awful, and it's made him feel vulnerable to the whims of fate. It's understandable, yet eerie to see in someone like Trace.

"Me too," Gabriel murmurs.

"Take care of each other," Trace says, more tenderly than Darrek has ever heard him before. "Get some rest."

Gabriel nods, says, "Go on. I'll call you in the morning."

―⚭―

Kyle wakes early, long before Darrek and Gabriel. When he begins work on the new doorframe, to replace the one he busted, Ben keeps him company in the garage. He tries to make as little noise as possible. Darrek and Gabriel hadn't asked him to make a new doorframe, but Kyle feels he needs to do it for his own peace of mind. Plus, it feels good to keep his hands busy while his mind whirs.

His phone keeps buzzing. The sound it's making is the alert for incoming messages, not calls. Ben squints warily at Kyle whenever it happens, wondering probably who could be sending so many of them so early in the morning.

"You gonna check those?" Ben asks when Kyle makes no move toward his phone.

"Nope. Busy," is all Kyle says to him. The truth is Kyle doesn't trust his reaction, should he go to look at what the messages contain. He's got a pretty good idea anyway, of what they are.

Doing his best to disguise his nervousness, Kyle feels quite certain he's going to have some confessing to do today, once he figures out how. His hands tremble, but he keeps his back to Ben so he doesn't see and hopes the warmth of the garage keeps his face flushed when everything in him sinks with cold dread.

He uses a hand saw rather than the loud circular saw so as to not wake Darrek and Gabriel, who are asleep nearby. Soon, though, they hear water running in the pipes, the first sign they've awoken.

"You okay down here if I go up to check on them?" Ben asks, looking quite eager for visual proof of Gabriel's good health.

"Yep. Go ahead," Kyle answers, impatient to finally get a look at his messages while unobserved.

Ben knocks gently on the closed bedroom door, hearing low voices beyond it.

"Yeah. Come in," Gabriel calls from inside.

Inching the door open, Ben sees them in bed—Gabriel and Darrek. Darrek is half-asleep and bare-chested, covered in a sheet and blanket, his arm slung possessively around Gabriel's equally bare chest as he spoons up behind him.

"How you two doing?" Ben asks.

"Good," Gabriel answers with a drowsy grin. "Forgot how nice it is to sleep in my own bed."

"Bad dreams?"

"Nope."

"How about you, Dare?" Ben inquires.

"Not too bad. Didn't sleep as much as Gabe. Too much on my mind, I guess."

Darrek seems somewhat embarrassed to be still in bed with Gabriel in a questionable state of undress, maybe still also wondering what particular part Ben played in his evening at the party while bound and unaware. But the look Ben gets from Gabriel is cozy and inviting enough.

"How's Kyle?" Gabriel asks, maybe so that Darrek doesn't have to.

"Good. He's fixing the door," Ben says with a little roll of his eyes that says it couldn't be helped. "Maybe a little skittish, but that's nothing new. He slept well enough, far as I could tell."

"I'm glad."

Ben sees Darrek sigh, dragging his fingers lazily through Gabriel's short hair and watching the strands move. Slowly, Ben approaches the bed. When he gets to it, he sits on the edge.

"I need to see," Ben tells Gabriel under his breath, the words barely loud enough to be heard. "Not that I don't trust you...."

With his own sigh, but a subtle grin, mainly in his eyes, Gabriel holds out his wrists. Taking them each in hand, Ben turns them over, examining the scrapes and shallow cuts from the handcuffs. Darrek continues to comb his fingers through Gabriel's hair, making his skin break out in goosebumps under Ben's fingers. Gabriel then rolls onto his back and Darrek presses a kiss to his temple while Gabriel draws back the edge of the sheet.

It's not as bad as Ben feared. The release of worry leaves him a little lighter. Reaching out a hand, he oh-so-gently caresses the inside of Gabriel's bare right thigh. With a feather-light touch, Ben shifts Gabriel's cock, the skin reddened in patches. The backs of his fingers drag against the inside of Gabriel's leg again, before he withdraws his hand.

"If he'd scarred you—" Ben starts, angry.

"But he didn't," Gabriel finishes.

Darrek's opened hand flattens over Gabriel's heart, his fingers brushing back and forth there. Ben catches his eye, and it feels like many layers of emotion are communicated between them. Fear, gratitude, shared devotion, surrender, revelation, lust, and realization are all there, in varying amounts.

"Okay," Ben says in surrender. "Need anything while I'm up here?"

"Nah, we're good," Gabriel smiles. "We'll be down soon."

"All right." Ben stands, going to the door. "Better go back to keeping an eye on Kyle. God knows what he's up to now."

―◻―◻―◻―

When Ben has gone, Gabriel rolls over to face Darrek. Darrek's fingers comb back through the hair at Gabriel's temple, his warm brown eyes filled with so much heart-stopping affection, all Gabriel wants is to lose himself there. For the rest of his life, all he wants, all he needs is to be by Darrek's side, loving him and being loved so devotedly in return.

Leaning in, Gabriel places a soft, gentle kiss to the swell of Darrek's lower lip. Opening reverently, frowning with need, Darrek moans when Gabriel's tongue enters his mouth. He undulates against Gabriel's body, getting off on the kiss, the closeness and security of being together. Despite everything, they are together, and they're going to be okay. They belong to one another and nothing will ever change that. No matter what life tries to throw at them, they will survive it and thrive, because they are loved and cherished.

It's everything Gabriel has ever wanted.

Smiling with all of the love he has for Darrek, his partner through it all, Gabriel caresses down his lover's body. Each touch, every brush of his fingertips over Darrek's velvety soft, sleep-warmed skin sends tingles of pleasure and happiness spiraling outward throughout Gabriel's body.

"Love you," he whispers against Darrek's lips.

Exhaling with a sigh that slips into a moan, Darrek echoes the words, saying his own, "Love *you*."

Caressing lower, the firm heat of Darrek's erection brushes against the backs of Gabriel's fingers. Darrek's frown deepens and he pulls away from the touch of Gabriel's lips, turning his face towards the pillow under his head instead.

The apology radiates from him, more stark than any words.

Gabriel takes firm hold of Darrek's cock, further proof of his love and desire, repeating the words, "Love you, Dare. Let me love you. Love you forever...."

He shifts downward, kissing Darrek's collarbone, his sternum, his newly pierced left nipple. Darrek rolls onto his back, still frowning against the onslaught of Gabriel's gentle trail of kisses, the tidal wave of his affection.

Scraping his teeth over Darrek's side, the muscles etched deeply, Gabriel sighs, "Mine," and sucks at the spot before moving even lower.

"Gabriel," Darrek groans, even harder now. He pushes up against Gabriel's grip on his cock.

Gabriel finds Darrek's hip, biting gently at that, too. Rasping the word, "Mine."

Humming, Darrek is trying futilely to fight back his lust, to control himself and try not to want what Gabriel is lavishing upon him. But Gabriel knows if he persists, Darrek will succumb.

"You don't have to," Darrek whispers, still so scared for Gabriel, but not scared for himself anymore, Gabriel sees. That fear has been dispelled.

Smiling as he recognizes that, Gabriel says, "Of course I do."

He settles between Darrek's thighs and takes a long lick up the underside of his reddened, swollen cock, sealing his lips around the head in a kiss before pulling off, catching Darrek's gaze and growling, "Mine."

Licking the taste of Darrek from his lips, rubbing firmly up his shaft, maintaining eye contact, Gabriel shivers with want as Darrek moans, "Yours. Fucking yours."

"Love you, Dare," Gabriel smiles.

But all Darrek can do is moan. He rocks up, taking Gabriel's mouth when it falls upon him, devouring him and his ability to speak entirely.

Clasping the back of Gabriel's head as it moves upon him, Darrek gives himself over completely, as he's always done, trusting so much, giving everything. And Gabriel falls, taking everything, consuming his lover's gifts and devoting himself anew.

Kyle holds his phone like a talisman. It's time, now that he has finally heard from Nicky. The photos are saved on Kyle's phone. Kyle needs to act, to confess what he's done, and it's going to be hard. It's going to suck and be messy, and he'll probably get in deep trouble for it with more than one important person in his life. He still has to do it though.

But it feels different than when he was coming to terms with the abuse, when self-harm was the only way out of the cramped cell he was mentally locked away in. Then, he still felt strong and determined to follow what seemed the only path available to him. The more minutes that pass, ticking like a timed bomb on a short fuse, the more he's transported back through all of the years and years. Kyle stops feeling like an adult with a life of his own, with a partner and a good future ahead of him, and returns to the old crippling uncertainty of his teenage years. He feels exactly like he did on those afternoons when he knew he shouldn't go over to Darrek's house to see him, Kyle's best friend in the world, because a monster lived there, too. Love for Darrek drove Kyle on in those moments, knowing no one else was aware of what they'd suffered through, and therefore wouldn't even know to watch out for Darrek, to look for signs that something bad had happened or was on its way again.

Was it the right decision to ask Nicky to do what he did? Kyle asks himself and doesn't have an answer. The fact of the matter is that now people know. Darrek's family, certainly, know about what Kyle set in motion at Jerry's funeral. Things like that don't stay contained or quiet. They blow up. The danger of getting pierced with emotional shrapnel is real. It's not an option to keep what he knows to himself any longer.

When Ben appears in the doorway between the house and the garage, the air itself becomes thicker. Kyle floats there, unable to move, stewing in his self-created chaos. Frowning slightly, Ben scrutinizes Kyle's expression for clues and asks, "What's up?"

The words Kyle knows he has to say and the confession burning to be voiced stick in his throat. The reality of what he's done and still intends to do make him weak, and afraid in the old ways. The bad ways.

There's no clever way to get out of this, no way around. He has to push through. But when Ben steps closer, taking hold of Kyle's hand, Kyle is faced with his moment.

"Come in the house and sit down. You're pale," Ben says, tugging him toward the door, the house, and the people in it. The body Kyle has betrayed, punished, and tormented decides for him, refusing to move an inch until he speaks up. His feet feel nailed to the earth below him.

"What's wrong? Kyle?" Ben asks suddenly.

The caring makes it worse. Guilt, sadness, weariness of all of it hit him at once. Trembling, growing even paler, he sniffs and hangs his head.

"I'm sorry," Kyle moans softly, a whisper of sound.

The collective fear these two little words instill is like its own monster, rising up before him, as Ben cups Kyle's face in both hands, caressing his cheeks with his thumbs as he says, "Hey, look at me. Kyle? We've been through this. You have nothing to apologize for!"

Kyle can't stop the tremors racking his body and he wants to throw the damned phone, smashing it to pieces before it can do more harm. But Ben just tries to comfort him, smoothing his hair, pressing his lips to Kyle's cheek, whispering, "It's okay. It's okay." And Kyle has never loved him more.

It seems such a simple thing, the speaking of a truth, the act of releasing a handful of words into the air. It's not, though. Not really. Kyle understands, then, how Trace must have felt in those moments before telling them everything he did about his past, Jerry, and Harry. The courage it must have taken leaves Kyle in awe of the man.

Feeling tangled up in how much he doesn't want to say what he needs to say, Kyle tries to get it out. God, how Kyle wishes he could just say he doesn't feel well and drive away, letting them all make their own assumptions and leave it at that. He knows, though, that his feet won't move one step in any direction until he does this. The time for silence and secrecy is done.

Sounding very young and very afraid, even to his own ears, Kyle says, "I have something to show Darrek."

The truth is a push. Ben pulls back to look at Kyle with confusion.

Staring, Ben says in a hushed voice, "You're scaring me."

And all Kyle can say in reply is, "I'm sorry."

Chapter 41
See It to Believe It

Kyle does the only thing he can to explain. He hands Ben the phone.

A single image glows on the tiny screen and Ben holds the phone like it's on fire, afraid to touch it, or maybe wanting to drop it or throw it away just like Kyle wanted to. Silent tears stream from Kyle's eyes, his hands folded in front of his mouth. Ben turns off the phone. The hand holding it drops to his side.

Then he gathers Kyle up, pulling him into a hug with a sighed, "C'mere."

"I had to," Kyle hisses desperately, needing Ben to understand.

"I know. It's okay," Ben promises, taking a deep breath and letting it out.

"I have to show him. He needs to *see it*," Kyle growls, disgusted and angry all over again.

Ben lets him go and steps back, gazing with a carefully masked expression at the house beyond the doorway.

"Yeah, he does," Ben agrees. "Let's do this. Then we're going home."

"Okay," Kyle sighs, even managing a small smile. "Thanks."

He sees a flash of it then, in Ben's expression. How Ben would tear the whole world apart with his bare hands and teeth if it helped spare Kyle more pain. He would do anything to erase the terrors and abuse he has suffered, and would gladly put himself in harm's way without a second thought if it did anything to protect Kyle, who Ben loves with his whole heart. And Kyle knows, through and through, with every fiber of his being, how very lucky he is.

"I love you," Kyle says, like it's yet another truth he's embracing in order to set himself free of old ties.

"I love you too," Ben replies.

With Ben's devotion strengthening him, Kyle walks to the door hoping maybe it won't be so bad after all.

―◻︎―◻︎―◻︎―

The four of them—Ben, Kyle, Gabriel, and Darrek—stand in the living room, feet from the door Kyle broke down the day before in his haste to destroy something certain to cause Darrek pain. And, funnily enough, Kyle is now preparing to show Darrek something which could cause him just as much pain.

"I need some space," Kyle says to Gabriel. "I need to just tell Darrek. Please, Sir."

Maybe the 'Sir' is inappropriate but Kyle and Gabriel both know he's unable to not use the honorific, especially in circumstances involving stress and heightened emotion. Eyes locked on each other, Kyle sees the effect the title has on Gabriel, ringing back through the months to that moment in the park, late at night, when Gabriel told Kyle to say it if it made him feel better. There's a small, but noticeable flicker of gladness behind Gabriel's eyes upon hearing it, the proof that the bond is still there, despite it all. The respect, and yes, even the trust never really goes away. Kyle does trust Gabriel, as he trusts Darrek. Kyle will always trust Darrek, inherently, as he will always love him.

"It's okay," Ben assures Gabriel, taking him by the arm. "We'll sit in the kitchen. We can see them from there."

"You know what this is about, don't you?" Gabriel accuses.

"Just give them a chance to talk. This is important. You trust me, don't 'cha, Gabey?"

Ben's not actually smirking, but Kyle sees the mischievous grin in his eyes all the same, as Gabriel does too, surrendering with slumped shoulders and a heavy sigh.

"Fuck you, Knox," Gabriel murmurs, turning to the kitchen.

"Oh no, fuck *you*," Ben replies, gesturing widely to the kitchen table to usher Gabriel along. He throws Kyle and Darrek a wink before turning to follow, grabbing at Gabriel's ass. "Over the table…

up against the fridge..."

"Knock it off," Gabriel argues halfheartedly, looking torn between worrying about what's about to happen in the next room and his own instinctive reactions to Ben's insatiable lust. Kyle knows the feeling. It's hard to say no to Ben when he wants you that much.

Ben asks, "You don't have any scotch or rum in the cabinets, do you? You've got that 'fuck me, Daddy' look in your eyes. Maybe if I get you liquored up—"

"Stop," Gabriel says tiredly, sliding into a chair at the table. "God, you're an asshole."

Ben takes a seat across from Gabriel, his feet planted widely, sitting back comfortably, and pats his thighs. "Come sit on my lap."

Gabriel actually starts to move like he's going to get up and do as asked, then catches himself and frowns at Ben. Kyle snorts with laughter and Ben throws him a smile before turning back to Gabriel and becoming instantly serious once again.

"Hey! I gave you an order. Get your ass over here."

"I can't hear you," Gabriel says, clapping his hands over his ears and resting his elbows on the table.

"That's cute. It's really that fucking hard for you to resist me," Ben says with awe. Gabriel pretends not to hear him. There's a long, silent pause, then Ben says sharply, "Look at me, you little cunt."

Gabriel's eyes snap up immediately, flashing dangerously.

"Gotcha," Ben smiles. "Where's your rum?"

"We don't have any," Gabriel grumbles, keeping a wary eye on Darrek and Kyle, who are both watching the show in the kitchen rather than talking like they're supposed to be doing.

"And how sorry are *you*?" Ben laughs.

"Really fucking sorry, actually," Gabriel retorts. To Kyle he says, "Would you get on with it, please? I have this one to deal with until you're finished."

"Good luck with that," Kyle says.

"God, they're amazing," Darrek mutters, shaking his head.

"Aren't they though?" Kyle grins.

Darrek gestures to the couch. Kyle sighs and relents, going to take a seat.

The first thing he does once they're both sitting side by side in the living room is take the phone out and set it on the coffee table in front of them. It's off, though. Before he can show Darrek the pictures stored on it, he has to start at the beginning and explain.

"Okay," Kyle breathes, rubbing his hands on the tops of his pants. "So, do you remember Nicky? Senior year, prom night?"

There's a pause, and it's so quiet, Kyle knows it's because Ben and Gabriel have stopped their sexual banter in order to eavesdrop. Then Darrek says, "Yeah, that guy you were boning in the pool."

Kyle laughs, impressed, and looks over and up at Darrek's face. "Wow, so you figured it out, huh? I thought you believed Nicky was a chick who snuck away before you showed up."

"Oh, come on. What did you say his name was? Sunscreen?"

"Tanner," Kyle grins.

"I didn't know you were screwing him then," Darrek allows.

"Not really. I mean, I knew but I didn't know, if that makes any sense. I've never really forgotten about that night, how sick it made me feel seeing you with that guy, all cozy and friendly. All I could think was, he should be with me, not this other kid. It was a pretty big clue which I did my best to ignore."

"You acted like you wanted to bite his head off."

"Yeah," Darrek groans, rubbing a hand over his face. "What in the hell does this have to do with him, anyway?"

Kyle takes a deep breath for courage. "I still keep in touch with Nicky. He still lives there, you know. He's a townie. Once in a while I send him an email asking how things are back home. Not that I think of it as home anymore, but anyway… I asked Nicky to do me a favor. A big favor. I may have kind of… bribed him."

"Jesus, Kyle," Darrek groans. "Money?"

"Money and videos. *My* videos from Diadem. Some, not all." He glances over at Darrek again and bursts out laughing, incredulous. "Holy shit, you have that look on your face again—that pissed-off expression you had on prom night when you walked in on me and Nicky! They're *public videos*, Dare. They've been for sale for years. You know this. God, you really don't like him, do you?"

Nostril's flaring, bristling visibly with anger, Darrek inhales through his nose and blows the air out his mouth. He's radiating the same possessive fury he did that night in high school, catching Kyle with another guy for the first time, even if he didn't know for sure what had really been going on. Kyle said they were friends, and the girls, their dates who never existed, had taken off just before Darrek arrived.

"The hell is wrong?" Gabriel shouts from the kitchen, sensing Darrek's unease.

"Nothing!" Darrek calls back.

"Dare just hates the shit out of my old love interest, that's all," Kyle says loudly.

"Does Ben know?" Darrek asks Kyle more quietly.

"Not specifically, yet, but Ben was fully present for the filming of said videos and was the one to orchestrate their sale, so yeah, I'm sure Ben doesn't give a fuck."

"Are you talking about me?" Ben shouts from the next room.

"Kyle gave his sub videos to some prick he used to fuck in high school," Darrek says loudly to Ben. "As a *bribe*."

"Thanks, Dare," Kyle sighs, rolling his eyes.

"Fine by me!" Ben calls.

Kyle gives Darrek a triumphant smile, which falters when Ben adds, "He comes near Kyle though and I'll break his dick off and stuff it down his throat. Then I'll kill 'im."

Wearing Kyle's previously triumphant smile, Darrek seems to calm down. "Thanks Ben!" he says.

"No problem."

"Moving on!" Gabriel yells, aggravated.

"Yeah, moving on," Kyle agrees.

"Why were you bribing Mr. Sunscreen?"

Rolling his eyes again, biting back his retort and choosing to bypass the bitchy comment, Kyle waits. Then he says, "Nicky's bribe was the videos. The money was actually for him to use to bribe someone else."

"Wow, this just keeps getting better," Darrek groans sarcastically.

Kyle doesn't know how to say the next part. He knows it's going to sound awful, because it *is* awful. He draws his feet up onto the couch, folding them under him, curling forward and rubbing the back of his head. As he shrinks in on himself and stays quiet, he feels Darrek reacting to his posture and mood.

"Just tell me, okay?" Darrek beseeches softly. "Don't do this. I'm not gonna hurt you or bite your head off. I'm sorry for getting angry about Nicky."

"It's gonna sound really bad," Kyle confesses, curling up even more, unable to look at Darrek or the phone. "What if you hate me for this?"

"Hey, I wrote down my solemn promise years ago not to hate you, remember?"

"This is different."

"No, it's not. Whatever it is, I will *never* hate you, Kyle. I'm incapable of hating you."

Kyle hears the words, but they don't really penetrate. When he begins restlessly, viciously scratching at his left arm, Darrek grabs Kyle's hand to still it and says, "Stop. Stop hurting yourself and just talk to me. You can tell me anything. *Anything*. I owe you my life, my… my fucking *sanity*. Let me help. Just talk to me."

"I had him break into the morgue." He says it fast, to get it out, then starts trembling, knees drawn up to his chest, hands wrapping his head. Waiting for it, the backlash and the pain, not knowing how to explain his actions or his logic now that the time has come, Kyle is startled when instead he feels familiar arms embracing him, unwinding his clawed hands, rubbing the sides of his arms to comfort him.

"I'm right here, okay? Not going anywhere. Just breathe. You're okay," Ben tells him, whispering by Kyle's ear.

Out of the corner of his eye, he sees Gabriel picking up the phone, sitting with it beside Darrek and turning it on.

Then there's a soft gasp. "Oh my god."

The image is a photo of the corpse, post-autopsy. Jerry's pale chest has been sewn back together, his eyes and lips sewn shut as well. There's no visible sign of the broken neck or the stroke he'd suffered, but by those stitches and the pallor of his skin, there is no mistaking it's him and that he's quite dead.

"There's more. Go to the next photo," Kyle murmurs.

Ben gently takes hold of Kyle's hand.

Gabriel and Darrek are silent.

"I had to, Dare," Kyle says, pleading for understanding. "They had to *know*. Your *mom* had to know. He didn't deserve an honorable death, or their grief."

The photo is a close-up shot of the words Nicky wrote across Jerry's pale forehead and chest after the first photo was taken: PEDOPHILE. BURN IN HELL.

"He used a permanent marker and they must not have been able to clean it all off, because his service was supposed to be open casket. After that they changed it to closed casket. Nicky promised to spray paint it across the tombstone, too, but I don't have photos of that. Not yet at least. I swore I'd erase these images after showing you. Nicky erased them, too. His cousin works at the morgue, so that's how he got access. The guy lied and faked signs of a break-in to take the heat off of himself. After I told him about Jerry, Nicky was more than happy to do this. Said he didn't care if he got caught or not, and neither do I."

Gabriel continues to swipe his finger across the phone's screen to switch from picture to picture. There are shots of the wake and the funeral, too.

"Nicky said there weren't many people there," Kyle says. "Just a handful, really. Your mom was upset, but who knows if it was for Jerry or because of what we did to his body, or whatever. Your brother, Steven, and Sara were there, but Nicky said they didn't cry or anything. Your brother kept checking his watch like he was eager to go.

"I had to see it, Dare. Maybe it's just me, but I had to see that he was really gone to believe it. I thought maybe it would help you find peace, too. I'm sorry. I know you didn't ask for this. You didn't ask for any of it."

"Neither did you," Dare replies, his voice sounding strained and rough. He's still staring at the phone, but after a moment sits back and lets out a heavy exhale, sagging slightly. "I uh."

"Are you okay?" Kyle asks him.

Arms crossed, hand masking his mouth, Darrek looks to be processing it all. His eyes are glassy but then he laughs, blinking as a few teardrops spill over and slip down. Gabriel turns to Darrek, taking his hand. Darrek takes another deep breath and lets it out with a groan, letting his head fall back for a moment.

"Hey," Gabriel says softly, trying to draw speech from him.

"God, it *helps*," Darrek laughs, heartbrokenly, and squinting a little as he tries to make sense of it all. "He's really… God, he's really gone, isn't he?"

Darrek sits forward, takes the phone from Gabriel, "Let me see it again."

"Baby, maybe you should—"

"Just let me," Darrek murmurs, flipping through images until he finds one of his mother, from afar. He makes a motion on the screen with his fingertips to zoom in on it and looks at it more closely. "She knows," he declares. He blinks and hands the phone back to Gabriel. Sitting up a little straighter, he looks sideways at Kyle. "You can see it in her face. She *knows*."

"He can't hurt you anymore," Kyle tells him quietly. "And neither can she. It's *done*, Dare. It's *over*."

When Darrek continues to stare at nothing, dumbstruck, Kyle asks, "Does it really help?"

A smile is there, then gone, overtaken by the ache. Darrek clears his throat and looks around his home, his gaze settling on the table that used to hold their telephone. With beautiful, glorious relief, Darrek laughs and nods.

Smiling all the way down to his toes, Kyle reaches out and takes Darrek's hand.

"Thank you," Darrek tells him in a thick voice.

"No more secrets. Don't be scared anymore, okay? There's nothing left to be scared of."

Gabriel stands and takes a step or two closer to Kyle, beckoning with a nod of his head, holding out a hand, he says, "C'mere."

Kyle gets to his feet and moves into Gabriel's arms, letting himself be hugged. "Thanks for that," Gabriel murmurs to him.

"Closure," Kyle replies, looking at Gabriel in such a way as to convey to him he would give him the same gift if he could.

"Closure," Gabriel agrees.

That night, Darrek and Gabriel sleep once more in their own house, in their own bed, with Sierra curled up by their feet, and there are no bad dreams or sleepless hours spent listening for a call that will never come or a knock at the door to fill them with dread. They both know whatever comes next will be better, and they can handle it because, for Darrek at least, the door leading to everything which has haunted him has been shut. There are no more footsteps in the dark, no more danger creeping up to his bed. There is just silence and the gentle snores of Gabriel beside him. And that is good.

Chapter 42
Slow Surrender

The phone keeps ringing. The shrill chime is a razorblade's edge dragging across Trace's already-frayed nerves, so he takes a page from Darrek's book and doesn't answer. He simply sits there, staring at the phone. The pre-paid, disposable cell sits upon Micah's desk in his home office, tidied and repaired since the incident with Moira's videos. The cracks are still there, though, but Trace kind of likes the cracks. Because shit is fucked up and to have it all glossed over would be a cruel lie.

Some of the crown molding on the far wall is smashed in. The baseboard is chewed and dented under the new coat of paint. There's a hole punched through the drywall at the edge of the built-in bookcase but a carefully hung print of one of Micah's favorite surrealist works by an artist named Ramaz Razmadze covers the gash.

The phone is still screaming. Trace wants to take a sledgehammer to it and dump the pieces through the hole in the wall to be lost for decades or centuries until that fine house crumbles and looters sifts through the remains.

"Not going to answer that?"

"What d'you think, smartass?" Trace answers, sucking hard on the end of his cigar, an Ashton that's as smooth as he could ask for. "I kept answering for a while, but not anymore. It's all bad news," he exhales, blowing smoke. "Bad fuckin' news, every time."

"How bad?" Gray asks, leaning against the edge of the desk Trace is seated at, folding his arms and gazing curiously down his nose.

Trace rolls his head on his shoulders, hearing a crack. He shifts his booted feet wider and slides lower on the carved wooden seat, gripping the armrests. It's perfect timing for Gray to show up now, and seek Trace out. It just adds to Trace's unease because even through the fog of worry clouding his ability to see things as clearly as he usually would, he can tell Gray has something to say. And that's not good at all either.

"Louis Rousseau, Barbara Day, and Alex Dustan have disappeared. As in *vanished* off the face of the damn planet. As in *disposed of*. They just happen to all be informants on The Company, working with FBI and all of the rest of those assholes with the feds and now they're just… poof. Gone. Guess you could say it was the feds that got them off the grid, except I heard Yasha and his wife are being put in witness protection. But that was just the start of it. This fucking thing," Trace picks up the phone after it stops ringing and pushes a few buttons to silence it. "Just keeps giving me news about more people signing off, dropping out of sight, telling me to do the same, 'cept I'm as far off the fucking grid as I'm gonna get."

"What about Diadem?"

"What about it?" Trace says, knowing the road this conversation leads down is lined with mines and IEDs. "I've kept my personal information off the website. Clients know me as Trace, and nothing else. In videos I keep my face masked or off-camera."

"There's always a record, a trail to follow."

"How stupid do you think I am? I invite you to try. Please. Please try."

"It's meant a lot to you, Diadem," Gray says coolly, countering Trace's increasing volume with a lowering and softening of his. "But you know your priorities."

"**This is my fucking life**. *This!* This *place*. These *people*." He takes the cigar from his mouth and glares up at Gray, almost wanting him to twist this around, to pull seniority and give Trace the punishment he knows is coming his way, one way or another.

"No one's asking you to abandon them, Tracey."

"My ass they aren't," Trace growls, grinding his teeth, chewing on the anger. He laughs bitterly, popping the cigar back between his teeth. In a subtly softer tone, he adds, "Just say it already, I can't fucking stand it."

Gray clears his throat, staying mum.

"I know you didn't come in here to ask about the goddamned phone."

"There are... concerns."

Trace laughs again, much more hysterically this time. "Fuck me."

"The state of security at Diadem is deplorable and must be corrected before normal operations can continue. The MC is asking to have you brought before them to account for the decisions you have made—"

"Kiss my ass, precious," Trace says. "No. Stop right fucking there."

He stands up, wanting to do this when he's eye level with Gray and not looking up to him like his perfectly submissive, obedient fucktoy.

"I am not hiring some staff of goons to breathe down my neck when I'm with a client, or sit in a dark room jerking off to the CCTV footage and busting a fucking nut at the expense of my boys and my clients. That ain't my style and you know it. No one encroaches on my privacy. Not even you and your damn high and mighty pals in the MC. You look in my eyes and tell me again I'm going to go back with you with my proverbial tail between my legs, spread my cheeks and take the brutal fucking they'd give me for running Diadem my way instead of theirs for so long. I dare you, bright eyes. Try me, please."

Trace gestures widely, holding his ground, biting his lip and raising his eyebrows, waiting for anything but knowing how Gray will likely respond.

All he does is smile. It's so controlled, emotionless and aloof that Trace wants to punch him in the teeth to pretty the smile up a little.

"Wrong time to mention it, I'll give you that. Think it over. Calm down. Then, we'll talk again, before we leave."

Trace inhales deeply, holds the breath and closes his eyes.

It's all hot air. It's all bullshit. Gray plays by another rulebook. Trace can talk a good game, but if Gray says the MC demands Trace's presence, he will appear, for no other reason than to protect his family, his staff, and his boys. They could take Diadem *and* his kids from him. No amount of bitching will change it.

"Goddamn it, man," Trace groans, completely deflating.

Gray smiles slightly to see it but says, "I'm sorry."

"No, you're not," Trace counters, but without enthusiasm. "If I nullify the issue, will that be good enough for them? Or do I gotta update my passport?"

Nodding, Gray does at least have the decency to look sorry for Trace as he answers, "That'd be enough. And it would help you stay safe." Gesturing to the phone, he adds, "Give things time to settle. Keep your head down. It's for the best."

He's trapped. Fighting it will only make the bleeding worse.

When Gray motions for him to come closer, Trace can't even pretend to hesitate. He walks right up to his old love and lets Gray kiss some of the furious ache and fight away. It's angry and passionate, with teeth and the old push and pull, but it soothes the burn when Trace finds himself yielding, letting Gray take over, take charge. Gray's fingers grip him hard by the arm and the hip and Trace prays for bruises to rise.

They break, gasping.

"Wouldn't mind you coming with anyway," Gray murmurs.

"Maybe someday. Not for them. For *you*."

Gray smiles, and Trace laughs, a smooth, rolling sound that fades off and away. It's not over yet. The others need to be told of what's been decided. He owes them explanation for more than just Diadem, too. It's time to trust them and stop holding back, hiding behind excuses.

"Your boys will understand," Gray assures him.

"Jesus, I hope so."

―◻―◻―◻―

The power sander whirs noisily away in the garage. The radio is playing, too, but Gabriel can only really hear the music when Darrek takes the occasional break. Sitting a few feet away from the workbench where Darrek is making progress on beginning his table and chairs order, Gabriel taps away at his phone, reviewing some of his latest photography project briefs, brainstorming ways to give each of his clients what they're looking for and coming up with some rough estimates to provide them. He's not even apprehensive about returning to his workspace. Every time he's in there, from now on, he'll just think to himself, 'See what you get, motherfuckers? See what happens when you fuck with me and mine?' It doesn't make him afraid, it makes him stronger. So, he looks to the future, to his work and his clients, eagerly.

Sierra is curled up at his feet, watching Darrek work and simultaneously guarding Gabriel. Whenever Gabriel thinks about moving or standing, Sierra quickly gives him a big-eyed look convincing him to stay where he is, keeping her company and idly scratching behind her ears.

When a familiar truck pulls up, though, Gabriel groans with sudden dread. No one hears it, lost in the din. After a few seconds, Darrek catches sight of the vehicle at the foot of the driveway in his peripheral vision, lifts his goggles and shuts off the sander.

"What's this about?" he calls back to Gabriel, the loudness of his voice overcompensating for the earmuffs doing their best to protect his hearing. He realizes he's shouting and pulls them off. Gabriel can't help but smile, even as the new arrival instantly sparks concerns.

In dirty old jeans which hang from the tight swell of his ass, a black sleeveless shirt showing off the broad muscles of his back and his impressive biceps flexing, Darrek looks good enough to eat or string up in chains again for a nice, hard, slow fuck. His hair is tied back in a knot at the nape of his neck and Gabriel has the almost unquenchable urge to yank on it, draw his sexy, sweaty slave's head back and expose his neck for biting. The local rock station has become audible once more. Sierra gives the truck an abrupt bark of greeting, redirecting Gabriel's wandering attention to the issue at hand.

"No fucking idea," Gabriel admits. "Wasn't expecting him or anything."

From the truck with the driver's side window rolled down, wearing one of his big, cocky, typical grins that always cause Gabriel to instinctively brace himself for trouble, Ben calls, "Hey, baby.

Get in. Let's go for a ride."

Darrek raises an eyebrow at Gabriel who puts his phone away and gets off his chair, despite Sierra's whine of protest. "Why? No."

It's telling that Ben directed the comment at Gabriel alone and not both him and Darrek. That's not a good sign, especially coupled with that fake-ass smile meant to distract and coerce.

"No?" Ben echoes. "Come on. Let's have some fun."

"No way, Knox. You've got that look on your face."

"What look? That's offensive. You're imagining things. Get in." The too-bright, paper thin smile stays firmly plastered. Ben isn't giving an inch. He looks half ready to wrestle Gabriel into the truck if he has to, which makes Gabriel want to protest that much harder.

Thinking it's probably another good clue as to the seriousness of the situation that Kyle has been left home, Gabriel asks, "Where's the other one? Why's it just you?"

"Listen to you with 'the other one'. That's also offensive."

"Fuck you. No. Go home. I'm done. No more. Enough."

Somehow, the smarmy grin gets wider. "Oh, there's *always* more, Gabey! Haven't you learned anything yet?"

"Just fucking tell me. Just..." he waves the inevitably shitty news over, through the air, inviting it. "Just get it over with."

Darrek has walked over to him. Gabriel notices this with a quick sideways glance as a shadow falls over him. Darrek doesn't seem to have any more idea about what's going on either, though, from the dark, controlled look to his face. Eyes sharpened, jaw clenched, wiping his hands on a rag, he plants himself by Gabriel's side, which is where Gabriel always likes to have him anyway. It helps a little as the butterflies start swarming in his gut.

Ben says, "Trace requires your presence at a meeting of all of Diadem's Doms and Dommes, former and present."

"Oh fuck me," Gabriel groans, hating it so much already.

"Already have, sweetheart. Don't pussy out on me now."

Knowing he does, indeed, sound like a pussy but unable to help it, Gabriel whines in complaint, "*Why* though? Why?"

With a resigned sigh, Darrek turns toward him and gives his shorter, slighter Master a brief, strengthening hug, then pulls back to kiss Gabriel's forehead. Whispering, "You'll be okay. I'll be here if you need me. Love you." Then he turns and goes back to Sierra and his workbench.

"How sweet," Ben remarks fondly.

"Come home soon," Darrek says from the garage.

"Yeah, okay," Gabriel replies in surrender.

Ben doesn't give him any more helpful clues as to what the good fuck is going on during the drive to Micah's place. He does, however attempt to reach across the cab toward Gabriel's lap but Gabriel knocks Ben's hand away every time. He's not in the mood.

They get there and Ben doesn't pull all the way around back. He stops in the middle of the long driveway, toward the front of the property, even though there's room to continue on to where they usually park. When he looks expectantly at Ben, all the answer Gabriel gets is a nod of Ben's head to the door and a curt, "C'mon."

There is no part of Gabriel that wants to get out of the truck, but the ways Ben could theoretically try motivating Gabriel to get out are less pleasant alternatives than doing so willingly.

The two of them walk, side by side, around the house to the back. What Gabriel sees as they get a clearer view of the back yard gives him a better idea of what they're walking into.

There's a pickup truck loaded with boxes parked in the driveway. One of Trace's old, but driveable 'project' cars is parked there, too. That's not what worries Gabriel. What worries him is that Trace has a pistol in his hand, a cigar in his mouth, and with both hands is aiming for some empty beer bottles lined up a distance away on top of a fallen log.

He cracks off a shot and a bottle explodes. Micah is sitting on the back stoop with his head in his hand. Alyssa is beside him, looking at least as concerned about the gunfire as Gabriel feels.

"Oh goddamn it," Gabriel says on the exhale, coming to an abrupt halt. Turning to Ben, he says quietly to him, "This isn't good. I'm leaving."

"Well, it *could* be good," Ben suggests uncertainly. He frowns with steadily increasing doubt as Trace fires the gun again. "Maybe. Ah, who'm I kidding, at least he's not shooting people."

"Does he shoot people?" Gabriel asks in a whisper.

Ben shrugs, then claps him on the back. "Not today! That's all that matters. Come on. Buck up. You've got nothing to worry about, you're his favorite."

"I'd prefer not to be sober for this," he tells Ben as Ben takes Gabriel's hand and drags him toward Trace.

"Join the club." Speaking up, Ben calls to Trace. "Good evening, sir! How about we holster the motherfucking handgun, eh? You're scaring the children."

Trace pivots, lowering the gun, engaging the safety. Then he does, indeed, holster the weapon.

"Good, you're here," Trace says, rolling the cigar between his teeth. "This won't take long. The target practice is just to make sure my aim's still decent. I plan on keeping this on me all the time for the foreseeable future. Safety concerns and all."

Closing his eyes against his profound certainty of imminent doom, taking a deep breath in through his nose, Gabriel feels Ben squeeze his shoulder supportively.

"You two," Trace calls to Micah and Alyssa. "Get your asses over here!"

"Okay. I give up. Who died now?" Gabriel asks, unable to take it anymore.

Trace smiles in a way Gabriel doesn't like at all. It's a smile so cold and evil, his balls draw up protectively. Trace sucks on the end of the cigar, then pulls it from his mouth.

"Diadem," Trace says simply.

"The fuck does that mean?" Ben demands instantly, getting angry fast.

"Means it's done, kid. Closed for business. You're all officially unemployed." To Gabriel, he adds, clarifying, "Well, 'cept for you, babydoll."

Dumbfounded, Gabriel has no response, no reply.

Ben growls. Micah winds an arm around Alyssa who's got a hand over her mouth and eyes full of tears. Micah doesn't seem surprised at all, just sad.

"The Master's Circle have given the fuckin' decree that Diadem can't continue operations without enhanced security put in place, and *that* happens over my dead fuckin' body. But I've also, hmm."

He pauses and Gabriel watches with horror as Trace is momentarily too furious to form words. That upsets Gabriel more than anything and he takes an instinctive step closer to Ben, who takes his hand. And somehow, being so scared he needs to hold hands with Ben just makes everything worse.

Continuing, biting on every piece of every word, Trace says, "Some friends from my time with my previous employer have been going missing. The feds are rounding up others in order to place them under protection. I shouldn't be in too much danger since I've already sacrificed my damn name, my family, my possessions, my appearance, and everyone I ever fucking knew before meeting any of you or coming here. I even lost my damn *voice* for them." Trace laughs bitterly.

There's a tense pause where none of them breathe or move or hardly blink. A subtle change comes over Trace then, who has always been the fiercest of them, the wildest and roughest of them. He sags slightly before standing straighter. When he next speaks, the tone of his voice is fractionally higher, the sounds smoother, more elegant, rolled together with hints of both New York and British accents. It doesn't sound like Trace at all.

"None of you are in any danger, but I can't risk it. If they're actively trying to clear the board and anyone who has ever been on it—anyone with any questionable loyalty—they could track me through Diadem, if they tried hard enough. These people... they're ruthless criminals with no conscience or morals and I can't take the chance of them coming here. They would hurt you, all of you, if it helped them get to me. I won't let that happen."

Shaken, Gabriel finds his voice and asks, softly, "Who are you?"

"It's safer if you don't know, sweetheart," he's told by the man who has been the heart of Gabriel's makeshift, adopted family since he was a homeless teenager. "I love you too much to tell you. Micah and I will be finding somewhere new to live. It'll be close by, but off the public record. It's best if they don't know where we are. My priority is doing whatever I can to protect you all, even if that means calling in help, or getting... creative."

The cigar is placed back between Trace's teeth. His body gains the tension and posture it had before. His voice is once more that of the Trace they know when he says, "This is who I am. Thought you all should know who I was, since I'm through pretending I've always been Trace. Trace is a cover. He's the way I protect all of you, but I'm a hell of a lot more than that. I'm fuckin' sorry to do this to ya. All of ya. Know that. I ain't perfect. I've made some big fuckin' mistakes and they're catching up with me."

"We've all made mistakes," Gabriel tells him. "We're grown-ups. You don't have to make up stories to spare us pain. We *know* pain."

"I know, babydoll. Thanks for that," Trace smiles with plenty of affection.

"If any of you need help paying bills until you find something new, Trace and I will step in and cover any expenses," Micah offers.

"We're still family. Just gotta be more careful for a while," Trace adds.

Gabriel looks over at Ben beside him. Ben appears stunned and maybe a little pale, his expression perfectly blank. Gabriel lets go of his hand and walks to Trace, who wraps him in an embrace, his mouth pressed against Gabriel's hair.

"I'm sorry," Gabriel murmurs to him.

"'S'okay, beautiful. It's just a job anyhow. Life goes on."

Chapter 43
Patrick's Family

"Where's your head at?"

The hair at the base of Micah's skull is gripped tightly and pulled, forcing him to tilt his head back, away from the wall he's shackled to. When he feels warm breath over his neck, he exhales heavily, eyes closing with pleasure as teeth scrape over skin beaded with sweat.

That's Trace.

He's entered, slowly, and moans like he can't help it. It's been at least an hour, maybe two, and he's past the point of being able to filter or control his reactions. He's just raw and exposed, as he likes to be.

The cock impaling him tugs back and a hand rubs up the center of his spinal column, following the curve of his back to the base of his neck.

"Where's your head?"

That's Patrick.

He can hear the difference. Hell, he can *feel* the difference. Patrick is sweeter, more dangerous, the unknown. Micah had been relaxed, his muscles loose as he took his pleasure, riding it out to an eventual completion. Hopefully. Upon detecting Patrick, though, he tenses up with self-consciousness. It's like suddenly finding yourself in bed with a stranger.

The sex starts to hurt from the combination of Patrick's force and his own nervousness, and he hisses through the ache. Patrick slows down and begins to stroke Micah's erection. Letting his head fall forward, braced against the wall, Micah moans sharply. His fingers curl inward, balling into fists.

"Answer me."

"Different places, Sir." It's the most honest answer he can think of without giving away more than he wants to. Earlier in the evening, Micah and Lilianna had gone for a walk through the woods at the rear of the property. She was concerned about Trace, but also for Micah. Actually, most of her concern was for Micah. It was nice, to witness her blatant fear for his welfare. Perhaps being freed from the responsibility to be the person caring for Micah and easing his stress is dispelling some of her resentment, helping her find her peace. He hopes so. He sincerely wants her to be happy. He understands her concern, though. Diadem has been Micah's outlet, his biggest and best distraction from everything he lost along with Moira.

"It's not permanent," he had told Lilianna.

"But what are you going to do in the meantime?" she asked, delicate frown lines creasing her brow.

"Help Trace and the others any way I can. Stay useful. I'm not sure what that means yet."

They walked a little farther with branches snapping under their heels as they picked their way along, and birds darting through the branches overhead.

A gruff, hard-as-iron, male voice pierces the fog of his daydream, memories of wandering in the woods with the woman who used to be his wife, but doesn't belong to him anymore. "Who am I?"

He tries to piece together the answer from those few syllables and the way the hand on his hipbone grips, drawing him back. His reply is instinctual.

"Master."

"What's my name?"

"*Master.*"

The column of flesh inside him draws out, leaving him empty and wanting. Footsteps sound behind him but he doesn't turn to look. Voices murmur in conversation. He hears them decide on something, with a definitive, "That one, I think."

"Come away from the wall, slave."

Hands draw his hips backward, his wrists together and enclosed in shackles above him, the chain they are linked to stretches to its limit and still they draw him back until his back is bowed to maintain the position. A stainless steel cock ring is then attached around the base of his scrotum. After one glimpse at it, he chooses to look at the wall instead. The heavy ring pulls at his sac, stretching it out and making him grunt. When a chain with a metal ball on the end is clipped to the ring, it stretches his sac even more and his mouth works around a low groan of complaint.

Something cool, thick and wet rubs between his cheeks, over his tender orifice.

"Open," is the short command he's given and he doesn't look, he just obeys. Tilting his chin up, he opens his jaws wide and feels the phallus pass between his lips and slide back into his throat. At the same time, the toy between his cheeks is angled differently and inserted into him in one smooth stroke. A rough cry of heady, intoxicating pleasure is surprised out of him. It gets him to open his eyes and all he sees is Gray's hand steadying the flesh colored dildo, sliding it far back into Micah's throat, then pulling it out so he can momentarily suckle the tip. A hard shudder works through him. The toy fucking his ass isn't being handled as gently as the one in his mouth. It puts iron in his cock and his balls try to draw up, but can't due to the sizable weight pulling them down. Micah writhes.

"Steady," he's warned. It sounds like Trace but he can't be sure. Wondering deliriously if it counts as a foursome instead of a threesome due to Trace's multiple identities, all present and accounted for, Micah chuckles around the phallus before Gray slides it deep again.

The longer it goes on, the more desperate he becomes. Taken at both ends, he feels ready and able to come spontaneously at the slightest word of permission. Moans sharpen into soft keening whimpers of supplication. He keeps his body open and spread for fucking but can hardly stay still. His hips pump slightly, riding the toy up his ass, making the ball hanging from his scrotum swing in a gentle arc and he sucks the silicone cock filling his mouth, feeling their eyes on him, seeing everything.

The ball stretcher is removed. Micah whimpers, desperate. When a hand massages his testicles, he humps the air, seeking some kind of friction. The long, thick toy fucking his ass triggers his prostate and he undulates, eyes rolling up, sucking away at the dildo Gray holds in his mouth.

"Eyes open," Gray orders.

Micah chances a look at the man. His cock jumps at the sight of such hunger in the Master Dominant's eyes.

"Would you like to come?"

Micah whimpers, pleading, unable to speak. The cock down his throat pulls out, so he rasps, "Please, Master Gray."

The toy up his ass pulls out, too, replaced instantly with Trace's flesh. Gray slides the toy back down into Micah's throat and every fiber of Micah's body feels it, the attention they give him, the ways they make him feel. Desire is like electricity coursing through his skin, making his hairs stand on end and he can't be quiet or stay still. Wild, frantic noises emit from him as he's taken deeper and harder.

"Then come," Gray whispers by his ear as he gently strokes Micah's shaft.

Micah shudders and orgasms abruptly. The strength leaves him and he hangs from the chain holding his wrists and from Trace's grip on his hips. The phallus is removed from his mouth. Gray drags an ice cube over Micah's skin while Trace pumps away, riding Micah until he's cursing, growling with his release.

They take him down and lay him out on the bed. Trace — or maybe Patrick — wipes him down, cleans him off. A cool cloth is laid across his brow. Gray offers a bottle of water with a straw.

"Stay with him while I shower?" Patrick asks Gray.

"Of course," Gray answers with a subtle smile and a nod.

The door to the bathroom closes over slightly, though not all the way as the light goes on in there, then the shower as well. The sound of water beating against tile fills the silence. Gray stays by Micah's side, watching him carefully.

"It's good he can be himself with you now. He needs that," Gray says.

"I have to ask you something," Micah says suddenly, knowing he has to seize the moment. It might be his only chance. The dark cloud that had been hovering over him and his family left him feeling so empty and despondent. Suddenly, he realizes it's not so any longer. He's been reinvigorated with trust and faith, even hope. The light of possibility hasn't burned out yet.

―⚭―⚭―⚭―

"Yes?"

"Patrick's daughter...." That's as far as Micah gets before words fail him. There's a look on his face like he's not sure what he's asking or what he wants to know, exactly, but the wanting itself is plain enough to Gray.

"What about her?" Gray asks.

"He says she's better off without him. Has he really never tried to make contact with her?"

"Mm," Gray hums, glancing toward the bathroom door. "Never."

Gray has been through those arguments with Patrick so many times, he knows the futility of expecting him to reach out to his daughter. There's been too much danger, too much darkness surrounding Patrick for too long. He'd sooner die than place her in the path of any harm, real or imagined. Gray is certain of it.

Micah says, "How do you know?"

Gray smiles.

He remembers that moment, after he'd seen everything, learned everything, and went to find Patrick in their bed. His jet-black hair was much shorter then, tousled from sleep and sex, as it always seemed to be. He was always particular about keeping his jaw shaved smooth, free of any trace of stubble, his features so handsome that Gray knew every time he laid eyes upon Patrick why The Company had scooped him up so quickly, and why he'd always been so popular with subs and Doms alike at the MC. But in that moment, knowing what he knew, Gray saw so much more than his lover and partner, lying in that bed. He saw everything Patrick never wanted to know he had.

"Have *you* contacted her?"

"No, I haven't contacted Heather," Gray answers slowly, deliberately.

"Heather," Micah echoes, grasping at the name like a lifeline tossed to a drowning man at sea. "You know her name."

"Of course."

"What else do you know?"

I know her eyes, her laugh. I know how she's an echo of him, in the purest sense. The world has taken so much from Patrick, but he was able to give something back, something so breathtaking. She lives for him. She lives in every way Patrick never could, without fear of danger or threat. She's free while he lives in shadows, in chains. She's everything to him. She means so much to him, he can't stand to get close nor even think of her for long. She's his angel, his baby girl. She always has been, always will be.

"I know she's safe, and healthy," Gray tells Micah, a man with his own dear angel, constantly with him in his heart, if not in actuality. "She's engaged to be married. She's a teacher in upstate New York. Does it surprise you that I know all of this, Micah? It shouldn't. She's important to me, because she's part of him."

―⬭―⬭―⬭―

Micah feels it then, lying on the bed with Gray at his side. A piece of his heart that had rotted away, left like an open sore for so long, pulls together, mending. That handful of words, proof that Trace's legacy, his child, is important not only to Micah but also to Gray overwhelms him, the joy and relief is so immense. Like a cleansing rain, he lets it wash out of him. He takes Gray's hand and holds it, so grateful he can hardly breathe.

"Thank you," Micah manages after a while, trying to compose himself before Trace—or maybe Patrick—joins them again. "That means a great deal to me."

"You're welcome," Gray replies, so steady and composed while Micah feels like a raw, emotional mess.

"Can I please have her last name? Maybe an address?"

"Eyl. Heather Eyl. What would you do with her address? She doesn't know about her biological father. She wouldn't understand your connection to her if—"

"I realize that. I just... it would help me to know where she was. To know she's *there*. Does she look like him?"

Gray drops his gaze to his lap. Urgent curiosity causes Micah to sit up straighter, eager for Gray's answer, scrutinizing the sad sort of smile on his face.

"Please," Micah whispers.

"She does," Gray admits quietly. "Very much so."

All the air leaves him in a rush, with a soft sigh of wonder. Folding his hands over his mouth, Micah chuckles softly. He dries his eyes with a tissue Gray hands over and Micah gives him a glowing smile.

A minute or so later, the tall, dark figure of Micah's true love enters the room, his hips wrapped in a towel. Micah immediately climbs off the bed and goes to him, wrapping his arms around in an embrace full of contentment.

"What's that for?"

"I just love you," Micah admits. "All of you."

Returning the embrace but frowning slightly, it's definitely Patrick who answers, saying, "You should be resting."

"Excuse me," Gray says, taking his leave and exchanging a glance with Patrick.

"Thank you," Micah calls to him before he's gone. Gray nods to him and slips from the room.

"Lie down," Patrick says adamantly when Micah makes no move toward the bed.

"Lay with me?"

"Go on."

Micah's smile grows when Patrick does lay down with him, propped on his side and looking down the length of Micah's body.

"I guess you don't have any photos of what you looked like," Micah observes. Patrick shakes his head. "I can't picture you with short hair and no beard."

"Good."

Softly, seeking to help but not knowing how, Micah asks, "What can I do for you? How can I make this easier?"

"No worries, love. I'm fine. How are you feeling?"

"Fine. Tired, maybe."

"Watching you with Gray is...." he sighs, glancing over to where the chain hangs from the bolt in the wall. "Incredible. It's nice to have the different parts of my life come together like that.

Everything's always been so separate; some of my energy was always dedicated to keeping things apart. Now, with you, feels like everything's as it should be."

"Mmm," Micah smiles. "I agree wholeheartedly. I was keeping things apart, too, in different ways, with Lily. I'm so glad her and I can still be friends, and be in each other's lives. There was always a sense that if I let her go, she'd never look back because of how I'd treated her. So, I'm grateful. I'm lucky. And being with you is always so… easy. You kow, I remember when you used to love watching me submit to Ben, too. It's kind of a pattern of yours. And I guess it's not a fluke that you're with another switch," Micah grins, rolling over onto his stomach and stretching out. Patrick caresses up and slowly down from Micah's shoulder, along his back, over his ass to his thighs, then up again.

"That's something you've got on ol' Gray, there. He was never up for switching with me. So," Patrick says, thoughtfully, "if we bring in people we trust to play with you, and I watch?"

Micah shivers, skin pebbling. Patrick's fingertips tickle downward, coming up between Micah's legs to fondle his aching balls. Spreading his legs apart and humming with pleasure, Micah surrenders and answers, "Anything you want."

"*Anything*? Really?"

"Really."

"Mm, I like the sound of that." He leans in and kisses Micah's lips. "Love you, Micah."

"Love you too, whatever your name is."

The hand on his balls grabs and pulls sharply. Laughing, Micah groans.

"Smartass."

Chapter 44

Parting Gifts

"You and Jack really danced with Kyle?"

"Oh yeah," Jan laughed.

"Mm," Darrek frowns. "Can't picture it."

"That a challenge?"

"A challenge?" Darrek repeats, confused. They're standing in Darrek's home, which has become Darrek and Gabriel's home, and will stay that way for the foreseeable future, much to Darrek's pleasure.

"Yeah. Here." Jan digs his phone from his pocket. After he fiddles with it for a few seconds, dance music starts to play. He sets the phone on the kitchen counter and waves Darrek over. "C'mere."

"Seriously?"

"Seriously," Jan chuckles. Floorboards creak overhead. That would be Gabriel and Jack checking out the dungeon in the second bedroom and all of the various BDSM gear and furniture Gabriel has stored up there.

"I don't really dance," Darrek says doubtfully, walking forward anyway and letting Jan draw him into his arms. He slings one arm behind Darrek's waist and pulls their hips flush together. Then he starts moving, taking Darrek with him, dipping his hips in a swaying, swiveling, rhythmic motion, their knees slightly bent and stances wide. "Wow. Okay. This is counts as dancing? It just feels like I'm trying to rub off on you."

Jan laughs again, looking up at Darrek's lips while biting down on his own lower lip in a sweet, sexy way. Darrek enjoys getting such an up-close view of Jan, remembering their kiss and unconsciously leaning in a little closer. He's pretty sure the "dancing" isn't going to fly with either Gabriel or Jack, or both, once they hear the music and come downstairs, so he savors it while it lasts.

"The hell is this?" Gabriel asks a minute or two later, after Darrek fails to hear them descend the stairs, too wrapped up in breathing in the tantalizing scent of Jan's cologne, savoring the feel of Jan's hands pressing against Darrek's lower back and gazing down into his eyes.

"Jan's showing me how they were dancing with Kyle," Darrek explains without breaking eye contact with Jan.

"Oh. Makes sense now. *Kyle* may consider that dancing. The rest of us call it dry humping."

"What're you on about?" Jack grunts, looking up from his phone. Once he sees Jan and Darrek pressed together, as they stop dancing but hesitate to part, Jack's eyebrows go up and he just says, "Oh," before going back to his phone. "Dare, Gabe says you take orders?"

"For furniture? Yeah. Sure."

"Jack likes your work," Gabriel grins, his thumbs hooked in his jeans pockets.

"Fuck right I do," Jack murmurs, scrolling through pictures. He holds up one taken of the bench made with custom holes and openings. "How about this one?"

"Sure," Darrek shrugs. "Whatever you need. I'd have to get some measurements from you so the spacing is correct but I can shoot you an email about it, work out the dimensions and all. Shipping would probably be a bitch, but I'd make it sturdy enough to survive transport."

"Peachy," Jack smiles.

"The benefits of screwing a carpenter," Gabriel says to Jan.

"Looks like it," Jan agrees, going to look at the photos from over Jack's shoulder. Pointing at one, he asks Jack, "You're gonna show these to Gray?"

"Fuck yeah I am," he says enthusiastically, angling his head to the side for a better view of the next picture. He clears his throat and turns the phone off. "Oh, got something for you two. Parting gifts, you could say."

"Ooh! We got you something too," Darrek says eagerly. He gestures over a shoulder at the laundry room, then turns to go fetch the bags he knows are in there, trying not to trip over his own feet as he does.

When he comes back with the bags in hand, he sees Jan petting Sierra again, crouched down and scratching behind her ears as she gives him a wet kiss for his trouble. It makes Darrek smile, feeling embarrassed about the gifts they'd found and knew right away would be perfect, just hoping Jack and Jan like them and aren't offended.

Unable to wait, he hands them over without ceremony, giving one each to Jack and Jan. Jack hands Gabriel a package, too, and Jan hands one to Darrek. They all open them simultaneously.

Jack starts laughing right away, taking the hat and putting it on his head.

"Fuck me; the Americans are taking the piss. This is bloody fantastic," he grins.

"You like it?" Darrek asks.

Jan shakes his head and points at the matching hat in his hands. It's a black baseball cap with white lettering, reading 'Brits Suck.' "You know he's never gonna take this thing off, now. It's perfect, Dare. Thank you. Open yours."

Gabriel already has his opened and starts laughing with a hand over his face. Darrek looks at him with a confused and eager expression but Gabriel doesn't show him what the shirt in his hands says. After a pause, he pulls off the plain grey t-shirt he had been wearing and puts on the new one, which is a lighter grey color and says in simply designed typography, 'When I grow up, I want balls as big as that,' with an arrow pointing in Darrek's direction.

"Oh my god!" Darrek exclaims, then collapses with hysterical laughter, doubled over and holding his side when it cramps. When he eventually composes himself, he sees how cute Gabriel looks. He's blushing, hands planted on his hips and lower lip bitten shyly though he's smiling. "That's amazing. How did you even get that?! Holy shit. Gabe, you have to wear that *everywhere*."

"Open yours!" Jan says impatiently.

Darrek groans, still laughing. He keeps catching Jan's eye in a way that makes his stomach flip-flop. "Oh, I'm afraid to look now."

He pulls from the package a shirt of his own, in an appropriately enormous size. The front is printed with a message that hits home for Darrek in a couple of ways. His laughter fades away, replaced then overtaken with a feeling of warmth and optimism he knows will stay with him, even when the others have to take their leave. His expression softening, Darrek holds Jan's gaze, smiles and says, "I love it."

Gabriel comes around behind him to see what it says. "That's a bible thing, right? Put it on."

Clearing his throat, Darrek pulls his shirt off, momentarily and illogically self-conscious about being temporarily bare-chested in front of men who have seen him naked, spread, and fucked into delirium. He's hyperconscious of the collar around his neck, too, but wouldn't take it off for the world.

He gets the new t-shirt on, and is glad to find it fits. The message printed on the front reads, 'This Goliath does kink, not stones,' referring to the biblical warrior whose story is told in the book of Samuel.

"Fucking perfect," Jack grins.

"Yeah," Jan agrees, and Darrek can't help but note the differences in the ways Jack and Jan are looking at him — Jack with warm friendship and admiration, and Jan with something more bittersweet and lustful.

"Oh hell," Darrek sighs, going over and gathering them both up in a group hug.

After a moment, Jack waves Gabriel over too, saying, "Get in here."

"Jesus," Gabriel groans, laughing again as Darrek gathers him up too.

"You guys are awesome," Darrek says. "Thank you. It sucks you have to go."

They separate, and it already feels like goodbye when they haven't even left yet.

"Oh, we'll see you again," Jan says with a smile.

"I hope so."

"And you owe me an email," Jack adds.

"Okay! Okay," Darrek grins. "I haven't forgotten."

"Get home safe, okay?" Gabriel says to them, but speaking mostly to Jack. "Take care of yourselves."

"Yes, Sir," Jack smiles.

Trace stands on the porch, watching the limousine driver load bags into the trunk as Gray shakes hands with Micah. It's still quite a head trip to have the past, present, and future together like that, looking each other in the eye. It helps cement him in his life, not a transient any longer, but a man with ties so strong, nothing that comes his way could ever sever them.

Jack and Jan have already said their goodbyes. Wearing the ridiculous hats which came from Gabriel and Darrek, they're busy making sure they haven't forgotten everything before getting in the car to go.

Then Gray is standing before Trace, holding out a hand. "Tracey," he says solemnly.

"Bright eyes," Trace replies, fitting his hand inside of Gray's.

"Thank you for having us."

"No sweat."

More quietly, with more audible emotion, Gray says, "It was good to see you."

"Amongst other things," Trace winks.

Gray laughs.

"Will you consider coming back to London?"

"Anything's possible," is Trace's noncommittal reply. Gray is slow to release Trace's hand. After hesitating, he pulls Trace in for a brief hug. As they step back, Trace adds, "Take care of those kids of yours." He knows some of what Gray has been through in attempting to do the right thing for both Jack and Jan, but especially Jack. He hopes the help they were able to provide with the video of Jack will be enough to correct the problem. The pessimistic part of him, which has been through hell and back, doubts it will. With any luck, he's wrong and things will be fine.

"I try."

"I know you do," Trace says affectionately. "If you ever need more help...."

He lets the offer hang there, between them, as an open invitation for Gray to interpret at his leisure.

Gray nods. They lock eyes and the moment draws out. Sincere regret, sadness, and heart-stopping love infuse Gray's expression, there and gone.

"Be careful," Gray whispers, and Trace can hear the fear there, which scares him more than anything.

"Yeah," Trace nods, clearing his throat, blinking the wetness from his eyes. "I try."

Gray lingers. Trace tips his head toward the car, saying gruffly, "Go. Go on."

Unable to watch Gray go, Trace lowers his gaze and stands his ground. He hears footsteps leading away, doors closing, and the engine starting. Tires crunch over loose gravel and asphalt as the limousine rolls away, taking Gray, Jack and Jan with it to God knows where and for what. Taking a deep breath, letting it out in a heavy sigh, at first all that's left behind is pain.

When he feels Micah's arms encircling him, Trace laughs with profound gratitude. He's not alone anymore, and never will be again, because he carries Micah, and all of his kids, in his heart, where they will never get hurt and they will always be happy, and loved. Accepting Micah's love greedily, he feels how lucky, how fortuitous his life has been, and realizes he doesn't regret a single thing.

"What do you say we get out of here, get some dinner, some drinks, then start our search for a good hideout?" Micah asks. Trace has already cleared the important things from his own home, which he's officially abandoned until the dust settles. Everything he needs in the world is either parked in the driveway or holding him, wearing an eager, adventure-hungry expression. Micah has also expressed his willingness to pack up some basics and go. The house will be sold off, the ghosts left behind to haunt someone else.

"Abso-fuckin-lutely. I'll follow your lead, love," he replies, taking Micah's hand. He presses a kiss to the side of Micah's face.

Together, they descend the steps, ready to see what the night may bring them.

Chapter 45
Company

"What'cha writin', Ben?" Darrek calls over the screech of the circular saw Kyle is using. Kyle frowns down at the pencil marks on the 4x4 piece of lumber, his eyes hidden behind goggles, blond hair hanging over his forehead. Darrek grins to see Kyle's diligent concentration, and raises his eyebrows at Ben.

"Smut!" Ben shouts back, while helpfully miming an obscene gesture.

"Awesome! Can I read it?"

"I just started, you jackass. Gimme some time to flesh it out a little." He hunches forward around the glow of his laptop's screen. The new arrangement is Ben supervises while Darrek and Kyle tackle carpentry orders whenever Kyle's not working a construction job. It gives Darrek and Kyle time together, rediscovering a sort of normalcy and companionship they haven't enjoyed in years. Ben's presence gives them all peace of mind, including Gabriel. He doesn't leave Darrek and Kyle alone, even for a bathroom trip, but Darrek is okay with that. It's in Ben's nature to be in total control of a situation, as it is in Darrek and Kyle's natures to obey without a second thought. The dynamics simply help them all feel more at ease in their appointed roles.

The past day or so, Ben has taken up residency in the cleanest corner of the garage in which they've set up a work space and computer terminal specifically for him to use. The position gives Ben a clear view of the garage and both Darrek and Kyle's work areas. While Darrek and Kyle work out the plans for the table and chair order, deciding who will do what and when, Ben has been on the phone almost constantly with Trace, jotting things down in notebooks or just frowning strangely at nothing in particular while staring out into space. This is the first time Darrek has seen him doing a bunch of actual, prolonged typing, but Ben seems really serious about it.

"What kind of smut?"

"*True* smut."

"Okay. So, like an autobiography?"

"*Bio*graphy."

"It's Trace's life story," Kyle supplies, when Ben doesn't clarify. "Names and places are changed, but the rest is the same. It's kind of his 'fuck you' to the people hunting him, I guess."

"Wow, really? That's so cool," Darrek gushes. "Now I really have to read it."

"I told him it was a great idea," Kyle says, shooting Ben a look.

"Oh, don't give me that 'I told you so shit,' blondie." Ben scratches at his head and punches a couple of keys.

"Like I always tell him," Kyle says. "He's really good at not being full of shit. I think it's great he's finally decided to use that particular talent to write some nonfiction, now that he doesn't have to jerk off random guys for money anymore."

Both of Ben's hands slap down on his thighs. He sits back and gives Kyle a look so full of exasperation and dark willingness to drag Kyle into a corner and spank the hell out of his ass that Darrek actually backs off a step.

"Really?" Ben says sharply. "Really, Kyle? How many times do I fucking have to spell it out for you? It's SMUT, not motherfucking tight-assed, hoity-toity non-fiction!"

Hands braced on the edge of the counter, Kyle calmly flips his hair out of his eyes with a toss of his head. "Whatever," he replies coolly. "It's an amazingly responsible pursuit and I'm proud of you."

Ben points a finger at him, his mouth a tight, hard line as he seethes, "So help me god, I will come over there and wash your mouth out with soap if you say that shit to me one more time."

"I love you, too," Kyle winks.

"God damn it, Kyle! Your sentimental logical bullshit is ruining my creative flow!"

"You two are ridiculous," Darrek says seriously. "I mean it. Completely."

"Get back to work, young'uns! Enough chit chat," Ben calls, typing away again. "I don't see a table or a single damn chair over there yet and that's only your first order of many." "He's been like this for days," Kyle sighs, shaking his head. "Trace has been almost just as bad, though. Micah came over for a drink or five last night just to get a break from the constant profanity-laced overexcitement. Plus all of the sex talk has given them, like, *constant* wood and too many dirty ideas."

"Kyle," Ben calls. "Which rule are you breaking right now?"

Kyle sighs again, licks his lips and manages to cover a smile just as it starts to curls his lips up at the edges. "No talking about you like you're not here?"

"That's fucking right. I'm writing, not deaf. Get the fuck back to work or I'm taking you home."

"Yes, *Sir*," Kyle says, saluting.

"Keep it up. I'm making a mental tally for later when I take it all out of your ass," Ben says softly, giving Kyle a look of warning.

"Shit," Kyle hisses, shifting the wood in front of the saw blade and losing the smile instantly.

"Jesus," Darrek laughs. "It's gonna be like this every day with you two, isn't it? Wow."

"Every fucking day," Ben agrees. "You're welcome, by the way."

"Thanks, Knox," Darrek replies, still laughing.

They each turn their focus back to their work. The sounds of intermittent typing and sawing fill the air as Darrek rechecks the measurements on the chair he's building. For a while, everything is calm and fairly quiet.

Then, suddenly, Sierra begins to bark crazily in the backyard. Her alarm causes Darrek to look up from his sketch. There's another shriek from the circular saw in Kyle's area. Seeing the car parked across the end of the driveway, and the man getting out of it, Darrek reaches out and lays a hand on Kyle's shoulder. The saw turns off as Kyle looks around.

Ben is out of his chair in an instant, looking ready and able to kick ass and take names. He storms forward, going to Darrek, who's the closest to the front of the garage, getting between him and the person approaching.

Maybe Ben sees the resemblance, or just senses the bad vibes. When he yells, pissed off and mean, "Hey! Back the fuck up!" as the newcomer circles the car and starts to walk forward, Darrek moves first. He puts a hand on Ben's chest, and lets him see the calm Darrek feels reflecting in his expression.

"It's okay. I've got this," he tells Ben.

"The fuck you do. Is that—"

"Yeah. I've got this," Darrek says adamantly. He turns to walk from the garage, getting a quick glimpse of Kyle, the goggles shifted up to his forehead, too stunned to move or speak. "Stay here," Darrek tells Kyle.

Kyle just nods tightly. Ben goes to stand with him.

With Sierra still barking angrily, Darrek takes a few steps forward. Before him stands a human being he never thought to see again in the whole of his life.

With the dreaded moment finally upon him, a confrontation he never wanted to have to make, Darrek feels ready. He's not scared anymore. The trials he's been through have helped him to know himself, what he wants, and what he won't tolerate.

The most accessible weapons are the pieces of lumber stacked a few feet away, the 4x4 segments for the chair legs easy to grip and swing. Instead, distantly, he thinks of the gun, wanting to feel it in his hand, cool and deadly, as he says what he knows he needs to say. He wonders where Gabriel moved it to. The gears turn in his head, trying to narrow down the list of possible ways this could go.

At first, Darrek isn't able to decide on a course of action. He could say something to make it clear he's not the stupid, weak-willed kid he used to be. He could let his fists ball up as tightly as they want to before letting the punches fly. Or, he could release Sierra from the yard and command her to attack, have her chase the newcomer from the property for him.

"We didn't know, okay. *I* didn't know," Darrek's brother Steven says in a quavering voice. Darrek is amused in a dull, disinterested way to see how much taller and muscular he is than his older brother. If it came down to a physical fight, Steven would stand no chance at all.

Soft and deadly, with so much wrath contained in the barely whispered words, spoken slowly with each sound carefully enunciated, Darrek says, "Get... the *fuck*... off of my property, you son of a bitch."

"I get that you hate me, Darrek," Steven says, holding up his hands, palm out. "You have perfectly good reasons to. But after what was done to Dad's body—"

Darrek continues, "I'm gonna count to three. Then I'm going for my gun. Turn the fuck around and leave. One...."

Jittery, looking everywhere at once, at Darrek, bigger and meaner than ever, at Ben and Kyle in the garage, at the fenced-in yard with Sierra ready to defend her owner, Steven yells, "Mom is a wreck! I keep thinking back to when we were little, things that happened and I couldn't explain but now they make sense—"

"TWO."

"We're still your family! Talk to us! We should *talk* about this!" Steven shouts, his voice breaking. He's walking backward, though, glancing behind himself so he doesn't trip.

"THREE."

Darrek moves, walking swiftly for the front door. He gets three paces before stopping abruptly, changing his mind, forsaking the idea of weapons entirely. Pivoting on a heel, he runs for his brother who does trip, then, as Darrek attacks. Scrambling back to his feet, he's unable to escape Darrek bearing down on him. Grabbing Steven by the shirtfront, Darrek delivers a brutal, furious punch which connects with the middle of Steven's face. He feels his brother's nose break under his fist.

"*That's* for fucking my fiancé," Darrek sneers. "You are *not* my family. You don't come here again, or call me, or write, or *anything*. If your conscience is disturbed by finding out our father was a fucking abusive, sadistic, evil pedophile, that's *your* goddamned problem. Take it up with a shrink because I want nothing to do with you."

"God it's true, isn't it?" Steven gasps, horrified, cupping his hands under his nose to catch the blood flowing freely from it. "*It's all true.*"

"Now, I go for my gun. We don't tolerate trespassers. Don't be here when I come out," Darrek growls. He tosses his brother backwards, releasing him, and turns, taking long strides toward the front door once again.

Steven yells at Darrek's back, "For what it's worth, I'm sorry! Darrek, *I'm sorry*! I'll go. I'm leaving, okay? I'm going."

Darrek gets to the door, pushes through it. The gun isn't by the door where it used to be. He checks some drawers but before he gets farther than that, hears the sound of an engine revving. When he glances over at the opened door, he sees the sedan which had pulled up in front of the house driving away at high speed.

Just like that, the moment he was dreading so much is over.

It's *over*.

Letting out a heavy breath, he grips the edge of the sideboard, hanging his head and trying to calm down. His heart pounds in his chest, adrenaline pumping through his system.

Ben and Kyle hurry over to check on him.

"Are you okay?" Ben demands. He holds Darrek's gaze, wrapping a hand around the side of his neck and generally looking him over like he's evaluating Darrek's vitals after a particularly rough scene. It makes Darrek want to smile, glad Ben is there, and that he's such a devoted friend.

"Yeah. I'm fine. Just startled I guess. Didn't see that coming."

He knows he should call Gabriel at work, and let him know what happened. First, he lets himself calm down.

"Were you really going to get the gun?" Ben asks.

"Maybe. Not really. I don't even know where Gabe left it, to be honest. I just wanted to freak Steven out."

Darrek leaves the house and closes the door behind him once Ben and Kyle are out too. They all go back to the garage.

"You're seriously fine?" Kyle asks, looking doubtful.

"Yeah," Darrek assures him. His abrupt state of high alert slowly relaxes into a wonderful, clear-headed steadiness. "I think I've wanted to do that, to chase them off my property, for a while now. I knew they'd come eventually, after everything with the calls."

Kyle says, "I just have to say, I'm so happy I got to see you punch that fucker in the nose. Did you see all of the blood?" He mimes it running down his chin with his fingers. "He's had that coming for *years*."

"Hell yeah, he did. God, that felt good," Darrek sighs, "just for the Sara factor alone. But getting to tell him to get lost and sending him running like that was even better. He was *terrified* of me. I mean, he didn't even have the balls to finish a thought let alone try to stand up to me."

"You were incredible, Dare," Kyle grins. "What a loser, thinking you owe him some sort of explanation or whatever the fuck. And what the hell did he ever do for *you*? Just close that door and move on."

"Exactly."

He realizes how invigorated he feels. Some more of the dread that has been with him since the phone started to ring, and before that too, held over since childhood, is suddenly gone. It has vanished along with Steven.

That's when Darrek realizes he's smiling. Taking another deep breath, he walks past Ben, who's watching him carefully, like he just wants to be sure Darrek isn't just pretending to be okay. Going through the garage to the back yard, Darrek finds Sierra. She jumps up, putting her front paws on him, her tongue lolling out. She gives him a happy bark and he gives her a kiss, saying, "Good girl. Who's my good girl?"

Ben comes up behind him, laying a hand on Darrek's shoulder. Darrek gives him a smile.

"I'm gonna call Gabe. He should know."

"I agree," Ben replies. He stays there while Darrek sits down on the back stoop. Sierra licks Darrek's face while he dials Gabriel's cell.

After two rings, it's picked up.

"What's up?" Gabriel says.

"Steven was here. My brother."

"Oh my god, Dare—"

"No, it's okay," Darrek says quickly to reassure Gabriel. "I stood up to him, told him to get off my property. He kept trying to talk about Jerry, saying how he didn't know, but now things make sense because of what was written on the body, and I guess from my call to Mom, too. He was *apologizing*, Gabe. And I um... I kind of broke his nose. Punched him in the face. When I acted like I was going inside to get our gun, he took off. He's gone now. Drove away. God, I just... I feel *good*."

He laughs, unexpectedly. There's stunned silence from Gabriel's end of the line.

"So y-you're okay?" he manages, stumbling over the words. "Ben's there, right? And Kyle?"

"Yeah. I told Ben I needed to handle it myself, but he was right there, too. They both were. I'm okay. I really am."

"You're sure? Look, I'll lock up. I'm coming home right now, okay? Do you feel safe there? Should I have Ben take you somewhere else, or—"

"Gabe. It's fine," Darrek assures him, still smiling. "Come home if you can. I would really love to kiss you right now."

"Tell Ben to keep an eye out, okay? Keep the phone near you. And Sierra—"

"Gabe," Darrek cuts in.

"Yeah?"

"I love you."

"Love you too, baby." He hangs up and Sierra tries to climb farther into his lap, giving him a happy bark, too.

"Exactly!" he says, agreeing with her entirely. She licks his face again and all he can do is laugh at it all, feeling so much lighter, so much freer than he has ever felt before.

"So, where are we going, love?" Trace asks.

Micah smiles with a mischievous gleam in his eyes, looking handsome in an impeccably tailored pair of dark grey pants and a crisp white shirt that looks so good against the darker hue of his skin, it makes Trace want to peel the clothes off of him and drag him right back into the bedroom.

"I can't possibly tell you," Micah says elusively.

Palming Micah's firm ass those pants hug so perfectly, Trace whispers, "Thought we had a no secrets arrangement here. Hmm?"

"Grab my ass all you want, we're still going, and I still won't tell you."

"You're not turning into a hardass on me, are you?" Trace teases. "With the hands-off, no questions, ball-busting tone, you kind of sound like someone else we know."

His hand slides down the smooth grey fabric, gripping the rounded muscle beneath. He's felt like more of a switch than ever lately, happily letting Micah fuck him for hours at a time, now that they had much less to distract them. Luckily for Trace, Micah tops as well as he bottoms, eager to give back just as hard for all he's gotten in the time they've been together, with Micah usually yielding so easily to Trace's every whim. Now, though, Micah gets to indulge all of his fantasies. He hasn't seemed to hate it, to put it mildly.

It's also another thing Gray was right about, damn him, Trace thinks with fond amusement, profoundly glad he took the advice to let Micah in even closer, being there to serve Patrick's needs as well. *Gray always knew he couldn't get this close, and play the switch as effortlessly as Micah. Instead, Gray opened my eyes to what a treasure I already had in Micah. Fuck, now I really owe him again, don't I?*

"Stop thinking with your dick. We've got places to be," Micah scolds gently, grabbing the pronounced bulge in Trace's pants and squeezing to punctuate the command.

Groaning softly, Trace replies, "Mmm, maybe you *do* know me, huh?"

"Maybe I do," Micah agrees, nipping at Trace's lower lip, looking ferocious enough to bend Trace over the porch's railing and do him right there. "The accent's still hot on you. Use it later when you're begging for my cock."

"Goddamn," Trace sighs.

"We're still going. Come on."

Trace groans again. Micah takes him by the hand and leads him from the front porch, down the path to the drive and up to the bike parked there. One the house's front lawn is a big, eye-catching For Sale sign. Half the house is empty now, with more and more cleared out every day, either moved to Lilianna's new place or to storage.

Micah gets on the bike first, with Trace pressing up close behind him. He palms Micah's flat stomach and breathes in the scent of his cologne with a happy hum.

"Close your eyes," Micah tells him. "Trust me."

"Always," Trace grins.

It's a short drive. When they roll to a stop and Micah cuts the engine, Trace finally opens his eyes.

"What's this?" he asks.

"You'll see," Micah replies, taking him by the hand once he's off the bike.

They've arrived at a local restaurant with quality food and good atmosphere. It's nothing fancy but it's not a dive either. When Micah gives his name to the hostess, she leads them up a short flight of stairs off of the main room. On the second floor is a smaller, private space with a bar, pool table, and a few tables. Waiting for them are Gabriel, Darrek, Ben, and Kyle. The first thing Trace notices is how good they all look. They're all dressed up a little and none of them seems worried, haunted, or even distracted. They just look happy, and smile widely, cheering for their arrival.

"What's going on?" Trace asks. "There an occasion I don't know about?"

"It's just thank you," Micah says after the hostess leaves them. Gabriel comes forward and hands them a pair of wine glasses. "For everything you do. We love you and wanted to make sure you know it."

Gabriel raises his glass and looks around to catch everyone's eye, briefly, before giving Trace his full attention as well as an expression full of warm affection. "Here's to Trace. We wouldn't have found each other without you, and you've given us more than we could ever ask. Thank you for making us family, and saving each and every one of us in so many different ways. I'm not sure we can ever full repay you, but we're gonna try our damnedest, even if it means saddling you with the lot of us for the duration. We love you, and we're glad as hell to have you."

"To Trace," Micah echoes, raising his glass as well.

"Here here!" Ben cries.

They all toast to him and drink. Trace's vision blurs for a moment as he blinks his eyes clear, trying to hide how happy it makes him to hear such things from people he's invested so much of his life and his heart in. He pulls Micah into an embrace. "Goddamn, love," he sighs. "This means *so much*—"

Micah kisses him quiet and Trace gets lost in him there, for a long moment, in not only being known and understood, but cherished and loved back so completely.

"I know we've both lost people, and parts of our innocence," Micah tells him softly. "And I might not be able to give you everything you've ever dreamed of, but I'm sure as hell gonna try."

"Love you. Love you so much, Micah," Trace vows.

He leaves Micah's embrace for a moment, going to Gabriel. Trace says to him, "Thank you, beautiful. Truly." He gives Gabriel a hug and a kiss on the cheek.

"Drink your wine! Come on, this is a party, not an orgy!" Ben calls.

"Yeah? Is that because Micah planned this instead of you?" Trace asks.

"Probably," Ben allows. "Drink up!"

"Saw that For Sale sign," Gabriel says to Micah. "You're really getting rid of the place, huh?"

"Yep," Micah nods.

"No more fuckin' around, babydoll. Time to relocate," Trace grins. Though his house is all closed up until sometime in the future when he's able to go back to it without fear of it being located by the people who are out to get him, Micah's house has officially been put on the market. Now that Lilianna has finalized her own plans to move in with Saoirse, Micah is ready to let his past go. But Trace has too many fond memories of forming his newfound family at his old place to be able to bear to part with it for good. Even if he can't be there, he likes knowing it's still his, and it's there, waiting for him.

Darrek smiles and comes up to shake Trace's hand, looking astonishingly confident. "Trace, thanks for being there for Gabriel and... well, everything. I owe you big time." Trace can't remember the last time he ever saw the boy so damned content. Joy beams from him. It's a hell of a sight.

"Lookin' good, Dare," Trace tells him, shaking with him. "Just glad it all worked out like it did."

"Me too," Darrek nods.

Behind Darrek are Ben and Kyle. Trace thinks about the trick he heard Kyle played on the corpse of Darrek's old man and looks Kyle in the eye. "How's it goin', blondie?"

"Awesome," Kyle says brightly, smiling so big, you'd think it was Christmas morning and Santa'd just left heaps of sex toys under the tree.

Trace loves the sight of them all there together, looking lighter and freer, each of the couples bonded in real, healthy ways. The storm of circumstance that had trapped them all, battering Trace until his entire identity fell apart, has lifted. Trace knows who he is now. He knows who he *was*. He also knows he doesn't have to leave anything behind anymore. He can take it all with him, into the future, and let the love grow.

"I'm glad we get to celebrate on our own, as a family. We've all been through a lot," Trace says. "You're all incredible people and I'm proud to know and love each one of you."

"Aww, c'mere you big lug," Ben gushes, pulling Trace in for a hard kiss on the lips. They break and Trace smacks Ben's ass to send him back to Kyle.

They each drink and chat while soft music plays. The lighting is warm, the company good. The mood is cosier, less stressful now that it's just their little circle. Trace overhears Darrek talking to Micah, saying, "You make him really happy, Mic. I can tell."

"I hope so," Micah smiles.

"Are you gonna miss your place?" Darrek asks.

Micah shrugs, "In a way, yeah. But it's time. I'm ready to go. It's always been too much house for me, anyhow. Kind of get lost in there, you know?"

Ben comes up to Trace, then, a pocket-sized notebook in hand, pen at the ready. Trace knows, right away, he's going to start asking for more details for the memoirs they're working on together. "Kid, lay off for one night, please," Trace asks.

Micah chimes in, saying, "We're here to have fun, not to work. You two have been at it night and day lately."

"But you've gotta tell me how it ends!" Ben exclaims. Turning to the others, he says, "Did you know Trace fucked a prince?"

"Trace fucked Prince?!" Kyle gasps.

"*A* prince, not *the* Prince," Ben clarifies.

"Well, he does have a nice ass," Kyle murmurs.

Gabriel leans forward over one of the tables and says, "Well, now you *have to* tell us about it."

"Or I can make ya's wait for the damn book," Trace counters.

"Did you get to go to his castle?" Kyle asks eagerly. "Did he ride a horse? Did he have perfect hair? Did he carry a sword?"

"Jesus Christ," Trace sighs, shaking his head and laughing. "Yeah, some kind of sword...."

They all shoot the shit for a while and it feels so good to be together without a care in the world, for a few hours at least, Trace never wants the night to end. Gabriel is standing with his hand inside Darrek's, Ben has his arm slung around Kyle's shoulders, and Trace lingers at Micah's side with his hand on Micah's waist, feeling the smooth texture of his shirt against his firm, hot body beneath. They're each where they should be, where they fit.

Trace takes a look around at how blessed he is, chuckling to himself, thinking how funny and wonderful it is, the way fate turns and turns again. For someone who has given away so much, he's utterly humbled to realize life has provided him with everything he could have asked for.

If you enjoyed this story, you can sign up for a free membership at ForbiddenFiction and discuss it with other readers and the author at the *Forgive Us* story page.

We do our best to proof all our work, but if you spot a text error we missed, please let us know via our website Contact Form.

Acknowledgments

There are a lot of people I need to thank for their help in bringing this book to life. First of all, I need to extend profound, heartfelt gratitude to Jack L. Pyke for consenting to our shared world project, The Society of Masters, and agreeing to lend me her boys for a while. I hope I have done them justice for you, Jack. As one of your biggest fans, I also absolutely can't wait to see what my boys get up to when they come to visit yours across the pond. Thank you for your faith in me, your guidance, editorial brilliance, and your kindness, most of all. This book would never have been possible without you. Gray, Jack, and Jan will always live in my heart, where I'll try to keep them safe from harm and, possibly, once in a while, let them get into even more mischief with the men of Diadem, if only in the playground of my imagination. Gray will forever be whispering to Trace in corners, watching Jack dance with Kyle while Jan lets Darrek talk his ear off about dogs.

Gratitude also must go to D.M. Atkins for daring to facilitate this partnership. Thank you for letting us be part of your vision, Dany, and for helping my world grow broader than I even dreamed it could. It's been one of the greatest pleasures of my life.

Thank you Rylan Hunter, for your skill and insight as you navigated me through the mine-field of merging worlds, characters, and plotlines. Your priceless guidance continues to transform my writing in beautiful ways.

Thanks also have to go out to my research support crew. Fortunately, I am surrounded by some wickedly talented, intelligent people. Denys, Jeannine, Jim, Raj, and Jenn, thank you for your insight and expertise in everything from mechanics to how to torture a man with only the supplies in a photography studio. Thank you to Rose for being such a wonderful listener. Thank you to my husband for giving me everything—time, love, patience, hope, and courage.

I am truly blessed and I honor each one of you.

About the Author

Lynn Kelling began writing in order to tell stories that weren't afraid of the dark, didn't hold anything back and always strived to be memorable, forging lasting attachments between character and reader. Her inspiration comes from taking a closer look at behaviors and ideas lurking at the fringes of life — basically anything that people may hesitate to speak of in mixed company, but everyone wonders about anyway. Her work is driven by the taboo in order to expose the humanity within it. Lynn is an artist, designer and lover of any form of creative self-expression that comes from a place of honesty and emotion, whether it's body art or opera. She has had multiple novels published, has written over fifty works of erotic fiction of varying lengths, and always has several novels in progress.

Works by Lynn Kelling:

Deliver Us series - novels:
Deliver Us (Book 1)
From Temptation (Book 2)
Forgive Us (Book 3)

Deliver Us series - prequels & extras:
Expected Lies • Never Happened

Whatever the Cost series:
Whatever the Cost
Between Here and There • Trick and Truth • Escape

Bound by Lies

Twin Ties series:
My Brother's Lover (Book 1)
Twin Affairs (Book 2)

About the Publisher

ForbiddenFiction.com is a publisher devoted to writing that breaks the boundaries of original erotic fiction. Our stories combine intense sexuality with quality writing. Stories at Forbidden Fiction.com not only arouse readers through sensations, but also engage them emotionally and mentally through storytelling as well-crafted as the sex is hot.

ForbiddenFiction.com is also designed to be a social reading environment. You'll have fun even if just reading the latest post each day, yet you will have the chance for so much more. Readers and authors can be part of ongoing discussions of specific works and individual authors as well as more general topics.

Sign up for a FREE Membership today at ForbiddenFiction.com

Made in United States
Orlando, FL
09 March 2023